THE
GLASS
BUTTERFLY

THE
GLASS
BUTTERFLY

LOUISE MARLEY

KENSINGTON BOOKS
www.kensingtonbooks.com

KENSINGTON BOOKS are published by

Kensington Publishing Corp.
119 West 40th Street
New York, NY 10018

All Kensington titles, imprints, and distributed lines are available at special quantity discounts for bulk purchases for sales promotion, premiums, fund-raising, educational or institutional use.

Special book excerpts or customized printings can also be created to fit specific needs. For details, write or phone the office of the Kensington Special Sales Manager: Kensington Publishing Corp., 119 West 40th Street, New York, NY 10018. Attn. Special Sales Department. Phone: 1-800-221-2647.

Kensington and the K logo Reg. U.S. Pat. & TM Off.

ISBN-13: 978-0-7582-6568-5
ISBN-10: 0-7582-6568-9

First Printing: September 2012
10 9 8 7 6 5 4 3 2

Printed in the United States of America

For my mother,
June Bishop Campbell

Heroism, sometimes, is less a shout than a whisper.

ACKNOWLEDGMENTS

This book owes much to the assistance and guidance of some very special people. Many thanks go to my sister Sarah Phillips, for her advice on professional therapists; to my cousin, attorney Nancy Sorensen, for legal insights; to the fine writers and great friends Sharon Shinn, Kay Kenyon, Brenda Cooper, and all of the Tahuya Writers, for their invaluable feedback.

Very special thanks go to the Puccini Museum of Torre del Lago and its helpful staff, and especially to Simonetta Puccini, granddaughter of the composer, who so kindly and personally answered my e-mails (without mentioning my occasional errors in Italian!).

I'm grateful, too, for the delightful company of Susan Witt, Joel Butler, and my husband, Jake Marley, on our pilgrimage to Villa Puccini, where we absorbed the music and the memories of Giacomo Puccini with the greatest joy.

Many thanks also, and again, to my excellent editor, Audrey LaFehr, and my patient and helpful agent, Peter Rubie. This book couldn't exist without them.

1

Santo Dio, come si fa?

Holy God, what is to be done?

—Sharpless, *Madama Butterfly*, Act Two

Tory loved the way the slanting October sun filled her office. The woods around her house were mostly eastern cedars and sugar maples, but one venerable oak tree spread its branches just outside her sliding glass door, and the sun reflecting from its red and yellow leaves splashed gold-tinged light across her desk. It shone on Jack's high school portrait in its braided leather frame, and made the faint gold butterfly gleam from the green depths of the Murano glass paperweight.

The easy chair where her clients sat faced the profusion of colorful leaves. The view seemed to soothe them, and to encourage them. With her back to the light, she could watch their faces as she listened to them talk, and give free rein to her intuition.

She relied on her intuition—her little fey, as her grandmother had called it—more than anyone knew. It often prompted her to ask the right question, to focus on the right problem, to suggest the perfect exercise. It could be immensely helpful, though it was an erratic companion, sometimes somnolent, occasionally so subtle she almost missed it, often so intense she could hardly bear it. Nonna Angela had warned her about that. On the same day she bestowed the Murano glass paperweight on her little granddaughter, she reminded her that her fey could be a curse as well as a gift.

Nonna Angela had been right. Today, Tory's fey had failed her utterly. The light, pouring so generously through the glass door, seemed to darken as she watched her client's freckled face change and close, her pale eyes grow flat and dangerous. The air in the office grew chilly, and the looming presence of the black revolver, so recently discharged and now locked in the file cabinet, made Tory's stomach crawl. Still her fey had not warned her.

Her client said, "You're my therapist. I'm supposed to be able to tell you everything."

Tory sat very still. The key to the file cabinet seemed to grow bigger in her jeans pocket, its cut edges sharper, its brass heavier. It felt as if it might surge forth under its own power, tear right through the denim, leap out to set the gun free from the locked drawer. Tory answered in as level a tone as she could manage. "You're a police officer. You must know there are limits to confidentiality."

"No. I don't know that." The client's voice was even, too, but Tory felt certain it was more easily achieved. Her tone had always been uninflected, oddly flat. The woman in the easy chair seemed to have become a stranger, unrepentant, unmoved, detached from all they had talked about over the months of their association.

Tory would think this later, when she had time—too much time—to reflect on what had happened. Her fey had failed her, or perhaps that was simply an excuse. She should have known better than to count on her fey for insight and understanding. She had forgotten the dark side of her gift, the weak side, and so she had failed everyone—her client, her client's victim, her son, and herself. She had waited too long, and said too little. Her habit of silence, cultivated through a difficult childhood, a sad girlhood, long years of standing alone in her world, had been her undoing.

2

❧

Ch'ella mi creda libero e lontano
sopra una nuova via di redenzione!

Let her believe I'm far away and free,
ahead to a new life of redemption!

—Dick Johnson, *La Fanciulla del West*, Act Three

Vanishing, Tory Lake discovered, was not all that difficult a thing to accomplish. When the moment came, when it was the only path left to her, it was simply a question of taking one step at a time, putting one foot in front of the other, and wasting no time in looking back.

The money was a great help. Her fey had prompted her, months before, to begin laying cash aside. She kept an old cracked suitcase in the back of the spare room closet, and she began tucking bills into it, twenties, fifties, an occasional hundred. It never occurred to her that it was an odd thing to do. The growing cache of money soothed the nameless anxiety she had begun to suffer, that clouded her days and woke her during the uneasy nights.

She could see, now, that the anxiety had begun when the client first came to her office, but at the time she hadn't made the connection. She only knew that it comforted her to know the cash was there. It had become automatic for her to add to the pile, and on nights when she couldn't sleep, she counted it.

With Jack away at college, she often woke in the small hours.

Her eyes would open in the solitary darkness, and she would lie for a time listening to the whisper of the night wind through the cedars, wondering if sleep would return. When it didn't, when the thread of anxiety wound itself through her chest and quickened her restless pulse, she would get up, pad on her bare feet to the closet, and pull out the suitcase.

The suitcase was the ancient cardboard sort. She had kept it long past its usefulness, but the suitcase, and the Murano glass paperweight, were all she had left of her grandmother. Even after all these years—after the loss of her mother, her father, the humiliating end of her marriage—Tory missed her Nonna Angela. She had been, by the time Tory was born, a wizened Italian crone with age spots and frizzy gray hair. She had been the only reliable source of affection in her granddaughter's life. The suitcase she had carried from her Italian home when she came to America as a war bride was nearly in shreds now, decaying and musty, but Tory couldn't bring herself to part with it. The spongy feel of the cardboard brought her visions of an Italian lakeside village, a hopeful young woman, a wedding in a tiny stone church, a meager trousseau to carry to her new country.

The suitcase had a new use now, securing Tory's stash of money behind lining so threadbare it was nearly transparent. She felt as if Nonna Angela were guarding it for her, and in the sleepless pre-dawn hours she would open it on the unused bed in the spare room and count the bills.

It had reached, by the time she needed it, an amount just over ten thousand dollars. The night she realized that, counting and sorting and banding the bills together, she went back to bed and slept soundly, sensing that some goal had been achieved. Her fey was satisfied. She was ready—for whatever it was.

When it came, it wasn't what she had expected, but then, she hadn't known what to expect. There was no time to think about it, nor was there time for regrets, or for arguments with herself over what she should have done or not done. She understood too late what the anxiety had been about, but that was gone, its last remnants washed away by the clear water of the Winooski River, where her Escalade now lodged among the boulders, doors open, leather seats soaking in the current.

It was not only her anxiety that had disappeared. She felt oddly still. Her body moved, but her emotions were frozen, like the surface of a pond in winter. It seemed better to be encased in ice, a carapace of protection that froze solid the moment she made her decision. Currents of feeling might roil somewhere beneath it—guilt, regret, anger, sadness—but she couldn't sense them. She didn't want to. She dreaded what she might feel if the ice cracked and broke.

She had tumbled out of the Escalade into the icy water, and hidden herself beneath the jut of the riverbank. When she heard the engine of Ellice's car roaring down the hill, she emerged, wet to the waist, her feet shockingly cold in her sodden sneakers. She worked her way back to the house to retrieve her money and, in haste, to bandage her arm. The cut was deep, and it hurt, but she was pretty sure it hadn't reached the muscle. She smeared some antibiotic ointment under the bandage, but she wasn't really concerned about infection. She kept her kitchen knives, like everything else in her house, immaculately clean. Obsessively clean, Jack would have said. In any case, she had more pressing concerns. She took an extra bandage, and set about preparing her departure.

She changed her sneakers, jeans, and underwear for dry ones, and put the wet things in the washer. She threw in some detergent and started the machine. She hurried to her office, but briefly, then ran upstairs, breathless with the need to hurry. She pulled the suitcase out of the spare room closet and wriggled the cash out from beneath the lining. She slit the lining of her warmest jacket, a black down L.L.Bean she'd had for years, and stuffed the fat rubber-banded packets of money inside. She slid the file in after the money, and secured the lining with small gold safety pins. Inadvertently, she caught sight of herself in the mirror, and saw that the jacket puffed around her, making her look like a cooked sausage. She patted the lumpy parts, trying to smooth them down, then gave it up as a waste of effort.

She replaced the suitcase, making sure the old coats and sweaters hung in the closet just as they had before, although she couldn't think who would notice. Not Jack, certainly. Perhaps her friend Kate, if she thought of it.

Kate. Kate would suffer, too. Tory hated having to cause her pain, but she couldn't see how to prevent it. She went down the hall to the kitchen, where the teakettle still rested on the stovetop, her cup and infuser ready on the counter. She left them where they were, testaments to her interrupted day. She hesitated in front of the refrigerator, but decided against taking anything from it, even though there was no one to inventory its contents. In her frozen state, she was sure she couldn't eat anything, anyway.

She pressed her hands against her forehead, thinking hard about how to do this. There should be no hints of anything missing, no evidence to indicate she had ever returned. The washer would run through its cycle and stop. There were CDs in her treasured Bose system, but she would leave them behind. She stood for a moment in the doorway leading to the garage, taking a last look at her beloved kitchen with its warm red accents, Le Creuset cookware hanging from the rack, her mother's wedding china showing through the glass-fronted cabinets. It was surreal, gazing at all this as if with a stranger's eyes. The next people to see it would indeed be strangers, she imagined. They wouldn't care about the thin Lenox teacups, the cut-crystal wine decanter, the polished granite of the kitchen island. At the moment, she didn't care, either. One day she might. She might miss her home, and her life. She would certainly long for her son, but that was the whole point. This was all about him.

She closed the door that connected the kitchen with her office, and went out into the garage. She took a single bottle of water from an open case, and walked away through the woods, leaving her house unlocked, the lights on, phone jack unplugged, and the sliding glass door to her office open to the wind.

She stuffed the bottle of water into one deep pocket to free her hands to push aside low-hanging branches. As she worked her way through the brush, she tried not to leave broken twigs and crushed leaves behind her, evidence of her passage.

The down jacket felt surprisingly heavy, the cash and the file folder dragging against her back, the water bottle bumping her left hip. There was something hard and heavy against her right hip, too. She put her hand in that pocket, and caught a breath of surprise.

When had she picked it up? She couldn't recall. She had dashed into the office for the file, then up the stairs for the money—but somehow, in her office for the last time, she had seized up the Murano glass paperweight. Jack might know that was missing. Kate might notice, too—she had always admired it—but Tory could hardly go back now to replace it. There would be no point in dropping it here, on the forest floor. She would have to carry it with her. It had been a strange thing to do. An impulsive thing. The only thing she had done that didn't make sense.

Underneath the paperweight she found her red felt beret, crushed but unharmed. She wriggled that out of her pocket, and pulled it on.

She wondered how long it would be before someone came looking for her. Her next client wasn't due until Monday. Jack was at school, and as they so rarely spoke, she wouldn't expect to hear from him before Thanksgiving. Kate and Chet had their grandchildren for the weekend. It could be three days before anyone discovered she was missing.

When they figured it out—Kate, or her next client—they wouldn't find anything in her house to help them. There would be no clues, except perhaps for the missing paperweight. They wouldn't find much, in fact, until they found her car.

Her folder of opera CDs was still in the console of the Escalade. It would be a convincing detail. It was one thing everyone knew about her, even her clients. They often smiled as they walked around the side of the house to her office door, hearing Verdi or Mozart or Puccini pouring out into the clear mountain air.

In a quarter of an hour, Tory broke free of the heaviest woods, thick with old trees she had kept to give her house privacy. She turned north, off her own property, and began walking faster. She wasn't precisely sure where she might come out of the forest, but she meant to stay well away from the river and the crashed car. The woods were quiet except for the faint susurration of evergreens stirring in the wind. Two tiny kinglets, birds she loved for the elusive flash of their golden crowns, sang from the trees. Their rhythmic tweet-and-warble rang like crystal through the cold air, but she didn't look up to find them. In this surreal hour, they stirred no appreciation in her.

She moved like an automaton, a creature programmed to take one step, another, doing her best to hide her trail. She skirted heavy patches of underbrush, followed deer paths when she could find them. She drank the water, but she kept the plastic bottle tucked into her jacket instead of burying it, worried it might be found. She pressed on even when she grew tired and her knees and hips began to ache. Blood from the wound on her arm soaked through the bandage she had taped over it, and stained her sweater. She stopped to change the bandage, pressing the new one as tightly over the cut as she could, and it seemed to stop. She rolled up the bloody bandage, and put that in her pocket, too. Her feet began to ache in her second-best sneakers, but she observed that from a distance, as if it were happening to someone else, not the woman encased in ice.

The weight of cash inside her jacket steadied her. She would buy food, eventually. She wasn't cold. She could spend the night in the woods if she had to. It all depended on where she came out.

Ice Woman was impressively calm. She knew, from years of counseling clients, that she couldn't avoid acknowledging the shock and guilt forever, but for right now—oddly—all she felt was a sort of triumph. Clinically, she could judge it to be a bizarre reaction, but crisis responses were idiosyncratic.

She scrabbled down one side of a dry ravine and climbed up the other, stopping at the top to catch her breath. As she leaned against a cedar, looking down on the wooded valley she still had to cross, she remembered that she had felt a single stab of premonition during Ellice Gordon's first appointment. It was familiar to her, a dull, abstract pain piercing her chest from front to back. It always presaged some significant event. Why had she ignored it?

It was a pointless question. She had ignored it because there was nothing else she could do. She hadn't known then what it meant, and it hadn't come again. It was no use wishing things had been different. Her ordered life had become profoundly disordered. Tragedy had struck, and she could neither deny her failure nor change the outcome of events.

Only one thing mattered, and that was to keep Jack safe. Ice Woman was determined to succeed at that.

She started down the slope into the valley, skidding on the mat of leaves and moss and needles that softened the forest floor. For now, she told herself, she would be grateful for the impulse that had moved her across the car seat, made her shove open the passenger side door, given her the impetus to throw herself out into the water. She could have been crushed as the Escalade tipped over the rocky bank and fell the thirty feet to the river. Had she had time to think it through, she might have decided she was safer in the car, behind the airbag, but there had been no time. And she had known, when she saw Ellice climb out of her patrol car and stride to the top of the bank to stare coldly down at the wreck, that she had done the right thing at last. The only thing she could have done.

She kept moving, pressing north and a little bit east. After several periods of walking, resting, and walking again, she broke out of the woods to find herself on the two-lane road that led to the town of Randolph. She walked up it for a time, grateful for the gravel shoulder, which was so much easier to navigate than underbrush and carpets of leaves and dropped branches. Dusk began to obscure the hills, but the darkness was helpful. When headlights flashed ahead or behind her, she stepped down into the drainage ditch, huddling with her head down until the vehicle passed.

Randolph was just big enough for her purposes. She didn't

know anyone there. She did most of her shopping in Sherburne Center, or even all the way north in Montpelier, but she had driven through Randolph once when Jack was in high school, and she remembered the little lane of used car dealerships with their hungry signs and strings of gaudy lights.

Her feet hurt in earnest by the time she spotted the lights of the town ahead. She turned off the main road to walk down a gravel-strewn street that led away from the town center. Around her lights shone from modest wooden houses. Children ran and shouted in their yards, and dogs barked as she passed. She thrust her hands into her pockets, and did her best to look like a woman taking her evening exercise in well-worn sneakers and comfortable jeans, a battered red beret on her head. She tucked her hair up under the beret, pulling the front down over her forehead. She might be blonde, brunette, or gray-haired. No one would be able to tell.

Darkness was complete by the time she found the lane of used car dealers. She eyed them as she passed, hoping a possibility would jump out at her. The strings of lights swinging in the breeze made the hoods of used cars and outdated trucks glimmer with false promise.

When she spotted a lemon-yellow VW Beetle at the front of one of the seedier lots, she turned in. The salesman who hurried toward her had thin, pimply cheeks and a wisp of mustache that made him look as if he belonged in junior high.

"Hi!" he said, with an eager smile. "I'm Adam." He thrust out his hand. The nails were too long, and she found herself reluctant to touch him. She shook his hand anyway. He couldn't be much older than Jack.

"Hi," she said hoarsely, then cleared her throat. She hadn't spoken for hours. She tried again. "Excuse me. Hi." She felt as if she were watching herself, observing her performance, assessing the efforts of the woman behind the ice to behave naturally. "This is kind of a cute car," she said. She couldn't actually dredge up a smile, but she spoke in as bright a tone as she could manage. "I thought my daughter might like it."

"Oh, absolutely!" he said. He withdrew his hand, and she felt the slight scrape of his nails against her palm. That made her shudder. That, of all things, after what had happened? The touch of someone else's nails? Ridiculous.

"How old is she? This is a great car for a girl," he said. He opened the door, and pointed to the bud vase attached to the dash. "They all love those," he said. "And I'll bet she loves yellow. Girls love yellow."

"Well, yes," she said. "I think she does. And it's an automatic, so that's good." It was tempting to say more, but Ice Woman stopped herself. The less information she offered, the less he'd remember about her.

"Special gift?" he asked.

She said, "Birthday."

"Birthday, nice, nice. What a nice mom! How much were you thinking of spending?"

She bent forward to see what the card on the windshield read, then leaned inside to check the mileage. Okay, it already had 120,000 miles on it. But it was a VW. Surely it could manage a few more. She straightened, and said, "About half what you're asking, actually. That's a lot of miles."

He smiled, and nodded. "Absolutely, absolutely. You know how it is. That's a starting point." He looked up at the office, little more than a lighted cubicle in the darkness, and she realized he was alone on the lot. The light showed the office was empty.

She glanced pointedly at her wrist. She had been wearing her wristwatch when she left, just a Timex. Now it was the only jewelry she had left to her. "Look, Adam," she said. "Can we get to the end point? This was sort of an impulse, and I need to—"

"Oh, absolutely, absolutely. Make me an offer, and I'll call my manager."

It didn't take long after that. She offered him eight hundred, and could tell by the way his face lit up that it was going to be enough. There was a bit of awkwardness when she slipped into the office restroom and came out with eight hundred in cash in her hand, but they got through it. He gave her a curious glance as she counted out eight hundred-dollar bills and one fifty to cover the sales tax, but he didn't say anything. When he asked her to step into the office and sign papers, she folded an extra fifty and slipped it into his hand. She said, "My daughter will come and do that tomorrow, okay?"

"Well—I guess that would work. I'll just say you're driving the car on approval." He pocketed the bill, his cheeks flushing guiltily.

Ice Woman persuaded the salesman to fill the gas tank. Within half an hour she was climbing into the car, inserting the key into the ignition, praying the thing would start. The salesman stood by, watching, no doubt joining her in her prayer. When the engine obediently came to life, a look of relief passed over his pimply features. She put the car in gear, and Adam stepped back, waving and smiling. Ice Woman waved back, then gunned the engine, zipping out into the street with a little rush that made the bud vase wobble in its holder. She glanced into the rearview mirror as she drove away, but Adam had gone back into his office, and was grinning as he spoke into a telephone. Someone, at least, was happy tonight.

Tory turned her eyes back to the road, searching for street signs as she tried to get used to the little car, adjusting the mirrors, locating the windshield wipers. She turned south toward Hartford, where she could catch Interstate 91. She wished she could go north, but crossing the border without identification was out of the question. She could find a map at a service station, but she thought for now she would just let her sense of direction guide her. She didn't know where she was going, in any case. Just away. As far away as she could possibly go, and as quickly as she could accomplish it.

She drove off into the night, pushing the little Beetle as fast as she dared. After half an hour, she pulled off the beret and tossed it into the passenger seat. She didn't look back. She didn't think, and she didn't feel. Ice Woman.

*   *   *

The Beetle was no Escalade, but despite its rattles and coughs, it carried her steadily south and then west, on roads with numbers and names she didn't recognize. She bought coffee and a hamburger in a drive-through at about midnight, but not before pulling on the beret again to hide her hair. She was careful to keep her head down, handing over her money without looking up at the clerk's face. She had slipped the bill out without noticing it was a fifty, but there was no demur. She pulled out again into the road, and ate the burger as she drove. She bought gas in a self-service station with one of the twenties she'd gotten from the fast-food place. The restroom was locked, but there was no one around, so she went around to the back and squatted in a square of weeds and gravel. In moments she was on the road again.

The radio in the VW worked fairly well, but she couldn't find a classical music station within range. She drove on through the night in the hard silence of solitude.

She wondered, vaguely, how Jack would take the news of her disappearance. Of her apparent death. She hoped he wouldn't be too unhappy. Despite the distance between them—call it what it was, an estrangement—she was certain he cared about her. She had known many clients who resented their parents, but that didn't mean they didn't love them. She had often taken comfort in that knowledge.

Jack was safe now. As long as she was gone, he was safe. It was the only thing that made her feel anything, though it was more an absence of anxiety than a concrete feeling of relief. Better to lose a parent than to face the mindless fury of Ellice Gordon.

"It takes time," she had said to traumatized clients. "Give yourself time."

Time was all she had left. Time, and a gutsy old yellow Beetle. And a bit less than ten thousand dollars in twenties, fifties, and hundreds. She would count it, eventually. Work out how long it would last. Decide what to do next. For now, she drove, and watched the highway signs spin by.

By midmorning, with the cool autumn sun at her back, she knew she had to stop and rest. She left the freeway when she saw a sign for a town called Meadville. It seemed big enough to hide in, but not so big she couldn't find her way back to the freeway. It would have been better, she supposed, to stop when darkness fell again, but her eyes were burning and her hands aching from holding the steering wheel. She could yearn for the easy steering of the Escalade if she allowed herself to do it, but she resisted. Instead, as she pulled into the back parking lot of the simplest motel she could find, she patted the dashboard of the VW. It was doing its job to the best of its ability. It wasn't the little car's fault it wasn't a Cadillac.

She pulled on the beret again and went to register in the motel office. The clerk was elderly, peering at her through thick glasses with black plastic frames. When he asked for a credit card, she said she had forgotten it. "You'll take cash, though, right?" She gave him her most feminine shrug, spreading her hands helplessly, and he nodded.

"Just fill this out." He pushed the form across a cracked counter that looked as if it had been lined with a leftover sheet of linoleum.

She wrote down an address in New York, not knowing if such an address existed or not. She made up a license plate number for her car, hoping the clerk wouldn't walk all the way around back to check. She took the key, thanked him, refused the city map he offered, and made her way up a set of splintered stairs to the room he had given her. It didn't look like there were any other guests, but she didn't mind that. That meant there were no maids with carts of sheets and towels to encounter, no people to notice or remember her. She let herself into the room, locked the door, drew the blinds, and tossed the beret onto a chair. She used the bathroom, then folded back the thin coverlet of the bed and kicked off her sneakers. She kept her jacket on, falling onto the dingy sheets and tucking the inadequate pillow under her cheek, and fell asleep at once.

When she woke, the room was dark, with only a dim band of

light making its way through the blinds from the hallway. She groaned at the ache in her back and neck, and rolled gingerly off the bed. She went into the bathroom and flicked on the light, avoiding the mirror. She showered, trying to keep the bandage on her arm dry by holding it out of the stream of water. She would have to buy more bandages. The cut might take a while to heal. It didn't feel hot or swollen, but she didn't want to remove the bandage to have a look.

She soaped herself twice, and washed her hair with the tiny bottle of shampoo provided for her. There was a bottle of lotion, too, and she used it all, rubbing it into her arms and legs and over her heels and her face. The last of her makeup was gone now, and when she finally faced the mirror, her face looked bare and somehow purified without lipstick or foundation or mascara. Different.

When she had toweled her hair until it was reasonably dry, and tucked it up into the beret, she put on her clothes again. She wished she had taken time to wash out her panties before falling asleep, but it was too late now. It was time to be on the road again.

The hour, she learned from the car radio, was after midnight. That was good. No one would see her leave, and with any luck, no one had noticed her arrival, either. She followed the road back toward Interstate 91, stopping first for another hamburger and a large paper cup of coffee. She took the paperweight out of her jacket pocket and placed it on the seat beside her. "You're all the company I have, Nonna Angela," she said. The green glass sparkled dully, and the gold butterfly appeared and disappeared in the intermittent freeway lights.

As she passed the "Welcome to Ohio" sign, Tory gave it a victory salute. She could do this. It was hard, and it was lonely, but she could do it.

That was a good thing, because she had no other choice.

3

❧

Tu che di gel sei cinta, da
tanta fiamma vinta, l'amerai anche tu!

You who are girded with ice, conquered
by such burning passion, you will love him, too!

—Liù, *Turandot,* Act Three

The ocean was gray and cold looking, with rolling waves that splashed and broke on the sandy beach and left irregular lines of brackish foam. A great rock, nearly black in the muted light, rose against the backdrop of the sea and the cool gray sky. Tory pulled on her coat, and stepped out of the Beetle into the gravel parking lot of the viewpoint. Seagulls swooped and cried above her head, and some sort of little long-beaked bird—a sandpiper, maybe—trotted here and there on the sand. There was no one else around, though rows of beach houses stretched to the north and south. She turned up her collar against the chill wind as she stepped over a weathered log that marked the end of the road.

The end of *her* road. She had traveled as far west as she could. Unless she were to turn south into California, her trip was over.

She had driven straight across the country, stopping only when she was too tired to drive any farther, subsisting on fast food and the occasional apple from a convenience store. She was wearing drugstore lingerie under the jeans and sweater she had started with. At the same drugstore she had bought a box of hair dye and a pair of scissors, a fake leather purse, a toothbrush and toothpaste, and a tube of hand cream.

At a diner in Wyoming she had picked up a *USA Today* someone had left behind. When she turned past the front page, she found a photo of her Escalade, nose jammed into the rocks of the Winooski River, open doors crumpled by its headlong rush to the bottom of the bank. The headline of the article read, "Missing Vermont Therapist," and there was a blurry reproduction of her license photo. Swiftly, she closed the paper and thrust it under the seat. She didn't want to read it, and she didn't want to risk someone seeing a picture of her. That day she cut her hair and dyed it, and tossed the beret into a Dumpster.

"It was so odd," she mused aloud, when she was on the road again. She had laid the paperweight carefully in a layer of plastic shopping bags, worried it might roll off the seat and crack. Through the long days of driving, she had taken to talking to it, speaking her random thoughts aloud as if Nonna Angela could hear her. "Missing Vermont Therapist, I mean. It didn't seem to apply to me at all." She had read once that for an actor, stepping onto the stage in a role meant thinking and moving and *feeling* as her character would. Putting aside everything else, anything that didn't belong in the world of the play. She was doing that. She was on her own stage, in her new role.

And now, her character would stop traveling.

When she had seen the sign, just off Highway 101, she had felt that familiar pain, like a dull arrow piercing her breast. This time she understood what her fey was telling her, and she obeyed it. The moment she turned off the highway, the pain eased, and as she followed the signs it lessened swiftly, until she could hardly feel it. As she drove over a concrete bridge into the rather rustic-looking town, the pain subsided. To her right, the ocean tossed in the misty light. Ahead, simple two-lane streets ran past businesses and restaurants and the sorts of shops tourist towns featured. Most of these were closed, and there were almost no cars on the streets. The season was over. October in this northwest coastal state must be at least as cold as October in Vermont, and no doubt considerably damper.

Tory stood in the viewpoint facing the beach for half an hour, watching the waves dash themselves against the big rock and listening to her intuition. The movement of the water held her gaze, called to her in some way she couldn't have described. For so many days there had been nothing, and no one, that seemed significant. Now, on this rocky beach, the breakers seemed to catch the rhythm of her heartbeat, to draw out the tempo of her breathing. Ice Woman still admitted no feelings, but she didn't want to leave the sea's edge.

Her face was chilled and her fingers were stiff with cold by the time she turned back to the Beetle, but she had decided. Her journey was over.

She climbed back into the Beetle, saying, "We're here. We're done driving." The paperweight, from its plastic nest, glowed green and gold in the gray light.

Tory glanced to her left and right, deciding which side of the town would be best to explore. To the north were hotels, inns, restaurants, all oriented toward the view of the ocean and the great rock anchoring the beach. It seemed to her that the residential streets stretched in the other direction. She cranked up the heat in the Beetle, backed out of the parking lot, and turned south.

With no map and no directions, she began driving through neighborhoods, more or less at random. Some streets were little more than packed dirt, while some were paved, but without sidewalks. The houses ranged from tiny cottages to the sorts of mansions rich people built as their weekend homes. She eyed them all, watching for rental signs, turning this way and that, always keeping the beach and the water in sight.

After twenty minutes of this, when she was beginning to think she would need to buy gas for the Beetle, she found herself on a windswept, narrow dirt lane lined with beach grass and the occasional boulder. She passed a broken bench, obviously meant to face the big rock and the ocean. It had collapsed on its concrete apron, tilted off its iron frame. "Someone should fix that," she said. The houses here were small, built close together, with postage-stamp yards and no garages. They were shuttered, garden gates locked, yards empty, everything put away for the winter. "I don't know," Tory mused aloud. "Maybe we should go back—"

But there it was. Its shingles were worn to a silvery gray, its white shutters in need of paint, its tiny square of yard worn down to the dirt. One of the shutters hung askew. A waist-high picket fence surrounded it, with crooked posts and a wooden gate missing two boards at the bottom. A sign tacked to the fence read "For Rent by Owner."

Tory turned the Beetle into the short driveway and turned off the engine. There was no garage, or even a carport, but the Beetle wouldn't mind. It would do for now.

"Where are your things, Ms. Chambers?" Chambers. Chosen because there were a lot of them in the telephone book of the last motel she had stayed in.

The owner of the cottage was Iris Anderson, a lean, weathered-looking woman of about sixty. She eyed the empty Beetle as she unlatched the battered gate.

Tory hadn't thought of this. "I'm having them shipped," she blurted.

Of course she needed things. Everyone had them, carted them around in satchels and boxes and luggage. It wasn't normal not to have cartons to unload, suitcases to unpack. She had nothing but the fake-leather drugstore purse with her few possessions in it. That, the butterfly paperweight, one client file, and a coat full of cash. It was an assortment sure to cause comment.

Iris Anderson assessed her with a sharp gray gaze. "Knew you were coming to Cannon Beach, then?"

Lifting the corners of her lips in a smile felt to Tory like lifting heavy weights. "I've always wanted to live here," she said.

Iris Anderson nodded, evidently satisfied. "We hear that a lot. Not usually in the wintertime, though."

"I love the water in all weather. And please call me P-Paulette." She should have practiced saying that more. And should have chosen a name that didn't come from an opera, but it was all she could think of. There hadn't been a Paulette Chambers in the phone book.

"I will, thanks. You can call me Iris." Iris produced a heavy, old-fashioned key from her cloth shoulder bag, and unlocked the front door. "I always keep one key, just for emergencies. This is for you—" She held it out. "I hope you won't lose it. There are only two."

"I'll be careful."

Tory stepped in through the front door of the cottage, and knew without a doubt she had done the right thing.

"There's only one bedroom," Iris said. "And one bath. Do you have much company?"

"No. Not really."

Iris glanced over her shoulder. "No family?"

"Not anymore."

"Hard to believe. A pretty redhead like you."

"Well, thank you. But I'm all on my own."

Iris raised one iron-gray eyebrow, but didn't say anything else. She stood aside so Tory could take in the room.

It was impossibly simple, even austere. It was as different from her own home as it could be, but that gave Tory a sense of security. A worn armchair faced the picture window. A floor lamp stood near it, beside a wood-burning fireplace. A short sofa, even more worn, faced the fireplace, with a low and obviously cheap coffee table in front of it, all of it supported by a braided rug. The kitchen opened directly to the right, and a door that must lead to the bedroom opened to the left. Tory crossed to this door, and looked in to see a double bed covered with a beige chenille bedspread. Beyond the bed a door stood open to a bathroom just big enough to hold a chipped porcelain clawfoot tub and a sink with a mirrored cabinet.

Iris came to stand behind her. "No shower, I'm afraid," she said. "I rent mostly to summer people, and they're only here a week or so at a time. They don't mind, and they use a hose out back to wash off the sand."

Tory's smile felt more natural this time. "I like it. I'll just glance at the kitchen."

The kitchen was simple, too, but the stove was gas, which was nice. To say that the refrigerator was old was an understatement, but it was spotlessly clean. Iris said, "There are a few pots and pans, and some dishes. Probably you'll want to push those to the back and use your own, since you have things coming."

"Probably." It seemed safest to agree. Tory began to wish Iris would leave. She seemed nice enough, but she wanted to be on her own, to *taste* the house, to gaze out through the front window at the waves rolling against the beach and splashing the sides of the big rock.

Iris saw her glance at the view, and led the way to the window. The two women stood side by side for a moment, watching the water. "This is why people come," Iris said. "And why I keep the place."

"Have you had it a long time?"

"It belonged to my folks. They lived in Portland. Used to bring us out here weekends."

"It's perfect for me," Tory said. "I don't need much room, and I can manage the price."

"The rent goes up in the spring," Iris said.

"I understand. Maybe by then I'll have a job."

She wished she hadn't said that. Iris turned to face her. Tory saw the older woman measuring her again. She was curious, but she had the right. It was, after all, her house. "What kind of work do you do?"

Tory looked away from Iris's canny glance, back to the constant movement of the water. "Anything I can get," she said.

"Really? I would have guessed you were a professional of some kind. Teacher, nurse, maybe a librarian."

Tory shook her head, keeping her gaze on the ocean. "No."

Iris was even more curious when Tory went into the bedroom to take off her coat and hang it in the closet, then came back with the deposit and the first month's rent in her hand. "Cash?" Iris said when she saw it.

"Is that a problem?"

"Well, no, of course not. It's just—usually people write a check, since I don't do credit cards." Her brows drew together suddenly, furrowing her forehead. "I don't do things under the table," she warned. "Everything goes on my tax forms, just so you know."

Tory hadn't begun to think about taxes, Social Security, any of the myriad other details that constituted modern life. "No problem," she said. Her throat felt dry, and she was suddenly very, very tired. Too tired to be clever. "I'm just between banks right now, that's all. It might take me a couple of weeks to find a new one."

"You took your money out in cash?"

In other circumstances, Tory might have been impressed by the woman's tenacity, but she wanted nothing more than to be alone, to soak in the bathtub with its rust stains and old-fashioned faucets, and then sit in the rented armchair and stare at the surf. She said, a little more sharply than she intended, "No. Not all of it," and turned away from her new landlady.

"So," Iris said after a moment's pause. "There are sheets on the bed, and towels in the bathroom. There's a charge to change them each week, though, so if you have your own—"

"I do," Tory said. "They'll be here tomorrow."

"Good. That's good. Then I just need a signature on this rental agreement." Iris still looked a bit wary, but Tory took a motel ballpoint from her drugstore bag, carried the form to the kitchen table—Formica-topped and much-scarred—and signed it. She had created a former address and memorized it, and she wrote that in.

Iris took the form and glanced at it. "Georgia?" she said. "You don't have a Southern accent."

"I was raised in the Midwest," Tory said smoothly. This much, at least, she had rehearsed. She had also invented a college degree from a tiny school she had seen on her trip, and imagined a family background. She hoped that for now she wouldn't need her made-up history. She was beginning to feel she couldn't stand on her own two feet any longer.

Iris seemed to sense this. She put out her hand, said an abrupt good-bye, and was gone a moment later, spinning down the dirt lane in a fairly new white Acura sedan. Tory looked down at her copy of the rental form, and saw that Iris also lived in Cannon Beach. She could stop by the cottage at any time. Tory would have to be ready.

She folded the rental agreement and tucked it into a kitchen drawer next to a pair of rusty scissors and a pizza delivery menu. She pulled the faded cotton curtains across the picture window, shot the dead bolt on the front door, and turned toward the bathroom.

She slept without dreaming, without even turning over. Rain woke her in the morning, a steady, rhythmic beating on the flat roof of the cottage. Lacking a bathrobe, she pulled the chenille bedspread around her and padded to the window to open the curtains. She couldn't see the collapsed bench from this vantage point. Rain obscured the beach and the surf, and made muddy rivulets in the dirt lane. The little yard soaked up the water as if it had been yearning for moisture. Tory thought she might even be able to get a little grass to grow there, if she tried. Odd, that she was thinking of a lawn. Did ice women plant gardens?

She drew the curtains again, and went to put on her clothes. She couldn't remember exactly when she had last eaten, and her jeans were so loose she was afraid they might not stay up. First, she thought, food. Then, with some calories to fuel her brain, she would think how to acquire the things that would make her seem respectable. Make her character come alive.

She found a tiny restaurant on the main road of the town, and ordered eggs and coffee and toast. It tasted so good in her mouth it surprised her. It tasted like—life. Like she was still alive. She ate everything. When she had drunk a second cup of coffee, she paid her bill—breaking another fifty—and went back to the Beetle. She turned north, back on the coast highway, where she had spotted a sign for a Costco store the day before.

Three hours later she possessed a new Costco card, four place settings of china and flatware, a set of thick glass tumblers, a skillet and saucepan, towels, a radio, and a prepaid cell phone issued to Paulette Chambers. She found a pair of jeans a size smaller than the ones she had on, and two thick sweaters to go with them. She chose two novels from the laden tables of books. She bought frozen pizza, some frozen fish and vegetables, and three bottles of red wine. She paid for it all with hundred-dollar bills. No one seemed to care if Paulette's birth date and Social Security number were fictional. No one blinked at the cash. Her identity was established.

She was on her way back to the highway when she spotted an antiques store just off the road to her right. On an impulse, she turned the Beetle into its muddy parking lot. There were only two other cars there, and it occurred to her that she didn't know what day of the week it was. She had lost all track of time.

The sign on the door said the store was open, so she parked and climbed out, taking care to lock the car with all her new things stuffed into the backseat. If anything was stolen, she could hardly call the police. It gave her an odd sense of vulnerability, of being without a form of protection she had always taken for granted.

The interior of the antiques store was the exact opposite of Costco's. Where Costco was full of the smell of new plastic and cardboard and the rubbery reek of tires, the antiques store smelled of age and dust and history. A middle-aged woman in an acid-green pantsuit nodded hello from behind a glass cabinet that served as her counter. It was littered with small pieces of paper, a telephone, and an oversized calculator. Tory nodded back, then turned to stroll down the first aisle she came to.

She immediately regretted buying her dishes and silverware at Costco. This place was stuffed with things she could have used, and some of them had no fault except their age. Partial sets of dishes, of silverware, of Depression glass, filled the cabinets. Tory gazed at them, struck by the thought that once they had been as new as the things now packed into the back of the Beetle. People had bought them, used them, incorporated them into their lives. What had happened to the woman who stirred bread dough in that pottery bowl, or the child who drank milk from that pink glass?

She touched the glass, thinking of Jack when he was small, laughing at her across the breakfast table. They hadn't laughed together in such a long time. *Oh, Jack. Sweetheart. I'm so very, very sorry.*

She clenched her teeth with a jolt of alarm at the rush of emotion that swept over her. She couldn't allow it. She could *not* feel. She didn't dare. She pulled her hand away from the pink glass, and breathed sharply to release the tightness in her throat.

When she felt she was in control again, she turned to another display. She picked up a soup bowl, and her fey sent a faint vibration through her fingers, as if the users of it had left an imprint, an invisible mark of history in the simple implement. She kept the bowl, and picked up a matching one to nest inside it. She found a ladle, and a rolling pin that resonated with memories of Thanksgiving pies and Christmas cookies. She picked up a saltcellar with a tarnished silver lid and a tiny matching spoon. The woman from the counter, seeing, came and took the things from her, carrying them back to the cash register to wait for her to finish shopping.

Tory bought six vintage cloth napkins and an embroidered apron with only a tiny stain at the hem. She chose two wineglasses with twisted stems that had no doubt once been part of a full set. She hesitated over a box of old LPs. She saw a precious recording among them of Risë Stevens's *Carmen*, but she made herself resist. She had no way to play it, and she had resolved to avoid that link to the past. Surely there would be a classical music station out of Portland. She would content herself with that.

She wandered around the store one more time, trailing her finger-tips over tasteless vases and lamps without shades, eyeing cabinets full of bric-a-brac. She was turning back toward the counter when a collection of framed photographs caught her eye. She picked one up, a picture of a woman in a dress from the forties, framed in Bakelite. Behind it was a photo of the same woman in a wedding gown, surrounded by a family in dress clothes. Tory gazed at the pictures for several moments. She could imagine, looking at the face of the woman, someone who was kind and maternal and sensitive. Someone she dared talk to.

Though she knew it didn't really make sense, Tory piled the pictures on top of the napkins and the apron.

It all seemed too easy. She could create an entire history with such things, invent a background made up of the bits and pieces of other people's lives. Could she create a future, too?

"You have some great things here," the woman said when she went back to the counter. She used the big calculator to add up the total. "Do you buy a lot of antiques? Would you like to be on our mailing list?"

"Oh. Oh, I don't . . . I'm not from here, actually."

"Tourist?"

"Yes—sort of." Tory thought she could have handled that better, but the woman didn't seem to notice. Probably saw dozens of tourists every day.

"I'll wrap everything so nothing gets broken."

"Thanks. I appreciate it." Tory counted out the money from her drugstore handbag.

"I love your hair," the woman said, as she began wrapping things in butcher paper. "I wish I could wear that color red. And wear my hair that short."

Tory touched her hair. She kept forgetting what she had done to it. She said, "I'm not all that sure I pull it off, either."

"No, you do! Really. Your skin and those eyelashes—I wish I had the courage not to wear makeup."

Tory's cheeks flushed. She could hardly connect herself with the person the woman was describing.

Her cheeks were still burning as she loaded her new-old possessions into the Beetle, and backed out of the parking lot. Her character must be working. Her new persona was as different from the old one as she could make it.

The rain had stopped by the time she got back to the cottage. She made half a dozen trips from the car to the house, then spent the afternoon stowing things. As Iris had suggested, she pushed the vacation-house utensils to the back of the kitchen cupboards, and put her own plates and glasses near the front. She found an empty drawer for the silverware, and a closet for the towels and sheets. She set the radio on one corner of the kitchen counter, where she could plug it in. She stowed her frozen food in the tiny freezer compartment. She stuffed the boxes for everything into the recycle bin behind the cottage, hoping no one was going to look in and realize almost everything she had was new.

Finally, she began unwrapping her antiques store purchases. Napkins went in a drawer, and the little saltcellar beside the stove. She hung the apron on a hook beside the refrigerator. She unwrapped the photographs, and carried them into the living room. She arranged them on the flimsy coffee table and stood looking down at them. They gazed back at her from their happy days, smiling, looking proud and—

Normal, was the word that came to her mind. It made her feel wistful, and then foolish. She, of all people, knew there was no normal. It wasn't just her own life that was fragmented and strange. She had counseled hundreds of people, and not a single one thought their lives were normal. These people, too, must have had their problems, their sorrows, their losses.

She turned resolutely away from the smiling faces of strangers. They were simply part of the set she was creating. The backdrop for the illusion she had invented, against which she would act out her new role. It would be good to remember that.

Nonna Angela's paperweight had been waiting on the kitchen table. Tory picked it up, cradling its cool, familiar weight in her hand. She carried it into the bedroom, and set it on the narrow bedside stand, beneath the lamp, where she could see it when she was reading in bed. It felt good to have it with her, though its elegance was out of place in this rustic house. She touched it with her forefinger, and said, "I guess we're home."

There was nothing left to do. She went back into the kitchen, found a corkscrew in a drawer, nestled incongruously next to a hammer and a rusty screwdriver. She opened one of the bottles of wine and poured a generous glassful, then walked aimlessly into the living room to stand beside the picture window and look out at the ocean.

She watched the gray waves swirl on the sand, and wondered if this was the moment it would all catch up with her, come roiling to the surface like those waves, to eat away at the ice that encased her. She sipped wine, and stared at the water. She didn't feel anything, not even relief that she had a home, that she had a few things to comfort her, that no one could find her. She was used to missing Jack, of course. That shard of her broken life rested in its customary place, tucked just out of reach in the tidy closet of her mind.

No, she felt nothing. Just a touch of surprise that she had pulled it off. Ice Woman.

She ate baked fish and steamed vegetables for dinner, drank another glass of wine, and went to bed with one of the novels she had bought. The last thing she did before turning out the lamp was to touch the Murano paperweight, and wonder at the impulse that had made her put it in her pocket when she fled.

4

Forse come la rondine, migreró verso il mare,
verso un chiaro paese di sogno, verso il sole!

Perhaps like the swallow I will migrate toward the sea,
toward a bright country of dreams, toward the sun!

—Magda, *La Rondine,* Act One

The heat that rolled in from the swampy shore of the lake was the sort to wilt starched collars and turn linen tablecloths as limp as dishrags. It was thick and damp, a weight of late-summer heat that oppressed everyone's spirits. It made the villa seem cramped and crowded. The *signora* quarreled with the *signore* and snapped at the cook. Doria, the maid, dripped perspiration as she stood over her ironing board. Signor Puccini, with an irritated oath, stamped into his gun room, chose a shotgun from the rack, and strode away through the garden. His gun dogs rose from their kennel to follow him, but even they moved languidly, tails drooping in the heat. Doria, seeing, snatched up Puccini's hat from the hook near the back door and ran after him into the garden.

"Maestro!" she called, but softly. Elvira Puccini's second-floor bedroom, with its small balcony and painted shutters, faced the garden, and the window was open to receive the breeze from the lake. "Maestro, the sun—you really must wear your hat!"

Puccini had already gone out through the scrolled iron gate. He turned back, scowling, but his expression softened when he saw it was Doria trotting after him. He took a few steps back, raising one hand to show he had heard her. His field glasses hung around his neck on a leather cord, and he had put on his tall boots for tramping through the muck of the swamp. He reached across the gate and took the hat in his fine, strong fingers. "Doria," he said. He shifted his ever-present cigarette to the other side of his mouth. Lines of anger still marked his cheeks, and his full lips pressed tight beneath his brush of mustache. He shook his head, as if with the movement he could shake off his fit of temper. "My little nurse! You're the only one who stays calm in this weather."

"You must take care, maestro," Doria said. She shook one small finger at him. "My mamma would scold you for not covering your head in this heat."

He grinned suddenly, showing strong teeth yellowed by smoke, and she smiled back at him. "I tell you, Doria," he said, "I am deathly weary of being scolded by women. But since it's you—" He made a small, ironic bow as he accepted the hat from her hands. "And out of deference to Signora Manfredi, I will certainly wear the hat."

Doria nodded, satisfied. He looked much more youthful when he smiled, and that pleased her. She bobbed a hasty curtsy before she picked up her skirt and dashed back into the house, hurrying lest her mistress glance out the window. She paused when she was safely inside, and stood in the music studio to watch through the zinc screen as Puccini shouldered his gun and turned toward the lake, the two shaggy dogs at his heels. The last thing he did before he disappeared from her sight was to tilt his hat at a jaunty angle. Doria chuckled, but her smile faded as she turned to resume her chores. The *signore* was always kind to her, and appreciated her efforts. The *signora* was another matter, but the *signore* didn't seem to understand.

She found the kitchen peaceful. Old Zita, unwrapping a ball of mozzarella on the wooden counter, whispered that the *signora* was lying down with a cold compress. That was a relief to them both.

Elvira Puccini was famous for her temper, not only here in

Torre del Lago, but in all the cities the Puccinis visited. The heat made her worse, of course. Indeed, the sweltering temperatures made everyone cross. The best way to manage Signora Puccini, in such a situation, was to stay out of her way. At least today she had vented her ire on her husband and not on her servants. It was something to be grateful for.

Doria put away the ironing board, then fetched her bucket and rags from the cupboard, taking great care not to bang or drop anything. She dropped an extra dusting cloth into the front pocket of her pinafore apron before she went to clean the studio.

The maestro's studio was her favorite room in the house. She liked it even better than the bathroom, though she loved that, too, with its big white bathtub and a thick rug to step on when you climbed out. The bathroom of Villa Puccini had its own plumbing that delivered hot and cold water. It was nothing like being at her mother's simple house, where a tin tub had to be carted into the kitchen once a week and filled with kettlefuls of water heated on the stove. Here in Villa Puccini, you simply turned the brass taps and waited in delicious idleness for the water to flow in.

The studio, though, was the place where magic happened. In this room the maestro sat composing into the late hours, sometimes even right through the night. It was lovely, with windows facing the lake and walls covered with paintings of flowers in Florentine urns and lined with shelves full of books in Italian and French. The piano and the desk fitted together, so the composer could sit in his swivel chair, turning back and forth between the keyboard and the desk while he labored over his manuscripts and flicked ash from his cigarettes into a cut-glass ashtray.

There had been friends with him last night, Father Michelucci, Alfredo Caselli, and the poet Pascoli, drinking and playing cards while the maestro worked. Glasses and empty bottles littered the card table. Doria carried those into the kitchen, and emptied the maestro's ashtray. She dampened her dust rag, and began wiping up ashes and crumbs of bread and cheese. She cleaned the grate, polished the mosaics of the fireplace, and stretched on tiptoe to dust the inlaid mantelpiece.

When she turned to the black walnut piano she pulled the special dust cloth from her pocket. With reverence, she wiped down each separate key, thinking of the mystical notes that trickled through the darkness to her little room behind the kitchen. Though she took care not to sound them, it seemed the music vibrated through her fingertips anyway, a sensation both marvelous and faintly disturbing. She lifted the lid of the piano to polish the underside, then closed it, so no new dust would fall on the keyboard. She cleaned the candle sconces set into the carved front, and replaced the old stubs with new, unburned candles. Despite warnings from his doctors about his eyesight, Puccini still preferred to compose by candlelight, complaining that the electric lights—though he had gone to such pains to have his house supplied with them—were too harsh and glaring.

Doria had clear instructions about the sheets of music paper on the piano and on the desk. She carefully lifted the pile to dust beneath, and set them back in the precise order—indeed, the precise formation—he had left them. When she touched the pages, more music seemed to sing through her fingertips, chords now, and fragments of melody. She paused with her palm hovering over the manuscript. *La Fanciulla del West*, it said at the top. It was still a thin packet of pages, the opera only half begun, but she heard the music in her mind, the opening chords, the first fragments of the melodies. She couldn't read the music—a village girl like herself was lucky to be able to read at all—but every note the maestro played imprinted itself on her memory, and if she only had time, she felt sure she could connect the marks on the page with the sounds the maestro played.

It was a dream come true to work in the same house as the composer of *Edgar* and *Tosca*, *La Bohème* and especially *Madama Butterfly*, her favorite above all other operas. Sometimes singers came here to Torre to work with Puccini. They rehearsed through the long evenings, trying out the arias, listening to the composer's comments, arguing, laughing with their big, beautiful voices.

Doria loved those nights, and when the opera was *Madama Butterfly* she knelt beside the window in her little room behind the kitchen, listening as intently as if she had a ticket to sit in one of the great, gilded boxes of La Scala.

She knew the story of *Butterfly* by heart, though she had never been to the opera. Even the poorest of inhabitants of the village knew all of Maestro Puccini's operas. People hummed the tunes in the streets, and paused to listen outside Villa Puccini when the composer was playing through a score. The butcher sang arias from behind his counter. The priest and the doctor huddled over cups of *espresso* or glasses of *vin santo*, disputing the merits of *Bohème* and *Manon* and *Butterfly*.

Of course, *Madama Butterfly* was the greatest of all the maestro's works. Doria would never understand why there was any argument about that, nor why it had not been instantly hailed as a masterwork. Not only was the music glorious—she could sing all the way through Un bel dì herself, though she only did it in private, when no one could hear—but the story was irresistible. Beautiful Cio-Cio-San, little Butterfly, thought the naval officer from America really loved her, had truly married her, saved her from her life as a geisha. Poor Butterfly, who named her little son Sorrow for the heartache that was to come. Even thinking about Butterfly kneeling above the bay, watching for her beloved's ship to return, brought tears to Doria's eyes. Then, when he did come, he brought his American wife, and wanted to take Sorrow home to raise in America! It was too cruel.

Sometimes, when Elvira Puccini had one of her bad days, Doria thought of Cio-Cio-San. Butterfly's story reminded her how dreadful things could really be for a powerless girl. She was no more than a few heartbeats away from being as helpless as Cio-Cio-San, destined for a life of drudgery and too many children. She blinked, and shook off the thought. It didn't have to be the same with her as it was with her mother! And she had the Puccinis to thank for that, even the *signora* with her uncertain disposition!

Doria finished with the piano and moved around to the desk. She dusted the surface, under the blotter, around the bronze base of the lamp. She wiped ashes from everything, including some that had spilled onto the wooden floor. She placed a fresh packet of cigarettes near the clean ashtray. She dropped the cloth into her bucket, and stood back to admire her handiwork.

Only one thing looked out of place. The maestro treasured it, because his beloved mother had given it to him after the premiere of *Madama Butterfly*. Doria loved it, too, because the older Signora Puccini had always been kind to her. When Doria was nursing the maestro after his car accident, his mother sometimes brought her little things—a book, an embroidered handkerchief, a box of chocolates at Christmas. Doria had seen Puccini caress the little paperweight with his fingers. She expected it made him feel connected to his mother. He had grieved so terribly when she died.

The paperweight was from the island of Murano. It was a delicate green, with a cunning little gold butterfly somehow set deep inside the crystal. It usually rested on the stack of music pages, to keep them from blowing about when the window was open, but it had somehow been moved to the edge of the desk, where it rested in a precarious position. Perhaps he had been holding it, toying with it. She leaned forward, and set it into its proper place. It was enchantingly cool and smooth, and she imagined she could sense the sweetness of Albina Puccini through her lingering fingertips.

"Doria!" The screech came from the kitchen. Guiltily, the girl pulled her hand away from the paperweight, bent to seize her bucket, and hurried out of the studio.

Elvira was opening drawers, cupboards, even the icebox, slamming each shut when she didn't find what she wanted. Doria said hastily, "I'm here, signora. Do you need something?"

"I can't find my locket, the one Giacomo gave me!" Elvira straightened, spinning in a whirl of full skirts. The white gauze of her summer-weight frock was so sheer Doria could see the shape of her plump legs in their white stockings. Her own dress was plain brown cotton, made from remnants her mother bought in the market at Viareggio.

"Did you take it from my dressing table?" Elvira demanded.

Doria, with a start, lifted her gaze to the *signora*'s face. Her natural temper flared, making her cheeks burn. "No, signora!" she said. "No, of course I didn't!" *Veramente*—did she expect to find her locket in the icebox? She was mad. *Pazza.*

"I told you to dust the bedroom, not to rearrange my things!" Elvira's dark eyes, her only good feature except for her abundant black hair, narrowed.

"I didn't! I mean, I did dust, but I didn't touch—"

"*Cretina!* How could you dust if you didn't touch?"

Doria judged that silence was the best answer to this. She stood still, her jaw set, her bucket hanging from her hand, and waited for the storm to pass.

Elvira strode across the kitchen, her leather heels clicking on the flagstones, until she stood so close to Doria that the scent of her perfume and the odor of her perspiration made the girl's nose twitch. "I know what you're up to," Elvira hissed.

Doria said, mystified, *"Cosa?"*

"Oh, yes. Don't think I don't notice how you look at my husband! It won't do you any good, I can promise you, my girl. If you keep it up, I'll have you out on the street, *subito!*"

She was gone before Doria grasped her meaning, and when she did, her hands shook so with fury she almost dropped the bucket of wash water. *Look* at him? Look at the maestro? The idea that she might even consider him as a possibility—a romantic possibility for herself, a peasant girl from Torre del Lago—was so preposterous she could hardly believe the *signora* had said it.

She had only just pulled herself together enough to empty the bucket out the back door and hang her wet rags on the clothesline in the back garden when she heard her name once again, shrieked this time from Elvira's window. "Doria!"

She ran for the stairs.

"Doria!"

Tory startled awake. She found herself sitting straight up in bed, her pillow thrust aside, the chenille bedspread sliding to the

floor. She blinked in the darkness, surprised by the damp coolness of the air inside the cottage. Ocean air. Not lake. Autumn-
cool, not July-hot. What had she—

As she shook off the last shreds of sleep, she realized it had
been a dream. It was only a dream, one of those vague, shadowy
processions of unlikely events and unfamiliar people. She put a
hand to her forehead, and found her hair damp from the heat of
that place she had imagined. How strange that her dream should
seem real enough to make her perspire!

She sat on the edge of the bed, fighting her disorientation.
When she got to her feet, the chill air brought goose bumps to
her thighs. She picked up the bedspread to pull around herself,
careful not to knock over the paperweight on her bedside table.

She was already in the kitchen, digging in the lowest cupboard
for a teakettle, when she remembered. She stopped, one arm
reaching past her new cookware. She was crouched on the
linoleum floor, gazing at the darkness beyond the windows.

The paperweight. It had been in her dream. How odd that
was, after all these years. She had grown up with that object.
When her Nonna Angela moved in with them, the small Tory
had watched her unpack, fascinated by the strange objects that
came from the old cardboard valise. The paperweight had been
the very last, the most precious, wrapped in layers of tissue
paper. Nonna Angela had smiled, and rubbed it with her fingers
to clear away any dust before she set it on a shelf where it would
be out of the reach of a curious child. Why should such a thing
show up in a dream?

Symbolic, she told herself. Something of home and family, all
lost to her now.

She found the teakettle, straightened, and went to the sink to
fill it. As it heated, she turned on her new radio, and twirled the
dial until she found the classical station. The signal was strong
and clear in the uncluttered night air. With a cup of tea steaming
gently in her hand, she went to the little living room. She opened
the curtains before she sat in the armchair, tucking her bare feet
up beneath the bedspread. She gazed out at the glimmer of light

on the waves below the beach. The rain had stopped, but clouds still obscured the stars. No other lights showed along the dirt lane. She felt more alone, more isolated, than she ever had in her life, even more than when her grandmother died. At least then she had her parents, inadequate though they were.

She listened to the ending movement of a Brahms string quartet, sipping tea, trying to let the dream fade from her mind. It was interesting that it still bothered her, though she had been awake for the better part of an hour. It was only a dream, after all, and not a particularly unpleasant one.

What had actually happened to her, in real life, in the clear light of an October day, was the stuff of nightmare. Why wasn't she dreaming of Ellice's furious face, the cold shock of a knife blade slicing her skin, the bruising flight into the woods, the Escalade smashed at the bottom of the gully? Or dreaming something even worse, the thing she most dreaded—Ellice with Jack in the sights of her gun?

Instead, her first dream since her real-life nightmare had been a complete fiction, about people she didn't know, a place she had never seen, objects that meant nothing to her.

Except for Nonna Angela's Murano glass paperweight.

In other circumstances, she might have found it all humorous, but Ice Woman had no laughter in her. She didn't have any feelings at all—except for those she had felt in the dream. The therapist in her found that intriguing.

5

Ah! triste madre! Abbandonar mio figlio!

Ah! sad mother! To abandon my son!

—Butterfly, *Madama Butterfly*, Act Three

Jack stood in the foyer of Our Lady of the Forests, accepting the sympathies of his mother's colleagues and clients. They shook his hand, murmured regrets, eyed him and each other with curiosity. Father Wilburton stood beside him through it all.

Jack thought this was particularly kind, since he barely knew the priest. He had stopped coming to Mass when he decided, at the age of fourteen, to become an atheist. The Garveys were atheists, and as a teenager, he had admired everything about the Garveys. The Garveys, though, had been gone a long time. Father Wilburton was here, and his quiet presence at Jack's shoulder felt good, a little island in the sea of grief and fear that tossed around him.

The police, in a painful and awkward interview, had taken pains to make it clear they considered Tory's case a "death investigation," not a missing persons one. Still, the event today hadn't been a service, since there was as yet no body and no declaration of death. It had been a gathering, a memorial, really, worried people coming together in the Fellowship Hall beneath the sanctuary. There had been coffee, cookies, lemonade. Tory didn't have many close friends—in fact, she really only had one—but she had a long list of clients and associates. Father Wilburton encouraged people to step up to the standing mike on the little stage usually reserved for Christmas pageants and spelling bees, and say a few words about Tory. Several did, and Jack listened in stony silence, trying to make sense of it all.

Nothing about the day seemed real. His heart thudded, and his eyes burned, but even those sensations felt as if they belonged to someone else. It was like watching a scene from one of his mother's beloved operas. Somber people, dressed in the dark colors of mourning, shook hands, embraced, murmured softly to each other. It all felt stagey. Jack had the bizarre notion that he could turn it off at any time, like turning off the television. If he could just find the right switch, it would all disappear.

It wasn't that he didn't care. When the dean of his college called him into her office to tell him his mother was missing, he had been speechless with shock. He had stumbled out of the administration building, forgetting to say anything to the dean, barely able to see his way on the stairs. She wanted to send someone with him, to stay with him. He had merely shaken his head, trying to process the news. For hours he could hardly breathe for grief and fear. And guilt.

His hands shook as he packed a few clothes for the trip home. His mouth was so dry it took him three tries to explain to his roommate what had happened. When he was finished packing, he found himself sitting uselessly on his bed, staring at his suitcase. He couldn't organize himself enough to call a taxi. His roommate finally did it for him, and even offered to come with him. Jack had refused, pulled himself together enough to get into the taxi, go to the station, buy a ticket. He stood on the platform, numb with horror, until the train arrived.

It was when he was in his seat, staring in misery at his reflection in the night-darkened window, that it struck him. He didn't know how he knew, but he did.

Fresh guilt assailed him. He had scoffed at Tory's premonitions, even mocked her for them. She had stopped telling him about them years ago. Now, here he was, alone on a train, having heard the worst possible news, and he was unable to fight off the conviction that it was all wrong.

Sitting in the cramped train seat with his legs stretched under the seat in front of him, Jack stared at the lights of houses flashing past, and examined the strange sensation.

He could only barely remember what Tory had told him about her little fey, as she called it. He couldn't have been more than twelve or thirteen, just old enough to act scornful of anything his mother did or said. He remembered her saying it was like something stabbed her in the chest. Jack didn't feel that at all. He felt it as a sudden knowledge tingling in the middle of his head. It carried an irrational surety words couldn't explain, and it gave him a slight feeling of vertigo, as if he had just done a somersault.

Tory wasn't dead. His mother wasn't lost. She hadn't vanished. They were wrong when they said she was. It didn't matter what they said, what they told him. He knew. Somehow, somewhere, Tory was still in the world.

The steady clack of the train wheels on the iron tracks seemed to underline his conviction.

That conviction had not left Jack, and it added to the sense that he was acting, here in Our Lady of the Forests. He was playing the part of the bereaved son, and he wasn't doing very well at it, but he couldn't think what else to do. Who would believe him if he tried to explain? The sheriff who had shaken his hand, pursed his lips, and looked as if he might cry? His high school counselor, who hugged him and said, "Call me if you want to talk"? Father Wilburton would no doubt tell him it was natural to feel the way he did. He would say he was in denial, the first stage of grief. Jack knew enough about his mother's profession to have picked up that bromide, but it didn't fit.

Tory's best friend and closest neighbor came up now, car keys rattling in her hand. "I'll drive you home when you're ready, Jack." Kate was a middle-aged woman, possibly ten years older than Tory. She looked even older than that, especially today.

But then, Tory had always looked young, even to the critical eye of her son. The clear blonde of her hair never seemed to change. She was lean and muscular from doing her own chores around the place. She didn't wear a lot of cosmetics, but she didn't need them. Her skin was clear and smooth, often flushed from walking in the fresh air.

He was sure he had never told her any of that. Never complimented her, at least not for a very long time.

He swallowed, and told himself he would think about all of that later. "We can go now," he told Kate. "I think everyone's left."

They turned toward the front doors of the church, with Father Wilburton beside them. Jack stepped out into the gloomy light of the late October afternoon, pulling up the collar of his wool blazer against the cold. He was waiting for Kate to follow him outside when a big woman, as tall as Jack and with broader shoulders, hurried up the steps from the street, taking them two at a time. She was sandy-haired, with freckled, ruddy cheeks, and she thrust out her hand to Jack with an abrupt movement that made him take a sudden step back.

"Sorry I'm late, Jack," the woman blurted. "I was on duty."

Jack hadn't noticed until that moment that the woman wore a police uniform, with a heavy Sam Browne belt and a black handgun strapped into its holster. The thick vest beneath her shirt gave her a barrel-chested look. Her hand was big and strong looking.

The officer hesitated with her hand outstretched, then let it drop. "You don't know me."

"No. Have we met?"

The officer shook her head. "I've seen your picture in your mother's office. I feel as if I know you. I just wanted to tell you how sorry I am about Tory."

"Thanks." Jack felt Kate move uneasily beside him, and he managed to say, as he had said to so many that day, "It's kind of you to come."

"I guess I missed everyone else."

Kate said, "There's a guest book. Please go in and sign it."

Father Wilburton said, "This way, officer. We brought it up into the foyer."

"I'll come back for that, Father," Kate said.

The policewoman nodded to Jack before she followed the priest into the shadows of the church. Kate took Jack's arm, and guided him down the steps toward the parking lot.

"Who was that?" Jack said.

Kate shook her head. "I don't know. That's a sheriff's deputy's uniform."

"Mom never told me she had a police officer as a client."

"Honey, there are probably a thousand things she never told you. Therapists aren't supposed to talk about their clients, are they?"

Jack didn't answer. It wasn't just that Tory hadn't discussed her clients with him. He and his mother had stopped talking a long time ago. That is to say, he had stopped listening to her, and she, bit by bit, had grown silent in his presence. The thought made his throat ache.

Kate started the engine of her Honda, and backed out of the now-empty parking lot, turning toward the park road. "I'm going to fix you some dinner. I've already told Chet I won't be home."

"That's not necessary."

"I thought you might be lonely."

Jack gazed out the window as they left the sparse neighborhood of the church and drove up toward the park and the few houses that dotted the familiar hillside just outside its boundary. "I couldn't wait to get away from here," he said. "And now I wish—I wish I could put everything back the way it was."

"That's natural. It's a terrible loss for you—for all of us—but I know Tory wouldn't want you to grieve too much."

It burst out of him, before he realized he was going to say it. "I'm a lousy son."

For a terrible moment, Kate didn't say anything. He took her silence as an acknowledgment of the truth of what he'd said. When she finally spoke, she said only, "You're young, Jack."

"Twenty," he said bitterly.

"Well. Twenty is young, though you might not think so. You're still finding yourself."

He made a small, involuntary noise that might have sounded rude. He hoped not. It was really a sound of pain and regret. He didn't know how to explain that to her.

She glanced at him, and he saw tears in her eyes, tears she had managed to resist during the memorial. "I hope you can have good memories of her," she said, her voice a little too high. "She was—remarkable." Her voice cracked on the word, and she turned her head away.

He didn't dare answer for fear his own voice would break.

They drove for a while in unhappy silence. Jack watched the stands of trees grow thicker as they climbed the hill. The maples were like flames of red and gold against the dark green backdrop of the eastern cedars. The beauty of it hurt somehow, as if it were a reproach.

When they were getting close, Kate said, "I wish you'd reconsider staying at our place. You'd be so welcome, Jack. All the kids are gone, and—"

He shook his head. "Thanks, Kate, but I'll be fine."

"Not nervous?"

"Nervous? No."

"Well, I would be," Kate said frankly. "Since no one really knows what happened."

Jack turned his head to look at Kate's plain, familiar profile. "You're the only person willing to talk about it," he said.

Kate kept her eyes on the road. "The police talk about it, surely."

"Well, yes. The sheriff's people. They always say the same thing. 'We're doing all we can.' " He shrugged. "I think it's shorthand for 'We don't have a clue.' "

"Honey, if Tory drowned—" Kate winced as she spoke the word.

"I know that's what they think. They said there was no reason to think she's alive." They had dragged the river, they told him. Searched the banks, below and even above the site of the accident, and found nothing.

Kate nodded, pressing her trembling lips with her finger. After a moment, she said in a choked voice, "It could be months before they find her."

"Yeah. If ever."

Kate touched his shoulder with her soft hand. "It hasn't hit you yet, I'm afraid."

"It doesn't seem real." He watched the familiar flicker of a porch light here and there. He knew every house, every family that lived up here in the foothills. They passed Kate and Chet's driveway, with its funny mailbox in the shape of a doghouse, before they turned into his own. Tory's mailbox was a tasteful gray-and-white rectangle, matching the paint of her house. The driveway was long and twisting, a narrow lane with a neat and fairly new layer of gravel. It looked as if she had raked it recently. It led nearly to the top of the hill, where the house had a view of the valley to the east and the park to the west. They had lived in it, Tory and Jack, as long as he could remember.

Jack had decided, at the age of fourteen, to blame his mother for everything—for having no father, no siblings, no other family. He understood, later, that it made no sense, but he hadn't gotten around to telling her that. Or maybe he just hadn't wanted to say it, and receive a therapist sort of answer about adolescents and their feelings. Sometimes he thought, when he was still a teenager, that she must not really care, or she would be angry, scold him, shout at him the way other mothers did. The way Mary Garvey shouted at her kids and her husband.

But Tory wasn't like that. She was . . . contained. Controlled. He rarely saw her show emotion except when she was listening to music.

The silence of the house, as they got out of the car and approached the front door, added to the strangeness of the day. When Tory had been here—and Tory had always been here when Jack came home, something that used to irritate him and now filled him with desperate sadness—music had met him, pouring out through the front door, or through an open window in summer. If it was early in the day, it was baroque. Bach, Vivaldi, Handel. If it was afternoon, Tory would have progressed to classical—Haydn, perhaps, or Mozart. Jack would always know the workday was over if the music that greeted him was opera. He had resented it, felt as if she was imposing her own tastes on him and anyone else that came into her sphere. He had often plunged up the stairs to his room to play opposing music, punk or metal or even country, cranking it up as loud as he dared.

Other times he would come upon her, curled up in the wide stuffed chair beside the Bose system, headphones on, tears streaming down her cheeks as she listened to some music she particularly loved. He hated finding her like that. It was embarrassing, as if he had caught her without her clothes on.

He had been, he thought now, the cliché of a teenager. He hadn't improved much as a young adult, either.

Now, opening the front door into the quiet house, the full impact of his mother's absence struck him like a gust of winter wind rolling out from the empty hallway. He froze on the doorstep, with Kate behind him.

"Are you okay, honey?" Kate murmured. She put one hand on his back, not insistently, but gently. Her hand wasn't slender, with firm, muscular fingers, like his mother's. It was plump, the palm soft and warm. "Do you want me to go in first?"

Jack shook his head. "No, I'm good," he said, but he couldn't get his legs to move.

Kate said, "Right," and stepped past him into the hallway. She turned on the porch light and the hall light and then stood, holding the door wide, giving him time.

The lights helped. Music would help. Kate left Jack to carry his suitcase up to his room, and she went to the kitchen to start putting a meal together. Jack trudged up the stairs, and stood uncertainly outside Tory's bedroom. The door was open. The bed was made, everything looking neat and tidy as always. A book lay facedown on the bedside table, open at the place Tory had stopped reading. Without going in, Jack could see that a bathrobe hung on the hook of the open bathroom door. A towel had been used and then spread to dry over the rack.

He turned away to his own room. He tossed his suitcase on the bed, and looked around at his things, carefully kept just the way he had left them. His Little League trophies lined the shelf above his desk, where his college thesaurus and dictionary still rested. His bookshelves were orderly, dusted, his old favorites waiting in neat rows. The same old band posters, curling now at the edges, studded the walls. His bathroom had towels on the rack and soap in the dish.

"Goddammit," he muttered. It was all just as he had left it, although a good bit tidier. She had kept it ready, as if she expected him to return at any moment. Or hoped that he would.

A single, painful sob forced itself through his constricted throat. "Goddammit," he said again. "Mom—I'm sorry. I'm going to find you, somehow, so I can tell you that."

6

❦

Vedete? Io son fedele alla parola mia.

You see? I am faithful to my word.

—Manon, *Manon Lescaut,* Act One

"I don't know what else I can do," Doria said. She cast her mother an exasperated look. "*Veramente*, Mamma, I work from before the *signora* is awake until she goes to bed at night. I've been there five years, and no one knows the house as well as I do! I clean, and I scrub laundry, and I iron the sheets and the curtains. I help Zita with the cooking, and I serve at table. I always wear my apron, and I never complain."

"You must have done something to make her angry." Emilia Manfredi dusted her floury hands over the sink, and gathered up the scraps of dough to roll another sheet for the ravioli.

"No one has to do anything to make her angry!" Doria pressed harder on the stone pestle, grinding the basil and garlic together. The pungent scent of pesto filled the room. "You can ask Old Zita, and she'll tell you, Mamma! The *signora*'s angry all the time. That's why no one else will work there!"

"Lucky for you!" Emilia snapped.

Doria clacked the pestle angrily against the rim of the mortar. "You don't know what it's like! She's so mean the *signore* calls her his policeman, did you know that?"

Emilia clicked her tongue. "That's not a nice thing."

"But she is like a policeman, Mamma, giving orders, shouting, always trying to catch someone in a mistake. The maestro stays away all day with his dogs and his friends, and Zita hides in the kitchen, but I have to go upstairs, downstairs, in and out all day, and be silent all the time besides."

"You should always hold your tongue! You're only the housemaid."

"I'm not the housemaid here, Mamma! Surely I can speak in your house?"

"Hmmph." Her mother slapped the mound of dough with an angry hand. "You'd better not lose your job, Doria. You would have no place to go."

Doria stopped, the pestle poised and dripping crushed basil. "No place to go?"

Signora Manfredi reached for the rolling pin, and began to spin it over the dough. "There is no room here, Doria, you know that. The house is overflowing as it is."

"It has always overflowed!"

"*Sì, sì, sì,*" her mother said. "It has always overflowed, and I'm tired of it."

"That's hardly my fault!" Doria said with asperity. "I'm not the one with six children!"

Emilia tossed her head. "We take what God sends us, Doria."

Doria sighed, a little ashamed. "Yes, I know. I'm sorry, Mamma."

"Well, never mind. In any case, you have a good job, in a good house."

"You don't need to tell me that. I love it there. I like taking care of Signor Puccini."

With deliberation, her mother laid down her rolling pin and folded her arms beneath her pendulous bosom. She fixed her black eyes on her daughter. "You are behaving yourself?"

"What do you mean?"

"You know what I mean."

"Behaving myself!" Doria clicked her tongue, and ground the pestle into the basil leaves once again, turning and turning it in the mortar until a green paste began to form.

"Answer me!" her mother snapped.

Doria let the pestle fall, its handle dropping into the sticky pesto. She turned, and matched her mother's posture, arms folded, chin thrust out. "You think I'm sleeping with Signor Puccini? Why not just say so?"

Her mother's eyes hardened. "Watch your tone with me, Doria Manfredi! It's a good question. Everyone knows about the *signore!*"

"You shouldn't listen to gossip, Mamma. Not about the maestro, and most certainly not about your daughter!"

"It wasn't about you," Emilia admitted, dropping her gaze back to the sheet of ravioli dough. "They say there is someone, but no one said it was you." She took the dough in her hands, but she looked up under her thick eyebrows at her daughter. "I would defend you. I know you're a good girl."

"A good girl!" Doria gave the pestle an irritated twist. "I nursed him, Mamma. When he was so injured in the automobile crash, all those months he couldn't walk, I did everything for him. The *signora* wouldn't do it, I can tell you! She wouldn't touch a bedpan, or wash him, or do any of the hard things. I was the one to sit up with him when the pain kept him awake."

"*Sì, sì, sì.* Everyone knows that, *mia figlia.*"

"She never thanked me, either."

"She is the *signora*, Doria. It's her house. She doesn't have to thank you."

Doria sighed, suddenly weary of it all. She wished, after all, she had simply held her tongue. One day, she prayed, she would learn to stay silent. "The maestro is kind to me."

"That's as may be," Emilia snapped, giving the dough on the floured table a sharp turn. "But he has a taste for young girls." Her eyes glittered a warning. "You must take care. And keep your mouth closed! You always did talk too much."

"It's a family tradition!" Doria responded. Emilia only grunted, but her lips twitched with something like humor.

Still, Doria felt impatient with her mother. She stood for a moment, staring at the rack of ancient cast-iron skillets on the wall, then pulled her apron over her head with both hands. It caught on her hairpins, stinging her scalp the way her mother's words had stung her spirit. She ripped it free, and threw it at the hook beside the kitchen door. She missed, and the apron fell in a heap of printed cotton on the plain wooden floor.

"Where are you going?" her mother asked. "What about the ravioli?"

Doria didn't turn back. She heard the thump of the rolling pin as it struck the floury board, stretching, thinning the dough. Her mother's ravioli were the best in Torre, but she couldn't bear the thought of them now. "Give my share to someone else," she said. "I'm not hungry after all." She slid out through the door, letting it bang behind her. Her mother didn't call her back. She was probably just as happy, Doria thought, to have one fewer mouth at the table.

Doria trod angrily through her mother's tiny garden, where fennel and parsley drooped in the sun. She stepped down the single stone step directly into the dirt lane. The heat was so thick she felt as if she couldn't breathe. It was her half day, and she had meant to spend the afternoon with her family, to return to Villa Puccini after the Puccinis had finished supper, when the *signora* had retired upstairs and the *signore* retreated to his studio. Now Doria didn't know where to pass the afternoon. It was too hot to sit in the *piazza*. She had no money for a café, because she had just handed over all her wages to her mother. Her room behind the kitchen at Villa Puccini would be nearly hot enough to boil Mamma's ravioli.

As she walked, picking the sweat-dampened fabric of her dress away from her skin, she thought longingly of the cool fragrance of the maestro's beloved garden. He had ordered it planted with sweet bay and privet, and the heart-shaped leaves of a Judas tree shaded a small wooden bench. Perhaps, if she were very quiet, she could sit there for an hour. She had a book in her pocket, one the maestro had given her. An hour's solitude, reading in the shade, would soothe her temper and cool her hot skin.

Hopeful, she turned toward the lake, where Villa Puccini rose in modest splendor above the lakeshore. She loved the house, she was sure, even more than the maestro did, and he loved it very well indeed.

She had been a young girl when the renovations of the old watchtower began. Everyone in Torre del Lago had been thrilled to have Italy's most famous composer come build his house in their village. Step by step, they had torn the old building apart and rebuilt it, painted it, plumbed it, even connected it to the marvels of electricity and the telephone. Doria was thrilled to be the one allowed to care for Puccini's "golden tower," as he called it, with its yellow stucco and scrolled iron entryway, its neat shutters and clean, elegant lines. The artist Nomellini came to paint the walls of Puccini's studio, and everyone in Torre heard about how the dampness that pervaded everything around Lake Massaciuccoli crept into the new villa and ruined his work. He had to return to reconstruct his pictures on tapestries of canvas.

Villa Puccini made Doria's own home, where six children crowded into two bedrooms, seem little more than a noisome hut perched along a dirt lane.

When she reached the gate of the villa, there was no one about. The house was so quiet she could hear the lap of the water below the road. The *signora*'s painted shutters above the little balcony were closed against the sun. No sound came from the kitchen, nor did Puccini's brown-and-white dogs come romping out to meet her as they always did if he was home. No doubt he had taken his big motorboat out to the little island where he went to fish or hunt or just find some peace. The dogs, the rough-coated *spinone*, loved going out in the boat, hanging over the bow with their long tongues dangling and their ears flattened by the wind.

Doria kicked off her shoes and stripped off her black cotton stockings before she settled herself on the bench. It was blissfully cool in the shade, and she wriggled her toes in the patchy grass as she pulled the book from her pocket. She turned the pages carefully, silently, and read.

It was called *Il Fuoco—The Flame*. She didn't truly like it. It was the sort of thing Puccini read. He liked this writer because he also wrote plays, and the maestro was forever seeking out plays he could turn into operas. This one, though, would never work. Even Doria, with her paltry education, could see that. There was a great deal of sex in it, which made her squirm. Despite her mother's dour warnings, Doria knew nothing of sex beyond what she had read in novels. Still, she meant to read *Il Fuoco* all the way through so she could talk about it with Puccini, if he should ask.

She was lucky to be able to read, to have learned so easily from Father Michelucci. Most of the girls in Torre, and the boys, too, for that matter, could barely write their names. Despite this bright new century and nearly new country, many Italians had no schooling at all.

For a happy hour she relaxed beneath the Judas tree. In this relentless heat, she doubted anyone beside Puccini would be out of doors. If he wasn't in his boat, he might have tramped up into the hills in search of a breeze. He often did that, his gun slung over his arm and the dogs panting happily at his heels. She hoped he had remembered his hat.

She sighed beneath a gentle wave of drowsiness. Bees buzzed in the roses twining through the wrought-iron fence, and an occasional lazy bird twitter punctuated the sweet silence of the afternoon. Doria's eyes drooped, and the book sagged in her hands. She gave in to the moment, and lay back on the bench, her knees up, her skirts arranged so they covered her modestly but allowed a bit of air to caress her hot calves. With a feeling of pure self-indulgence, she drowsed through the warm afternoon as if she were a lady of privilege.

She woke to the damp scrape of a pink tongue against her cheek and a blast of hot dog breath. With a start, she sat up, crying, "Buoso, stop!" Her protests did nothing to prevent the dog from slathering her with affection. She tried to push him away at the same time that she struggled to pull her skirts down to her ankles. Bica, the bitch, galloped up the path behind Buoso, and the two dogs quarreled, forcing their heads into Doria's lap as she groped beneath the bench for her shoes and stockings. She dropped one shoe, and Bica grabbed it in her teeth and shook it fiercely, as she might an unlucky mole that crawled into her path.

"Buoso, Bica, down!" Puccini called as he paused to latch the gate.

Doria leaped to her feet, laughing. She had stockings in one hand, a shoe in the other. The hounds had knocked her book to the ground, and she bent hastily to pick it up and brush bits of grass and dirt from its cover. Clutching her possessions in front of her, she tried to regain her dignity by bobbing a swift curtsy.

"That's a good way to stay cool," the maestro said, nodding toward her bare feet.

Doria tried to twitch her skirt so it would cover her toes, but her dress was too short for that. Her feet embarrassed her. They were like bird feet, with long, narrow toes and high arches. Worse, they were dirty now, smudged with dust and grass stains. She sidled away, hoping to escape to her room to set herself to rights.

"You're reading *Il Fuoco*!" the maestro said cheerfully. He was wearing his broad-brimmed hat, but he was in shirtsleeves, and he had dropped his braces so he could wear his shirt loose outside his trousers. Now he took off the hat, and slapped dust from it against his knee. He had a bag with a couple of fat birds in it, and he looked happy, dark hair falling across his sunburned brow, a rime of dust on his thick mustache. Why, she wondered, had such a man married Elvira? The *signora* was old and sour in comparison with her husband's boyish charm. Even at the great age of fifty, Giacomo Puccini was a handsome man.

Doria took another sidelong step toward the kitchen door. "I'm halfway through," she said. "I mean—" She held it up. "I mean the book."

He said, "I didn't like it all that much. His plays are better."

Doria said, "I think they must be, signore. This book, it's all about sex and not about—" She closed her mouth abruptly, and ducked her head. Her mother was right. She should learn to keep silent about things she knew nothing about.

He said, "You're quite right, Doria! Sex isn't the least bit interesting unless the characters are interesting."

In fact, it was just what she had been thinking, and his agreement gave her a little glow of pleasure. She took another step, her head down, watching the impression her bare feet made in the grass, little claw marks like those of a hen scratching for ants. The dogs pressed close to her, nuzzling her legs, asking for tidbits. She slipped them treats from time to time, when Elvira wasn't looking, and she saw by Puccini's grin that he knew that. He couldn't know, of course, how she nestled with them sometimes on the grass. They were her only source of physical affection, and she adored both of them, despite their antics.

She patted the dogs, and muttered, "Go on with you, now. I don't have anything!"

Puccini fell into step beside her, and at that moment, with a talent for timing only Elvira Puccini seemed to possess, the shutters of the second-floor bedroom window flew open, clacking against the outside of the house, and the lady's head appeared.

"Doria!" she shouted. "You haven't touched the ironing!"

Doria lifted her head. "Signora." Sudden anxiety made her voice rise, and it sounded plaintive. "Signora Puccini, it's my half day."

"Your half day?" Elvira exclaimed. "And you spend it gallivanting in the garden?"

Puccini said, "Elvira, let her be. She can spend her half day as she likes."

Doria drew a small, dismayed breath. Surely he must know by now that any argument could set off one of Elvira's tantrums. Even at this distance she could see the *signora*'s face darken, her eyes contracting like those of an ill-tempered crow. Doria tried to hurry around the side of the house, toward the kitchen door, but it turned out that, too, was a mistake.

"Where are your shoes? Your *stockings?*"

Elvira sounded like a crow, too. She screeched and cawed and quarreled, and once she got started, nothing would stop her. Doria stopped where she was, and held up her single shoe and the wad of her stockings. "Here they are, signora."

Puccini laughed, and Doria thought he was trying to lighten his wife's mood. "Look, Elvira, Bica has the other shoe! I think she's trying to kill it."

Elvira said, "I won't have anyone in my house running around barefoot like a common village slut!"

"I—I was just reading in the garden—"

"What are you doing with my husband?"

Doria turned to the maestro, hoping he would explain, but Puccini had evidently comprehended what was about to happen after all. He slipped quietly in through the iron-and-glass bow window that connected the garden to the house, and disappeared. Even the two dogs abandoned her, trotting after their master. Doria felt a flush of resentment burn in her cheeks. She stared at her long toes, afraid to show her angry face. "Nothing, signora," she said. "I wasn't doing anything. I was asleep on the bench when the *signore* came home."

"Hah!" Elvira said, and slammed the window shut with a bang.

"Hah!"

Tory jerked awake. It was still dark, and cold. Only the faint ghost light of the sea found its way through her open bedroom door to shimmer on the mirror above the bureau and sparkle faintly on the gold butterfly in the paperweight. She lay a moment, rubbing her eyes, trying to orient herself. She put her hand to her chest, and found her skin hot, her nightgown damp with perspiration.

There had been new people in this dream: a mother, and a man who seemed vaguely familiar. Thinking of him made her uneasy for some reason she couldn't identify. It seemed if she could just concentrate long enough, remember what she had

dreamed, she might know who he was, or at least who he represented in her psyche.

But then, the dream would evaporate soon enough, as dreams
did. Sometimes her clients had felt their dreams were significant,
that they held clues to their waking lives. Tory, though she listened and encouraged the lines of thought they created, had
never been convinced. For her, a cigar was always just a cigar. Or
so she had thought.

She threw back her blankets and put her feet on the cold floor.
So different from the warm, patchy grass in the world of her
dream. She was cold here, even in the daytime. Perhaps her
dreams were just her suppressed longing for a warm, sunny cli-
mate.

She had found a long zippered sweatshirt on the remainder
table at a little shop on the main street of the town, and decided
it would work as a bathrobe. She pulled it on, and zipped it, letting the hood hang down her back. She put on a pair of thick
socks, and padded out to the kitchen to fill the teakettle. The
stove clock read four A.M. Too early to go for a walk, too early to
eat breakfast. Too late to try to go back to sleep.

She turned on the radio—early music, Hildegard of Bingen,
she thought—and carried her teacup into the living room. It was
becoming a habit, she feared, waking on East Coast time and sitting in the armchair watching the tide creep up the beach. Solitude was becoming a habit, too. She tried to think when she had
last spoken with anyone other than the clerk at the market,
which was hardly conversation, or the station attendant who
pumped gas for the Beetle.

It was time, she told herself, to do something different. Idleness didn't suit her. She needed to go out, to find something to
do. She would have suggested that to a client who found herself
spending too much time alone.

She carried the bedspread out to the living room and settled
into the armchair, the blanket pulled up to her shoulders, to
watch the light grow over the beach and the ocean. The big black
rock—Haystack Rock, they called it—emerged gradually from

the gloom as the darkness of the sky lightened to gray, then to a dusky blue, with streaks of pink and lavender on the horizon. The rock hulked above the shallow waves, a sentinel guarding the coastline.

Watching dawn break over the water, so far from her home, made Tory long for her son. She wondered if he was all right, if he was back at school, if he was sad, or frightened, or . . . She thrust the thoughts away. In her dreams of that hot place she felt things—sadness, anger, even joy. Maybe that was the point of having the dreams. In real life, at least in *her* real life, feelings were pointless. She had done what she had to do. She closed her eyes, and let the cold sea air chill her mind and her heart, banish the treacherous stirrings of longing.

Her life had been ruled by taking care of Jack. She had ended her marriage to protect him, moved him away to a tiny place where no one knew them or knew their story. Nothing else mattered, even when he barely spoke to her, when she knew he longed to be part of some other family. This separation should be easier, surely, because their relationship was already fractured.

It didn't work that way, evidently. Even after all this time, the rift between Jack and herself made her heart ache. The pain was layered, like the water swirling in the gray morning light, ephemeral on its surface, but deep and dark and irresistible at its deepest point.

Be safe, Jack. Kate and Chet would watch over him, surely. They were natural parents, wonderful grandparents, much better at the whole thing than she'd ever been. She'd had no role models, of course—except for Nonna Angela—but that wasn't much of an excuse.

She let her head fall back, her tea cooling on the table beside her, and she slept again.

Doria bent over the ironing board in the kitchen, sweat running down her face and her chest as she labored over one of the maestro's high-collared shirts. She was still barefoot, despite the *signora*'s complaints. It was far too hot to wear stockings and shoes. The big black stove, though she kept the fire as low as she could, made the kitchen all but unbearable, but there was no other way to heat the soapstone irons. She swept the iron back and forth over the heavy white linen, and listened to Elvira's voice rise and fall in its unmusical way, upbraiding her husband for his imagined offenses.

The iron had grown too cool, and she put it back on the stove to heat while she took up the other one. She was so hot she feared her perspiration would turn the shirt limp before she could finish it. Indeed, the air was so humid she doubted the shirt would keep its shape until she could stow it in Puccini's wardrobe. She knew what that meant. Elvira would bring it back to her in the morning, demanding she do it all over again.

She had seen an advertisement in *Il Secolo Illustrato* for an electric iron, which sounded wonderful, but Elvira would never consent to buying one for Villa Puccini. She was too old-fashioned, and too tight with her *lire*. The only reason the villa had electricity at all was because the *signore* insisted on the newest and best of everything—his house, his cars, his boats—even a telephone! Zita refused to touch it, but Doria yearned to be the one to answer its strident call, to pick up the little black cone of the receiver and speak into the scrolled mouthpiece. She knew just what she would say, if she ever had the chance. She would speak very clearly, in her most courteous voice: "*Pronto!* This is Villa Puccini, and Doria Manfredi is speaking to you."

She was not allowed to answer the telephone, though. The *signora* had decreed that only she or the *signore* should answer the telephone, and when it was she, she croaked into it like the big black crow she was. "Villa Puccini!" she would shout, as if her voice had to reach over the distance without any assistance. "Who is that?" It was disgraceful. Doria knew she could do it much better.

She sighed at her own spinning thoughts as she bent over the ironing board. The heat made her heart pound, but there was a mountain of laundry in the big wicker basket, and she feared the worst if she didn't get it done. She swore to herself, pressing the flat-felled seams until they hissed, that her next half day she would stay away from the house, even if it meant hiding in the woods!

The dogs lay flat on the flagstone floor near the pantry, their tongues lolling. Elvira wouldn't like that, either, but Doria wasn't responsible for what the dogs did. For that, the crow could caw at her husband.

She was taking a short break, sponging her forehead with cold water at the sink, when she heard someone coming. She hurried back to the ironing board, where she seized up one of the irons to show she was working. The kitchen door opened. To Doria's relief it was Puccini, carrying one of his big guns, broken in half for safety, with the muzzle pointing downward. He set the gun beside the door and crossed to the sink. He turned the brass tap, and let the water run until it was cold, something Doria never did. "Too damned hot in here," he said as he filled a glass. "You should iron after dark, when it's cooler."

She shrugged. "The *signora*—" she began.

"I know, I know." He put his head back and drank, emptying the whole glass, it seemed, in one gulp. He put the glass down, and reached into his pocket for a cigarette. "You think she's mean-tempered," he said.

Doria kept her eyes on the shirt, turning it so she could iron the yoke.

"It's all right. I understand. Everyone thinks that," he said. "Her life hasn't been easy." The smile had gone out of his voice, and it throbbed slightly, musically. With sympathy for Elvira? Doria didn't know. He added, with what she thought was an admirable show of loyalty, "Her first husband was a grim man. She had to leave her son with him when she—when we moved to Milano."

Doria lifted the shirt, and smoothed the sleeve out along the board. Everyone in Torre knew of the scandal. Elvira had abandoned her first husband and her son to run off to Milan with Giacomo Puccini. No one in society would speak to her for a very long time, and she was cut in the street by everyone she knew. They were poor, also, when they first came to Torre del Lago, and it had been years—not until after the success of *La Bohème* and *Tosca*—before they were able to build Villa Puccini.

And then, of course, there was the affair with Corinna.

Doria didn't like to think of it. It bothered her to imagine Puccini in bed with some other woman. Of course she heard Elvira and him together sometimes. She couldn't help that. Her room was just under theirs, and though she covered her head with her pillow, the thumping of the bed and the squeaking of the springs were unmistakable. But they were a married couple. It was proper for them to enjoy each other, even though they were terribly old. It was the idea that the *signore* would make such thumps and squeaks with someone else that made Doria feel uneasy.

Of course the *signora* had behaved shamefully to Corinna, and in the most public place. The enormous umbrella she had used to strike her rival, in full view of everyone on the street, still rested in the stand beside the back door.

Doria turned the shirtsleeve to iron the other side. A drop of perspiration slid from her cheek and fell on the linen, and she dabbed at it quickly with the hem of her apron.

Puccini expelled a wreath of smoke that rose slowly through the hot air. "Doria, you know, sometimes . . ."

She looked up at him from beneath her eyelashes. He was staring out the window at his garden browning in the relentless sun. "Signore?"

He took another drag on his cigarette. When he breathed it out, the kitchen filled with the toasty scent of tobacco. Doria inhaled, savoring the taste, liking it because it had been in his lungs, had been exhaled through his lips.

"Sometimes we make bad decisions, but we have to live with them. You're young. You don't know that yet."

"I'm nearly twenty-one," she said.

At that he turned to look at her. "So young!" he repeated. "Half my age—less, even." His eyes were liquid and shadowed, like the depths of the lake where the sun seemed never to reach. She liked looking into them, and she was sure his thoughts were deeper than hers, more complex, more knowing. "You should be out in the village, Doria, spending your time with young people, not here with old folks like us."

"I don't want to be out in the village, signore. I like it here."

He twinkled at her. "No young man, my little nurse?"

She tossed her head. "The village boys are boring," she said crisply. "They talk of nothing but how well they shoot, how much they can drink—how many girls they go to bed with!"

He laughed aloud. "You always say what you think, don't you, Doria?"

She dropped her eyes. "Oh, no, signore. A girl like me doesn't dare say what she thinks." She could have said that what she wanted was not to go into the village, but to go to school, to study in Milan, the way the maestro had. She would never speak such a desire aloud. The whole idea was laughable.

He gazed at her, still smiling. "Sometimes, my little nurse," he mused, "I wish I were young again. Just like you are! If I had known what I know now, I might do things differently."

"But, signore, you—you are—" She couldn't think of the words. Surely he, who had everything, who had achieved so much, should not entertain regrets. She looked down at the shirtsleeve, and ironed the same spot again.

"I," he said, "am old and tired."

It was ridiculous, but how could she say so? It was precisely as Mamma had said. She was only a housemaid. She had no authority to scold the great Puccini, to point out how wrong he was. She could only wash his clothes, run his errands, clean his studio. Admire his music from a reverent distance.

He ground out his cigarette in one of the ubiquitous ashtrays, nodded to her, and picked up the shotgun. The two dogs, grunting, lifted themselves from the floor, and followed him out of the kitchen. There was a bit of banging and bustling as he racked the gun. A moment later the piano sounded through the hushed, overheated house.

Doria paused, the iron in her hand. He had gone back again.

Back to *Butterfly*. It must be comforting to him, that great aria, the one everyone had been singing before the opera even opened. Un bel dì vedremo . . .

She pictured the devoted Cio-Cio-San, little Butterfly, kneeling at the doorway of her house, looking down on the bay with Sorrow beside her. "One fine day we will see the smoke on the far horizon . . . the white ship sails into the port . . ." Butterfly, not knowing yet that she had been betrayed, sang her beautiful song of waiting for her beloved, pouring out her longing for him to return to her.

Doria took the shirt from the ironing board and folded it neatly. Butterfly had dared to dream of something beyond her station, a happiness not granted her by birth. Doria understood perfectly. She and Butterfly were both village girls, born to do as they were told and accept what came their way.

Doria couldn't go to school, but she could at least hold on to what she had. She could stay here, in Villa Puccini, where she had a room to herself, enough to eat every day, an ordered house. She could listen to the music coming from the studio every night, and serve the genius who created it. It was a small ambition, surely, a modest wish! Hardly the stuff of grand opera.

She pulled another shirt, stiff with starch, from the basket, and shook it out on the ironing board. She took up an iron, spat on it to test the heat, and began again, keeping her ears pricked to any sound of fresh trouble from abovestairs.

Tory woke with perspiration beading her forehead and her neck. A drop had rolled over her cheek to fall on the hood of the sweatshirt, and that had woken her. The sun slanted directly onto her face, and her legs beneath the chenille were hot and itchy.

She couldn't remember ever having resumed a dream after being interrupted, but then she couldn't remember ever dreaming repeatedly about the same people, the same place. The whole thing was so strange, as was the feeling of anxiety that stayed with her even as she got up to return the comforter to the bed and pour out the cold tea. She put the kettle on the stove again, and moved briskly about the cramped kitchen, taking eggs from the fridge, putting bread in the toaster, staying busy until the unwelcome feeling passed.

As she settled her breakfast on the cracked Formica of the table, it occurred to her that now she understood what her depressed clients had tried to explain, what it felt like to have no feelings of your own. It was what her own mother must have felt, this flatness. This disconnection. It was too bad that she understood it more deeply now, when it was too late to help anyone else. She hoped some other therapist had taken her practice, contacted her clients, claimed her files.

All except one, of course. That one lay where she had stowed it, hidden in the bottom drawer of the rickety bureau in the bedroom. She hadn't looked at it. She hadn't wanted to think about it, but she remembered the look on Ellice's face, the weight of that cruel black gun, the horror of an innocent man's death. . . .

And she had done nothing. Nothing but run away.

She spread jelly on her toast and took a bite, but her appetite faded at the taste of the food in her mouth. She abandoned the eggs, left the toast uneaten, and went into the bedroom.

She opened the drawer, and stared down at the file folder. Her conscience flailed beneath the ice that encased her. Someone else could suffer. Some other therapist might be at risk. She had to do something, to take some action—but what?

There was Jack, and Jack came before anything. Whether he knew it or not.

She shoved the drawer shut with her foot, and stood for a moment, thinking, then hurried to pull on jeans and a sweater. She took the hammer and screwdriver from the kitchen drawer, and carried them out into the little yard. She knelt beside the gate in the picket fence, and began to pull nails from the broken slats.

7

Ho tante cose che ti voglio dire,
o una sola, ma grande come il mare.

I've so many things I want to say to you,
or one only, but big as the sea.

—Mimì, *La Bohème*, Act Two

Jack squatted before Tory's personal filing cabinet and pulled open the top drawer. He had put off this chore for too long. It was past time to face what was in it, deal with the mortgage and the bank and the insurance company, get it all to the lawyer's office. The lawyer said she would inform everyone, make arrangements for payments and cancellations. Kate had offered to help. He had told her he could manage, but now his heart quailed at the orderly row of folders with their official-looking names. It was all meticulously organized, of course. That was Tory. Everything about her was disciplined: her appearance, her house, her practice—just not her son.

He closed his eyes for a moment, his elbows on his knees, his forehead on his closed fists. "Jeez, Mom," he muttered. "I feel like such a shit."

He had been thirteen when he'd started spending all his time with his friend Colton's family, the Garveys. There was hardly anything left of his own family. His crazy grandmother had finally died, and his grandfather, too. His great-grandmother, the Italian one from some little village in Tuscany, had been gone long before he was born. If he had ever met his father's parents, he couldn't remember them. He thought he remembered his father, but he had been just a toddler, and he knew it was possible he had created that memory.

The Garvey family seemed perfect to him. They had three kids, a dog, a rambling, messy house, and two parents. There were pictures of relatives stuck here and there, grandparents, cousins, aunts, and uncles. Colton's dad liked to throw a football and watch sitcoms. Colton's mother worked in her garden all the time and never, to Jack's knowledge, vacuumed her house or folded laundry. They didn't listen to music, they didn't go to church, and they didn't have regular meals or bedtimes or—it seemed to Jack—any rules at all.

Jack had really liked that dog. He remembered a time when his mother had come to pick him up, and the dog had rushed up to her in a flurry of muddy paws and unwashed, shaggy coat. She had drawn back from it, pulled her coat hem away from it as if it might have fleas.

In fact, she always seemed edgy when she came to that house where he had so much fun, where there was a father and boys to roughhouse with, where no one asked him to pick up after himself, where they ate pizza from the freezer and chili from cans. He had said something snotty to his mom in the car on the way home that day. Tory had glanced at him, and her eyes reddened, but she didn't say a word. When they got home, she asked him to put everything he was wearing into the washer.

Colton's family fell apart when Jack and he were both sixteen. The Garveys moved away, taking the dog with them. By then Jack had fallen into the habit of excluding Tory from his life. He didn't tell her about his baseball games or class projects. She went to Parents Night right up until he graduated from high school, but they never talked about his teachers or his class work. She tried to help him with his college applications, but he took them into his room to work on, bringing them out only when he needed a signature. She tried to explain once, when he was a junior, about his father, but he told her he didn't want to talk about it. She subsided into her customary silence, and that was the end of it.

He never told her that he already knew all about his father. He and Colton had looked him up on the Internet, something Tory wouldn't think of because she didn't use a computer. It had been ridiculously easy, because he and his father had the same name.

Colton had been impressed that his friend's father had gone to jail, as if somehow that made Jack tougher, cooler. Jack hadn't felt any tougher, though. Going to jail for embezzlement was lame and embarrassing, and dying in a car crash two weeks after he got out was just stupid. Jack made Colton swear not to tell anyone.

Jack had thought his mother must be relieved when he went off to school in Boston, but now he wondered. He lifted his face from his hands and looked around her office. There were pictures of him everywhere, a snapshot, two school portraits, a copy of his prom picture with—God, he couldn't even remember the girl's name. He had only dated her twice. As soon as she started calling his cell phone, he lost interest.

On the filing cabinet, in front of where he now crouched, his senior picture looked out from a braided leather frame. He had posed against a maple brilliant with fall colors, head to one side, a cocky grin on his face. "Arrogant bastard," he told his image.

A memory surfaced, suddenly, of a kid in his English lit class. He hadn't thought of that guy in years. They were discussing some nineteenth-century novel with a protagonist who was an orphan, and the kid had said that losing a parent made you grow up overnight. He wished he could talk to that guy now. He'd been right.

Jack blew out a breath, and started stacking the folders on the floor beside the cabinet. The phone on the desk rang, but he had stopped picking up, because most of the calls began, "Hi. I was one of Tory's clients, and I'm just wondering . . ."

He sat back on his heels, waiting to hear who it was.

"Jack, it's Kate. Are you there, honey?"

With a humiliating jolt of relief, he lunged for the phone. He raked his thigh painfully on the corner of the file drawer as he picked up the handset. "Kate," he said. "Yeah, I'm here."

"Hi." She waited a moment in sensitive silence, and he thought she must hear the stress in his voice. "Are you all right?" she asked at last.

"Yeah. Yeah, I'm fine."

She gave a small laugh. "Jack, you sound just like your mom. She would never admit to being upset."

That gave him another twinge, and he sagged against the desk, rubbing his smarting thigh with his palm. "Well," he said. "I finally got around to her—to Mom's—the files."

"I'll come get you, then, and we can go to the lawyer's."

"Kate—the clients keep calling. What do I tell them?"

"The police have all of Tory's client files for now—but you can refer them to the lawyer. She'll know what to say."

"There was a notice in the paper."

"I know. And Tory left specific instructions for her clients to be notified should anything happen to—to disrupt her practice. I'm pretty sure they should all have received the lawyer's letter by now. I'm told not all therapists are that careful. She seems to have thought of everything."

"Instructions? You're talking about her will."

There was a little pause, and he sensed Kate trying to find the right words. She gave a click of her tongue, and he thought, wryly, that she had given up the search. "Jack, I'm so sorry. There's just no easy way to talk about this stuff. Do you need to see someone, maybe? Father Wilburton, or a counselor?"

"No. I'm good."

She was silent again, and he knew she was feeling helpless and worried. Just as he was. He said, "Don't worry, Kate. I can manage here, I really can. Everything's in perfect order."

"No surprise there, right?" she said. "I always told Tory she should leave at least one mess, somewhere. Something to make her human."

"Yeah. Well. She had my bedroom," Jack said, and managed a little chuckle.

"I heard about that! My kids were just the same, believe me." Another laugh, just light enough, just short enough so he knew she had not forgotten, that she understood he was struggling. Kate Bingham was an awfully nice woman. He wondered why he hadn't appreciated that before. He'd always just thought of her as Tory's friend, older, fatter, duller. Another mistake to add to a growing list.

"So, did you—did you want something?" he asked. He stared down into the open file drawer, and saw a fat, neat file with his name on it. He looked away.

"Honey, the police called here, and they spoke to Chet. I guess they—well, it was the sheriff's office, and I suppose they thought someone older should talk to you first. They're done with your mother's car."

"Oh." Jack straightened, and walked to the window of the office to look past the oak tree into the woods beyond. A pretty hummingbird feeder, empty now, twirled on its chain just beyond the sliding glass door. November sunlight, cool and faintly yellow, sifted through the stand of cedars. The sugar maples had shed most of their leaves, and the ground was thick and bright with them. Tory had loved this time of year, gathered huge armfuls of leaves to fill baskets here and there around the house, filling the place with the scent of the woods. He wondered what she put in the hummingbird feeder, and if he should refill it.

"Chet can help you decide what to do with it," Kate went on. "It's a good car, and it's only two years old. You probably want to have it repaired."

"Will the insurance cover it?"

"It should. There will be some paperwork."

Jack chewed on his lower lip, watching a gray squirrel dash through loose red leaves. "Yeah," he said after a moment. "I think I'll get it fixed. Do I have to go get it?" The idea of seeing the car, with its crumpled hood and broken door—the door, presumably, his mother had fallen through—made his belly go cold.

"Chet can do it," Kate said. "Okay if we handle that for you, then? I'll call the sheriff back. Chet will make the arrangements."

"Thanks, Kate. And thank Chet for me. I really appreciate you guys helping me out."

"It's nothing," she said, with firmness now, and a touch of briskness. "Now, listen, honey. You've been staying alone over there for too long. Won't you come and have dinner with us? And Chet was asking when you're going back to school. He offered to drive you to the train when you're ready."

"Look, Kate, it's really nice of you. Both of you. I'm just—I'm okay here, for now."

The squirrel reached the trunk of a sugar maple, and scrambled up, its fluff of tail swinging behind. Jack turned back to face Tory's desk, with its photos and its big calendar blotter, dotted with notes in her cramped, precise handwriting. The chill crept up from his belly and into his heart. He felt as if he had a rock in his chest. A cold, unforgiving rock.

Suddenly, he wanted nothing more than to get off the phone, to go to his mother's collection of CDs, and play something, anything. He wanted to hear her music.

Kate released him in a few moments, saying she would let him know about the car, making him promise he would call her in the morning. He promised, as much to get off the phone as because he would have anything to say by morning. He went into the living room, leaving the file drawer open in the desk. He walked to the cabinet holding his mother's collection, and pulled down a CD at random.

Mahler, Symphony no. 5. He popped open the jewel case and lifted out the CD. Mahler was as close as his mother would allow herself to get to Wagner. She had said so often. He put the CD into the Bose, and wandered into the kitchen as the attenuated melodies and ponderous harmonic progressions began to fill the house. He felt a bit better with the music playing. He felt connected to Tory.

Was his hunch right, or was it wishful thinking, guilt over having been a bad son, a difficult teenager, a distant young adult? He found a picture of the two of them behind a row of cookbooks, and took it down to hold in his hand. Kate had snapped it at his graduation, and he remembered the moment. His mother had put her arm around him, pulled him close to her. It had been a long time since they had been that close physically. He remembered often feeling as if there was a fence between them, a barrier of some kind, not of their own making, but holding them apart. He gazed at the picture, wishing he could call back that moment, turn and hold his mother in both arms, let her hug him as tightly as she wished.

She looked nice in the picture, her hair clipped up, a simple short dress showing her trim legs. It was only two years ago, and he looked with fresh eyes at her fair hair, her clear, smooth skin, the faint lines around her eyes, the deeper ones around her mouth. He couldn't remember ever looking at her as a person. As a woman.

But maybe young men didn't do that. Maybe if he sat down with a therapist—like Tory—that's what he would hear, that young men were that way, that their mothers weren't women, they were . . . mothers.

His had done the best she could. He wished he could tell her he understood that.

He put the photo back on its shelf behind the cookbooks. No, it wasn't wishful thinking. She wasn't gone. He could—he could *feel* her. Wills, police, the wrecked car, the lawyer—none of it changed anything. Jack wandered into the living room and gazed out at the mountains of the park, their wooded peaks going blue with early dusk. He listened to the swell and crash of the Mahler symphony, and wondered what he should do.

By the time full darkness settled over the house, Jack began to wish he had accepted Kate's invitation after all. He didn't want company, exactly, but the house seemed to echo with emptiness. Tory disliked drapes that might block her view of the woods, so the big picture window in the living room and the sliding glass door to her office were uncurtained. With the lights on, the glass was black and reflective. He saw his every movement, his mussed-up hair, his ragged Red Sox sweatshirt. He felt exposed to the night.

He went around the house, checking that the front and back doors and the office entrance were locked. He peeked in the utility room, where the washer and dryer were now clean and empty. There had been a few things in the washer, a pair of jeans, sneakers, a shirt. He had dried them and put them away. The ironing board—as always—was folded up into its frame. He had never seen it out, and he didn't know why they even had one. If there was an iron in the house, he didn't know where. Tory had a thing about ironing.

He turned out the lights in the living room and in her office, and confined himself to the kitchen, where he could draw the curtains over the sink and close out the darkness. He could watch the small television Tory kept under the cabinet while he made himself dinner.

At first he had avoided the TV. The news endlessly replayed the photos of the Escalade at the bottom of the ravine, its doors open like empty arms that had dropped their burden. But now, it seemed, with nothing new to report, everyone had lost interest. There had been blood on the upholstery of the car, but it had been Tory's, and there hadn't been much of it. The Escalade appeared to have some damage to its rear bumper, but no one knew how long that might have been there. There was no explanation for why Tory might have driven into the woods instead of down her driveway, but the police seemed to think that wasn't particularly suspicious.

Father Wilburton had explained all of this to Jack in a gingerly fashion, as if the twenty-year-old young man in front of him might break down or fly into hysterics. Jack listened, his head down, his teeth clenched. There had been so little blood, the priest said. Not enough to prove that—

Jack had thrown up his hand, made him stop talking about blood.

Misunderstanding, Father Wilburton had changed the subject. He went on to speak gently about sorrow, support groups, the comforts of faith. Jack had listened to his little homily in polite silence.

Jack switched on the television, but he kept the volume low, letting the news drone softly while he pulled one of Kate's casseroles out of the fridge. She had taped instructions to the lid. He pulled those off, set the oven temperature, and slid the dish onto the top rack. While the oven ticked, warming, he looked through the kitchen cupboards for things he should give away or throw out before he went back to school. He found the knife block in a lower cupboard, and gazed at it for a moment. Hadn't it been full? His mother liked CUTCO knives, and he remembered her saving up for a set, filling every slot in the knife block. One of the slots was empty now. It was a small thing. He doubted anyone who didn't know Tory would even notice. It probably didn't mean anything. He'd find the knife somewhere else, or perhaps she had sent it in to be sharpened or something.

In the pantry he gazed at the shelves full of coffee and sugar and pasta and cereal. He carried a bag of steel-cut oatmeal back into the kitchen. He was trying to judge from the label how long it would keep when he heard the sound.

He reached out to flick off the television. He listened, hard.

It came again, a click, as of glass on metal, a subtle sound that might have been the click of the furnace going off, or the house settling, or the oven still preheating.

Jack's skin prickled with sudden goose bumps. It wasn't the furnace. It wasn't the oven, either. *Okay, big guy,* he told himself silently. *You said you'd be okay. Prove it.*

With a grimace, he took the marble rolling pin out of its holder, and hefted it in his hand. It wasn't much, but it was something. He crossed the kitchen, opened the swinging door, and sidled through, letting it shut soundlessly behind him.

He stood for a breathless moment in the darkened hallway. For long seconds he heard nothing. The rolling pin was cold and heavy in his hand, and he thought how foolish he was going to feel when he put it back—

There it was again. It was louder this time, a lot louder. It came from Tory's office, and it was followed by the unmistakable sound of the glass door sliding open.

Jack drew a quick, shivery breath, and lunged for the door to the office. He banged it open, and palmed the light switch, the rolling pin at the ready and his heart hammering beneath his sweatshirt.

The relief that washed through him left him weak in the knees. He was sure his face was white, and he had drawn a deep breath, prepared to shout at someone. Instead, what came out was scratchy and thin, more breath than sound. "Dammit! You scared the shit out of me!"

It was the woman from the memorial service, the sheriff's deputy. She was in uniform, her wide-brimmed hat pulled over her forehead, her gun belt drooping around her waist. She carried some sort of tool in her hand. She had one foot inside the sliding glass door, and her hand still rested on the latch. Her eyes widened, the pupils expanding in surprise. "Jack!" she exclaimed. "What the—I thought you were back at school!"

She swiftly tucked the tool, a sort of flat metal thing, into her shirt pocket, then turned her back on him to shut the glass door.

He let the rolling pin hang by his side. It felt huge and embarrassing, evidence of his nervousness. "You—what are you doing here?" he asked. His voice sounded high and childish.

She turned back with deliberation, and it crossed his mind that she was choosing her words. The back of his neck tingled.

"You should be careful about locking this door," she said.

He made sure his voice dropped to the proper register. "I did lock it."

She shrugged her wide shoulders. "It was open."

It was an impasse. He repeated, "What are you doing here, officer?" He hadn't spoken to a lot of cops, but he was pretty sure that was the right way to address her.

She grinned now, and took off the hat, revealing short, brushy hair. "You can call me Ellice," she said. "My name's Ellice Gordon." She took a look around the office, her glance pausing at the open file drawer, then resolutely continuing its circuit. "I just came up to make sure everything was okay here. I, uh, I saw the light from the road."

"I didn't hear your car."

Ellice shrugged again. "I hiked up. It's good to get out from behind the wheel sometimes." She took a step farther into the office. Her hand, with the hat in it, dangled beside her thigh, the same side as her holstered weapon. She had pale eyes, with light, reddish lashes. She gazed at the upholstered chair where the clients sat with something like nostalgia.

"Were you one of Mom's clients?" Jack asked, and then wished he hadn't. It was probably violating her privacy or something. He never met his mother's clients. Client privacy was one of the reasons she had a side entrance to her office.

Ellice Gordon didn't seem to care. She nodded, without looking at him. "Yes," she said. "For quite some time. She was—" She gave a shake of her head, and looked up at him again. Her eyes were oddly flat, though their color was so light. "She was great," she finished. "But you're her kid. You know that."

"Yeah."

The officer's gaze swept him in what felt like a professional way. She grinned when her eyes fell on the rolling pin. "Weapon?" she said.

"I thought someone was breaking in."

"I'm sorry about that. I would have rung the bell if I knew you were here." She tilted her head toward him. "Scared, up here by yourself?"

"No. No, I'm not." The rolling pin felt like it had grown three sizes in his hand. He wriggled it self-consciously against his thigh. "I'm good."

"So I see." Pointedly, she dropped her gaze to the rolling pin again, then returned to his face. "Well, be careful to lock up next time, okay?"

"Sure." Jack thought he should probably say something else, but he didn't know what. The officer gave another look around the office, her eyes lingering on the open file drawer, before she took a step back toward the door.

She jerked a thumb back toward the desk, and the drawer. "You need some help with your mom's files?"

"No. Thanks."

"But the client files, and so forth . . ."

"Those are gone. The lawyer has them."

Her sandy eyebrows lifted. "Gone?"

"Yeah. First, I guess the cops looked at them—oh, sorry. Do you hate that word?"

She grinned again, freckled cheeks creasing. "We're used to it."

"Yeah." Jack shifted his weight so he could lean against the doorjamb. He would have liked to put down the rolling pin, but he was stuck with it now. He tucked it under his arm in what he hoped was a casual manner. "Yeah, so the cops went through them and then they went to the lawyer's office. I guess in case someone wants to take over the practice."

She nodded, and put her hand on the latch. "Okay, then. We're keeping an eye on the place for you. You'll be glad about that, I imagine."

"Thanks, officer."

"Ellice."

Jack didn't answer. Ellice pulled on her hat again, adjusted her belt, and slid the door open. She said, "Bye," closed the door, and was gone.

He waited where he was for a full minute before he crossed to the sliding door to check the latch. He knew, somehow, that he would find it broken. It was a simple hook latch, the hook bent now into uselessness.

"What the fuck?" he muttered. It could have already been broken, but he didn't think so. He had locked the door, tested it with his hand. He remembered doing it.

But maybe he was wrong. Maybe, with the police in and out of the house, someone had broken it, and not thought to tell him.

Maybe it broke while he was at school. He could have latched the door, tried it with his hand, and just thought it was secure.

He couldn't convince himself. He wished the officer had stayed away from the place. He didn't like her. He didn't like her at all.

He stood there, debating himself. He could call the Binghams. Chet would come and get him, but he'd have to explain this. After his bravado earlier, that was embarrassing.

He thought of his sports equipment, stacked in his bedroom closet. He ran up the stairs, opened the closet door, and found his old baseball bat standing in the corner. He ran down again, a little breathless with hurrying, and dropped the bat lengthwise into the base of the sliding glass door. It fit as if it had been designed for the purpose.

That would stop her, he thought.

But stop her from what? He wished he knew.

8

Si, mi chiamano Mimì, ma il mio nome è Lucia.

Yes, they call me Mimì, but my name is Lucia.

—Mimì, *La Bohème,* Act One

"I guess you haven't gotten around to opening that bank account," Iris said. She stood in the doorway of her pretty Cape Cod house, her arms folded, her gray gaze bright and piercing.

Tory held out the envelope with the cash in it for her second month's rent. "No," she said, a little huskily. "Not yet."

Iris accepted the envelope, but her eyes never left Tory's face. "That's a lot of cash to have lying around."

"I know. That's why I brought it over, instead of mailing it."

"I haven't seen you in town at all."

"Oh," Tory said, striving for an offhand tone, "I've been around. The market, you know. The library." At least she had gotten a library card. And with that and her rental agreement, a driver's license.

Iris nodded. "It's small, our library, but I like it."

It was tiny, in truth, a building of weathered wood nestled in a grove of trees. Tory had stocked her cottage with books from the Friends of the Library sale, most costing no more than a quarter. There had been CDs, too, but she hadn't bought any. She had nothing to play them on. "It's very nice," she said now, a little stiffly. She found, suddenly, that she wanted to get away from the piercing gaze, get back to her cottage and her view of the wintry ocean. It had surprised her, this morning, to hear the date on the radio. She had vanished herself more than a month ago.

Jack's fall quarter would be almost over, a time she had always looked forward to. Strained as their relationship was, she loved having him home for vacations. Even though he spent most of his time with his friends, it had been a comfort to her to know he was in the house, was up in his room dropping clothes on the floor and leaving his bureau open with T-shirts and socks hanging out of the drawers. She had learned not to touch any of those things while he was still home, but to wait until he had gone again to put things to rights.

She wondered where he would go now. And if Ellice knew that, too.

These thoughts rushed through her mind all at once, a little tide of them, and she blinked to push them away.

Iris misunderstood the blink for tears. Tory could tell by her voice when Iris said, "Paulette. Are you all right?"

"Yes! Yes, I'm quite all right. Thanks." Tory's voice sounded tight in her own ears, even angry. She hadn't intended that. She took a step back, down the first stair, and turned toward the driveway where the yellow Beetle waited, a spot of color against the green and gray landscape.

"Wait, Paulette." Iris came out of the doorway, pulling her worn cardigan closer against the sharp wind from the ocean. Her house was several blocks from the beach, about a half mile north of the cottage, but she had a good view of the water and even a glimpse of Haystack Rock. The rock dominated everything in the town. From Iris's porch, the rugged tip of it was easily visible, and with that access came the wind, straight off the water. Tory felt it on her neck and nipping at her ankles. Iris's gray hair spun in lank strands in front of her eyes. "Wait a moment. Come in and have a cup of coffee with me."

Tory hesitated, searching for a polite way to demur. There would be questions, not just about the cash, but everything else. The only way she knew to be safe was to be solitary. To be silent.

She had tried, once, to do something about Ellice. It had been bad, standing in a pay phone box on the main street of town, where anyone could see her and wonder why she didn't use her own telephone. She had leafed through the pages of the phone book until she found the government listings. She chose the FBI. Who else could she call?

The woman who answered wouldn't take her report. "Just give me your name," she kept saying, until a rush of anxiety stilled Tory's voice and made her slam the receiver down. Now, with Iris's curious gaze on her, her throat closed again.

"Come on," Iris repeated, and Tory knew she had waited too long. Iris put out her hand. She touched Tory's arm, but briefly. "Cold out here," she said. "I'm ready for another cup."

Tory found herself, a moment later, stepping over an enormous gray cat just inside Iris's door. She let her black coat slip from her shoulders as Iris reached for it. Iris hung it on a vintage mirrored coatrack, and gestured with her thin arm toward the kitchen. Tory, feeling tense and defensive, walked through a living room furnished with a deep gold sofa and a mahogany armoire into a kitchen shining with hanging copper pans and sparkling glassware on open shelves. A bird feeder in colored glass, empty now, hung just outside the window above a big stainless-steel sink. All of it reminded her, painfully, of her own modern kitchen and carefully designed living room. She could see why Iris preferred to rent the rustic cottage and have a more formal home for herself.

Iris waved her to a stool at a long granite-topped island. As Tory slid onto the stool, her hands swept over the cool stone, and a wave of nostalgia made her blink again.

This time, Iris was busy with the coffeepot and didn't notice. Tory cleared her throat. "Your house is beautiful," she said.

"Thanks," Iris said. "Cream?" She turned, a vintage pottery creamer already in her hand.

Tory had to smile at the creamer. It was made in the shape of a dairy cow, black-and-white spotted, with exaggerated eyelashes and full red lips.

"There, now," Iris said in her dry voice. "You look better when you smile."

Tory looked down at her linked fingers on the speckled granite. "I'm sorry if I seem unfriendly," she said. "I haven't had much to smile about lately."

"I guessed that."

Tory braced herself, sure that the questions were now to come, but her landlady brought down coffee cups, took spoons from a drawer, set four homemade cookies on a saucer, and laid out napkins. She braced her hip against the counter while the coffeemaker gurgled, and looked out her kitchen window at the branches of a spruce tossing in the wind. Light refracted through the glass bird feeder cast red and yellow spangles on the angles of her face. "Big storm coming," she said. "I think I'll send Jimmy Wurtel over to repair the broken shutter on the front window of your cottage. I should have done it earlier, but our weather's been so mild. The shutters help to block the worst of the storms, keep a bit of heat in. You'll be glad to be able to close them."

Tory said, "Iris, I can fix a broken shutter. Do you know what it needs?"

"Not really. I just noticed it was hanging loose when I met you there."

"I can figure it out. Let me do it."

"Are you sure?"

"Yes. I'm used to repairing things."

The corners of Iris's mouth lifted a bit, and Tory was tempted to tell her she, too, looked better when she smiled. "I'll bet you can do it yourself, at that," Iris said. "You look the type to do your own chores."

"I'll just need some tools. Maybe some nails, or screws if that's what's broken."

"Everything's in that little shed in the backyard. Tools are on the wall, and hardware is in the drawer of the workbench."

Tory, thinking about shutters, had a sudden vision of the house in her dream. It blocked out Iris's bright kitchen, and she saw, as if she were sitting in the little garden, the painted shutters and the iron-framed entryway baking in the summer heat. She had forgotten that image until just this moment, but now it was so vivid she could almost feel the sun burning her shoulders. It was so *real*. For one disorienting moment, it seemed more real than the cozy kitchen she was sitting in.

"Too strong?"

Tory, startled, looked up at Iris's raised eyebrows. "Sorry?"

"Your coffee. Is it too strong?"

Bemused, Tory made herself lift the cup, taste the brew. "No, it's delicious. Thanks."

"We like it strong here," Iris said. "Something about the cold and damp, I think."

Tory bit her lip to try to ground herself in the moment. Cold and damp. That was real. The burning sun of her dream wasn't, but it felt—she felt—

She shook her head sharply, and put down the cup with a bump. It didn't break, but coffee slopped over the edge onto the speckled granite. She dabbed at it with her napkin.

This shouldn't be happening. She had done so well, kept it all at arm's length, but now these dreams—they shouldn't be troubling her waking hours, too. She dropped the napkin, and pressed her fingertips to her forehead. "Sorry, Iris," she said again. "I think I may be coming down with something."

"I think you came with something, honey. Something you already had when you arrived in Cannon Beach."

Tory looked up at her. Her mouth opened, her lips parted to speak a denial, but the remark was so unexpectedly cogent that she couldn't find the words.

Iris, sipping from her coffee cup, lowered it and gazed at Tory with her sharp gray eyes.

Tory wondered fleetingly if she had looked that way when she sat behind her desk and watched her clients, listening to them, listening to her fey. She felt a prickle of alarm in her chest. She swallowed, and said faintly, "I—well, I—"

Iris put up a narrow hand. "It's okay, Paulette," she said. "None of my business. I just wanted to give you coffee, honest."

Tory said, with a rueful twist of her mouth, "I like the coffee."

"Better have a cookie with it." Iris pushed the cookie plate toward Tory with one finger. "You don't look like you've eaten much this month."

"Well—no, not a lot." Tory obediently took one cookie, and bit into it. It was perfect, sprinkled with cinnamon and sugar, soft and crunchy at the same time. Her mouth suddenly watered, and she ate the rest in two big, swift bites.

Iris took one herself and nibbled at the edge. "Our storms can be exciting," she said casually. "High winds, a lot of rain, sometimes thunder and lightning. But not to worry. If it were something big—tsunami or something—there's a warning system. You'd know."

"Tsunami?" Tory brushed crumbs of sugar from her sweater, and took another cookie. "That sounds dramatic."

"Would be, if we ever had one."

"You haven't, then?"

"Not since seventeen hundred." Iris got up to pour more coffee. "And despite what you may think, I was *not* around then."

Tory chuckled, and bit into the second cookie. She felt, for a moment, almost normal. The moment of danger had passed, and the richness of the cookies felt good in her stomach, the sugar soothing the raw edges of her nerves. "Seventeen hundred—there wasn't anybody around here then, was there?"

"Natives. Stories of a whole tribe being wiped out. Tree rings fixed the date."

"Well, I'm not worried about a tsunami. But I'll do the shutter today, just the same."

"Great. Saves me having to pay Jimmy. I appreciate it."

"That's okay. I don't have much to do right now." Iris fixed her clear gaze on her again, and Tory wished instantly she could call the words back. It wasn't smart, surely, to imply—to reveal—that she was used to being busy. She remembered Iris saying she thought she must be a nurse, or a librarian—

Had the news from Vermont reached here? Was anyone looking for her?

Jack . . .

Tory's sense of feeling normal subsided, and the cookies that had tasted so good suddenly felt like stones in her belly. It felt more normal, more usual, to be tense and withdrawn.

Jack—oh, no. This isn't safe.

Tory got to her feet, and carried her cup to the sink to rinse it. Over her shoulder she said, "I'll get to the shutter now, Iris, before the storm reaches us. Thanks again for the coffee."

"Any time." Tory wasn't sure how she managed to get back to the hall, retrieve her coat, say good-bye, and make her way out to the Beetle. She hoped she had been polite. Iris hadn't done anything, really, but give her coffee and chat with her a little. She was friendly, that was all. And she really hadn't pressed her for more information.

Tory gunned the noisy motor of the Beetle as she drove back to her cottage, fighting a mixed reaction of remorse and embarrassment at how she had behaved in Iris's kitchen.

At least she could do a really, really good job on the shutter.

She had been hammering nails when she and Jack had their first real falling out. As she chose some small nails to repair the crosspiece of the broken shutter on the cottage, the details of that day came back to her in all their unpleasantness.

Jack had been just fourteen, beginning to get tall, shoulders widening, a wisp of mustache appearing on his upper lip. His feet seemed to have become enormous almost overnight, and he had begun to spend a lot of his time with his friend Colton. She had asked him to stay home that afternoon to help her put together a lean-to for a cord of firewood that was coming.

"I don't know anything about building," he had said.

"You can learn," she answered, digging through a paper bag of nails she had picked up at the hardware store. "I don't know much, either, but we can figure it out."

He grumbled a bit about playing ball with Colton, but she didn't pay much attention. When she began to fit the pieces together, hammering nails while he held the wood in place, he said, "That doesn't look right."

She had just barked her elbow on a board, and she snapped, without thinking, "I thought you didn't know anything about building!"

He dropped the end of the board he was holding. It splashed in a leaf-strewn puddle, soaking his jeans and his sneakers. His voice broke in that way it had begun to do, in that way that later seemed to foreshadow the rift between them. "You think you know everything, Mom! Well, you don't!"

She looked up at him, her little boy on his swift way to manhood. He stood above her like a stranger, his hands on his hips, his mouth drawn into a scornful line, his cheeks suddenly blazing with color. Her lips parted to say, *I know I don't, sweetheart. I know that,* but he didn't give her a chance.

"Why can't we be like the Garveys?" he demanded.

She stared at him in dismay. Her son, her sweet, easygoing boy, was glaring at her, and his breath was coming too fast. His eyes were suspiciously bright, and she thought for a moment he might burst into tears. That would have been the Jack she knew. "Jack," she began. "Tell me what this is about. The Garveys? Is there something about them you—"

He interrupted her, his voice squeaking, then dropping so he sounded like a strangled frog. "Don't go all therapist on me, Mom, I'm telling you! I just want to have a normal family!"

What could she say? She *was* a therapist. It was the way she thought, the way she reacted. That didn't mean that the anger on his face, in the tone of his voice, didn't hurt. It did. It hurt too much to put into words.

She had promised herself she would never be the bitter, complaining parent her father had been. She would not make her child responsible for her happiness, or blame him for her troubles. Now, surprised and wounded, she crouched on the carpet of wet leaves, any words she might have spoken frozen in her mouth. She stared helplessly at the hammer in her hands, and the tears, it turned out, were in *her* eyes, not his. She had to bite her lip to stop them from falling.

The Garveys. Mr. Garvey was a salesman of some kind, maybe insurance. Mrs. Garvey seemed to spend all her time in the garden, or buzzing around town in her station wagon. Tory had only been inside the house once, and that had been chaotic, cluttered, full of shouting kids and a blaring television no one seemed to be watching.

Be like the Garveys? It wasn't possible. Not for her.

Jack stamped away, leaving her to deal with the pile of lumber on her own. She didn't call him back. It would pass, she thought. It was one of those sudden rushes of hormones, a flood of heat and feeling, and it would subside. Her boy would be restored to her.

She struggled on with the lean-to, finding ways to brace the supports, to nail one end of the boards and then pivot them up to nail in the other. She scraped her ankle—at least on the other side, to balance out the bruised elbow—and she broke two fingernails, but she managed to get the frame up. She stood back to look at it, knowing it was no thing of beauty, but feeling certain it would do the trick when she got the roof on. Maybe Jack would help her finish it.

When she thought she had given him enough time, she dusted the leaves and sawdust off her jeans and went in through the sliding glass door. She washed her hands in the little powder room, where she had towels and soap ready for clients, and then she went upstairs.

Jack was sitting in front of his computer. When she came in he blanked the screen and jumped up. "You could knock, Mom," he said.

"You're right." She stopped inside the door, resolutely ignoring the clothes-strewn floor and unmade bed. "You're right, I should knock."

He rolled his eyes, as if her compliance was yet another irritation. She felt a flicker of anger in her chest, but she repressed it. "I just came to apologize."

He stood beside his desk, one hand on the back of his chair, the other thrust into the pocket of his jeans. He said, without quite looking at her, "Yeah. Me too."

If only she had let it go at that. If she had backed out of his room, gone back down the stairs, left him to come to her when he was ready.

But he looked so gangly and out of proportion, so awkward and vulnerable and—and *lost*—she just wanted to gather him into her arms, comfort him, assure him this difficult time would pass. She crossed his room, and reached for him.

It was such a small thing. A tiny thing. It was tiny the way the stab of an ice pick is tiny, the wound deep and penetrating. Hard to heal.

The moment her hand fell on her son's shoulder, he shifted away, slid out from beneath it as if her touch repelled him.

She drew her hand back suddenly. She thought she might even have gasped. He had never done that before, shrugged her off in that dismissive way.

She turned from him without speaking, and hurried out of his room, fleeing down the stairs and out of the house. She went back to the lean-to and started on the roof, blasting nails into the asphalt shingles as if she could undo the morning's events by the sheer force of her will. She broke one of the shingles in two, and with a curse, spun it into the woods with all her strength. The effort made her slide on the wet leaves, and her feet flew out from under her. She landed hard on her rear end, dropping the hammer and scattering the stack of shingles. She looked up and around, fearful Jack had seen her fall, dreading the disdainful look on his face.

She was spared that humiliation. He wasn't there, either outside or at the window.

It was nothing. It was a silly disagreement, a misunderstanding. But she was wet and tired and alone, and she had buried her face in her hands and sobbed.

Yes, she thought now, as she fitted the end of the broken slat back onto the crosspiece of the shutter, it had been a small thing.

It should have passed, an unhappy day that faded as time went on, a moment of friction like those that came to every family, soon forgiven, eventually forgotten. Instead, fueled by silence and strain, it grew. There was no one to mediate between her and her son, no grandparents, no father, no siblings. Sometimes she wanted to rage at him for being impossible, for being inconsiderate or ungrateful, but she remembered her father's rages, and she held back. She didn't want to be like her mother, either—withdrawn, remote, shrinking away from her family more every year until she finally shrank herself right into an institution, leaving Tory with a father who was furious with the world, with his wife, with Tory, and—she understood, though it didn't help—with himself.

Sometimes it was all right between Jack and Tory. There were moments they seemed to communicate, their lives to intersect in the old way. Mostly they were separate, and distant. Jack spent every possible moment at the Garvey house. Tory, clinging to the idea that it would all blow over one day, carried on in silence. Therapist or no, she didn't know what else she could do.

She finished the shutter with no difficulty. She had grown adept, these past years, at using a hammer, a screwdriver, a wrench, even a hatchet. She did it alone. She made Jack's meals, drove him to school, took him shopping for clothes, and all the while, though he was right there in the house, she missed him with a physical ache that sometimes drove her nearly mad.

Kate wanted her to meet someone, to go out to dinner, to have her own life. Tory had no energy for that, no inclination, though she was grateful for Kate's concern. She didn't know how, without Kate Bingham, she would have survived that period of her life. Only Kate knew the truth about Jack's father, and only Kate understood how she felt about her son.

It crossed her mind, as she put away the tools in the shed behind the cottage, that Kate might be suffering her loss more than Jack did. She and Kate had often chatted on the phone, met for coffee, even hurried to get supplies together when a big winter storm was coming. Chet brought his tractor over to plow the snow from her driveway, and kept an eye on things on the rare occasions she was away from home. She drove by their house when they were away visiting their kids. She knew they cared about her, and she knew they must be terribly hurt by what had happened. She also knew they would watch out for Jack. It would be okay—at least as okay as it was possible to be.

Oh, Jack. Son. Be safe.

She went inside the cottage to change out of her jeans. She glanced down at the bottom drawer of the bureau, where the file rested, and a sudden urge to get rid of it seized her. Burn it. Destroy it. Make all it represented disappear, just as she had made herself disappear.

She squeezed her eyes shut against the sudden vision of a man being shot, of blood flying everywhere, of smashed bone and the thud of flesh striking pavement.

She forgot about changing her clothes. She found herself, moments later, back in the toolshed, seizing the hammer and a Phillips screwdriver, filling her pockets with nails and screws, grabbing an ancient pair of leather gloves. She stalked out of the cottage and down the beach until she came to the collapsed bench on its little apron of cement.

She knelt beside it, and began pulling the bent screws out of the iron frame. The rising wind whipped at her hair and tugged at her jacket as she shoved and kicked the frame back into place. She straightened boards, hammered new nails, inserted new screws. She worked until it was too dark to see, but when she finally rose and stood back, the bench was intact again, facing Haystack Rock and the shadowed vista of waves and clouds and sand.

The promised storm roiled the water, and the first rain began as Tory gathered up her tools, brushed away the prints of her knees and her sneakers, and walked back up the beach. She didn't look back at the repaired bench, but she thought that tonight, at least, she could sleep undisturbed.

9

Io non son che una povera fanciulla oscura e buona a nulla.

I am nothing but a poor girl of humble birth,
and good for nothing.

—Minnie, *La Fanciulla del West*, Act One

Doria sang fragments of melodies to herself as she bent over the sink in Villa Puccini, peeling fat cloves of purple garlic for *aglio e olio*. Old Zita bustled about in the dining room, laying the table in readiness. Despite the oppressive heat, the oven blazed, roasting the ducks Puccini and his guests had bagged the day before, and which Zita and Doria had spent the morning scalding and then plucking. A fresh basket of ironing waited near the back door, but there was too much cooking to be done for Doria to get to it now. In any case, in this heat, it would be far better to do the ironing after dark.

Tonight, there would be no reason not to wait. Elvira had gone off to Milan to visit her daughter, Fosca, and would be gone most of the week. Puccini and Ferruccio Pagni had driven to Viareggio to see a litter of hound puppies. Doria had hurried to clean the studio the moment they departed, though the next morning it would be cluttered and ash-strewn all over again. Puccini was hard at work on *La Fanciulla del West*, but it wasn't going well. The evening before, she had heard him cursing the librettist, complaining that the play wasn't working.

She smiled now, thinking of it, as she dropped the garlic cloves into a shallow pan of olive oil and sprinkled salt over them. The opera would be wonderful, of course. The maestro always doubted himself. He agonized over every bar, every chord, every phrase, but the magic always happened in the end. She wasn't at all worried. She had listened to the fragments trickling from the studio late at night, and she knew. It would be magnificent.

Zita came back into the kitchen, extra napkins draped over her arm, and nodded approval at the garlic soaking in olive oil. "I just wish I had some fennel for the ducks," she said. "I used the last of ours in the *ragù* yesterday."

"Mamma had some in her garden, the last time I was there." Doria wiped her hands on the kitchen towel. "Would you like me to fetch some?"

Zita gave her a whiskery grin, and patted her arm. "You're a good girl, Doria. Yes, some fennel would be *buonissimo* for the sauce!"

"I'll go now." Doria untied her apron, and laid it over a kitchen chair.

"Take that extra bird hanging on the porch," Zita said. "That will make your mamma happy, I think, with so many people to feed."

"*Grazie!*" Doria, in her bare feet, padded out to the porch and took down the duck hanging in the shade. She slipped it into a canvas bag, and pulled her straw hat from its hook. It felt good to be able to move about as she wished, without having to explain every step she took to the *signora*. She felt no compunction at all over her errand. She would take the gift of a duck to her mother and return with the fennel in no time. She would wash her feet, change her wilting frock, put on a freshly starched apron, and be ready to help Zita serve.

Her mother, stirring a pot of soup, scowled suspiciously when she came in through the kitchen door. "There's no need to look at me like that!" Doria said. "I'm not staying." She pulled the duck from her bag and held it up by its feet before she laid it on the table. "Zita needs fennel for the maestro's dinner. I told her there was some in your garden—I didn't think you'd mind—and she sent you this."

Her mother's face softened. She put down her long spoon, and crossed to the table. "Well, now," she said. She poked the fat, promising shape of the bird beneath its glossy feathers. "Well. We haven't had a duck in a while." She looked up at her daughter as if she didn't know what to say next.

"Fennel, Mamma," Doria said again. "We need fennel, and I saw some in your garden."

"*Sì, sì, sì!* Fennel." Her mother waved her free hand in the direction of the garden. "I have lots of fennel. Help yourself." She laid the duck on a wooden board and turned her back on her daughter as she reached for a big pot to scald it in. "It's nice to have duck." She began to pump water into the pot, the muscles of her arm flexing as she worked the handle. "Although," she added, as if to herself, "you could have plucked it for me."

Doria pressed her lips together as she took her bag out into the garden. She would not, she told herself, let this nice day be spoiled by her mother's crossness. She crouched down beside the bed of fennel. The heat had browned their feathery tops, and when she pulled them, the bulbs slid easily out of the dry dirt, perfuming the air with their faint licorice scent. She took six, shook the soil from them, and dropped them into her bag. She straightened, brushing dirt from her dress, pulling her hat brim down over her eyes against the brilliant sun.

"Doria—" She looked up to see her mother standing in the doorway.

"Yes, Mamma?"

"Tell Old Zita—tell her, *grazie.*"

"I will."

"And, Doria—"

Doria couldn't help another sigh, anticipating some new criticism. "Yes, Mamma?"

"Take care of yourself, *mia figlia.*"

"*Cosa?*" Doria felt a brief quiver of unease that had nothing to do with her mother's temper. Her mother could be cross, but when she sounded like this, it was best to listen.

"I had a dream. Two nights ago."

"What was it?"

"My house was full of people, all in black, everyone crying. Someone was dead, but I don't know who."

Doria nodded, accepting this. Everyone in their family knew that if Emilia had a dream, it might mean something, or it might not, but it was never good to ignore it. Their father had made a fatal error by dismissing one of Emilia's dreams. They could be hard to interpret sometimes, and sometimes they were just the result of too much salt in the pasta, but all the Manfredis took note of Emilia's dreams.

Doria, lifting her hand in farewell, saw the lines of worry and fatigue etched in her mother's dark face, the streaks of gray in her black hair. It occurred to her, with a little shiver, that her mother was not all that much older than Elvira Puccini. She looked elderly by comparison. *Un' anziana.*

She said, with a twinge of regret at the lack of affection between them, "I will take care, Mamma. Don't worry."

As she stepped down into the street, her mother called after her. "It's nice to have the duck. Even if I have to pluck it myself."

Doria laughed to herself as she set out on the trudge back to Villa Puccini, her long bare toes scuffing puffs of yellow dust from the road. Her mother was as predictable as sunrise and sunset. She scolded and complained, but she had managed to feed six children and hold her modest house together with no one to help her. Signora Puccini would have crumbled under such pressure!

The hot sun baked the top of Doria's head, even through the crown of her straw hat, and sweat trickled down her ribs and back. Still, it was lovely to be walking through the village, swinging her bag with its fragrant harvest, calling greetings to her neighbors. She was looking forward to a festive evening, serving the maestro and his friends. She and Zita could relax over the leftovers after the sun had gone down and the worst of the heat had dissipated. Best of all, there would be music pouring from Puccini's studio.

She looked down at her dusty chicken feet. Before any of that, she must wash!

She was just passing the little stone church when she was seized by a sudden urge to go in, to spend a moment in the cool silence, perhaps light a candle to the Virgin and ask for—for what? She had everything she wanted at this moment. Perhaps she would just kneel in the alcove and offer her gratitude. She stopped at the door, and did her best to clean her bare feet before going in.

After the brilliance of the sunny afternoon, the dimness of the church blinded her for a moment. She paused beside the font, just inside the door, and waited for her eyes to adjust. Candles flickered near the altar, and the inviting fragrance of incense filled the space. Doria drew an appreciative breath through her nose, and turned toward the alcove where a painted statue of the Virgin kept watch.

She was bending to light a candle when she heard a light step behind her. She turned to see Father Michelucci coming up the central aisle. He smiled when he saw her, and came to stand beside her.

"Doria," he said. "Are you well?"

"I am, Father," she said. She bobbed a shallow curtsy. "And you?"

"Very well indeed. I'm to join you tonight at Villa Puccini."

She smiled and held up her bag. "I have some fennel here for the duck sauce. The dinner should be very good! Zita is already hard at work."

"Signor Puccini speaks well of you, Doria." The priest's eyes twinkled at her. "You make me proud."

Doria ducked her head, blushing with pleasure. "I do my best for the maestro, Father."

"I'm sure you do." He patted her shoulder, and she lifted her head again. He was her favorite person in Torre del Lago. Well, perhaps her second favorite, after Puccini. Father Michelucci was barely taller than she was, slight and wiry in his black robes, gentle in his speech. The best memories of her childhood had been in his company, in the peace of his little classroom. It was Father Michelucci who encouraged her to read books, to listen to music, to allow her to imagine something better for herself than laboring all her life to feed a flock of children. He had been the one to recommend her to the Puccinis after the maestro's automobile accident. She had been eager to apply for the job, and delighted when they accepted her. That was, of course, before she knew how many servants Elvira Puccini had driven away with her temper, but even so, she would not have passed up the chance to work in Villa Puccini, to have electricity and the telephone and a room of her own, and best of all, to hear the maestro create his wonderful music.

Father Michelucci had aged, but the lines in his face and the gray in his hair seemed as gentle to Doria as his manner of speaking. He asked, "And how do you get on with the *signora?*"

Doria had to duck her head again to hide the hot stain that spread over her cheeks. "I do my best, Father," she said, staring down at her long, bare toes.

"I'm sure of that, Doria. I know you always do your best."

At these encouraging words, she lifted her head and looked into his face. "She hates me," she whispered.

Father Michelucci drew a breath, and his lips parted, but for a long moment he didn't speak. When he did, Doria could see he chose his words with care. "Doria," he said softly, though there was no one else in the church. "I don't think she hates you."

"Oh, she does, Father! She shouts at me, and criticizes everything I do!"

"She has a bad temper."

Doria rolled her eyes. "My mother has a bad temper. The *signora*'s is *evil!*"

The priest's eyebrows drew together, and the lines around his eyes deepened. "You must be careful around her."

"*Sì, sì,*" she said. "I try to do everything just the way—"

He shook his head. "I don't mean the housework," he said. His voice dropped further, and there was a tinge of urgency in it. "You know the stories, I think. I have to say, Doria, a woman so unhappy is capable of many things."

"She should not be unhappy. She has a beautiful house, a talented husband—"

"She knows he does not love her."

Doria gazed at the priest in wonder. "She knows . . . ?"

He nodded, and his gaze swept away from her, up toward the Virgin with her blue painted robe and her hands pressed together in prayer. "He married her because he felt he had to," he said sadly. "But the wedding was held here, very late at night, and in secret. Puccini had the church windows covered, so no one would see and talk about it. This is a shameful thing for a woman."

"But everyone knows they are married!"

"Yes, they know now. But for so long, she was still married to her first husband, and there was someone else Giacomo loved."

"Corinna," Doria breathed.

"Yes. The very night of that secret wedding, Elvira made Giacomo promise never to see Corinna again. He made the promise. He had to, really. There was pressure from all sides, and there were the children to think of. But I saw tears in his eyes when he agreed to it."

"*Che peccato!* He really loved her," Doria sighed, imagining the maestro, so boyish and funny and charming, pining for love of a girl he could no longer have, and tied to Elvira through duty. "That's so sad, Father!"

Father Michelucci put a firm hand on her arm. "Just know that your mistress has good reason to be unhappy."

"Yes, Father."

"Still, she can be—let us say, unpredictable. Take care, Doria."

"I'm not afraid of her, a fat old woman like that!"

"Doria! She is your mistress, after all."

"I know. And I do my job better than anyone else could!"

"Yes." He looked thoughtful. "I worry, though, Doria. There's something about her—"

Doria smiled at him affectionately. "Don't worry, Father. Everything will be fine."

"I hope so." He blessed her then, making the sign of the cross over her bent head. They said good-bye, and Doria went out into the brilliant sunlight again, blinking after the dimness of the church. Two warnings in one day! That couldn't be a good thing. But, as she set out toward Villa Puccini, the bag of fragrant fennel swinging at her side, it was hard to feel anything but contentment. At least for now, with the *signora* away, there was nothing to worry about.

She let herself in through the garden gate and went to the back, where she could pump water into a bucket to wash the dust from her feet and ankles. She had just stepped into the bucket, lifting her skirt to keep it out of the water, when she heard the sharp voice above her head. "Where's that girl?"

Doria gasped in dismay. The *signora!* But she wasn't supposed to return until Sunday! She heard Zita's murmured answer, though she couldn't make out the words. Zita was probably trying to help the *signora* with her valise, which would normally be Doria's task. Elvira snapped something else at Zita, drowning the cook's explanation for Doria's absence. With anxiety clutching in her throat, Doria stamped up and down in the muddy water to rinse her feet as best she could, then hopped out to dry them on the grass. She crept in through the door, careful to let it settle quietly into its frame, then hurried to find her shoes and stockings.

She didn't waste time on her hair or her dress, but dashed up the narrow stairs.

"I'm here, Zita," she said, at the *signora*'s door. "Signora, I'm right here. Do you—"

Elvira and Zita were struggling with the front hooks of the *signora*'s corset. Her traveling costume, a skirt and fitted jacket of cream-colored broadcloth, lay in a heap on the floor, with her pleated shirtwaist on top of it. Doria saw, with a little flicker of revulsion, that it was stained yellow in the armpits, and would be horrible to wash. She forgot that in a moment, though, as the *signora* said, with tears of frustration in her voice, "Oh, Doria! *Grazie al cielo!* The hooks are stuck, and your fingers are thinner!"

Doria moved to assist the older woman. It was stiflingly hot in the bedroom. The curtains and shutters had been kept closed throughout the *signora*'s absence, but it hadn't helped much. Elvira's body radiated heat that Doria could feel even before she touched her, and her cheeks and throat were painfully flushed. Her hair, no longer contained by the wide-brimmed hat she had tossed onto her dressing table, fell every which way. She smelled of perspiration and sour breath. "I have to hurry," she quavered. "Before Giacomo returns. I can't let him see me like this."

Elvira looked utterly miserable, and she panted with effort. She gave a sob of relief when Doria finally freed the hook from its snag of fabric and the heavy corset popped open. Beneath the layers of silk and boning, Elvira's body was drenched with sweat.

"There, signora," Doria said. "There, now, that's better. I'll mend this later. Zita, the *signora* needs a bath filled, don't you think?"

Elvira said plaintively, "A cool one, Zita. I fear this heat will be the end of me!" Zita hurried off, and Doria helped Elvira out of her sodden shirtwaist and handed her a dressing gown. She went to the window and pulled the curtains aside enough to open it. A faint breeze stirred the heavy air in the room, and Elvira, with a sigh, collapsed onto the lacy stool before her dressing table. "Do you know where Giacomo is?"

"He went to Viareggio, signora. A hound bitch there has a new litter."

"*Mamma mia!* All we need is another dog slobbering all over this house!" Elvira began searching through her heavy hair for pins, pulling them out and tossing them onto the dressing table. "Get my ivory cotton dress out for me, Doria. I hope you ironed it!"

"*Sì, sì, sì!* It's hanging just here." Doria opened the walnut wardrobe and pulled out the dress. It was light as a feather, with panels of lace inset into the lingerie cotton. She glanced back at

Elvira's substantial form, hoping the *signora* could still fit into it. She grew stouter every year, another cause for her to lament. She would have to put on a fresh corset.

Elvira caught her backward look, and scowled at her. "What's wrong?"

"*Niente, signora,*" Doria said hastily. She draped the dress invitingly over the bed. "You see? It's all ready for you."

Elvira said, "My Fosca received an invitation to a house party on Lago di Garda, and there was no room in the car for me, or so they said. I meant to stay longer, but . . ." She gave a gusty sigh. "Children are so thoughtless. See you treat your mamma with respect, Doria! A mother's life is a hard thing!"

"*Sì, signora.*" Doria hung up the traveling suit and took the soiled shirtwaist under her arm. "I'll just set this to soak. Your bath will be ready soon." She made her escape, pattering down the stairs and on through the kitchen. She checked on the water flowing into the bathtub, then went back to the porch to pour soapy water over the shirtwaist. She sprinkled an extra measure of bluing over it, but she wasn't sure she would be able to get the stains out even so.

Zita was at the counter, rubbing potatoes with olive oil. She glanced up at Doria when she came back into the kitchen. "Did you get the fennel?"

"Oh! I forgot! Yes, it's right here." She handed the cook the bag, and saw her glance inside, nodding with satisfaction at the size of the bulbs. "Mamma says to thank you for the duck."

"Good. Good. You can slice these for me, then."

"Yes, and Zita . . . Mamma had a dream."

Zita stopped her work, her greasy hands poised over the dish of potatoes. "Emilia had a dream? What was it?"

"She said people filled the house, all of them weeping."

"*O Dio.*" Zita sketched the sign of the cross. "Just like when your poor pappa died."

"Yes, I suppose. But it might mean nothing!"

Zita shook her head, and resumed oiling the potatoes. "In

Emilia's line," she said dourly, "there is always the *fé*. You have to remember that."

"I don't have it, Zita."

Zita flashed her a look, her black eyes glinting in the bright kitchen. "You are mistaken, Doria *mia*. *I* don't have the *fé*, though I always wished for it. But you will one day. Every woman in your mamma's line does, sooner or later."

Doria shrugged. "*Chi sa?* There is no sign of it yet. If I had it, I might have known the *signora* had returned!" She grinned at the old cook, but Zita scowled, and shook her head so her frizzy hair flew around her face.

Doria took the fragrant fennel bulbs out of her bag and laid them on a cutting board. She was folding the bag to stow in the pantry when she caught sight of the basket of ironing. She had forgotten all about it.

All she could do now was hope that the *signora* didn't notice it waiting here, still undone. Perhaps she would go to her bed when the men retired to the studio for their cards and music and talk, and give Doria the chance to get through it.

A sudden wave of weariness swept Doria as she took up the first fennel bulb and cut off its long, feathery top. She might, with luck, get this basket of ironing done before another was ready and waiting, but it was a faint hope. That lacy dress of the *signora*'s had to be laundered and ironed every time she wore it, and she would no doubt want it again soon, in this heat.

A moment later, the *signora* came through the kitchen on her way to the bathroom. As Doria wiped sweat from her forehead with the back of her arm and began to slice the fennel, she heard Elvira sigh with pleasure as she sank into the cool water.

Zita's dinner was a great success with the gentlemen, although Elvira complained that the soup, a lovely thick *ribollita* using up the heels of the previous day's bread, was a peasant dish and shouldn't be served to guests. Peasant dish or not, none of the diners left scraps in their wide pottery bowls. Zita grunted with satisfaction when Doria carried them back into the kitchen and muttered something about nothing being wrong with good country food.

Doria, dressed in a fresh skirt and her long, voluminous apron, helped Zita to plate the servings of duck in fennel sauce, laying the filled plates in front of each guest, careful not to let the sauce spill onto the clean tablecloth. Signor Caruso winked at her, and said, "Elvira, how lucky you are in your housemaid! My own Ada would envy you."

The maestro, with a wave of his cigarette, said, "The best in Torre, friends!" Elvira smiled, and nodded to Doria, but her eyes were cold. Doria made a shallow curtsy, and escaped to the kitchen.

She told Zita about the compliment. "I suppose I'll be scolded for that, too," she said tiredly. "The *signora* didn't like it, I could tell."

"Never mind," Zita said. She was arranging slices of almond cake on small china plates, but she paused to pat Doria's arm. "The *signore* appreciates you, and that's what matters."

Doria stretched to reach down the delicate gold-edged Murano glasses from the china cupboard, and set them on a tray with a decanter of *vin santo*. With great care, she carried the tray back into the dining room. As she slid it onto the tablecloth, she felt Elvira's burning gaze on her every move. It made her hands tremble, and when she tried to pour out the wine, a few drops spattered across the tablecloth.

"*Attenzione!*" Elvira snapped.

Doria glanced up at her, sensing the triumph in her voice. She murmured, "*Sì, signora,*" as mildly as she could, but she knew, as surely as if Elvira had said so, how pleased the *signora* was to see her make a mistake in front of the guests. She managed to serve the wine and the dessert plates without further incident, and carried the tray back into the kitchen, but her cheeks flamed.

As Zita moved to damp the fire in the oven, Doria said, "Zita, leave the fire. I have ironing to do."

Zita turned to her with a motherly click of her tongue. "You've been up since dawn! You should go to bed. If you don't rest, you'll be ill."

The sympathy made Doria's eyes prick with tears. She pressed them away with the heels of her hands. "I have to, Zita," she said. "You know the *signora* will be angry if she sees the basket full in the morning."

"She wasn't even supposed to be here," Zita grumbled. She banged the saucepan into the dishwater and began scrubbing at it with sharp, angry movements. "No reason you couldn't do the ironing in the morning."

"I know. But it can't be helped. At least it's a bit cooler now."

"Well, you go on and get started, then. I'll clean all this up and clear the table when they're done."

Casting her a grateful look, Doria fetched the irons from their cupboard and set them on the stove. The house was still warm despite the late hour. Mosquitoes buzzed outside the zinc screens, and white moths flickered through the darkness. Doria heard the scrape of chairs as the dinner guests rose from the table and moved into Puccini's studio. She listened hopefully for the *signora*'s step on the stair, and when it came, she allowed herself a breath of relief. As Zita carried the last of the dishes back from the dining room, Doria began on one of Elvira's flounced petticoats, careful to press each layer as smooth and flat as possible without scorching the delicate material.

Zita soon finished the dishes, and wiped down the wooden counter in the kitchen. "I wish I could help you with that," she said, as she took off her apron and folded it. "We should ask the *signora* for another ironing board."

"Oh, don't do that!" Doria said with a laugh. "She'll just say I should get it done faster."

"Ironing is ironing. You can't hurry it."

"Isn't that the truth? I wonder if anyone who doesn't iron understands that."

"Well, *carissima*, try not to stay up too late. I'll let you sleep in a bit, shall I?"

"I'm all right, Zita. Thank you."

"Sogni d'oro."

"And you." The sound of the piano began in the studio just as Zita closed her bedroom door, and Doria smiled again. She wouldn't mind her chore so much if there was to be music. She shook out the petticoat, draped it carefully over its padded hanger, and hung it from the door frame. She pulled a lace-trimmed camisole out of the basket as the maestro began to play through the act that had been troubling him so. Caruso would encourage him, and that would be good. She worried about that. When he was unhappy, he smoked too much, and drank too much, and drove his boat and his car too fast, as if speed would spur his creativity.

You would think, she mused, that the *signora* would try harder to make his life more peaceful. He had almost died in the car accident, and it had been a whole year before he recovered. Perhaps Elvira liked that, though. All that year he was confined, she didn't have to wonder where he was or who he was with. She had been happy, then, for Doria to sit with him, talk with him, nurse him. It was only now, when he was strong again . . .

The music stopped, and when it started again, Doria stopped what she was doing to listen, the iron poised in midair. Signor Caruso was singing. First there was a bit of the recitative, a few notes and words, a pause, then the notes repeated before he sang the opening bars of the aria. His voice was strong and insistent, yet his *legato* was faultless. She could imagine, if she closed her eyes, that great, steely voice filling La Scala, echoing from the vaulted ceiling, thrilling through the balconies and the boxes. She put her head on one side, closing her eyes, relishing the phrasing, the liquid connection between the notes of the melody and the chords beneath Puccini's fingers.

There was something mystical about the music sounding through the warm night. It was like being in church, that same feeling of being above everything that was mundane, ugly, or harsh. The electric lights glowed yellow, making the kitchen cozy and private in the darkness beside the lake. The moths fluttered at the screens, like tiny *putti* gathering to hear the celestial music. Even the crickets seemed to cease their chirping to listen to Caruso sing Puccini's music.

Doria opened her eyes to find that her iron had gone cold. She replaced it on the stove, and took up the other, but it was cooling, too, as the fire burned lower. She left them both on the top, and went to the back door for another stick of wood. After she fed the fire, she had to wait for the irons to get hot again. She moved closer to the door that led to the dining room and the studio, leaning against the wall, listening.

Puccini was singing in his smoke-roughened voice, first one part and then another, and Caruso answered him. Caruso was to undertake the role of Johnson when the opera had its premiere in New York. How wonderful it was that she, Doria Manfredi of Torre del Lago, should be one of the first to hear him sing it! She imagined the singers in their colorful costumes, the set rising around them, the orchestra playing in the pit. She closed her eyes again, delighted to see it all in her mind's eye, to feel as if she were really there, perhaps in a fine gown with lace insets and gloves that reached all the way to her elbows—

She didn't hear Elvira's slippered tread on the stair, or her quick step across the kitchen floor. She didn't know she was there until she felt the hot, heavy hand strike her upper arm with a stinging slap. "What are you doing?" Elvira snapped.

Doria jumped, her eyes flying open, her mouth instantly drying. "I—I'm ironing, signora," she said faintly.

"You are not!" Elvira pointed at the stove. "Both your irons are right there, and you're standing idle!"

"But, signora, the stove was—"

"Don't argue with me! And why are you ironing at this hour?"

Doria had to clench her teeth to keep from snapping back that the *signora* had just accused her of *not* ironing. She rubbed her stinging arm as she crossed to the ironing board, and took one of the freshly heated irons from the stove. "It was a busy day, signora," she said, keeping her face averted. She heard the edge in her voice, but she couldn't help it. "I was helping Zita prepare the dinner. You saw that for yourself."

Elvira's voice rose, and Doria braced herself for the onslaught of temper she knew was coming. "You don't fool me, Doria Manfredi!" she began, interrupting the music, standing so close that Doria could feel the unhappy heat of her body. Doria kept her eyes on the ironing board, pressing the neck of the chemise smooth, flattening the lace with her fingertips. "You can't fool me!" Elvira repeated. "You're just trying to get close to my husband when you think I'm not looking. You think I don't see! You little tart, I'll have you out in the street—"

"*Non è vero, signora!*" Doria whirled, and her voice rose, too, full of resentment at the unfairness. "It's not true! You know it's not true!"

"*Cosa?* What did you say?" When Doria didn't answer immediately, Elvira pushed at her shoulder with an impatient finger. "What?"

"I said it's not true! I have told you before!"

At the same moment that Puccini put his head inside the kitchen to see what the noise was about, Elvira struck Doria again, smacking her shoulder with the flat of her hand. Doria, desperate to lift the iron up and away, to keep from burning Elvira, stumbled back into the ironing board. The board crashed to the floor, Elvira shrieked something about Doria trying to kill her, and the iron went flying, skidding across the flagstones to land with a fearsome sizzle against the base of the icebox.

Puccini shouted, "Elvira! What are you doing?"

She screamed back, "*Io?* I'm not doing anything! It's this brat of a girl trying to murder me in my own kitchen!"

Doria sucked in an outraged breath, and shrieked, "Liar! How can you lie to the *signore* that way? *You* struck *me!*" Puccini and Elvira both stared at her, speechless with surprise.

Doria, humiliated in front of Puccini, and with Caruso listening from the studio, burst into tears. She spun to escape from the kitchen, and ran out through the dark garden, racing toward the edge of the lake and its muddy solitude. Puccini called her name, but she didn't turn back. The dogs left their kennel and bounded after her, one on either side as she ran sobbing into the darkness.

Burning with shame and resentment, she found herself on the rough planks of the boat dock. She walked along to the end, where she crouched down, hugging her knees. Her tears ceased as she gazed into the dark depths of the lake. The dogs nosed her cheeks, then flopped beside her, panting. She put a hand on each of them, taking comfort in their company.

She could still hear the *signora* screaming her rage into the night, as if she were one of the divas come to coach a role with the maestro. The great difference was that Elvira's voice was so ugly, splitting the darkness with knife-edged fury. Elvira could stab a person with that voice.

The maestro must not have known her voice was like that. He couldn't have! Surely he would never have married her if he had.

Doria slipped out of her shoes, and let her long bare toes trail through the cool water. There would be no more music tonight. She felt a rush of sympathy for Puccini. He was trapped by Elvira just as she was, and there was nothing either of them could do about it.

10

❧

Sogni fugaci di chi nacque per gemere e tacer.

Fleeting dreams of one who was born
to moan and to keep silent.

—Tigrana, *Edgar,* Act One

Tory woke with someone's harsh cries echoing in her ears. Her sleep had not been undisturbed after all, though she had been exhausted when she finally pulled the blanket up around her. The same people had been in her dream, acting out a scene of anger and noise. She felt, again, as if she were the girl in the dream. As if she and the girl were the same person. It was a classic case of transference, she supposed, except that she seemed to be both therapist and client. It was as if, by imagining this girl's unhappiness, she was trying to work out her own.

She pushed back the sheets and swung her feet down to the cold floor. The paperweight reflected the faint light from the window, but everything else lay in the thick darkness of a starless night. The rain had stopped, though the wind still whistled at the eaves and rattled the shutters. Tory padded awkwardly to the bathroom, feeling her way, disoriented and out of balance. She used the toilet, then felt her way to the sink to wash her hands. She turned on the light over the mirror, squinting until her eyes adjusted. When she could see herself, she pushed back her sweat-dampened hair, and saw with alarm that a half-inch of pale roots showed beneath the red dye. What if Iris had noticed?

She flicked the light off again, and wandered aimlessly out into the living room. It was three in the morning, the worst hour of the twenty-four, the worst to be awake, the worst for worrying. A rush of anxiety filled her, a flood of helpless panic that made her mouth go dry and her heart pound.

Jack's okay. Kate will see to it.

She fought for calm as she stood beside the window, where the chill of the night crept through the glass and dried the perspiration on her forehead. She told herself it was just the hour. And the vividness of her dream. It didn't mean anything.

One of the hardest things about being fey was knowing the difference between premonition and anxiety. Nonna Angela had understood that, because she suffered the same doubts. She knew when a little boy from her village fell into Lake Massaciuccoli and drowned before anyone knew he was missing. She knew when her cousin, sixteen and unmarried, was pregnant. She saw her father's death the night before he was struck by a train and died.

On the other hand, she suffered terrible bouts of anxiety before her voyage across the ocean with her American soldier husband, yet their journey was safe and smooth and uneventful. It was a matter of faith, she told Tory, when her fey had made itself known. Faith. *Fé*, in Italian, which became fey in Nonna Angela's accented English. It was all the same, and it was both a gift and a curse.

When prickles of cold began to creep up and down her arms and across her chest, Tory made herself go back to bed, but she didn't sleep. She lay on her pillow, staring up at the low ceiling, listening to the wind and watching the light change as dawn made its slow way over the hills to draw faint sparkles from the tossing sea. The bout of anxiety faded as the light rose, and she felt calm again. Ice Woman.

When the clock said six, she got up. She dressed, and pulled on her coat, which was beginning to look a little down-at-heel. She filled a mug with coffee, a lidded cup some service station had given her. Locking the cottage door behind her, she wandered down to the beach, feeling small and alone on the sandy expanse. As she passed the bench she had repaired the night before, she glanced back at the cottage. The mended shutter looked perfect, the boards now secure. The gate was intact again, too, and swung smoothly on freshly oiled hinges. She had also, when no one was around, repaired the broken frame that held the recycling bins of the house behind hers, and straightened a tilting bike rack at one of the beach entrances, replacing its bent screws with fresh, unrusted ones. She wondered what people must think about her little improvements. It was a bit like the old children's story about brownies that sneaked around fixing things in the night.

The tide was in, bubbling far up, so she had only a narrow strand to walk on. She found a dry boulder and perched on it to gaze out over the gradually brightening water. The wind had eased a little, but it was still sharp and cold. She slid down onto the sand to sit in the lee of the rock, out of the breeze. She wrapped her arms around her bent legs and rested her chin on her knees.

If her dreams meant anything, she supposed, they meant she should face what had happened to her instead of burying it. She had often advised her clients to walk themselves through their traumas, alone or with a support group. She couldn't turn to a support group, of course, but she also couldn't rely on dreams to find her way out of the labyrinth of her feelings. Something terrible had happened—she had made at least one serious error, probably two—and it wasn't going to vanish just because she had fled from the consequences.

She pulled up the collar of her coat until it nearly reached her temples. She closed her eyes against the dance of light on the water, and let the image of Ellice Gordon—tall, sandy-haired, pale-eyed—rise behind her eyelids.

Ellice had been her client for nearly a year, and it was obvious from the beginning that she was angry. In her sessions she recounted, in an uninflected voice, a long list of resentments, hurts, and suspicions. She returned to them again and again. As she talked, her fury showed in the tightness of her features and the drumming of her fingers on the arms of the easy chair.

She had an unusual face. The nose and pale eyes, the long jaw, the straight eyebrows were all unexceptionable in themselves, but they seemed, in a strange way, not to fit together. It wasn't an ugly face, particularly, but it was—a difficult one, Tory decided. A difficult face to live with. She leaned back as she listened through that year, and watched the light of the seasons play across it.

The bleak winter light accentuated the lines of tension graven in Ellice's freckled cheeks. The spring sunshine was softer, filtered through budding leaves, and Ellice looked as if she might be just a little more relaxed, more receptive. The summer sun had been hard and clear, bringing red highlights to Ellice's short brush of hair, picking out her faint freckles so she looked boyish. In the fall—when the truth began to come out—the light had turned golden, reflecting off the sugar maples and the oak tree, but even that rich light couldn't bring a shine to Ellice's eyes.

They had talked about all sorts of things, family relationships, sexual orientation, the difficulties of being a woman in a man's field. Ellice related her memories of being bullied by her brothers, ignored by her father, berated by her mother for her unfeminine ways. Tory watched and listened, and waited for her intuition to help her help her client. She had believed, as time passed, that Ellice was beginning to trust her, though slowly. Ellice began to have moments of calm, even of laughter. She began to remember pleasant moments from her youth—baseball games, a fishing trip, a good teacher—instead of only miserable ones. Though Tory's fey had not yet given her insight into what troubled her client, she thought they were making progress.

Months of therapy passed this way, gradually delving into Ellice's past, into her feelings of being unloved by her parents, into her fears of being tormented by her brothers, into her sense of receiving no respect for her work. When Ellice admitted her recurring fantasy, Tory regarded it as a breakthrough.

Ellice seemed calmer that day than she usually did. She had

come straight from work. She was still in uniform, but she had locked her service weapon in the file drawer, something Tory required of her during a session. The key to the file drawer was safely in Tory's pocket.

That day Ellice didn't fidget with her collar or adjust her duty belt over and over as she so often did. She only brushed her short hair with her hand once or twice as she talked. She kept her eyes on the red and gold of the oak tree, and not until she was finished did she look at Tory, assessing the effect of her admission.

Tory had heard many confessions over the years—longings for revenge, stories of betrayal and tragedy, admissions of abuse given and received. She had never heard one like this. She kept her eyes away from the file drawer, where the big gun lay hidden, but she was painfully aware of its presence. It was a hot afternoon in early August, and the sliding glass door was open a bit to allow the breeze from the mountains to fill the house with fresh air.

She heard a nuthatch twitter its innocent song just as Ellice said, "When I think about it—when I think about actually doing it—I feel better."

"In what way do you feel better, Ellice?" Years of practice kept Tory's voice steady. The fantasy was disturbing, even repellent, but it was, after all, just a fantasy. A scene, created by her client's subconscious as an outlet for the emotions she was trying to discharge.

"I feel better because I'm not angry anymore." Ellice leaned back in the easy chair, crossing her long legs. Her freckled hands lay on the arms of the chair, the fingers relaxed, not tapping as they so often did. "It's like there's this big, tight bubble inside me, but when I do it—when I fire my weapon, and see someone go down—the bubble bursts. Like the bullet explodes the bubble."

"You often feel angry. We've talked about that."

"Furious." Ellice tipped her head back to rest it against the top of the chair. "Utterly, completely pissed off. Like I could punch someone in the face without a thought."

"So this fury inside you—this bubble—when do you feel it?"

Ellice's lips curled in a chilly smile. "People don't respect me. They've never respected me. When I think about that, when I remember how many of them have insulted me, betrayed me— that's when the bubble grows. It fills me so full I can hardly breathe."

"Can you be specific about the people, Ellice?"

One freckled finger lifted in a vague, dismissive gesture. "All of 'em. My brothers. My father. The guys in the department. The instructors at the academy."

"We've looked at some of these instances before. I don't think it's so much that these people—your colleagues, your parents, your brothers—not so much that they don't respect you as that you don't trust them. You've accomplished a great deal. Not many women could do what you've done."

"Yeah. But nobody else seems to get that."

"You might be surprised to find that they do. If you were to talk to your parents, for example—"

"No offense, but what the hell do you know about it? You don't see them, the way they look at me. You don't hear my mother whining about me not being married, not having children. She thinks my brothers are all so perfect, with their wives and families and fancy jobs. No one would believe the way they were when we were kids. The guys in the department pretend to treat me okay, but I know they all think I'm a dyke."

"Have they said so?"

"They don't have to." Ellice's fingers tightened, pressing into the upholstery. "I can tell by the way they smirk behind my back when they think I'm not looking."

"But you have friends in the department. You told me about having coffee with—"

"I don't have a friend in the world." This was said with bitter conviction.

Tory let a moment pass before she said gently, "Maybe, Ellice, they're afraid of you." She tried to soften her words with a smile. "You can be—fierce."

Ellice laughed, and sat up. "Good. I *am* fierce! And I *want* them to be afraid of me! You're not getting it, are you? This whole idea is about that, about pulling out my gun—" Her hand lifted from the chair arm, and hovered above her empty holster. Tory watched her, wishing she could delve beyond the façade, find the real woman behind the bluster.

"Pulling my gun," Ellice repeated, her laughter fading. White lines bracketed her mouth. "Blasting some poor bastard, just showing them what I can do. I wish someone—anyone, I don't care who—would give me an excuse!" She fell back again, blowing out her breath. She lifted her hand away from her holster, flexing the fingers as if she had just let go of her revolver.

Tory searched for her fey, but there was nothing. Strange, that her intuition would not respond to Ellice Gordon. She had to speak without it. She chose her words with care, walking the fine line between understanding and indulgence. "My sense, Ellice, is that the relief you imagine you would feel wouldn't last long. That bubble you speak of—it would grow again. I don't think you can burst it through violence."

Ellice's sandy lashes drooped, and then lifted again. She fixed Tory with her pale-eyed gaze, and showed her teeth. "Maybe not," she said. It was a wolf's grin. A predatory expression. "But I'd like to try."

Tory had to admit, though not aloud, that Ellice was right— she didn't get it. She didn't really get it until much later. Until it was too late.

Now, staring out across a beach two thousand miles from that sunlit office, Tory made herself face the truth. She should have taken action that same day. A therapist was supposed to report possible harm to herself, to someone else, or to the client. She should have known Ellice better. She should have understood this client was capable of acting out her fantasy.

But she hadn't.

A wave of guilt swept over her, as cold and dark as the Pacific waves washing the beach at her feet. The weight of responsibility bowed her shoulders, and she dropped her forehead to her knees again. There were cracks in Ice Woman's shell. She could feel them growing, fissures marring the glacial surface she had been hiding beneath. She couldn't stay frozen forever, she supposed. But she didn't know how she could face this failure in herself.

Suppose Ellice Gordon killed someone else?

But suppose, if she called to tell the police what she knew, Ellice turned on Jack? She had sworn to do it, and Tory knew she would. Her fey had surfaced in time to make that desperately clear. The knowledge had pierced her with a bolt more painful than the cut of the knife that had scarred her arm.

Ellice would choose Jack as her next victim if she thought Tory was still alive. If she thought Tory and the file could expose her. She would choose Jack because that would cause the most damage, the biggest explosion. She would use Jack to burst the bubble of her fury, knowing full well that would destroy Tory, too.

Every therapist knew the stories. Tory, like her colleagues, had been warned during her training that it could happen, that a client could turn violent. It was a cliché, she supposed now, that she had never believed it could happen to her. She had fallen into the classic trap, convinced that her relationship with Ellice was just what it seemed—respectful, productive, and if not amicable, at least reasonable.

She had spent the morning of that October day in her usual fashion. She had no curtains on her windows because she loved the trees and the natural light, and she always woke when the sun rose. In autumn the light had a special quality, colored by the turning leaves, angled by the turning Earth. She rose early that morning, and went down to the kitchen for her daily cup of freshly ground coffee before she went out to walk through the woods, enjoying the birds and the drift of spent leaves tumbling from tree branches to cushion the ground. She climbed hills and wandered through gulleys, walking for an hour at a good clip before she went back to the house to shower and dress for the day in jeans, a light sweater, a blazer thrown over everything. She had bought some nice Gravensteins at the farmers market the week before, and she sliced one and ate it with yogurt.

She touched the phone on its mount above the kitchen island, but she didn't pick it up. She would have liked to speak to Jack, but nine in the morning probably wasn't a good time. In truth, there were no good times. No matter when she called, he sounded impatient, distracted, busy with classes and friends and all the activities of college.

And that's the way it should be, she reminded herself. *He's busy with his life, and I wouldn't want it any other way.* Her calls to him had grown infrequent. She had fallen into the habit of waiting for him to call her instead. It didn't happen often.

Other parents used e-mail, of course, but she still hadn't gotten around to buying a computer and learning how to use it. She had put it off for so long now it hardly seemed necessary. She could still send Jack an old-fashioned postcard. That would be better. She would ask him to let her know when to expect him for the Thanksgiving holiday.

She clicked on the radio to listen to the news as she rinsed her bowl and filled the teakettle. She was bending to drop the fruit knife into the dishwasher when she heard the announcement that there had been a shooting in town. It made her straighten in surprise. Their town had so little crime that most people didn't bother locking their doors and often left keys in the ignition of their cars. To hear that something so strange had happened, the victim found in a parking lot outside a liquor store, was really odd. The sheriff's office didn't know much yet, apparently, about who the man was, but he was dead. Deceased, the announcer said, as the result of a single gunshot wound, and left to bleed to death on the pavement. Tory shook her head, saddened by the incursion of violence into her small, quiet town.

Tory heard the sound of a car outside. She turned off the radio, and set the teakettle and cups and tea bags on a tray to carry into her office.

Ellice was her only client of the day. She arrived still in uniform from her overnight shift. With the practiced air of routine, she unholstered her weapon and deposited it in the file drawer. She locked the drawer, then flipped the key neatly onto the desk blotter before she arranged her lanky form in the easy chair.

Tory pocketed the key before she sank into her own chair and regarded Ellice, who sat in a shaft of light that turned her pale eyelashes golden. Tory smiled, and opened her mouth to greet her.

It was at that moment that her fey, somnolent so long, hit her with all its force. The stab of *knowing* struck through her chest so powerfully she only just stopped herself from crying out. The suddenness of it shook her. Her smile died on her lips, and she felt the blood drain from her cheeks. She gazed in horror at Ellice Gordon.

She knew. Appalled and sickened, she knew.

It had been Ellice. It was Ellice's fantasy. She didn't need to ask how it had happened, or why, or what the order of events had been. She could see it, as clearly as if she had also been in that parking lot.

Ellice raised an eyebrow, and her pale eyes met Tory's as directly as always.

Tory's throat constricted. Anguish stole her voice and her breath, and the ache of her fey made her press a hand to her chest.

Ellice leaned back in the easy chair, crossing her long legs, her big hands relaxed on the arms. She said, with a wry intonation, "Good morning?"

Tory dropped her hand, and linked both hands together in her lap. She forced herself to draw a breath around the pain in her chest. She said slowly, "I don't think it's a good morning, Ellice. Quite the contrary." The pressure in her chest eased a little, and she watched as Ellice's eyebrows pulled together. Though her eyes didn't flicker, they looked dull, as if a shutter had been pulled.

"Well," Ellice responded. She was very still for a moment, and then her lips curled. "Do you want to talk about that?" She gave a brief, deprecatory laugh.

"You'll need to be the one to talk," Tory said. Her voice felt thin, fragile as the dry leaves falling past the window.

"What shall I talk about?" Ellice sat very still, only her eyes moving. She seemed not to blink, nor even to breathe.

"I think you know. No—" Tory leaned back in her chair, though her stomach crawled with tension. "No, Ellice, I *know* you know."

Ten seconds passed before Ellice spoke again. "Okay," she said. "I guess I do."

"Tell me about it."

Ellice glanced away, out into the sun-spangled woods. When she looked back at Tory again her face had changed. Her freck-led cheeks flushed. Her eyes glittered, and she leaned forward so abruptly that Tory flinched.

"Why are you surprised?" she said in a gravelly voice. "I told you what I was thinking."

"You told me it was a fantasy. Everyone has them."

Ellice grinned, a fierce expression that made Tory's stomach clench harder. "Everyone has them?" she asked. "Not like mine, they don't."

"Not exactly like yours, perhaps," Tory said. "But everyone has fantasies. They don't act on them."

"Are you sure of that?"

"I'm sure that acting on this particular fantasy was a tragic thing to do."

Ellice's grin faded. She braced her elbows on her knees and re-garded Tory for a long time. The silence in the office grew heavy, and the song of the birds in the cedars seemed to fade. Tory thought, for the first time ever, that Kate and Chet's house was too far away. She was alone on her hilltop with a woman who had done something unthinkable.

At last, Ellice straightened, and her gaze left Tory's face to drift back to the grove beyond the windows. "I was right, you know," she said in an offhand tone. "It was just as I thought it would be."

"That surprises me."

Ellice's gaze didn't waver from the trees. "Why? It didn't surprise me at all."

"I didn't think you were capable of it."

"You're disappointed in me."

Tory hesitated. Nothing in her experience or her training had prepared her for such a moment. "I'm—saddened," she finally said. "I'm sad for you, sad for the man you killed. I'm terribly sad that I didn't know this might happen."

"Nothing you could have done to stop it," Ellice said. Her fingers lifted and fell on the arms of her chair, a placid rhythm. "I did it, and I felt good afterward. That shocks you, I suppose."

Tory let that go. "How do you feel now?"

Ellice lifted one shoulder, and let it drop. "I don't feel anything," she said. "And I can tell you it's a fucking relief."

"You're saying that today you don't feel angry."

"That's right."

"You don't feel any sense of responsibility?"

Ellice shook her head, gazing out through the glass. A bar of ruby light reflected from the hummingbird feeder to glisten on one freckled cheek. "I'm not stupid, Tory. If I was going to torment myself with guilt, I wouldn't have done it."

"Did you have any excuse at all, Ellice? Any justification?"

"Sure." Ellice shrugged, a negligent gesture. "If I needed it."

"You don't think you need it?"

Ellice turned her head, and Tory felt she was looking into the face of a stranger. She couldn't recognize the client she had worked with most of the year, and that meant she had failed miserably to understand what was happening.

Ellice said in a lifeless tone, "I couldn't help it." She shrugged again. "It is what it is."

"But, Ellice," Tory said carefully, "surely you know I have to report this."

Ellice blinked, a slow flutter of her pale lashes. "What are you talking about?"

"A therapist has to make a report if a client is a real danger to herself or to others."

"I thought you had to keep everything between us confidential."

"A man is dead. You've admitted your responsibility. That's not confidential."

Ellice straightened in the armchair. She gave the impression of growing taller, bulkier, even though she didn't rise. "You're my therapist," she said. "I'm supposed to be able to tell you everything."

Tory sat very still. "You're also a police officer. You must know there are limits to confidentiality."

Ellice's hand moved, in an automatic way, toward her empty holster. "No," she said. "I don't know that." She added, with a truculent thrust of her chin, "I trusted you, Tory."

"And I trusted *you*, Ellice."

"You won't do it!" Ellice thrust herself abruptly out of the armchair, and stood over Tory, her fists on her hips. "You're just trying to scare me."

Tory rolled her chair back a bit, and rose. "I won't have to if you'll do it yourself," she said. She wanted to put the chair between herself and Ellice, but she forced herself to stay where she was, the desk at her back, the chair pushed to the wall.

"Do it myself? What the hell does that mean?"

"Tell the sheriff what happened." Tory's skin had begun to crawl under Ellice's hard gaze, and the key of the cabinet where the gun was locked began to grow heavy in her pocket. "I'll speak for your state of mind, of course."

Ellice barked a laugh that made goose bumps prickle on Tory's neck. "State of mind? I'll tell you my state of mind." She spun to one side, and took up Jack's graduation picture. She held it up, pointing to it. "I know all about you, Tory." Ellice's voice rose and thinned, reminding Tory of a crow's caw, harsh and cutting. "I know about your son, and where he goes to school. I know which dorm he's in, what floor, and what room. I know when he comes home, who he sees! I have *power* over you, Tory!"

Tory said, "I don't believe you would threaten Jack," but her voice faltered.

Ellice took one swift step around the desk. "Don't you?" Her hand flashed out, seizing Tory's wrist in an iron grip, and a rush of anger suffused her face, staining her cheeks red and burning scarlet across her neck. "You don't know me at all!" She yanked Tory close to her. "Report me, and Jack's next," she grated. "He's the next one I shoot."

And with that stabbing premonition, a sharp and unforgiving certainty, Tory knew it was true. Ellice would do just as she said.

She—Tory—was in real trouble.

Tory's arm felt small and thin under those strong fingers, but she had her own wiry strength. She pulled back, ripping herself free with the suddenness of her gesture. Now she did roll the chair between them, putting herself within reach of the telephone on her desk. "Ellice, please sit down, and let's—"

Before she could finish her thought, Ellice reached across the desk and ripped the telephone cord out of its jack. Tory jumped away from her, abandoning all pretense of calm, and dashed across the office toward the safety of the kitchen and the lock on its inside door. That lock was her protection. It was the escape route every therapist was supposed to have, but she saw now how paltry it was, how little defense it would give her. She was too late, and the door lock too little, but she tried anyway. She grasped the doorknob and pulled the door open.

Ellice came close behind, her long, strong arm stretching past Tory's head to slam the open door hard against its stop on the outer wall. The bang of wood against rubber made Tory's nerves jump. "Give me the key, Tory!" she commanded.

Tory crossed the kitchen, rounding the island, and pressed her back against the refrigerator. "You don't want to do this," she said.

"Just give me the goddamn key," Ellice said. She reached Tory in two strides. Her arm went around Tory's neck, pulling her off balance as she groped in her pocket with her other hand.

Tory, with the strength of a woman used to wrestling cords of wood, wrenched herself free. She spun away from Ellice and dashed toward the garage door. There was no outer lock on it, but her Escalade was there, and if she could get in, lock the doors—but she wasn't fast enough.

Ellice, with a motion so smooth and efficient it was as if she had planned it, snaked a knife from the pine block beside the sink, and came after her.

The whole scene was so humiliating that now, huddled beneath a boulder on the Oregon coast, Tory could hardly bear recalling it. Ellice had held the knife to her throat, then wrested the key from her jeans pocket through the sheer muscular force of her big hands and long arms. In the struggle, the knife had sliced Tory's forearm, the blade cold as it cut through her flesh, but leaving a burning slash of pain behind it. Ellice, the knife in one hand and the key in the other, tried to drag her back into the office. Tory needed no intuition to know that if Ellice succeeded in getting the gun from the file drawer before she could get away, she would never survive.

Blood soaked the sleeve of her sweater as she dropped and twisted. With a groan of effort, she kicked herself free of Ellice's grasp. The momentum sent her flying across the kitchen floor. She scrambled the rest of the way, leaping to her feet just as she reached the garage door. She blasted through it, jumped into the driver's seat of the Escalade, and hit the electronic lock a heartbeat before Ellice caught up with her. Ellice stopped where she was, assessing the situation in a flash, then whirled to go back into the kitchen. It would take her only seconds to reach the office, unlock the file drawer, and retrieve her weapon.

Tory hardly breathed, waiting for the garage door to open, winding up on its pulley at what seemed an agonizingly slow pace. Before it was fully up, she gunned the motor. Her muscles trembled with adrenaline. Every second seemed to last a minute, every minute an hour as she backed out of the garage, tires spitting gravel every which way. Ellice's patrol car blocked the driveway, and the trees on either side grew too closely for her to fit past. She cranked the wheel, and sped off in the other direction, around the side of the house, past the garden shed, out to the dirt lane used by plows and tractors. She meant to wheel around to the road from there, but before she could reach the lane, the patrol car caught her. It was more powerful even than the Escalade, and Ellice had no fear of using its weight and momentum. She drove the patrol car right up behind the Escalade, striking its bumper with hers. She forced Tory across the dirt lane and down the slope of the hill toward the Winooski River.

Tory tried to stop above the riverbank. She even set the emergency brake, but it did no good. The patrol car struck the back of the Escalade again, hard. It was terrifying, a blow neither measured nor restrained. It felt to Tory as if Ellice meant to go over with her, to careen both vehicles down the bank and into the river.

Time slowed down even further for Tory. Her car tilted, leaning forward in a dream motion, listing, sliding, falling. She barely heard the screech of metal on rock, of bursting glass, of her own harsh breathing. She saw the water rising toward her at a speed so stately she could distinguish the crevices in the boulders rising to catch her, appreciate the spray of water shining in the cool sunshine, pick out the colors of the gravel below the clear water where the hard surface of the riverbed waited to jolt her into unconsciousness. She had all the time she needed to slide to her right, to release the door lock. She had more than enough time— three seconds, five, which passed so slowly she could have divided them into milliseconds—to shove the door open with her foot. Without haste, she judged the moment when her car would hit the rocks, and at the perfect instant she threw herself out the side door and into the waist-deep water. She splashed through the water to hide herself behind the boulder.

At the touch of the frigid water of the river, time sped again to its normal pace, and she hunched down, wet to her hips, holding her arms above her head as if that would help protect her.

She heard the patrol car brake in the dirt and leaves above the bank, and she heard its door open and close. She couldn't see Ellice, but she could *feel* her, her sluggish fey engaged at last, fully focused on someone who wanted to hurt her. Who meant to kill her.

Now, weeks later, she was huddled in the same position. Her knees were in sand instead of the icy water of the Winooski River. She was many, many miles away from the crashed Escalade.

But still hiding from Ellice Gordon. It was for Jack, of course, but she was still hiding.

Why did she think now of her dreams, and the black-eyed tormentor who dominated them? What was her fey trying to tell her?

11

Vengono a darmi aiuto?

Are they coming to help me?

—Minnie, *La Fanciulla del West*, Act Two

"Paulette?"

Tory startled from her reverie. She jumped up, knocking over her half-full coffee mug so that the chilled coffee soaked into the sand. The wind struck her face as she straightened, and she turned her back to it. "Iris?"

Her landlady, with strands of long gray hair whipping around her narrow face, was coming down the beach. She wore a red plaid parka, far too large for her lean form, and a dilapidated wool cap pulled down over her forehead. When she reached Tory, she smiled. "Bit chilly for meditating on the beach, isn't it?"

Tory hadn't noticed she was shivering. When she looked down to shake out the last of her wasted coffee, she saw that her knuckles were scarlet with cold. She gave a diffident laugh. "Yes, I guess it is. I just like the water at this time of day."

"That shutter looks great, Paulette. And the gate, too. You've been busy."

"Thanks," Tory said. Her teeth began to chatter, and she clenched her jaw to stop them.

Iris encircled Tory with her arm. The familiar gesture made her stiffen, but there was a look of real concern on the older woman's face. "Come on," Iris said. "Let's get you inside and warmed up."

By the time they had trudged up the beach and gone into the cottage, Tory's hands were so stiff she could barely unzip her coat. She went into the kitchen to fill the teakettle, rubbing her fingers to warm them. Iris, seeming perfectly at ease, took the stool on the other side of the short counter. "What are your plans, Paulette?" she said.

"Plans?"

"For today, I mean. For dinner."

Tory frowned at her over the teakettle. "Dinner—?"

Iris clicked her tongue, and pulled off her battered cap. She twisted her gray hair back with both hands and contained it with a silver clip. "It's Thanksgiving," she said.

Tory put the kettle down slowly. Her fingers had begun to sting as they thawed. She looked past Iris, out to the tossing ocean beyond the picture window. "It can't be," she said, her voice cracking. Thanksgiving. She had been gone . . . nearly two months. Thanksgiving! Her heart cried, *Oh, Jack.*

"You didn't realize," Iris said.

Tory made herself breathe, made herself speak as normally as she could through her chilled lips. "No. No, I didn't realize. Time just—just slipped away from me."

"Well." Iris smiled, but Tory could see she wasn't going any-where. She said, "I'll wait while you bathe. You're coming to my place."

The refusal was on Tory's lips, but somehow she couldn't speak it. Iris looked across the counter at her, and though she grinned, her eyes pierced Tory's as if they could see past eye-lashes, through pupil and retina, right into her mind. "Come on," she said, with what, for Iris, was a gentle tone. "Only four of us— including you. Don't be alone today."

Without quite knowing how it happened, Tory found herself in the bathtub. The hot water stung her cold skin at first, and then felt wonderfully soothing. She soaked as long as she dared without being rude, and washed her hair. She toweled her hair dry, and pulled on clean jeans and a sweater and her usual sneakers. She eyed herself in the bathroom mirror, thinking of the photograph on her therapist's license picture, her hair styled, her eyes done up with mascara and shadow, her lips tinged pink. She didn't look anything like that now. Luckily, she had re-dyed her hair yesterday. No one could possibly recognize her, even if they'd studied her picture.

"I don't have dress-up clothes," she said to Iris as she emerged from the bedroom.

"You're just fine," Iris said.

"I can bring wine, at least."

"Good. Always welcome."

As if in a dream, as if none of it were her own doing, Tory got into Iris's car, the bottle of wine in her lap. "I could drive—" she began, but Iris shook her head.

"I'll bring you back," she said. "Just for today—be my guest."

Tory let her head fall back against the leather headrest, and watched the closed and shuttered houses drift past as Iris drove toward her house. She couldn't think what she was doing here, in this white car, going to a Thanksgiving dinner as if it were a normal thing to do. Something quivered inside her, faintly calling her to step back into the world. To thaw, as she had thawed her icy skin in the bath. She quelled the impulse, pressing her lips together, turning her head as if there were something interesting beyond the passenger window.

She wasn't at all surprised at the preparations she found underway at Iris's house. Thanksgiving dinner was a great American constant, she supposed. A turkey was roasting in the oven under a tent of foil. The table glittered with crystal and silver and china, and tapered candles waited in their holders to be lighted. Pies rested on the lovely old sideboard she had noticed when she was here before. Potatoes were peeled and ready in a big pot of water. It was all very much like—too much like—her own home had always been on this holiday. Could she get through it? She would have to. Then, as soon as she could, she would make her escape, back into her haven of silence and solitude. And she would be very, very careful.

She said, "Can I help?" Another constant. Courtesy. A semblance of participation.

Iris waved a hand. "You could whip cream," she said. "Or fill the water pitcher."

"The table is—it's lovely, Iris."

"You're not surprised?"

Startled, Tory laughed. "No! Surprised? Why would I be?"

"You sound a little surprised."

"No, not at all. Everything here is lovely."

Iris had shed her disreputable coat and hat, revealing a vividly printed red silk tunic and narrow black slacks underneath. She looked utterly different, sophisticated and elegant. She tied on a colorful apron before she went to the stove to turn on the gas under the potatoes. "You like things that are beautiful," she said.

"Doesn't everyone?"

"Oh, no." The wry smile had begun to feel comfortable to Tory, another danger. "No, some people like things to be sharp, or cozy, or edgy . . . but you listen to classical music, and buy vintage china."

"How do you know I listen to classical?" Tory asked warily.

"I hear it when I go by. Your radio, I think."

"That's right. There's a good station out of Portland. I don't have a CD player." She wondered if listening to classical music set her apart too much, even if it wasn't opera.

The potatoes began to boil, and Iris turned down the gas, then turned her attention to Tory again. "Paulette," she said quietly. "I won't pry, but it's obvious something's happened to you. You're not the only one. A lot of us who stay here in the winter are like that—refugees."

Tory couldn't think of a safe way to answer. Her own face, unfamiliar with its shock of red hair, glimmered back at her from the shining surfaces of Iris's kitchen. She looked away, to the bare branches of the trees in the garden. *Refugee*. It was a good word.

"Take me, for example," Iris said. She started spooning flour into a cruet, adding water and seasoning, shaking it.

It was the way Tory always made gravy, and she watched, bemused by the simple, familiar process. Automatically, not really expecting an answer, she asked, "You?"

"Yes," Iris said. She set the cruet down. "I told you I came here with my parents when I was a girl. But I married someone they disapproved of—with good reason, as it turned out—and we were estranged for the rest of their lives. My husband left me when they died. It looked as if I hadn't inherited anything after all, and apparently that was what he was waiting for."

"But you did inherit the cottage."

Iris's narrow lips twisted. "The cottage, and what there was of their estate. I lied to him. I'd figured it out by then. I knew he was no good, and that there was nothing to be salvaged of our marriage. I waited too long, of course, because my parents died before I could admit to them they'd been right all along. It was too late to make amends, and I'd lost contact with all my friends in Portland. I came here, and had to start all over."

"I'm sorry."

Iris shrugged. "Just telling you so you'll understand. We all have a story."

The implication, Tory feared, was that she should now share hers. She was relieved when the doorbell rang. The arrival of the other guests meant she didn't have to respond to Iris's gentle challenge.

Both of the others were men, gray-haired and quiet. They greeted Tory without curiosity, and she couldn't help, from her professional perspective, but notice that Iris was right. These men were as much refugees as she was. She didn't want to know what their secrets were. Perhaps she would never again be able to take on other people's secrets, to help to carry their weight—or to be responsible for them. Perhaps she should never have done it in the first place.

They all drank from the bottle of pinot noir Tory had brought as they made casual conversation. Jazz played softly, masked by the clink of glassware and china and the occasional sizzle of cooking. They talked about the wine, about slow business in the wintertime, about the storm the night before. No one asked anything personal beyond the "When did you come to Cannon Beach?" sort of thing. When Iris called them to the table, everyone rose to help carry dishes, a cutting board, a pitcher of water.

The turkey was perfect, stuffed with apples and lemons and a bundle of fresh thyme. "You make this just the way—the way I do," Tory said. *The way Jack likes it.*

"Oh, good," Iris said easily. She lifted her wineglass in Tory's direction. "We're more alike than you think, Paulette."

Tory hesitated, searching for a polite response, but one of the other guests chuckled. "No point in arguing," he said. "If Iris says it, it's true."

Tory felt a flush creep over her face. Iris grinned.

Only later, after the other guests had left and she was helping with the dishwashing, did Tory have the courage to ask about it. She was a bit drunk on red wine and pumpkin pie with Grand Marnier–laced whipped cream, and more relaxed than she had been in weeks. "Iris," she said, swabbing a pie plate with a sponge, "why did you say we're alike?"

Iris was laying neat slices of white turkey meat into a casserole dish. She didn't look up from her task. "I shouldn't have said it." Tory, watching her, saw one corner of her mouth twist.

"I don't mind that you did," Tory said. She rinsed the pie plate, and set it in the rack, careful of her wet fingers and the slippery glass. "But you don't really know anything about me."

"Well." Iris shrugged. "Maybe I'm wrong."

Tory turned back to the sink. She felt a bit confused, as if she didn't know where the conversation had gone. She told herself to stop talking. Silence was safer.

Iris snapped a plastic cover over the casserole. "Some leftovers for you," she said.

"Thanks. The dinner was delicious."

"It was, wasn't it? It's so good to see people eat around my table—I love that."

Tory had a brief flash of Jack at her table, tall and thin and always hungry. "I always did, too," she said softly.

Iris paused, her hand flat on the covered casserole. "I'm a lot older than you, Paulette," she said. "And I've learned it gets better. Whatever it is."

Tory had said those same words to so many clients. The realization made her stomach contract. She gave a small, convulsive sigh, and reached for a dish towel. "I know, Iris."

"But you can't see it right now."

Tory pleated the snowy dish towel between her fingers. "No," she said. She felt suddenly dull and tired, her defenses down. "No, right now it seems pretty grim."

Iris stacked the casserole with a plastic container of pie and one of cranberry sauce. "Do me a favor, will you, Paulette?"

Tory looked up, into Iris's cool gray eyes. Iris gave her a half smile, and Tory read sorrow and understanding and kindness in it. "Just promise me," Iris said. "That if it gets too bad—you'll call."

Tory couldn't think, at first, just what Iris meant. That was foolish, of course, and she realized it a heartbeat later. When she had said those words to her most troubled clients, she had meant them—she had meant them with all her heart.

She dropped her eyes again to the towel in her hands. "It won't get that bad," she said, but she knew she sounded unconvincing. It wasn't fair to Iris, who was trying so hard.

She put the towel down, and turned her face to Iris, hoping she would see the truth in her eyes. "You're asking if I'm a suicide risk," she said. "It's very kind of you to be concerned, Iris. I appreciate it very much. I promise you, though, I'm not at risk for that. Please don't worry."

Iris watched her as she spoke, then nodded. "Excellent. Thank you." She patted the stack of leftover containers with a brisk gesture. "It would be a tragic waste."

* * *

Tory returned to the cottage laden with largesse. There were not only the leftovers, but a CD player Iris swore was going to waste in a back bedroom. "I only have jazz recordings," she said, "but you'll find what you want to listen to, right? Try the library sale."

They carried the things into the house as the light waned over the big rock on the beach. Gulls cried their tritone song through the gathering dusk, and Tory, exhausted by the company and the day, dropped the leftovers on the kitchen counter with a sigh.

"I'm going," Iris said. "I know you're beat."

Tory nodded. "I am. But it was a lovely day, Iris. Thank you so much."

Iris set the CD player on the table. "You're welcome. It's good to be with friends."

Friends. Tory wanted to think that through, to sense how dangerous it might be. The idea of having to leave Cannon Beach because someone might guess her secret made her so tired she could hardly stay on her feet. It was why, every time she went to a pay phone and tried to call someone in authority, terror that the call would be traced or someone might guess where she was made her voice shake. She had tried again, two days before. This time she had called the attorney general's office in Vermont, but the result had been the same—disbelief, doubt, insistence on knowing her name. It had made her feel both helpless and invisible.

The lights in the cottage reflected in windows that were nearly black. She glanced at the clock on the radio, and saw that it was already five o'clock. Eight in Vermont, where Jack would be . . . what? Watching football with Chet, she hoped. Playing video games with Kate's grandkids. Or maybe at a friend's home, some friend who had a big, noisy family like the Garveys, two parents, kids roughhousing in the yard. But not alone, please god. Not alone.

She had a sudden, devastating image of that black revolver pointed at her son's lean belly, and a spasm of fear made her heart clench.

She tried to thrust the image away, to gather herself so she could show Iris to the door. Somehow along the way she found herself sinking onto the sofa by the cold fireplace. She wrapped her arms around herself, saying shakily, "Sorry, Iris. I'm just so tired. And a little drunk, still, I think!"

"You're not drunk," Iris said firmly. She came into the living room, and sat on the armchair. She leaned forward with her elbows on her knees. "You relaxed a bit today, and it all caught up with you."

"I suppose."

"It's a tradition with me, the refugee dinner. Different people come in different years. Some I know well, some not so much. It's not terribly personal, but it's comforting."

"It's so kind of you," Tory said. She couldn't remember how much wine she'd had, but she probably shouldn't have added sugar to the mix. She let her head drop back, and closed her eyes. The room spun a little when she did it.

"Well. No point in having a pretty house and nice things if you don't share them." Iris drew a breath, and Tory was sure that, now, she was going to rise from the chair, say her good nights, and go. She opened her eyes, anticipating this, but she found that Iris was looking at the family pictures she had bought at the antiques store. "Your folks?" Iris said.

With a quiver of shame at the deceit, Tory nodded. "Parents, grandparents."

"Looks like a nice family. All gone now, I suppose. Like mine."

"Yes." It was probably true, Tory thought. Otherwise, why were their photographs for sale in an antiques store?

Iris didn't seem to notice her reluctance to talk about them. She said, "Mind if I use the bathroom before I go?"

"No, of course not." Tory closed her eyes again as Iris went through the bedroom and into the bathroom. The door closed, and water ran. Tory thought how strange it was to have someone else in the house, to hear the cozy noises of someone other than herself. She was just marveling at how much of her life she had spent in solitude when Iris returned. She walked with quicker steps now, her shoes scuffing the floor in a nervous rhythm. Tory opened her eyes.

Iris had Nonna Angela's paperweight in her two hands. She held it out. "What's this pretty thing?"

The sudden pain of premonition, piercing her chest from breastbone to spine, took Tory's breath away. Her voice faltered. "It's—a paperweight. My grandmother's. She was a war bride, and she brought it from Italy."

Iris cradled it in her palms. The gold butterfly in the sea-green glass caught the light as her thin fingers traced the silhouette. "Not the grandmother in that photograph," she said. "That woman's not Italian." She wasn't asking. It was a statement, and it felt to Tory like an accusation. That was the trouble with lies, as she had often advised her clients. It was hard to keep them straight.

She said shakily, "No, she was—my other grandmother."

Iris set the paperweight on the table with care. "It's probably fragile, as old as it is," she said. "It reminds me of something, but I don't know what."

"Oh. Does it?"

"It seems familiar." Iris shrugged. "Strange, isn't it?" She thrust herself up from her chair, and was at the door in seconds, buttoning her jacket around her, pulling her cap down over her forehead. "Thanks for coming today, Paulette," she said. "I'm going to check in on you tomorrow, if that's okay."

Tory said faintly, "Sure."

Iris lifted a hand in farewell, and was out the door a moment later. Tory sat where she was, staring at the paperweight, for long moments before she finally rose and went to bed.

12

❧

Chi son? Sono un poeta.
Che cosa faccio? Scrivo. E come vivo? Vivo!

Who am I? I'm a poet.
What do I do? I write. And how do I live? I live!

—Rodolfo, *La Bohème*, Act One

Doria set the breakfast things ready for the morning, then turned out the lights in the kitchen. She stepped outside for a breath of fresh air, and paused to enjoy the light of a full white moon shining on the garden, glistening on the glossy leaves of the Judas tree and gleaming on the wrought iron and glass of the bow window. The crisp air of October was refreshing after the wilting heat of August and the humidity of September. Soon the Puccinis would be off to their apartment on Via Verdi in Milan, and she and Zita would be alone in a peaceful house, with nothing to do but begin preparations for Christmas. Zita, who was from Siena, would assemble the traditional seventeen ingredients for her famous panforte, and pretend to smack Doria's hand as she snitched hazelnuts and candied apricots from the mixing bowl. She would haggle with the butcher over prices for turkey and leg of lamb. Doria would scour Villa Puccini from top to bottom, and there would be no one about to make it dirty again until the *signori* returned.

She took off her apron as she went back inside. Before going to bed, she took a last glance into the dining room to see that everything was ready for the morning. She noticed the glow of candle-light coming from the studio, but she heard no conversation and no music.

She peeked in. The electric lights were off, but the candles burned merrily in their brass sconces on the piano. The room was in shadow except for bars of moonlight reflecting from the lake onto the carpet.

Puccini was in his chair before the piano, but not touching the keys. He had just lighted a fresh cigarette, and blew a ring of smoke, tipping his head back to watch it rise and break against the sculpted moldings. When he dropped his chin, he saw Doria, and saluted her with two fingers to his forehead. "Not in bed, my little nurse?"

"I was just going, signore. I thought perhaps you had forgotten the candles—it was so quiet in here."

"*Sì*," he said heavily. "Too cursed quiet." He tipped his chair back, and stared up at the ceiling again. "The music won't come."

"It will. You always say that, yet in the end, it comes."

"Not this time!" His voice was rough with smoke and tension. "I think this is the end, Doria. I'm a fifty-year-old has-been with a ruined leg and a career drowning in *cosettine!*"

"*Non è vero!*"

He waved a negligent hand, but she could see by the arch of his eyebrow that he was listening. Just so had he listened to her through long wakeful nights after his accident, when he relied on her to talk about anything and everything she could think of, to distract him from his dark thoughts and the pain in his leg. He was like one of her little brothers, in constant need of comfort and reassurance.

She took a step inside the door. "Signore, your operas are not little things at all. They are—" She gestured with her hand, as if she could snatch the word from the air. "Profound!" she finished. And with a touch of asperity, because he already knew how she felt about it, "Especially *Madama Butterfly*."

He snorted, not yet mollified. "That's the one they criticize the most. They say it's commercial. Cheap. A melodrama!"

"Then they don't understand the story," she protested. "Cio-Cio-San's story!"

"And you do, Doria?" He stretched out his arm to tap his cigarette ash into the cut-glass tray. "My little nurse? You think you understand?"

She tossed her head. "Of course I do! Cio-Cio-San and I have much in common."

He puffed on the dwindling butt of his cigarette, and smiled at her. "No one has sold you to an American naval officer, Signorina Manfredi!"

She folded her arms, laughing at him. "Not yet, in any case!"

He let his chair settle back to the floor, and ground out the cigarette. "I wish you to be happy, Doria. You should be out with young people in the evenings, not stuck here with all us old people."

"You're not old!" she insisted. "And besides, I don't want to be out in the village. I'm happy here, in your pretty house. Hearing your beautiful music."

His smile faded, and he stared up at his painted ceiling through a haze of cigarette smoke. "You pay a price, I think, my little nurse."

She shrugged. "We all pay in some way for what we want."

At that he laughed, but it was a bitter sound. It grated on her ear, and she flinched, fearful he would wake the *signora*. "You're too wise, Doria. We do indeed! Even I!"

She said with sympathy, "*Sì, sì. Lo so.*"

He grimaced, and straightened his right leg, rubbing at the thigh and groaning. "Doria, let's have a glass of port. I have no musical ideas tonight, in any case."

"I will bring you one, maestro."

She turned back into the dining room to pour a glass. She carried it back to him and set it on the desk, within his reach. "Are you sure you're well? Does your leg pain you tonight?"

He sighed, and reached across the desk for his box of Toscano cigars. "My leg always pains me, which no one but you seems to care about! Still, I'm well enough," he said. She took the cigar from him. She clipped the end with the little cutter, then handed it back. He stuck it between his teeth as she scraped a match on the matchbox, and held the flame for him as he drew. When it was glowing, he said, "There's no need to nurse me now, Doria."

"I don't mind."

"I know." He squinted at her through the smoke. "You're a good girl."

"*Grazie.*" Doria gave a shallow curtsy, and he chuckled. "*Buona notte, signore.*"

"Wait." He took a deep swallow of wine, and set the glass down again on his desk. He propped his left elbow on the piano above the keyboard, and played an idle chord with his right hand. "Are you very tired? Could you sit a while and talk with me, as you used to do?"

Involuntarily, Doria glanced above her head, as if she could see through the sculpted plaster ceiling and into the *signora*'s bedroom.

Puccini saw, and drew hard on his cigar. "Your mistress is asleep, I promise you." He pointed to a chair resting beside the card table. There were no guests tonight, and everything was as tidy as she had left it earlier in the day. "Pull that over. Just a moment's talk, to distract me. Perhaps my reluctant muse will wake."

Doria hesitated, torn between wanting to do as he asked and fear that Elvira would find her here, and misunderstand. The house had been more or less peaceful for a week, and she hoped it would stay that way.

He gave her his boyish smile, rueful and self-deprecating. "Please," he said, squinting through the smoke and tugging at his mustache with his free hand. "The opera is a disaster, and I can't sleep for worrying about it."

Doria gave a shake of her head, but she brought the chair close to the piano. He said, "Pour a glass for yourself, my little friend. Let's make the best of this dark and empty evening!"

Of course, Puccini didn't have to get up at dawn to begin the work of maintaining Villa Puccini, but Doria would never point out such a thing. Soon enough she could rest as much as she needed to, she and Zita. She went back into the dining room, poured herself a small glass of his excellent port, and rejoined him in the studio. He raised his glass to her as she sat down. "Good! I hate to be alone with my miserable thoughts—and this piano refuses to speak to me!"

Doria, rather primly, sipped the port. She sat with her legs crossed at the ankle, the glass held in both hands in her lap. Her eyes cast down, she said, "Maestro, the piano will not speak if you don't touch the keys."

He laughed, more merrily now. "You're a bossy one, aren't you, Doria? You love to tell your master what to do."

Her lips twitched, and she looked up at him from beneath her eyelids. "It's what we do with spoiled boys," she dared to say.

He guffawed, and a flush of pleasure rose up her chest and throat. It was the same laugh she heard so often when his friends were here, the *signori* from Milan who came to keep him company on the hot summer nights as he wrestled with his music. She took another sip of port to hide her blush, though it would make her head spin if she drank it too fast.

"My sisters tell me the same thing," he chortled. He drained his glass, and she took it from him, carrying it into the dining room to refill it. When she brought it back, she found him absently rubbing his leg with the heel of his hand and gazing at the manuscript sheets standing half-filled on the piano. His laughter had faded, and although he took the glass from her, he set it on his desk, and picked up a thick black pencil, marking a note on the staff, then another.

His mood had changed abruptly, as it so often did. It was like the autumn weather, sunny one moment, stormy the next. "You're going to work now," she said. "I'll leave you to it."

"No, no, not yet," he said. He put the pencil down, picked up his glass, and took a swallow. His eyes were still on the manuscript. "Sometimes I think if my leg would cease its infernal aching, I could write faster."

"Did you write faster before your accident, maestro?"

"Only when I was very young. Before—before I was distracted."

She knew what that meant, but forbore to say so. He meant Elvira, and the scandal that caused so much fury to circle around him, like a chain of thunderstorms, one after the other. His family, his friends, everyone had been shocked when Elvira abandoned her husband and her children to live with Puccini, and she knew they had badgered him endlessly to send her back to her husband and restore his reputation. He hadn't done it, and Doria thought they must, once, have been very much in love. Why else would they suffer the scathing looks and biting words of society? Why else had they stayed together through the years of poverty? Perhaps Elvira had been different then, more amiable. Perhaps she had been pretty, her voice sweeter, her eyes more tender. Doria took another delicate sip of wine.

These conversations in the dark of night were familiar to her from that first hard year of Puccini's convalescence, when she had come so eagerly to the beautiful new Villa Puccini to nurse the great composer in his recovery. The pain of his injured leg often roused him in the night. She would fetch whatever he needed, do what she could to make him comfortable, and listen as he talked. She heard him speak of his beloved mother, of his children, of his tumultuous relationship with his publisher, and with his librettists, who seemed to quit on a regular basis. She knew how desperately he feared failure, how much criticism stung him, how he loathed Wagner and adored Verdi and Mozart—all of it. She had learned a great deal about opera by listening to him. And sometimes, deep in the night, he had sung fragments to her—a bit of an aria, a line of recitative, even the melody of a chorus—and she remembered every one of them.

"So now," he mused, twirling his glass in his left hand, tapping the keyboard with the pencil in his right, "now I have made it worse. Distracted myself so I fear I will never write another note."

The dour tone of his voice made Doria look up at him. "What do you mean, signore?"

He sighed. "I brought this all on myself," he said, his voice little more than a scrape in his throat. "I know that now, but at the time—I thought it was only my fancy, my mood."

"I don't know what—" Doria began, and then stopped.

"No. No, I never told you. I thought you would not believe me. Elvira didn't." She held her breath, wondering what made him so gloomy.

The sky beyond the windows darkened suddenly, clouds folding over the moon, obscuring the stars. The night seemed to close around the studio. The only light came from the candles on the piano, flickering unsteadily over Puccini's cheeks. He was in need of a shave. His mustache drooped, a little overlong, and the shadows deepened the lines in his face.

"Premonition," he muttered.

"*Cosa?*"

He glanced up, one eyebrow raised, then down into the luminous darkness of the wine in his glass. The pencil was now motionless in his fingers. "I had a premonition. I've tried to convince myself I imagined it, that the medicines and the pain altered my memory of that night, but I know now it's not true."

"You've never told me this," Doria murmured.

"No." He emptied his glass again. She rose, and brought him the bottle, setting it next to the manuscript on the piano. His cigar had gone out. He dropped it in the ashtray, then groped in his pocket for a cigarette. When it was lit, he slumped in his chair.

"The night of the accident—it was so dark, you know, foggy, wet—it wasn't as if we had to go. Elvira wanted to—well, that doesn't matter. It wasn't her fault. I was the one who wanted to come to Torre, to get out of Lucca for a while. Everyone in Lucca was angry at me, my sisters, our friends—everyone." He uncorked the bottle, and refilled his glass to the brim. "We were just dressing for the trip, and the chauffeur was bringing the car around."

His voice turned to gravel, low and grinding and ominous. Doria's arms prickled.

"I remember glancing out the window as I was putting on my

coat, and noticing how dim the headlights of the car were through the fog. I felt—" He glanced up at her, unsmiling. "This is like one of my operas, I know. But I felt this overwhelming sense of dread. Of something awful about to happen."

"The *fé*," she whispered.

"Perhaps." He puffed fiercely on his cigarette, and held the smoke in his lungs for a long time before he released it in a cloud. "How different things might have been, if I had listened to my own heart. But I was so arrogant, so sure of myself . . . and now I have a wife who is never happy, a constantly aching leg, and my muse has abandoned me. I'm a wreck."

"You're not a wreck, signore," Doria said gently. She stood, and put her chair back beside the card table. "You are tired, and your leg hurts. You're a little drunk, and you're worried about the opera."

He flicked the manuscript with a dismissive finger. "Mademoiselle Minnie!" he said with a derisive snort. It was what he called the principal character in *Fanciulla*, especially when it was all going badly. "I hate her!"

"In the morning you will love her again."

He set his glass unsteadily on the desk, nearly knocking it to the floor. He took a last drag on his cigarette, and dropped it in the ashtray. Doria reached past him to grind it out, then blew out the candles, cupping them with her hand to keep the wax from splattering the piano. She handed him his cane, and offered him her elbow. "Let me help you to the stairs," she murmured.

There was a sob in his voice. "*Grazie,*" he said. He took the cane in one hand, and her arm with the other. "*Grazie tanto*, Doria *mia*. I'm sorry to be such bad company."

She clicked her tongue as a mother might, though she was thirty years younger than he was. She led him toward the stairs, and as she guided him up, he leaned heavily on her shoulder, his steps uncertain in the dark. "Elvira thinks I should not be alone with you."

"After all this time, that whole year I nursed you?"

"You know how she is," he said, with a theatrical sigh. "My policeman. She watches everything I do, every step I take."

A creak from inside the bedroom he shared with his wife made her shiver.

Noticing, he patted her shoulder. "Don't worry, Doria *mia*. She scolds and shouts, but it doesn't mean anything. It's just noise, because she's so unhappy."

"Yes, signore," Doria said.

"You should feel sorry for her."

"Yes," Doria said again. "Good night, now, signore."

She stood back, waiting until he was safely inside the bedroom, the door closed, before she went back down the stairs. It was nearly one, she saw from the hall clock. She would have to be up again in only five hours to begin preparations for breakfast.

She wondered, as she trudged wearily through the kitchen and into her own bedroom, at what Puccini had said. She tried to find it in her heart to feel sorry for Elvira, for his sake if for no other reason, but sympathy eluded her. Perhaps, she thought, as she stripped off her clothes and fell into her bed, she was just too tired.

13

Chi c'è là fuori nel giardino? Una donna!

Who is out there in the garden? A woman!

—Suzuki, *Madama Butterfly*, Act Three

Chet Bingham drove Jack home after the Thanksgiving dinner was over. Kate had insisted on picking him up that morning rather than letting him drive the Escalade. Jack was pretty sure they had been afraid he wouldn't show, and they might have been right. The whole day felt hollow, despite the crowd around the Binghams' table and the good food, music, and friendly conversation. In years past, Tory and Jack had always gone to the Binghams' for dessert. Jack liked the tradition. He had also liked the quiet dinner he and his mother had enjoyed at home.

He'd never said that, though. It was as if, by not telling her, he was retaining control somehow. It didn't make sense, and he had figured that out when he went away to school. It wasn't that she tried to control him unnecessarily—not really—he had seen how the parents of other guys, mothers in particular, called and e-mailed and generally hovered over every detail of their lives. It wasn't Tory who was controlling—it was Jack who couldn't bear to be controlled. It was one of the many things he meant to tell her, if—no, when—he got the chance.

Although it was hard to admit it, he was glad Chet was with him as he approached the dark house. Ever since the deputy's visit, he had been uneasy around the place, especially at night. Now the house bulked before him, its blank windows and oppressive silence daunting. "Can I give you some coffee?" he asked Chet.

The older man nodded, and climbed out of the driver's seat. "That would be great, Jack. I'd be relieved to have a moment away from the thundering herds," he said.

Jack knew he didn't really mean it. Chet, stout and graying and cheerful, adored his children and his grandchildren. It was obvious to everyone who knew him, however he might bluster sometimes and complain about the noise in his house.

They walked side by side up to the front porch, and Jack unlocked the front door. He opened it and switched on the lights. The mail from the day before—the mail from the whole week, in truth—still lay waiting on the hall table. Chet raised an eyebrow at the pile. "Yeah," Jack said. "I need to go through that."

"Tell Kate if you need help," Chet said. "She's good with that sort of thing."

"I know." Jack glanced at the stack of mail, then away. He went to the mailbox every day, pulled out the envelopes and circulars. He flipped through everything to see if there was anything that might be from Tory, some hint of where she was, before he added it all to the pile.

"There might be bills in there," Chet said.

"Yeah. I'll check it tomorrow." Jack gave Chet a rueful look as he led the way into the kitchen. He glanced around, and felt a rush of self-consciousness. It wasn't just the neglected mail. The kitchen—in fact, the whole house—was significantly less tidy than when Tory was here. Bread crumbs and smears of butter marred the granite countertop, and dirty glasses and plates sat in the sink, waiting to be put into the dishwasher. He pulled out the coffeemaker, saying, "Sorry about the mess."

Chet laughed. "Did you see our house, with all the monsters tearing through it?"

"Yeah. But there's only me here."

"I know, son. I'm sorry about that." Chet pulled one of the tall stools up to the island and sat on it with a little grunt, adjusting his belt as he did so. "Listen, Jack—I've been hoping to have a moment with you."

Jack was spooning coffee grounds into the filter. He glanced across at Chet, and saw that the older man was staring down at his folded hands. His round cheeks, so often creased in a ready grin, drooped. Jack braced himself. "Go ahead."

"It's just—well, Kate and I are worried about you."

"I'm doing okay."

Chet looked up, and gave Jack an approving nod. "Yes, you are. You've been doing great with all this."

Jack pushed the button on the coffeemaker, and it began to bubble. "The thing is—" he began, but Chet rushed on. A slight flush stained his round cheeks, and Jack was sure he had prepared his statement, and wanted to make certain he got it out.

"I spoke to the sheriff's office," Chet said.

Jack turned to face him. "Did you? Why?"

"Well." Chet cleared his throat. "I hope you won't mind, but you're so young, and all on your own. They thought it was better if it came from someone you know."

Jack kept his back braced on the counter. The coffeepot gurgled, and the darkness beyond the windows seemed to intensify. "What is it?"

"It's about declaring your mother—deciding she's really—" Chet pursed his lips, and cleared his throat as if he couldn't bring himself to speak the word.

"Dead," Jack said. He shifted his shoulders. "I understand that's what it's about."

"Right." Chet sighed, and folded his hands together on the counter. "It's just—man, it seems harsh."

"It *is* harsh." The coffeepot gave a final gurgle, and Jack turned to pick up the pot. He carried it to the counter, and set it on a trivet. As he took cups from the cupboard, he said, "What did the sheriff say?"

"Well, it's about this 'death in absentia' thing," Chet said. He took a cup from Jack, and poured coffee for both of them. "I don't know if this comes from the police or from a judge, but the sheriff said that if the preponderance of evidence—those were his words—if the preponderance of evidence points toward death, then the missing person is declared dead."

"I thought it took seven years," Jack said.

"Not always, I guess. After 9/11, they told me, there were a lot of declarations made in a hurry. They can make a death declaration whenever they think it's reasonable, and in Tory's case, it seems they do."

"That's why we're not having—what do you call it—probate?"

"You don't have to worry about probate," Chet said. "Your mom's will was clear, and it was up to date. Her usual efficiency. Everything goes to you, so—"

"But not if she's not dead."

"They think she is, Jack." Chet blew on his coffee, then set down the cup without sipping. "I'm sorry to have to say that to you, son, but it's been more than six weeks. We have to face the facts, tragic though they are." He gave Jack a sympathetic look, and Jack knew he should feel grateful. Chet was doing the best he could. He added, as if more persuasion were needed, "The sheriff called it 'the balance of probability.' The probability being that Tory is no longer alive."

"Yeah," Jack said. His voice was rough, and he shook his head, hoping Chet understood. "I got that."

"Have some coffee, son. Let's talk it through. You're going to have bills, the mortgage, life insurance, all the things we have to deal with when someone dies."

Jack filled his cup, and pulled a stool up to the island opposite Chet. "I appreciate that you're trying to help me. I do. And Kate, too—she's been great." He sat down, and fingered the cup. "Mom's not dead, though. She'll be back."

Chet gave him a sad, paternal look. For a moment Jack was afraid he was going to reach across the island to pat his shoulder, or worse, take his hand as if he were a child. He breathed a heavy sigh, and his plump cheeks drooped. He said, "It's natural, I'm sure. I don't know much about these things, but I suppose you haven't accepted it yet."

"It's not that." Jack turned to the side, angling his body so he didn't have to see the pity in Chet's gaze. "I accepted it at first. When the dean told me. It was a shock, and I was practically— well, I could barely move. But then, on the train, I knew—I just had this feeling—" He stretched out his legs, and stared down at his worn sneakers. "I know she's not dead, Chet. I can't explain it."

"I'm sure that's a comfort, but—"

"No!" Jack shook his head so his shock of hair fell over his eyes, and he had to push it back with his hand. "No, it's not a comfort! There's something wrong, some reason she's not here, and I have to find out what that is!" He made a fist on the counter-top beside his coffee cup.

"I'm sorry, Jack," Chet said quietly.

"It's okay. I didn't mean to raise my voice."

"Perfectly understandable."

A silence stretched between them, punctuated only by the hiss of steam from the coffeemaker and the rush from the furnace as the heat came on. Jack said finally, "I shouldn't have said anything. I knew no one would believe me. I didn't believe in Mom's premonitions, either."

"Did she have those?"

"All the time. She stopped telling me, though, after—I used to make fun of her. They were so weird, you know. Embarrassing."

"Yes." Chet gave a hollow chuckle. "There's nothing a parent can do that's worse than embarrassing his kid." Jack wished he could laugh about it, acknowledge that it was normal, something all families experienced.

Chet drained his coffee cup, and set it down. "Look, Jack," he said. "I sure don't want to be the bad guy here."

"You're not." Jack turned to face him, resting his elbows on the counter. "You're a good friend who's trying to help out a dumb kid."

"Not dumb. You're a smart young guy. But this is a hell of a situation."

"Yeah. It is."

"I think you should do your best to face the truth, though, son. The sheriff believes your mother died, and he's ready to declare that to the court. It will free up Tory's estate so you can manage things."

Jack chewed his lower lip, and twirled his coffee cup on the counter. He didn't want to argue with Chet. Not only wouldn't it do any good, but the poor guy had obviously been waiting for the chance to say this. He finally said, "What do you want me to do?"

"Well, nothing now. The sheriff will report to the court, and when there's a declaration of death, there will be forms to take to the bank, to the insurance companies, that sort of thing."

Jack felt a rush of irritation. This wasn't what they should be talking about. They should be trying to think where Tory had gone, how they could find her, what had made her flee, not how to take over her finances. He gritted his teeth against making some stupid remark that would just upset Chet.

"You okay, Jack?" Chet asked, in his grandfatherly way.

"Yeah. Yeah, Chet, I'm just thinking."

"Well. No need to worry about it just now. It will all take a bit of time." He climbed off the stool, and carried his coffee cup to the sink. "No reason you shouldn't go back to school," he said, feigning casualness. "Kate and I will keep an eye on the place for you."

Jack was on more certain ground here. "I took a leave of absence."

Chet paused, the cup in his hand over the sink. "I suppose I can't talk you out of that."

"Well, it's sort of a done deal. I called the dean—I've missed most of the quarter anyway. They call it bereavement leave, so I'm okay."

"Kate's not going to be too happy with me," Chet said, shaking his head. "That was my real assignment tonight, to talk you into going back to college." He turned to face Jack, leaning his back against the edge of the sink. His paunch strained at his shirt, and absently, he fidgeted with the waistband of his slacks. "I would think, Jack, you'd want to be with your friends."

"They e-mail me."

"No girlfriend?"

Jack shook his head. "No."

Chet put his head to one side, and smiled. He looked younger when he smiled, less weary. "Come on, Jack, a good-looking young guy like you? There must be girls. Or even—" He colored, and waved an embarrassed hand. "Well, I'm old-fashioned, but if you're not . . . I mean . . ."

Jack gave a brief chuckle. "I'm straight, Chet, if that's what you mean. And yeah, there are girls, but . . ."

"Nobody special, huh?"

Jack didn't know how to say it. He would have liked to confide in someone, someone with real-life experience. He'd even thought of it, once or twice. He'd considered going to the counselor at school, but it seemed such a lame thing to do, and he didn't know how he would find the words. He could hardly tell Chet, especially not right now, about his problems with girls. He liked them fine. There had been two or three he liked a lot, but the feeling didn't last. It never lasted. He figured there was something wrong with him, something that made him irritable and restive in his relationships. It was the same thing, he feared, that made him draw back from his mother. And hurt her.

All he said now was, "No. No one special."

"Just the same, Jack. You're too young to hole up here, spinning your wheels."

"I know. I'm going to go back. I'll go back when—" He stopped. He had been going to say, "When Mom comes back," but clearly, that wasn't a good idea. He was the only person in the whole damn world who thought she would return one day. Who believed she was alive.

He wished, suddenly, that he had just one person to talk to, to turn to, one person he could trust not to dismiss this powerful conviction. Ironically, that person would have been Tory.

"Well," Chet said, though he seemed doubtful. "You can, go back in the spring."

"Right."

Chet gathered up his jacket and keys, and stood irresolute in the middle of the kitchen. "Sure you wouldn't rather come stay with us, Jack? Kate would love to have you."

"I'm sure. You guys have been great, though."

Chet looked around at Tory's pretty things. "Not that I know much about kitchens, but this one is really nice."

"I know. Mom loves—loved this house."

"And you have everything, I know—when Kate needed something, she always called Tory. Whether it was a zester—whatever that is—or a wrench, your mom always had it."

"Everything but an iron. Mom hates those."

"Didn't like to iron, huh?"

"Nope. Nothing but permanent press in this house."

"I guess everyone has their little weakness."

Jack stood, and walked with Chet to the front door. "Tell Kate thanks again," he said. "The dinner was great."

"I will." Chet shrugged into his jacket. The lock on his car chirped, but still he hesitated on the doorstep. "Call us, son. Don't be lonely."

"Okay." Jack put out his hand, and Chet shook it with both of his. Finally, with obvious reluctance, Chet went down the steps, walked to his car, and climbed in. Jack waved farewell, then stepped back and closed the front door, grinning cheerfully as he did so.

When the door was safely closed, he let the smile fade. He stood listening to Chet's engine start, then the crunch of tires on gravel as he backed and turned and disappeared down the long driveway. It was a relief to have him gone, but only because of the questions Jack didn't want to answer. The protest he wasn't allowed to make.

Carefully, Jack locked the door, turning the dead bolt before he switched off the porch light. Behind him the house felt like a cavern, full of empty rooms and dark corners. He felt jazzed up by the coffee, and he was sure he couldn't sleep.

He scooped up the mess of mail from the hall table, and carried it into the kitchen. Might as well do something useful if he was going to be awake.

There were two psychology magazines, and he set those aside. He had thought about canceling the subscriptions, which he was sure Kate would have advised. Instead, he had started saving the issues in a grocery bag. It was beginning to fill up, the glossy covers declaring their topics—*Blood Sugar Levels in Depressed Patients, Treating ADHD without Drugs, Counseling Bereaved Children*—from the pantry floor where he stored the bag. Some nights, when he couldn't sleep, he imagined himself presenting Tory with the bag when she came home—not if, but when—as evidence he had known she would return. It comforted him.

There were two long, official-looking bank envelopes, and one from some sort of financial institution. He set those in a separate stack, to go through in the morning. There were Christmas cards in colored envelopes, and those he opened to arrange on the mantelpiece in the living room as Tory always did. He saved the envelopes, in case she wanted to write back to the senders. He sifted through a little pile of concert invitations on four-color postcards. She was probably on the mailing list of every musical organization in the state. Idly, nostalgically, he read several. He could guess what her response to each of them would have been. Mozart Christmas pieces, she would love. A recital of Puccini arias for New Year's Eve, a definite yes. A January evening of Mahler, maybe—she liked "The Songs of a Wayfarer." Wagner, absolutely not. He said aloud, "Sorry, Mom," and chucked the whole stack into the recycling bin. As he did so, a hand-addressed envelope that had slipped into the folds of one of the advertisements slid to the floor.

Jack bent to pick it up. He didn't recognize the handwriting. It looked like it might be another Christmas card, though it was a business-sized envelope. A Christmas letter, maybe, one of those photocopied things. He turned over the envelope to slit it open, and paused. A sudden chill stirred the hairs on his arms and the back of his neck.

The envelope had been opened. It hadn't been steamed, which

Jack was pretty sure would curl the paper and leave traces of water damage. Someone, he thought, had pried up the flap and then pressed it back down, but whoever it was had left wrinkles in the gummed edge. It was skewed, slightly but obviously crooked. Carefully, he slid his forefinger under the flap to lift it. He pulled out the contents—a Christmas letter, as he had thought—and it, too, showed evidence of having been opened, clumsily refolded, shoved back into the envelope.

Disturbed, he hastened to the pantry for the saved Christmas card envelopes. He looked at each, wondering if he had missed something. He tried to think what it was like to mail Christmas cards. Scrawl a signature, an address, give the envelope a quick lick or a dab with a sponge. They often weren't very well sealed, and he had opened these without paying much attention. He examined them now under the bright kitchen light. It was hard to tell for sure—in fact, he couldn't be sure about any of this—but one or two seemed to have been re-sealed like the letter.

He put them back, moving slowly now, thinking hard. There wasn't much he could do. The letters and cards might look to him as if they had been opened before, but then he had opened them himself, and no one would be convinced by his hunch. He didn't want to tell Kate and Chet, because they were already practically insisting he come and stay with them. If they thought there was something strange going on, maybe something dangerous, they would never let him be.

He picked up the long envelope once again, the pages of the Christmas letter forgotten on the granite countertop. He stood for a long moment, the re-sealed envelope in his hand. He knew what it meant. He had been hoping for someone to believe him, but not like this. This wasn't the support he had hoped for. This didn't feel good at all.

He was pretty damn sure, now, that there was at least one other person in the world who didn't believe his mother was dead.

14

*Diedi gioielli della Madonna al manto, e diedi
il canto agli astri, al ciel, che ne ridean più belli.*

I gave jewels for the Madonna's mantle, and I gave
my song to the stars, to heaven, which smiled with more beauty.

—Tosca, *Tosca*, Act Two

Tory startled when her cell phone rang. It had never rung
before. It was a cheap thing, something she'd bought at
Costco just because people expected everyone to have a phone.
But there was no one to give her number to.

She answered in a hesitant voice, and heard, "Hello? Paulette,
is that you?"

Of course. Iris. She had written the cell phone number on her
rental agreement. "Yes," she said, and had to clear her throat. She
hadn't spoken aloud at all today. She wasn't sure she had spoken
at all the day before, either, or to anyone except a grocery clerk
since Thanksgiving. Silence surrounded her, the silence of solitude, filled only by the music from her radio and the rush of
waves on the beach. She said again, "Yes, it's me. Hi, Iris."

"There's a job," Iris said. "You mentioned once you might
want one."

"Oh. A job?" Tory walked to the window to look out at the
rain-lashed ocean. Low clouds obscured the horizon, and the
great rock looked as if it were hunched against the storm. "Yes,
Iris, I—I might want a job."

"It's just seasonal. Doesn't pay much."

"That's okay." Tory knew she sounded noncommittal. The idea of a job—getting out of the cottage and meeting people—both thrilled and frightened her. The long hours alone made her anxiety rise and intensify until she felt she might jump out of her skin, but—when anyone looked closely at her, or asked her a question, the fear that had become her only companion shuddered in her belly.

She leaned against the cold window, and reminded herself that she'd done fine so far. Her made-up Social Security number and the hastily acquired cell phone hadn't made Iris so much as blink. They could hardly lead anyone to her. And she needed the money. Her little cache of bills was shrinking at an alarming rate. "Where is it, Iris?"

"Flower shop. They get really busy over the holidays, and Betty told me her daughter needs help handling the counter. Don't know if you've been in there, but they sell a lot of decor items, bric-a-brac, souvenirs, that sort of thing."

"I haven't been in," Tory said. "But I'm sure I could handle it."

Iris chuckled. "I'm sure, too. If you're interested, I'll call Betty."

"Yes. Thanks, Iris. It's nice of you to think of me."

"Nonsense. What friends are for."

As Tory pocketed her phone, she puzzled over Iris's remark. It was the second time Iris had implied they were friends, but were they, really? She supposed they could be. It wasn't like it was with Kate, but she and Kate had known each other for more than fifteen years. She knew almost nothing about Iris, while she knew everything about Kate Bingham. They talked about everything—well, almost everything. They were in and out of each other's houses, borrowing, lending, sharing in the way of true friends. Old friends, who understood feelings without having to explain them.

Suddenly, Tory missed Jack with a stab of pain so deep it was as if it were brand-new. It made her heart clench with despair. With an exclamation, as much sob as curse, she seized her coat and knitted cap and fairly threw herself out the front door and through the gate.

She walked as fast as she could across the damp sand, heading toward Haystack Rock. The rock, big and black and dominating, had become her cathedral, the place she went for respite, the place she could pour out her grief and worry, at least for a time.

Cold December sunshine broke through the clouds. The tide was out, but the winter breakers still swelled impressively high before they smashed themselves against the ancient boulders. Tory walked right to the tide line, letting her sneakers splash in the brown foam edging the beach. She gazed out over the restless water, and the pain in her heart eased just a bit, to a level that was almost bearable.

Why did water work that way for her? She had no idea. Except for a couple of beach vacations as a child, before her mother withdrew into illness and depression, she had never lived by the water nor spent much time on it. She remembered the feeling, when she drove the yellow VW right up to the edge of the Pacific Ocean, that her journey was done. In the weeks since, the water had become her solace.

It's okay, she told herself. We take comfort where we can. She wondered if it was because of the water in her dreams, that muddy lake lapping at the edge of the road. Her dream life was twining itself with her waking life, so that every event she dreamed of seemed to mean something profound.

She reached the giant rock, and walked as far around it as the water allowed. She took care not to step in the tide pools or to disturb the miniature beasts that inhabited them, the layered barnacles, the slow-moving sea stars, the curious formations of anemones. She had learned about the aggregating anemones, tiny beings huddled together in communities that shared a single mind and purpose. There was an opposite species, similar, but solitary rather than communal. These little, separate creatures curled in crevices of the parent rock, stubborn and alone.

Like me, Tory thought. *Stubborn and alone.*

She wondered if Jack was lonely. She hoped not, hoped with

all her heart that he had friends around him, people to share the burden that had fallen on his young shoulders. She hoped, also, that he would think well of her, in memory. That he would understand that the distance between them had been superficial, something that would have passed in time. She hoped with all her heart that he would know how much she loved him.

She couldn't think of her own parents that way. She remembered her mother's withdrawal into mental illness. She remembered her father's impotent rages. Had they loved her? Or were they too unhappy, too consumed by the tragedy of their own lives, to make room for her?

She wrapped her arms around herself against the cold. Nonna Angela must have suffered, too, in that unhappy household, yet she had never spoken of it. She had simply loved her little granddaughter, and shielded her as best she could. It must have been hard to watch the family disintegrate and not be able to do anything to stop it.

Tory stood for a moment in the lee of the rock, out of the wind, her hat pulled down past her ears and her hands thrust deep into the pockets of her now-shabby coat. She would take the job in the flower shop, if this Betty would hire her. It would give her someplace to go each day, people to talk to, work to take her out of herself.

She had to move forward. Do something. It was exactly the sort of thing she would have advised her clients to do, but it was surprisingly difficult in the actual event. She comprehended, now, the comfort of being still. Of being stuck. Ice Woman understood. She wondered if she would be able to let the ice break apart.

Oh, Jack. Be well, sweetheart. Be safe.

She pulled the collar of her jacket up to her chin, and retraced her steps around the landward side of the great rock, emerging into the wind with her sneakers wet and the hems of her jeans dripping foam. She angled up the beach toward the cottage, thinking she'd better leave her shoes outside, maybe even strip off her jeans just inside the door.

She had just passed the repaired bench when she stopped, and stood motionless.

Something was huddled against the gate of her tiny yard. She couldn't quite make it out at first, just a big, wet mound of brown and white. It took a moment for her to realize it was an animal. Its ears drooped against its matted skull. It was shivering, and when it saw her, the lift of its head seemed to be a gesture of hope. Its eyes, gleaming black from beneath long white eyebrows, pled for understanding. A dog.

Tory stared at it. She couldn't open the gate without making it move. She would have to speak to it, possibly touch it. She didn't like dogs. She had never liked them.

It wasn't that she was afraid of them. She had tried to explain that to her son, when he asked if they could have one. She thought at the time it was part of his attempt to be more like the Garveys, and she had talked too long, explaining that dogs required a lot of attention, company, discipline, space . . . He had stopped listening, she was sure. Finally, she admitted her real reason: that dogs made her feel sad.

"Sad?" he had said, with the disdain only a fourteen-year-old could affect. "That's stupid, Mom. Why should dogs make you feel sad?"

She remembered being caught by the question, pinned like a butterfly on a collector's board by her son's challenging blue gaze. She still wasn't used to that look, though she was to become accustomed to it before long. She said, weakly, "I know, Jack. It is a bit stupid, but feelings are—"

"Yeah, I know, Mom. Feelings are valid. You've said." He rolled his eyes, and shoved his too-long hair away from his face. It was nearly white-blond then, the way her own had been when she was a little girl, when her mother had still liked to brush it and braid it or smooth it into a long, spun-sugar ponytail. His hair had darkened to pale gold as he grew, just as hers had. He said, "So, aside from the counselor talk, why do dogs make you sad?"

It seemed the right moment to tell him about her mother—his grandmother, whom he barely knew—but it was hard finding the words. She had worked all through it during her training, had achieved a certain peace with the pain of growing up with someone suffering from mental illness. Explaining it to her son was different. It was delicate. She didn't want him to worry that the same thing might happen to her, or even worse, to him.

She had begun carefully. "It's complicated, sweetheart—"

"Mom, it's *always* complicated!"

"You're right about that, I guess." She wanted to take his hand, to make him sit down and listen to her. He stood in front of her, hands in his pockets. He slouched, shoulders forward, his spine curved over his concave chest as if to keep her from touching him. She said, "You know, Jack, I can't make it *not* complicated."

His gusty sigh should have warned her, she supposed, that he was in no mood for the family story. It had been weighing on her, though. Kate felt that the sooner he understood about his grandmother, the better it would be. Kate also thought she should explain about his father, and she hadn't done that, either. Kate was great at talking to her kids. Tory didn't seem to have the knack. Her talents as a therapist seemed to evaporate when it came to her son.

She began again. "My mother was sick when I was young," she said. "Mentally ill."

"Gramma? Mentally ill?"

"Yes."

"I figured—I just thought it was that thing old people get. Alzheimer's."

"Not in this case."

She could see that, for once, she had his full attention. He was silent for a moment, screwing up his face as if that would help him think. After a moment he said, "What does that have to do with how you feel about dogs?"

"Well—it's an ugly story. We had a dog, a little one. My mother lost her temper one day and—and she hurt it."

"Hurt it?"

Tory closed her eyes for a painful moment. Even now, all these years later, she could see the little thing, lying limp and lifeless. Only a dead thing could be that still, and even at ten, she had understood it. She opened her eyes again, and tried to speak in a level tone. "She killed it, I'm afraid. She didn't mean to, I'm sure, but—maybe she kicked the dog instead of hitting her child. We didn't know then—none of us understood how sick she really was."

"God, Mom. That's awful."

Tory was ashamed at the little spurt of gratitude she felt for his flash of sympathy. She hadn't, in fact, been particularly fond of the dog. It was snappish and cranky, older than she was. It had been shocking, though, to watch her mother lash out at it, and sickening to see its small body sprawled across the gray and white linoleum squares of the kitchen floor. Her mother, sobbing, had vanished into her bedroom, where Tory could hear her weeping all through the afternoon. The dog's body lay where it was, sightless eyes staring at nothing, until her father came home.

Jack leaned forward, and patted her shoulder with just his fingers. "I'm sorry, Mom," he said. "That really stinks."

She wanted to catch his hand and press it between hers, but she was already learning such displays weren't welcome. She had to content herself with the brief, voluntary contact. There was more she would have liked to tell him, but she was terrified of becoming one of those single mothers who turn their sons into the man of the house, load their young shoulders with adult burdens. She had counseled too many people who had grown up as a parent's confidante. It was never a good thing, and she didn't want to do that to Jack.

She never spoke to him again about her girlhood. She didn't describe the pain of ruined playdates, the embarrassment of strange calls when she was at school, summoning her home for nonexistent emergencies. She never told him how her father reacted to her mother's illness, the towering rages that left her cowering in her bedroom while he stormed around the house. She understood, eventually, that fear was at the heart of her father's fury, the fear of losing control, of losing his wife, of their entire life as a family coming apart. There had been no question of therapy, or counseling, only the awful day when her mother—who had ceased speaking, stopped eating, refused even to get out of bed—was taken away in an ambulance. Tory had been terrified of being alone with her father, but with her mother gone, his rages disappeared, too. He no longer shouted or broke things. He didn't do much of anything, in fact, but go to work, then come home to sit, silent and broken, at the kitchen table. Tory, by the time she was twelve, was keeping house, cooking, shopping, cleaning, washing clothes. Jack never knew any of this.

It was a great relief for Tory to go off to college, and it was there she discovered music. She went to New York with some friends to hear *Madama Butterfly* at the Metropolitan Opera, and the perfect beauty of the melodies and the harmonies was almost more than she could bear. The inevitability of Cio-Cio-San's tragedy overwhelmed her. Tory, the most reserved girl of all her circle, wept through the entire performance. When she went to bed that night, the arias whirled around and around in her head, perfectly memorized. She had the strangest feeling of recognition, as if she had always known this music. She began to search out CDs, go to every concert she could find, immerse herself in this unexpected pleasure.

Whenever she went home, it was like being in a prison of silence. She and her father crept around their hushed house, avoiding each other. The two of them made ritual visits to the mental institution to visit her mother, and on the way back they might assure each other she looked a bit better, she had said a word or two, perhaps she was on the mend, but neither of them believed it.

Jack never knew any of that. She poured it all out to Kate one day, talking and talking, a spate of words as if someone had opened a dam that was on the verge of cracking. But she never told her son.

Now, far from her son and her closest friend, she looked down at the shivering dog in front of her, and the intensity of her sadness was almost more than she could bear.

She tried to edge around the dog to open the gate, but when she did, it fell to its side, as if the only thing holding it up had been the support of the wooden slats. Its ribs stood up like those of a wrecked ship, each bone visible through wet fur. It shook visibly, wasted muscles rippling from head to tail. She stared down at it in an agony of indecision. She could leave the gate open, go inside, hope the dog could fend for itself. Perhaps it would get up and wander off. Or perhaps it would die, right there where it lay.

"You pitiful thing," she muttered. "You're like me—wet, alone, and miserable."

The dog's ears twitched, and it gave one small whine, as if in agreement.

Tory sighed. She couldn't do it. She couldn't go in and close her door, hoping the dog would disappear and solve the problem for her. She trotted up the walk and into the house. She grabbed a towel, and hurried back through the yard to where the dog trembled on the bare ground, the open gate looming over it like a coffin lid. She bent to wrap the towel around the thin body. At her touch the dog's tail, a bedraggled flag of brown and white fur, beat three times against the ground. Tory felt her heart beat in time with it, each strike of the wet tail a thud in her own chest. "Okay," she said softly. "Let's get you up. You don't want to lie out here in the cold."

She was surprised, when the dog struggled to its feet, at how tall it was. Its head reached her mid-thigh. It wavered on its long legs as she helped it up the walk. She kept the towel around it, worried it might have bugs or mange or some other doggy pestilence. Its shoulder bumped her knee as they made a slow, awkward progress up over the single step and into the cottage. Tory shut the door with her foot, then turned to start scrubbing the dog dry as best she could. It lay flat again, and she knelt beside it, rubbing its flanks and chest. When she gingerly lifted its head to dry its ears, its long pink tongue flicked out and scraped her cheek.

She chuckled in spite of herself. "We're a pair, you and I, dog. Lost and lonely, and more than a bit damaged." She rubbed it from head to tail, then picked up each big paw and dried those, too. It submitted with patience to her ministrations. She didn't know if dogs liked being rubbed, or if this one was just so tired— or ill—it didn't care. As the sand and water came out of its coat, she found no signs of injury or noticeable sickness. It—he—was just bone-thin and cold.

Tory coaxed him to get up, to move onto the rug in front of the easy chair. She had chopped wood the day before, and now she laid a fire with kindling and crushed newspapers and a nice dry log. In moments the fire crackled pleasantly, and warmth swept out into the chilly room. Tory, kneeling on the hearth, surveyed her unexpected company.

He was on his belly now, lying with his head on his paws, his eyes shining with firelight. His ears twitched as she came to her feet, adjusted the fire screen, sat on the edge of the little couch. "Listen," she said. "I don't know anything about dogs. I don't know what you eat, or what you need. I can probably afford to pay for one vet visit, but if there's anything seriously wrong with you—" The dog's long eyelashes swept down, then up. "I don't even know if Iris will let you stay here."

The dog sighed, a huge, gusting puff of air that came from his lean flanks and made his nostrils flutter. With a groan that sounded very like one of relief, he rolled onto his side again and lay flat, his head toward the warmth of the fire, his tail extended beneath the easy chair. His eyelids drooped.

Tory watched the dog breathe. He looked like some sort of spaniel, she thought, but she had no idea what kind. She bit her lip, trying to think of what she should do next. Water first, she supposed. He would need water. She had some hamburger in the refrigerator. She was pretty sure all dogs liked meat.

She filled a bowl from the tap, and put it near the dog's nose before she pulled her phone out of her pocket. She had to call Iris before she did anything else.

"Paulette. Did you change your mind?"

Tory caught a breath. "How did you know it was me?"

"Caller ID. I put your number into my phone. Don't you have it?"

Tory nearly took the phone away from her ear to look at it, then blinked at the foolishness. "No. No, this phone isn't much."

"I left a message at the flower shop. They're expecting you in the morning. Is that why you called?"

"It's not that, Iris, but thank you. I haven't changed my mind. I'll be there. What I called about, though—the thing is—" Tory glanced back at the brown-and-white dog, lying in front of the fire. She said helplessly, "Iris, it's this—this dog."

A long pause made her wonder if their call had been cut off. She was about to say something more when Iris said, "A dog?" in a wondering tone. It was as if Tory had told her it was a space-ship.

"This dog was—it was collapsed in front of the gate. Wet, shivering. Skinny. I didn't know what to do, but I couldn't just leave it there."

"What kind of dog?"

"I don't know. Big. Brown and white, long hair. He's kind of sweet." She rolled her eyes, embarrassed at what she had said. She didn't know, really, if the dog was sweet. He might turn into some sort of monster when he wasn't so tired.

There was another pause, but Tory could think of no way to fill it. She waited. It was as if she could hear the process of Iris thinking, all the way from her pretty house across town.

"Well," Iris said finally. "Actually, the rental agreement says no pets. But you—" She expelled a sharp breath, as if through her teeth, and it was somehow a sound of decision. "Paulette, you've done so much work on the place. It's never looked better. I would imagine when you leave, I'll never know there was a dog there."

"You know, Iris, I hadn't really decided to keep him," Tory confessed. "He just—he's lying there in front of the fire, and he looks—"

Iris laughed. "Like he belongs?"

Tory pressed a hand to her chest. The sudden, premonitory pain pierced her through. It took her breath away. She whispered, "Yes. He looks like he belongs," and the pain subsided.

"Well, then," Iris said brusquely. "More of a cat person myself. But you'd better keep him. Company for you."

Company. Yes. And something else, something Tory knew very well but couldn't guess at yet. Her heart thudded at the thought, that familiar sense that something was coming. She said through a dry throat, "Thanks. Thanks very much, Iris. Do you know if there's a vet in town?"

15

❧

Oggi il mio nome è Dolore.

Today my name is Sorrow.

—Butterfly, *Madama Butterfly*, Act Two

Doria stood, hands on hips, and looked around at the spotless kitchen. Old Zita had gone to her bed an hour before, but Doria had stayed on, scrubbing, polishing, tidying. The brass-and-steel *espresso* maker was filled and ready for the morning, and the table laid for breakfast. She was tired now, and she would have to be up early to begin it all again, but there was still the basket of ironing waiting for her. She put a stick of wood in the stove, and fetched the two irons from the pantry to begin to warm while she set up the ironing board.

Beyond the screened window the night looked thick and dark. Autumn often brought clouds and rain to Torre, gloomy days, murky nights, sometimes thunderstorms and great flashes of lightning that lit the clouds from within as if God had set them afire.

Doria set the basket of ironing on the table and went to fill the sprinkler at the sink. She yawned, wishing she could go to sleep. At least, if she had to iron, she could listen to the desultory sounds of the piano from the studio. Puccini was working on *Fanciulla* again.

She sprinkled water over a linen tablecloth, smoothed it over the ironing board, and picked up the first iron. Just as she was testing its heat with her finger, she heard his whisper.

"Doria!"

She turned from the ironing board, and found Puccini standing beside the sink. His cigarette hung from his lower lip, and he gestured with the glass of port in his hand, making the dark wine slosh over the rim. "You're still up," he said, grinning. "Good! I hate being alone when Mademoiselle Minnie is behaving badly!"

"Signore." She crossed to the towel rack, took the oldest one there, and bent to wipe up the spilled wine. "Your Mademoiselle Minnie will not behave if you drink so much."

"No, no, Doria *mia!* It's the other way around! I drink because she will not behave!"

Doria tutted as she folded the towel and replaced it. "You should go to bed. It's late."

"No, no," he said. "These are the best hours. These are the hours the music comes to me!" The slur in his voice told her he had drunk more this evening than usual. He took a step, stumbling as his weight shifted to his bad leg. She put out her hand to steady him, and he chuckled. "*Grazie.* You're very nice to an old man." Then, with a louder laugh, "An old drunken man!"

"You're not old, signore." She stood back, and shook her finger at him. "You are, however, quite drunk."

At this he guffawed, then clapped his hand over his mouth like a guilty boy. "Shhh," he whispered loudly. "You'll wake my policeman."

Doria pursed her lips to quell her smile, and said as sternly as she could, "You shouldn't speak so of your wife."

"No?" He leaned back against the sink, puffing on his cigarette, filling the kitchen with its toasty scent. "No, perhaps I shouldn't." Another laugh. "But I will! She dogs my every step, just like one of the *carabinieri* in their striped pants and silly hats!" He took another drink of port, and said in an undertone, "Have you *seen* her hats? *Mamma mia*, what contrivances! They lurk at the top of the wardrobe, hulking there in the shadows like—like monsters waiting to leap at me! I swear to almighty God they give me nightmares!"

Doria giggled before she could stop herself. Elvira's hats were the talk of the village. They seemed to grow larger and more elaborate every year, with great swaths of netting and massive collections of silk flowers. It was, Doria thought, a thing rich women did as they aged, compensating for lost youth with fancier dresses and bigger hats, the most expensive gloves and the softest shoes.

"Women," Puccini said with bitter humor, "have ruined my life."

"No, no, signore, surely not!"

"*Sì, sì, sì*, signorina, absolutely true!" He took his cigarette from his mouth to drain his glass, then stuck it back between his teeth, sucking on it so the tip glowed fiercely. "Women—my sisters, my wife, my mistresses—they steal my soul! They want to tell me what to do, where to go, whom to see—whom *not* to see. Their endless chattering drowns out the music in my head!"

Doria thought he had a good point. He needed to concentrate, of course, and they distracted him. His sister Ramelde came to Torre to harangue him for his offenses. His sister Iginia, the nun, wrote him scolding letters. His lover Corinna had even threatened a lawsuit! Of course, some of the fault must be laid at his own doorstep. He could have settled on one woman, and avoided the scandals and the arguments and the—

Puccini dropped his cigarette in the sink, and it hissed for a second or two before it went out. She saw the gleam of his teeth beneath his black mustache as he smiled. "Doria! Come into the studio with me," he said. "Listen to what I'm working on. You have a good ear! Maybe you can tell me what's wrong."

Doria's breath caught, and she gasped, "No, no, maestro! I know nothing about music!"

He put out his hand to catch her wrist, and tugged her roughly toward the door. He meant to be playful, she knew, but his grip hurt, and she couldn't pull away from him. "Just *un momento*,

Doria *mia*," he said, with laughter in his voice. "Just let me play you a little of Mademoiselle Minnie—talk to you about it—"

She trotted after him because she had little choice, but she protested at every step. "Maestro, your friends will be here to-morrow, Pascoli and Caselli. Play it for them! Ask them your questions!"

He paid no attention. "I hear you singing around the kitchen, and when you're cleaning upstairs," he said cheerfully. "You *understand* my music, Doria, I can tell you do! It touches you. It moves you!" As they passed through the dining room, he snatched up the port bottle from the sideboard. "Elvira doesn't understand anything about my work—except, naturally, for how much money it brings in." He released her when they reached the studio. He banged the bottle down on his desk, where he could reach it from the piano. He snagged an extra chair, then flung himself onto the piano stool. "Sit, my little friend, sit! You will help me with this beast of an opera!"

Reluctantly, Doria settled herself on the chair. It was ridiculous, of course. She knew nothing of how an opera should be composed, nor how to criticize its faults. Anything she knew she had learned in the long nights of the maestro's illness, when he talked on and on about arias and recitatives, staging and orchestration. All she knew about *Fanciulla* was that Puccini had been agonizing over it, that it was due in New York far too soon, and that he was terrified of a huge failure after the grand success of *Butterfly*.

She watched him turn the pages of the handwritten score, splotched here and there with cross outs and insertions and scribbled notes, and her heart throbbed with a mixture of pity and admiration. He was, despite his fifty years of life, like one of her brothers, all bravado and bluster one day, all doubts and despair the next. She wondered Elvira could not see that all her badgering only made things worse for him, only drove him farther away from her. The two of them were like petulant children, tormenting each other in some twisted game no one but they could understand, subjecting everyone around them to their tantrums and tumult.

Puccini played a few bars of a melody, and turned to her, his eyes pleading. "There!" he said. "You see? It's not working."

"No, signore," she protested. "It's beautiful. I don't know what to say, because I—truly, I don't even know the story of this opera. Of your Mademoiselle Minnie."

He spun on his stool to face her. He had picked up his thick pencil, and he held it ready in his hand, as if she were going to tell him just what to do and he would write it out. He said, "It's a terrible story, and Minnie is the ugliest name any of my heroines has ever had."

She gave a wry little shrug. "But she's American. Perhaps in America, it's considered a beautiful name."

He fumbled in his pocket for a fresh cigarette. "Not even an American could love that name! But I'm stuck with it, as I'm stuck with this play. I wish I had chosen the other play, but I've gone too far to stop now. It's due in New York! There's no time to start again."

Even the name of New York made Doria lightheaded with wonder and envy. She had never been to Milan, to the great La Scala. She could not even dream of going to the Metropolitan Opera in New York City, America. She sighed a little, and spoke gently, as she would have spoken to the very youngest and most spoiled of all her brothers. "Tell me the story, maestro. Something must have appealed to you, when you chose it."

"Oh, yes." He held the cigarette in his teeth while he struck the match. He drew a lungful of smoke, and blew it out in a big ring. "For one thing, the villain smokes cigars!" He laughed. "And they all shoot guns! Two of my favorite things."

"Who is the villain? And why do they shoot guns?"

He squinted at her through the viscous yellow cloud of smoke. "The villain is a *sceriffo*, in the far west of America—California. They all carry guns there, I think."

"What is a *sceriffo?* And who is this Minnie?"

"A *sceriffo* is a sort of policeman. And Minnie is a young

woman who keeps an inn," he said. He took the cigarette from his mouth and examined the glowing tip of it thoughtfully. "She keeps the inn, and all the men who come to drink there love her. She teaches them the Bible—"

"The Bible!"

"Yes, she's very virtuous." He winked at her. "But she carries a gun, too, right here!" He pointed one finger down the front of his shirt. "The *sceriffo* is furious because she won't marry him, and then a bandit comes to town, and she falls in love with him."

Doria smiled, imagining a girl with a gun and a Bible falling in love with a bandit. "And so," she said, "the *sceriffo* tries to arrest the bandit, and she pleads for the life of her lover."

"*Esatto!*" Puccini laughed again.

"Maestro, it seems a very good story for an opera."

He gave a negligent shrug. "I suppose. In this scene, Minnie plays a card game to try to save her lover." His laughter died, and he turned back to the piano. "It's not working." He played a few notes. "I want the singers—the *sceriffo*, and the virtuous Minnie—to sing recitative, back and forth, back and forth, as they play their cards—but there has to be tension, or it's just—it's just silly. Already there is so much in this opera that's silly. All the time they're playing the game, the bandit is hiding upstairs, wounded by the *sceriffo*'s gun."

"So many guns," Doria marveled.

"Oh, yes, many guns. I think Americans go around shooting each other all the time." He played the notes again, shaking his head, puffing gouts of smoke into the dimness of the room. "This could be a good scene, though, the bandit bleeding in the attic while the sheriff and Minnie play cards. . . ."

"Poor Minnie! She must be so worried!" Doria put both hands over her heart.

Puccini glanced over his shoulder at her. "I suppose she is." He eyed her. "Is that what you do when you're worried, Doria? Put your hands there, so?"

Embarrassed, Doria dropped her hands. "I don't know, signore. I suppose if I'm worried—if I'm afraid—my heart beats hard, and perhaps I put my hands there—" She did it again, one hand pressed to her chest, the other covering it.

"Yes," he said. "Your heart beats hard, because you're afraid— you're afraid he will die, and you're afraid you will lose—" He began a slow, repetitive bass with his left hand, and with his right he seemed to conduct, as if he could hear the orchestra in his mind. He chuckled, and said, "She cheats, you know," but he kept on playing. "She cheats the *sceriffo* at cards, and all the while her lover is bleeding . . . and the blood runs down through the boards and drips onto the hands of the cardplayers. . . ."

Doria held her breath, afraid of distracting him. The corners of the room lay in deep shadow. The last embers of the fire glowed from the hearth, but there was no other light except for the candles in their sconces. The candle flames flickered, their shifting light shadowing the deepening creases in Puccini's face, making him look even older than he was. He needed rest, she thought. He looked exhausted.

Suddenly, Puccini exclaimed, "Ah ha!" She jumped, but he laughed. "Very good, Doria *mia*, very good indeed! You see, I *knew* you understood!"

"But, maestro . . . I don't understand at all! I didn't say anything."

"You did, my dear, you did! There will be an *ostinato*, a beat in the orchestra, like Mademoiselle Minnie's heart beating with fear . . . with anxiety . . ." He scribbled something, and then reached for the port to fill his glass. Ruby drops scattered here and there on the desk, on the floor, on the lower keys of the piano.

Doria stared at Puccini, openmouthed. She hadn't understood more than one word in four of what he had just told her. Surely nothing she had said . . . she couldn't have . . . No. It was only that he figured out what was wrong on his own, even in his port-infused state. She shook her head, bemused by the vagaries of living with an artist. A fleeting wisp of pity for his wife clouded her mind. It could not be easy.

He sketched in a chord, and then another and another. Quietly, so as not to disturb his concentration, she rose, and pushed her chair back to its place beside the card table. She started through the dark dining room toward the kitchen as he began playing the new chords, filling them in with his left hand while he picked out the melody in his right. It would work, of course. He would change it, and change it again, but she could hear that the idea was there. He would mold it and polish it and turn it upside down and right side up again until it was just right. She had heard him do exactly that with *Butterfly*, the music growing, maturing, flowering over the months he labored over it.

The stove had gone cold. She would have to build up the fire to warm the irons again. She bent to pick up another stick of wood.

"Doria! What are you doing?"

Doria turned just in time to see Elvira burst from the stairwell in a whirl of long dressing gown and loosened black hair flying about her face. She looked for all the world like a *strega*, a witch from a child's fairy tale.

Doria put her finger to her lips. "Signora, the maestro is working!"

"Of course he's working!" Elvira put her hands on her hips and braced her big bare feet far apart as if ready for battle. "I heard you in there with him! What were you up to?"

Doria answered without thinking. "He asked me to help him."

"Help him! Do you think I'm a fool?"

"No, of course not, signora, and I did try to tell him I know nothing of—"

Elvira's thick brows were drawn so hard together they looked as if they must hurt. "Don't be ridiculous!" she snapped. "How could you help Giacomo, you of all people? You, an illiterate village girl!"

Doria sucked in her breath. Her temper flared at the insult, and she spoke more loudly than she intended. "I am *not* illiterate! I read as well as you do!"

"Don't talk back to me!" Elvira shouted.

They both realized, in the same moment, that the music in the studio had stopped. Together, they turned guiltily toward the door, expecting Puccini to come in, to remonstrate, to object to the noise.

He didn't appear.

Now the two women stared at each other. Elvira's eyes glittered, and Doria wished she had held her tongue. It never helped to argue with the *signora*. As they gazed at each other, the front door closed with a bang, leaving the house enveloped in a tense silence, broken only by the scratching and whimpering of the hounds at the back door.

Elvira hissed, "Those bloody dogs!"

Doria, cautiously, as if to move too quickly might set Elvira off again, slid the stick of wood she was holding into the stove. She closed the lid with a soft click. "I was just ironing the linens for the morning," she said. She pointed at the tablecloth as evidence of her industry. "The *signore* came in, and he asked me—that is, I told him I couldn't, but he—"

When Elvira didn't answer immediately, Doria looked up. Her mistress was leaning against the counter, one hand on her chest, the other buried in the unbrushed mass of her hair. Her eyes were closed, and her lips were trembling. Softly, Doria said, "Signora?"

Elvira made a small, choked sound. Her eyelids fluttered open, and Doria saw that they shone with tears. Instinctively, Doria started across the kitchen. She supposed she meant to comfort her mistress, perhaps to touch her arm or take her hand, small gestures she would offer to any unhappy person. Elvira, however, threw up her hand, and Doria stopped where she was.

"You can't know how terrible it is," Elvira said, her voice rough as gravel, "to have no one you can talk to. No one to share your burdens."

Doria twisted her fingers in her apron. Her lips parted, but no words came. What could she, a housemaid, say to her mistress? What words of counsel could she serve up?

Elvira barked a mirthless laugh. "You see? I can't talk to Giacomo—I can't talk to my servants—I am completely alone." She pushed at her hair with both hands now, and the tears in her eyes slipped over her cheeks. Another sob escaped her, an ugly sound, as if she were doing her best to hold it back.

Doria dared to whisper, "Signora, surely your children . . ."

Elvira closed her eyes again. "My children! My children have no time for me. They have their own families, their work, their homes—what do they care for their mother, who did everything for them?"

Doria couldn't speak her thought aloud, that Elvira had driven everyone away from her with her rages and tantrums. In any case, what good would it do now? Her mistress looked so utterly miserable, so lost. . . . It wouldn't help to point out the ways in which she had created her own problems. "Signora Puccini," Doria ventured, "why don't you—why not let me make you a cup of tea, and while you drink it, I'll brush your hair for you? That's always so relaxing, don't you think?"

Elvira's eyes opened and fixed on Doria. "Brush my hair?"

Doria, pinned by that dark gaze, squirmed a little. "I just thought . . . perhaps . . ."

Elvira sighed suddenly, and looked away, toward the darkness of the night beyond the kitchen window. "My mother's maid used to brush my hair," she said sadly. "When I was small. My mother didn't like to do it, because it was so curly, and it tangled. If I cried—because it hurt—my mother would throw down the brush and walk away, and her maid would finish for her."

"It's still curly," Doria said. "And so thick."

"Yes," Elvira said absently. "It's hard to brush even now." She turned her head to look at Doria again, but she didn't seem to see her. "If I had a lady's maid," she said, "that would help. If only Giacomo would agree to hire someone, find someone to do some of these things for me."

Someone else for Zita and me to look after, Doria thought, *and probably take my bedroom, as well.* She heard the crackle as the fresh wood caught fire inside the stove, and she moved to the sideboard to fetch the teakettle and fill it at the sink.

"Tea," Elvira said. "You're right. Tea would be good. Bring it to my room."

"*Sì, signora.*" Doria didn't turn as Elvira swept out of the kitchen. She heard her padding up the stairs, and she shook her head in bemusement. She had worked in this house nearly six years, and Elvira had never once, in all that time, told her anything personal. She had no real relationship with her mistress other than trying to anticipate her wishes and stay out of her path when she was in one of her moods. Was it possible the *signora*'s moment of weakness might improve things between them?

It was past midnight by the time she carried the tray up the stairs. She had wrapped a cozy around the teapot, and laid a cup and saucer and two biscotti on a clean pressed napkin. There was still no sign of Puccini. He had gone to the café, no doubt, and was now drinking *vin santo* with his friends. Doria suppressed a yawn as she shouldered the door open into Elvira's bedroom.

The *signora* was seated at her lacy dressing table, massaging cold cream into her cheeks. Doria set the tea tray next to her, and poured out a cup. Elvira, without speaking, picked up the cup with one hand and pointed to a hairbrush with the other.

It felt strange to Doria to pick up Elvira's hairbrush, to clean a few strands of the *signora*'s coarse black hair from its bristles. She had often brushed Puccini's hair, and washed and shaved him as well, when he was bedridden for so long, but Elvira was another matter. Even though it had been her own idea, now the thought of touching her, of being so close to her, made Doria's stomach quiver unpleasantly.

Elvira sipped from her teacup and set it down as Doria started on her hair. Doria did it the way her mother had when she was a little girl, brushing and brushing with regular strokes, smoothing snarls, loosening the long tangles. Elvira sighed, and her eyelids fluttered and grew heavy. In the mirror Doria saw her thick shoulders relax, the lines of her face soften and nearly disappear. She kept working, gathering Elvira's thick hair into a plait, smoothing it away from her temples and behind her ears. It felt rough and oily against her fingers, but she tried not to think about that. Elvira slumped a little, and for a moment Doria thought she might have fallen asleep, right there on the stool.

She reached the end of the braid, and tied it with a bit of ribbon that lay on the dressing table. When she released it, and stood back, Elvira's eyes opened. She glanced at herself in the mirror, and then at Doria. Her eyes suddenly narrowed, and her face tensed. "You think I'm old and ugly," she said.

"No, signora, of course I don't!"

Elvira went on as if Doria hadn't spoken. "You'll see one day," she said. Everything about her seemed to change all at once. Her lips thinned. Her shoulders hunched. Her forehead creased as if she had suddenly remembered all her complaints. She said in a sour voice, her mouth pulling down, "You'll see what it's like." She pointed a long, sharp-nailed forefinger at Doria.

Doria's own shoulders tightened. She still held the hairbrush, and she cast about her for a place to put it down.

Elvira's eyes began to glitter with incipient temper. "That smooth skin, that slender waist! You're going to find out it doesn't last. When I met Giacomo I was so slim, he used to say he had to shake the sheets to find me! But now—"

With a sudden motion, she shoved herself to her feet. She turned swiftly around, and Doria flinched. Elvira said, "You'll see! One day you'll be old and fat like me, and then you'll—"

"Signora," Doria interrupted. "Don't speak of yourself that way."

"I don't like the way you talk to me!" Elvira put her hands on her hips. "I never wanted you in this house, did you know that?" As her voice rose and sharpened, the fragile moments of peace evaporated like soap bubbles on a cold breeze. It was startling, Doria thought, how swiftly her mood could change. Perhaps Old Zita was right. *Pazza.*

Now Elvira thrust out her heavy chin. "Oh, yes! I wanted someone older, someone who knew how to nurse Giacomo. I certainly never wanted an ignorant village girl, but Father Michelucci told Giacomo—"

She broke off, listening. The door had opened and closed

downstairs, and footsteps sounded through the studio. "It's Gia-como!" Elvira hissed. Her temper had brought the lines back to her face. The cold cream settled into them, thin white worms outlining every crease and wrinkle. "Out! I don't want him to find you here!"

Doria understood, with swift feminine instinct, that Elvira didn't want her husband to compare the two of them. She backed toward the door, but she said as soothingly as she knew how, "Signora—I'm in your room every day, the *signore* knows—"

Elvira lunged at Doria, her big feet slapping on the carpet. She thrust at her shoulder with her extended fingers, as if she would push her bodily out of the room. Doria stumbled against the doorjamb, and rubbed her shoulder where Elvira's sharp nails stung through her dress. She wondered if Elvira had been this way with her children, pushing and shoving at them when words failed her. That would explain why they never wanted to see her. Her own mamma, though they quarreled so often, had never struck her, would think such behavior beneath her dignity.

Doria pulled the door open. Behind her, Elvira said, "Hurry! Hurry!"

It was too late to hide the fact that she'd been in the bedroom, though. Puccini was already at the foot of the stairs, and when he heard Doria's step on the landing, he tipped up his head, then, laughing, caught at the banister for balance. He was now very, very drunk; she could see that. She started down the staircase, and Puccini, his braces hanging loose over his trousers, started up it.

As they met, he said blurrily, smiling at her and grasping at her hand, "Doria *mia!* Not in your bed?" He glanced up at the land-ing, squinting as he tried to focus his eyes. "What are you doing up here at this hour, little nurse?"

She pulled her hand free, afraid the *signora* would come out of the bedroom and see. "I was—I braided the *signora*'s hair for her," she said.

"Oh! Oh! That was sweet of you," Puccini said. His hair was tumbled over his forehead, and he reeked of wine. He fumbled in his pocket for a cigarette even as he leaned toward her, nearly falling as he bent to smile into her face. "Such a sweet little nurse, aren't you? L-l-lucky Elvira!" and he did stumble then, missing the next stair and landing hard on his bad leg.

He groaned, and she put out her hand to support him. "Signore, go to bed," she said firmly. "And no more smoking, or you'll likely catch the house on fire."

He straightened with difficulty, still grinning, and released the cigarette back into his pocket. He gave her a mock salute, the edge of his hand unsteadily meeting his forehead. "Yes, signorina!" he said. "Nurse's orders! I'm off to bed."

Doria stood where she was, watching him struggle up the stairs and cross the landing to the bedroom. The door opened and closed, and she heard the thunk of his boots on the floor. She waited a moment, to see if Elvira would scold. Instead, she heard a soft murmur of voices, and Puccini's sudden laughter. The light went out, and seconds later she heard the noise of the bedsprings beginning to squeak.

Doria turned toward her own room, pursued by the rhythmic sounds of the marital bed, creaking and thumping and complaining. The house had grown cold, and she shivered as she unpinned her hair and hurried into her nightgown. By the time she slipped between her icy sheets, hugging herself for warmth, the sounds upstairs had ceased.

Perhaps the *signora* would be in a better mood tomorrow. She hoped Elvira had rubbed off the face cream before her husband saw her.

Or, Doria thought wickedly, as she nestled into her pillow, *perhaps she didn't.*

Tory woke, shivering this time instead of perspiring. She sat up, finding her blanket gone and the sheet pulled down to her waist. Blinking in the predawn darkness, she reached for the bedspread. She tugged at it, but it didn't move. She flicked on the bedside lamp.

The dog, though she had made a bed of towels for him on the floor, now lay next to her on the bed, a skinny length of brown-

and-white fur stretched across the foot in a tangled fold of beige chenille. His eyes slid sideways when the light came on, but his big paws didn't move. Only the plume of his tail moved, silently beating against the blanket.

Dogs. There had been dogs in her dream, scratching and whining at a closed door.

She lay down again, frowning into the vague dawn light, searching for meaning in the strange succession of her dreams. She didn't find it.

She reached toward the dog, and curled her fingers into his long fur. The gesture felt familiar somehow, natural. It must be instinctive, this link between canines and humans, bred into them both by centuries of cooperation. The dog's long pink tongue lolled, and the corners of his mouth curled upward as he panted.

"Are you smiling at me?" she demanded softly. "And who raised you to think you belong on the bed?"

His tongue disappeared, and his eyes closed again. Once his fur had dried, it proved to be silky and long, matted in places under his forelegs and along his ribs. She had spent a good part of the evening brushing him, an operation he was clearly accustomed to, lifting his paws when she wanted him to, submitting to scissors when some of the mats wouldn't give way to her hairbrush.

Gently, Tory tugged the bedspread out from under the dog, and smoothed it up again over her side of the bed. She was about to pull on her sweatshirt and go out to make a cup of tea to watch the light rise over the water, but on an impulse she slipped back under the blanket, and turned out the light. The quilt was warm from the dog's body, and having him there—calm, accepting, another breathing, living being—soothed her restiveness.

She snuggled deeper under the covers, washed by a comforting tide of drowsiness. Just as she fell asleep again, she felt a weight on her ankles, and heard the slight, contented groan as the dog settled his head across her legs. Tory, her dream forgotten for the moment, slept again.

16

Mi piaccion quelle cose, che han si dolce malìa . . .
che parlano di sogni e di chimere. . . .

Those things please me, which have such sweet magic . . .
which speak of dreams and of chimeras. . . .

—Mimì, *La Bohème*, Act One

There was no veterinarian's number in the slender telephone directory for Cannon Beach, but when Tory called information, it turned out a new vet clinic had just opened. She called the number, and the doctor himself answered. When she had explained the situation, he said, "No collar or tag? We'd better check to see if he's chipped."

"Chipped? I don't know what that means." Tory was standing beside the counter in her little kitchen, a cup of coffee in her hand. The dog lay on the rug in front of the fireplace, his eyes following her, his ears twitching at the sound of her voice.

"It's a microchip, usually inserted in the skin at the back of the neck. If it's there, it will tell us who owns the dog."

"Oh." Tory turned to face the back wall, not wanting to look at the dog—who might belong to someone, who might need to be restored to his rightful owner, his proper place. She tried to achieve a matter-of-fact tone. "I understand," she said. "I have an appointment this morning, but I'll bring him in after that, if that's all right."

"Oh, sure," he said. "We're not busy yet. We've just opened our doors this month."

"It will be about ten, I think. Maybe ten-thirty."

He chuckled. It was a nice sound, baritone-deep, resonant. "Walk-ins welcome," he said cheerfully. "Like a barbershop. See you then."

Tory drew a deliberate breath, closing her eyes for a moment to pull herself together. The dog wasn't hers, after all. Someone was probably desperate to find him, and she had to do the right thing.

She opened her eyes to find that the dog had come to sit in front of her, tongue lolling, ears pricked forward. She crouched down to stroke his smooth head, and his tongue lapped at her cheek. It felt warm and dry and slightly prickly.

"Clearly," she said to the dog in a husky voice, "I've been alone too long." The dog put his head to one side, watching her. "Breakfast?" she said, and he stood up, ears turned forward, tail wagging.

The night before she had fed him hamburger. He had drunk all of the bowl of water, and after she refilled it, drunk even more. The liquid sound of his eager lapping had been oddly satisfying. He ate all the hamburger, and when he was done, he flopped down on the rug with a sigh she interpreted as relief. This morning she gave him scrambled eggs, which seemed to suit him just as well as the hamburger. He made a circuit of the yard while she watched, a little anxiously. He seemed to have no inclination to leave, and he already looked significantly stronger than he had the night before. When she opened the door, he was right at her heels, eager to follow her back inside. He drank more water, then sat down in front of the door as if he was worried she might go somewhere without him.

She checked her appearance in the small mirror in her bathroom. She supposed she might have to buy some clothes, but for now the black Costco sweater and jeans and sneakers would have to do. The no-cosmetics look seemed to fit Cannon Beach just fine, as did the flame-red hair dye. She ran her fingers through her hair to fluff it, dipped her little finger into a jar of petroleum jelly and smoothed some on her lips, and she was ready.

She went back into the bedroom for her black coat. It looked really dilapidated now, the down shifted here and there to make lumps in strange places, but there wasn't much she could do about it. She paused for a moment, as she often did, beside the bureau where the file lurked in the bottom drawer. It was no wonder she had bad dreams. The file lay there like a monster hiding under the bed, waiting to pounce the moment she made a mistake. Another mistake, that is. It reminded her of all that was wrong, the mess she had created and that now she didn't know how to fix.

Jack. Son. Be safe.

She drew a deliberate breath, turned away from the bureau, and marched out of the bedroom toward the front door. As she reached it, the dog rose, tail waving, ears lifted. The sight of him moved something in her, softened her despite her resolve. She stroked him, and wondered, as she shouldered her handbag, if she was making things worse for herself. Ice Woman was impervious. This dog-patting, vet-visiting person was vulnerable.

She meant for the dog, big as he was, to ride in the back seat of the VW. She moved the driver's seat forward and urged him in. He jumped in with an impressive flowing motion, and she said with some surprise, "Good boy." Why had she thought dogs were difficult? He was as obliging a creature as she'd ever met.

Then, as she settled herself in the driver's seat, he slid past her right arm, his feet slipping as he scrabbled over the console. It took him only seconds to arrange his big body in the cramped passenger seat. Tory opened her mouth to object, but found herself laughing instead. The laugh felt strange, as if some involuntary process had seized her, a sneeze or a shiver. She couldn't remember when she had last laughed aloud. The dog turned his head, his long tongue lolling, the corners of his mouth curling in that expression that looked exactly like a grin. When she didn't object, he faced forward, looking out the windshield in the manner of one who knew just what he was doing.

"I guess I've been missing out on the whole dog thing," Tory told him. "Jack would have something to say about that. I wish he could see you." The dog cocked his head in her direction, listening. Her heart fluttered at the strangeness of the morning as she fired the engine, backed down the short driveway, and turned toward town.

She left the dog in the car, the window open, as she went into the florist's shop. The place was easy to find, right on the main street. As she opened the door, a bell above it tinkled, and someone called out, "Don't leave! I'll be right there." Tory glanced around at the shelves and racks holding assortments of souvenirs and postcards, ornaments and stationery. She walked forward, and found herself in a bower of vegetation, poinsettias, miniature pine trees with Christmas ribbon around their pots, bunches of carnations dyed red and green, a few arrangements with candy canes or snowmen stuck into them.

The woman who emerged from the back wore a florist's apron over a long purple skirt and yellow cowboy boots. She was startlingly young, dyed black hair cropped short, a stone of some kind sparkling in one nostril, and lips painted deep red. "Hi!" she said. "I sure as hell hope you're Paulette!"

The girl's energy swept across the counter like a gust of wind. Tory had to resist the temptation to take a step back, away from the fern-and-ribbon-littered surface. "I am," she said, but she sounded unsure even to herself.

The girl stretched her arm across the cluttered counter to shake Tory's hand. Her fingernails were short and square, painted the same vivid red as her lips. "Hey," she said, grinning. The deep color of her lipstick made her teeth look faintly yellow. "I'm Zoe. God, I love your hair. Wish I could wear red like that."

Self-consciously, Tory touched her hair. "Thanks."

"Are you gonna take the job? I'm about to go under here."

Tory couldn't help glancing around at the empty shop. Zoe gave a belly laugh that belied her slender frame. "I know, you're wondering why! But I have a list of orders a mile long, and Mom won't be back until next week." At Tory's puzzled glance, Zoe said, "Mom. Betty. She and I own the shop together. And trust me, this weekend things are going to be hopping. The holiday people are coming in. Two weeks till Christmas!"

"Two weeks?"

"Oh, yeah!" the girl exclaimed. "You haven't noticed?" She opened her eyes wide. They were ringed with mascara and smudged with navy-blue eye shadow.

Tory felt pallid in the face of Zoe's vitality, but she made her lips curve in a smile. "I've been distracted. Two weeks, my goodness! But yes, I'd like to take the job."

"Great! Can you come Friday?"

"Don't you want—I mean, an interview, references . . .?"

Zoe gave her a wide scarlet grin. "Nah. Cannon Beach, you know? Iris talked to Mom, and that settled it." She swept her arm across the counter, shoving the detritus off as if she had only just noticed it, catching it all in a metal wastepaper basket.

"That's all you need, that Iris talked to your—Betty?"

Another grin. "Yep. Iris collects people, you know. And she's never wrong."

"Okay, then," Tory said awkwardly. "Friday it is. What time shall I be here?"

When she went back to the VW, she thought she couldn't have been inside the shop for more than five minutes in total. The dog was watching for her, his nose stuck through the open window, nostrils fluttering as he sniffed the breeze. She climbed into the driver's seat and sat for a moment, trying to take it all in, trying to imagine working for someone like Zoe.

"Well," she told the dog, as she turned the key in the ignition. "That's an interesting girl. I'll bet there's no color she doesn't like."

The veterinarian's office not only looked new, with the landscaping still raw around its small parking lot, but when Tory coaxed the dog into the waiting room, it smelled new, too, of plastic and tiles and paint. The dog pressed close to her legs, and she kept her hand in his ruff to reassure him.

A woman in a cotton tunic printed with cartoons of dogs and cats stood up to frown at her. "Mrs. Chambers?"

"Miss, but yes. Paulette," Tory said.

The receptionist, fortyish and sturdy, wore no more makeup than Tory, and her graying hair was pulled back into a ponytail. Her lips tightened as she peered at the dog. She gave Tory a stern look, and pointed at a sign on the front of the desk. It read, "Please leash your dog."

A flicker of irritation lent energy to Tory's voice. "I don't have a leash. He's not my dog, really. I mean, not technically."

The woman, whose name tag read SHIRLEY, came around the desk to a rack on the wall where several leashes of different lengths hung. The dog crept behind Tory and sat there, tucked against the backs of her knees. Shirley chose a leash from the rack, and a chain collar to go with it. Still without speaking, she held them out to Tory. Tory accepted them, but she couldn't figure out how the collar worked, with its metal circles and sliding chain. Shirley kept her distance, and Tory supposed she was afraid of approaching a strange dog. She turned the chain this way and that, trying to see how it was meant to go on. Behind her, a door opened, and when the vet spoke, his voice was familiar from the phone.

"Hey," he said. His voice was even deeper in person, creating a faint vibration in the glass of the windows. "This must be our found dog!"

Tory glanced over her shoulder. A tall, lean man with silver-gray hair, startling above his olive complexion, crossed the waiting room and crouched beside her. The dog put his head around Tory's legs for a cautious look at the new arrival.

"This is him," Tory said. She held up the collar in one hand, the leash dangling free from the other. "I know you prefer a leash, but I don't—"

"No problem," the vet said. He wore a crisp white coat, and his hand, when he held it out to the dog, was meticulously clean, the nails pink against his skin. "Hey, there," he said softly. He cupped his palm, and the dog took a gingerly sniff. "We just like to be careful," the vet said, evidently to Tory. "Sometimes these fellows are scared, and they don't know what to do about it. The leash is a precaution."

"I didn't have one."

"Not to worry." He held out his hand for the collar. She gave it to him, and with a deft motion, he turned it into a perfect circle that slipped easily over the dog's head. The leash was clipped in place a second later, and the vet stood. "What do you say, big guy? Shall we go have a look at you?"

He turned, lifting the leash in his hand, and walked toward one of the two examining rooms. Tory watched, bemused, as the dog—she hadn't said so, but already she thought of him as her dog, though he had no name or anything else to tie him to her— walked obediently beside the doctor and into the exam room. At the door, the tall man turned, twinkling at her. He was much younger, she saw, than his silver hair implied. "Come on in, Mom," he said cheerfully.

Tory said, with a glance at Shirley, "I guess that's me," and followed. She went into the exam room, and as she closed the door behind her, she saw Shirley standing, hands on hips, watching as if to make sure Tory obeyed orders.

The vet, crouching again beside the dog, began looking in his ears, feeling his chest, running his hand along the dog's spine. He lifted the dog's lips and examined his teeth. "I'm Hank Menotti," he said, without looking away from the dog.

"Oh—Menotti. Like the composer?"

He smiled up at her. "Most people don't get that, but yes. Like the composer. A third cousin, or something."

"I'm Paulette Chambers."

"Right. We spoke this morning. Nice to meet you in person." He listened to the dog's chest with a stethoscope. When he palpated the dog's belly, the dog gave a slight groan. "It's okay, my friend," the vet said in a reassuring tone. "It's okay. It all feels good."

Tory watched, enchanted by the gentleness of this tall man. When he stood up, he filled the little exam room, towering nearly a foot above her. "He's thin," Dr. Menotti said. "Probably hasn't been eating much."

"He wandered in from the beach. He was soaking wet and covered in sand. He seems a lot stronger this morning than he did last night."

The vet nodded. "He was probably more exhausted than sick. He might have been running on the beach for quite a while."

"But how did he get there?"

Dr. Menotti shrugged. "It's hard to say. It could be he wandered away from one of the vacation homes, or jumped out of a car when someone stopped in town. I'll get the scanner. Just wait here a moment."

He went out through a back door. Tory sat down on a padded bench that filled one corner of the room, and the dog thrust his head into her lap. She fondled his ears. He pushed closer with a slight, anxious whimper, and she bent to press her cheek to his silky head. It felt so good to feel close to another living being that for the second time that day, her heart fluttered. "I know," she whispered. "I don't want to think about it, either."

Ice Woman was definitely melting. She wondered if the process could be reversed.

The vet came back, and Tory sat up, embarrassed to be found hugging a stray dog. Dr. Menotti said, nodding toward the dog, "Kind of a sweet guy, isn't he?"

"I think so. I don't know much about dogs."

"Really? You two have hit it off, though. That's nice." He came to crouch beside the dog again. He had a white plastic instrument in his hand, and he held it up to the back of the dog's neck. Tory could just see the little screen, upside down, flicker with numbers. The vet sat back on his haunches, and turned the scanner so she could see it right side up. "There's a chip there, all right," he said.

"Oh," was all Tory could say. She found she was gripping the dog's fur, and she made her fingers relax. "Oh, I see."

The vet was watching her. "You were hoping there wouldn't be."

"No, no, I—I just—Oh, it's silly. But I sort of like this dog."

"And he likes you, obviously." He stood up, unfolding his long thin frame with surprising ease. "We'll call the microchip company, see what turns up."

Tory came to her feet, too, but she kept her gaze on the dog. "Okay," she managed to say. The dog pressed close to her again, as if he sensed her emotions.

Dr. Menotti spoke as gently to Tory as he had to the dog. "In the meantime, he might as well stay with you, if you're willing. I can't see anything wrong with him, and there's no point in sending him to the shelter if we don't have to."

Tory nodded. "Yes, please do leave him with me. If you'll just tell me what he should eat, what I need to do . . ."

"We'll send some dog food home with you, and now you have a leash and collar. Otherwise—" He paused, and she looked up at him. He was watching her closely, and she felt her cheeks warm. "You're doing just fine, Ms. Chambers. The dog is in good hands."

"Paulette," she said.

"Paulette. Call me Hank." He smiled. "You and your friend here are almost my first patients in Cannon Beach. I'll give you a call tomorrow, if you'll leave your telephone number with Shirley."

At the reception desk, Tory brought out her wallet as Shirley began adding up the cost of the collar, the leash, the food, and the office visit. Hank Menotti said, "No, Shirley. Let's wait until we see if we find the owner. Whoever that is should pay this bill, not Ms. Chambers."

Shirley acquiesced, but she scowled as she said, "I'll keep the bill in a file."

Tory said, "Thank you, Shirley." Then, prompted by some mischievous instinct, she turned and put out her hand to the vet. "And thanks, Hank," she said, with a deliberate emphasis on the first name. She saw by the twitch of his lips that he understood. He shook her hand, nodded to the disapproving Shirley, and disappeared back into the exam room.

Tory gave Shirley a pointed smile as she led the dog out of the office.

*   *   *

As the early sunset glimmered over the ocean, Tory took the dog out on the beach for a run. She left the chain collar on, as that seemed to make people more comfortable, but she didn't bother with the leash. If he wanted to leave, he would leave. She didn't think he would. He waited for her as she locked the front door, and then as she unlatched the little gate. Not until they reached the beach did he start to run, chasing up and down the packed sand, his tail up and his tongue flying from his open mouth like a limp pink flag.

Tory trudged along the sand. It was really the first moment she had been able to ponder her dream of the night before. Caused by the dog's arrival, perhaps?

The dog seemed to have a limit to how far he wanted to be from her. He ran in front and then behind, but never more than a couple hundred yards away. A cold breeze sprang up as the sun dropped below the water, and Tory pulled her knit cap down over her forehead, tucking the strands of her hair underneath it. The dog frolicked at her side, then raced in circles around her on the wet sand. They must look so ordinary, a woman and her dog having a romp on the beach before dinner. She wished it was true. She wished with all her being that when she went back to the cottage, she could find Jack there, his big sneakers up on the little coffee table, playing a video game or texting his friends. He would be so pleased about the dog. She wouldn't care if he didn't say much. Just knowing he was there would be enough.

But that was fantasy. Jack thought she was dead. And the dog belonged to someone else.

She had been gone for two months. Jack would have started to adjust to her loss, just as she had adjusted to the loss of her grandmother, her mother, and later her father. She supposed she was beginning to adjust, too, to come to terms with the realization that she would never see her son again. It would mean never feeling whole, never feeling complete, but she had only herself to blame. The file lying in her drawer—and the threat it represented—held power over both of them.

The swift darkness encroached upon the beach, swallowing the big rock and the low dunes with their spears of marsh grass. A few lights glowed here and there through the dusk, but the holiday renters hadn't come in force yet. Scattered stars pricked the marine layer of cloud, but gave no illumination. Tory called, "Hey, dog! Let's go get our dinner!"

The dog, evidently untroubled by his lack of a name, bounded toward her, tongue and tail flying, and trotted by her side as she made her way up the dark beach toward the house.

Her step faltered when she saw the strange car outside the cottage. In the darkness, it was hard to tell the make, but it was an SUV of some kind, dark and boxy. It loomed behind the yellow Beetle. Tory had left the kitchen light on in the cottage, but the yard was dark. She approached the gate warily, the dog close at her heels.

When the door to the SUV opened, the interior light went on, and she saw who her visitor was. "Oh!" she said, relieved. "Dr. Menotti."

He smiled at her as he swung his long legs out of the car. The dog dashed ahead of Tory to sniff at the vet's shoes, then wind against him to be petted. Hank said, "I thought I'd come and give you the news in person."

Instantly, Tory's heart sank. Of course. He had found the dog's owner.

She tried to smile at him as she opened the gate, led the way up to the front door, and fished out her key. Her hand, she saw with dismay, was trembling, and she blinked to stop the stinging of her eyes.

It was ridiculous, of course, that she should cry about a dog. She who hadn't shed a single tear in all these weeks—over the loss of her son, her home, her livelihood—she could cry over a dog that wasn't even hers, a dog she had met only yesterday. It was textbook therapy material.

17

꧁꧂

Ah! quella donna, mi fa tanta paura!

Ah! that woman frightens me so!

—Butterfly, *Madama Butterfly*, Act Three

Night had fallen over the wooded hills by the time Jack drove the Escalade back from town, past Tory's tidy mailbox, and up the long driveway. The house ahead was dark. The mail—what there was of it—rested in a pile on the passenger seat. He had taken a box at the post office, and directed all mail to be delivered there. It was an instinctive decision, and he hadn't told Chet or Kate about it. He hadn't told anyone except the manager of the post office, an incurious sort who asked no questions.

The mail looked to be mostly Christmas cards, a few circulars, one or two bills. Jack still felt nervous when he saw the bills. Kate had helped him sort things out, just as Chet had promised, but the Lake finances were in a precarious limbo—no income without Tory's practice, but no life insurance until the death declaration was official. She had enough in savings to cover the mortgage and utilities for a few months, but after that he would really need the insurance.

That bothered him, and left him staring at the stack of bills with a sick feeling. If he took the life insurance, it was like giving up on her. It didn't feel right, but he didn't know what he could do. His school was expecting him back in mid-January, but how could he go back to classes, go back to college life, with his mother out there somewhere, possibly alone and afraid?

He'd tried to keep himself busy. Since Thanksgiving he had spent every day working around the place, preparing Tory's garden for winter, repairing anything he could find that was broken, keeping the house and the kitchen clean. Well, except for his bedroom. The clutter and mess there comforted him, made him feel less as if everything in his life had changed. Chet and Kate thought he was being mature and responsible. He didn't tell them that he was keeping the house ready for Tory's return. He didn't want to see that pitying look they would bend on him, the secret worried glance they would exchange.

When Kate said she was sure the death declaration would come in January, so he could collect the life insurance, he kept his head down so she wouldn't see the expression on his face. She no doubt thought that was grief.

It wasn't. It was anger. Not at Kate, but at whoever, or whatever, had driven his mother away from her home.

He pulled the car into the garage, carefully turning off the motor before he pushed the button to close the door. He gathered up the little stack of mail and the bag of groceries, and went in through the door to the kitchen. He flicked on the light, then stood, thunderstruck.

The kitchen—Tory's beautiful kitchen—lay in ruins. Drawers had been pulled out, their contents strewn across the floor. The pot rack with its expensive Le Creuset cookware had been ripped out of the ceiling to crash on to the glass-topped stove beneath it. Cupboard doors had been wrenched from their hinges, and the china and glassware swept out to smash on the tiled floor. The pantry door stood open, and Jack could see from where he stood that everything on the shelves had been dumped on the floor, packages opened and emptied. Flour and sugar and coffee and pasta lay in mounds on the floor, and someone had kicked through them, leaving trails of black coffee grounds, white crystals, and crushed macaroni, all leading to the litter of glass and porcelain in the center of the kitchen.

Jack stared at the mess. An icy feeling of dread crept up the back of his legs and into the base of his spine. He took one shallow breath before he crossed the kitchen, sneakers crunching on the mess, to peek into the office. He knew, by the cold breeze that chilled his face, what he would find there.

The sliding glass door to Tory's office lay in great transparent shards across the carpet. Her desk drawers were all pulled out, papers and pens and paper clips spilled everywhere. The file cabinet, too, had been opened, but had been empty, all the client files removed. Tory's private filing cabinet was also open, the files tossed this way and that. It looked as if the pictures had been thrown at the wall, and the standing lamp pushed over.

Someone was looking for something, no doubt, as with the mail. But someone was also angry. Furious. You didn't have to be a therapist, Jack thought, to see it. There was so much unnecessary destruction. It was excessive, melodramatic. It was as if someone had indulged in a giant temper tantrum.

As he turned, with glass crunching underfoot, he heard something else, some faint bump or creak. He froze, listening. He felt like a deer caught in headlights, not knowing which way to jump. The sound—if sound it had been—didn't come again, but Jack's nervous system was screaming alarms now. He seized the phone from Tory's desk, and punched 9-1-1 at the same time he strode toward the living room.

"Nine-one-one. What is your emergency?" The woman's voice sounded slightly bored, and Jack, staring at the wreckage of the sound system and the bookcases in the living room, could barely speak.

"I—someone has—there's been a break-in," he finally said. The word seemed meaningless as he spoke it, a word meant for broken windows or jimmied door locks, stolen computers or television sets. The devastation around him was so thorough, and so hateful, that he didn't think he knew the right word to describe it.

They exchanged a few words, he and the 911 dispatcher. Someone, she told him, was on the way. Jack stood at the bottom of the staircase, surrounded by the ruins of his mother's house, and dialed the Binghams' number. There was no answer. He left a terse message, trying to sound as calm as he could, but asking for Chet's help.

He heard the siren coming up the hill from town, and he crossed the mess of the living room to open the front door. The revolving lights on the patrol car flashed through the bare limbs of the trees, ghost lights in red and blue. The siren grew louder and louder as the car turned into the driveway and raced up the hill. When the patrol car stopped, gravel sprayed over the lawn. The siren ceased with a loud chirp, but the lights still spun, red, blue, red, blue, casting garish reflections across the dark windows of the house.

It seemed inevitable that the officer who climbed out of the patrol car was Ellice Gordon. The tingle in Jack's skull began the moment he saw her pacing toward him, carrying an enormous flashlight, its light dancing across the dark grass. He watched her come, his pulse pounding at the base of his throat. He had to force himself to stand where he was, to stand as tall as he could.

"Officer," he said, when she was close enough. He wished Chet had been home when he called. And he wished the sheriff's office had sent any other deputy but this one.

"Hi, Jack," she said. The look she turned up to him was unreadable. Her hair was so short beneath her sheriff's cap that in the darkness he could not have distinguished the color. She came up on the porch, and he remembered how tall she was. "You told the dispatcher you had a break-in?"

Wordlessly, he pushed the front door open, and stood aside for her to go in. He followed, and flicked on the overhead light. It was a chandelier, with five small bulbs around a large central one, and its light threw the whole mess into sharp focus.

The deputy whistled, a long, low sound. Beside her, Jack surveyed the wreckage afresh, and his skin began to burn with fury.

Ellice Gordon said, "Any idea who would want to do this?"

Jack blurted, without thinking, "Are you kidding? Whoever did this is out of his mind! I don't know people like that!"

The deputy turned her head slowly, looking down at him. Her pale eyes had a flat look to them, as if no light reflected from her irises. He felt caught by her gaze, like a rodent mesmerized by a snake. "Tell me what happened," she said. Her voice was flat, too, unemotional.

"I don't know what happened. I was downtown this afternoon, picking up—doing some errands, groceries, that sort of thing. When I came home—" He gestured with his hand, and saw that it was shaking.

She saw it, too. "No need to be frightened, Jack. Not now."

His jaw began to ache. He said through gritted teeth, "I'm not scared. I'm pissed."

She nodded. "Sure you are. I would be, too." She flicked off her flashlight. She walked forward to the kitchen door, where glass and porcelain bits sparkled in the light. She glanced toward the office, taking in the smashed glass door. "You found a way to lock it, I see," she said in an offhand fashion.

"Yeah. Didn't do much good."

She turned toward the staircase. "Any damage upstairs?"

"I haven't been up there. I—" He was going to tell her he thought he had heard a noise, but now he didn't want to say it. It made him sound like a scared kid. "I just thought I should call you guys first."

"Smart. I'll go up and have a look, if that's okay."

"Sure. Yeah." Jack stayed close behind her as she climbed, her long legs taking the stairs two a time. He wondered if she'd been upstairs before, if Tory had invited her up, or sent her up after a session. There was no reason for that he could think of. If clients needed a bathroom, they used the powder room off the office. The deputy seemed to know where she was going, though, passing his room with a cursory glance, pressing on toward the doorway of his mother's bedroom.

She stood there, turning the flashlight in her fingers. He

looked past her shoulder. Nothing was broken here. At first glance, in fact, it looked undisturbed, as if whatever maelstrom had hit the downstairs had not reached to the second floor. "He didn't bother up here, I guess," Ellice Gordon said.

"I guess," Jack said.

"So, it looks the same to you as when your mother disappeared?"

"Yeah, I think so."

The deputy took a last look at the bedroom, then turned away and started downstairs. She pressed a button on her shoulder radio and started talking to someone.

Jack was about to follow her, but first he took a closer look at Tory's bedroom. He'd been trying to keep things clean here, but he wasn't the greatest duster. In fact, he'd told himself to get in here with a cloth and polish her bureau, the marble top of her bedside stand, the curtain rods and windowsills. There had been dust on the surfaces, and there still was. There were tracks in it, though. And there was a smudge on the mirror, one he could see even from the doorway.

"Hey, Jack," the deputy said from the bottom of the stairs.

His head buzzed now so he could barely hear her. He turned and looked down.

"You shouldn't stay here alone," she said.

Was it a warning, or a threat? He didn't like it, either way. He said, "I'm not going to leave the house empty. Especially now."

"He could come back," she said. Was it his imagination, or did her hand twitch above the gun in its holster at her hip?

"Yeah. But I'm not going."

Her eyes narrowed slightly, but she made a gesture that seemed to say, "Up to you." "You need to go through the mess, see if you can figure out if anything's missing."

"I will."

"We'll make a report for your insurance company. You'll get an incident number."

"Aren't you going to—I don't know, check for fingerprints or something?"

Her smile was patronizing and dismissive at the same time. "It's not like on TV, I'm afraid," she said. "Unless someone's hurt, you know—or there's a really big theft—we don't do that. Actually," she added, shrugging, "we'll probably never get this guy. It's too bad, but it's the way it is."

That didn't sound right to Jack, but he didn't know how to press her. He also didn't know who the insurance company was, but he figured he could find it, somewhere in the trashed office. Kate would help—again. And Chet would help him repair the door.

They would want him to come and stay with them, of course, and it was tempting. It would be great to sleep one night without jumping at every creak the house made. His mother would want him to go to the Binghams'.

He wouldn't do it, though. He'd be damned if he'd give in to whoever did this, whoever was watching his mail, spying on his house. He stood in the front doorway, watching the deputy back and turn her patrol car. He didn't move until her taillights disappeared down the slope.

When he was alone again, Jack turned on the outside lights, and went out into the cold to the garden shed. There was a hatchet there, on the wall next to Tory's array of other tools—pliers, loppers, a shovel and a rake, a saw, a hoe, various trowels and hammers and wrenches.

He paused a moment, remembering how deft she was with all these things, how competently she had built raised boxes, repaired broken steps, cultivated her garden. Why had it irritated him so? It wasn't as if she had a choice. There was no one else to do those things for her. It would have been nice, he thought wryly, to have her able hands here now, to help him sweep up broken glass, sift through shards of porcelain and pottery for anything worth saving, and figure out whether it was possible to put the house to rights again.

He sighed, took down the hatchet, turned off the light in the shed, and went into the house through the shattered glass door. All he could do for tonight was to lock the office from the kitchen side to keep the heat in. He had brought a frozen pizza from the grocery store, and he could bake that, then close up the kitchen, too, and isolate the living room with its intact windows and un-broken door. Sleep, he was sure, was not going to come tonight.

All of Tory's pretty china was ruined. From the jumble of kitchen things he dug up a paper plate that wasn't covered in flour or fragments of glass, and put the pizza on that. He carried it into the living room, the hatchet under one arm, and arranged himself on the couch with the pizza on the coffee table, the hatchet next to it. Before he ate, he went back to the office for the baseball bat, still lodged firmly in the track of the sliding door, and for the phone. He brought them back with him to the living room, locking the office behind him.

He didn't turn on the television, or play music. He concentrated on listening, on watching the driveway for any movement. He ate his pizza, and drank a soda. At eleven, he turned out all the lights, pulled a knitted afghan over his legs, and sat in dark-ness in the crook of the couch.

He had expected to be nervous through the long hours of the winter night. Instead, strangely, he found himself thoughtful, re-membering things he usually tried to put out of his mind. He thought of Tory's face the day he had left for college, the deter-mined smile as she waved good-bye, the proud, pained set of her shoulders as she turned back to her car, alone.

He had wanted, suddenly, to jump out of the train car and call to her, to tell her—what? There were no words. He was an eighteen-year-old guy who had been mean to his mother for years, and he didn't know why.

He was mean to all women, in fact. He never meant to be. He often liked a girl very much—at first. But one date, or two, at most three—just about the time the girls began to think there was something special between them—his liking would change to restiveness, to resentment, to chafing against their expecta-tions. He couldn't understand it, but he thought it was some-thing about restriction. About interference. Or control.

He had felt that way about Tory. It wasn't fair, and it wasn't—

it wasn't real, he thought now. It was superficial, but he hadn't known what to do about it. It was all mixed up with the Garveys, with the contrast between their family life and his own. It was all mixed up with wondering about his father, then being ashamed of him. There was something beyond that, though, something he couldn't put his finger on. And now, this sheriff's deputy—all of his unease about women seemed to focus on her, seemed to be concentrated in her.

Who the hell was she? Why did he dislike her with such intensity?

Find Mom, he thought. *I need to find Mom. I can't move forward until I do.*

In the stillness, drowsiness began to overtake him. He let his head fall back against the couch cushions, and his eyelids drooped. Whatever the intruder had been looking for, it seemed clear he hadn't found it. That was why the destruction was so devastating. Whatever it was wasn't in the house, and the intruder had indulged in a spasm of anger and resentment.

Jack settled further into sleep, weary of trying to parse it all. *Just send me a clue, Mom. One hint. I'll come for you, I promise—if you could just—*

Just what? She must have a reason for staying out of sight, for letting everyone—even her son—think she was dead. She never did anything without cause. It was one of the most impressive things about her, that everything she did was planned, organized, well thought out. She must have a reason for this, too, a damned good one. He wished he knew what it was.

18

Forse la perla è già trovata?

Perhaps this pearl has already been found?

—Rance, *La Fanciulla del West,* Act One

"You must have news for me." Tory pushed the door open, and Hank Menotti followed her into the cottage. The dog went straight to the kitchen and stood waiting beside the stove, his flag of a tail waving, the corners of his mouth turned up in his canine smile.

"I see he's made himself at home," Hank said.

Tory made herself speak as casually as she could. "Yes, he seems to be comfortable."

"That's good. The thing is, the microchip company can't reach the dog's owners."

A little rush of hope spurted through Tory's breast. Impulsively, she said, "I want to hear about it, Hank. Can I offer you a drink? I only have red wine, I'm afraid."

"I'm Italian," he said, with a deep laugh. "I love red wine."

She brought out the two vintage glasses she'd gotten at the antiques store, and pulled a bottle of wine from the cupboard. Hank reached to take it from her, and when she took the corkscrew from a drawer, he held out his hand for that, too. For an awkward moment she was dumbstruck at the simple, chivalrous action of a man opening a bottle of wine for a woman.

She blew out a breath to settle herself, and he gave her a questioning look. "Are you okay? Were you worried?"

She took the glass he poured for her, and gestured for him to follow her into the living room. She had laid a fire earlier, and now she put a match to it. When it was burning, she took the armchair, and he sat on the couch, arranging his long legs beside the little table. She said, "I thought, when I saw you in the driveway, that you must have found the dog's owners."

The dog, giving up hope of food for the moment, settled himself beside her chair, his chin over her right foot. Hank looked down at him, and smiled. "No," he said. "The number they had is out of service, they tell me. I learned a bit about him, though."

"Did you?"

"Yes. Mixed breed, as we thought. Golden retriever and one of the big terriers, I'd guess—Airedale or wheaten, something like that. Neutered, which we knew. He's four years old."

"Are they still looking for the owners?" Tory reached down to stroke the dog's head. It had become, already, an automatic gesture.

"Unless the owners think to contact them, probably not. The company looked up the address, and there's someone else living there now."

"It's just strange that he would end up here, all on his own."

"Things happen. Dogs can get confused when they're staying in a rental house or a motel. Sometimes—although I hate to say it—their owners abandon them. Leave them along the road, so they don't know how to get home."

"That's awful. Surely no one would leave a nice dog like this one."

"He does seem like a good guy," Hank said. "He certainly likes you."

"Well, I saved him, I guess." Tory's cheeks warmed. "I've never had a dog before. I don't really know how to—well, how to do anything!"

"You're doing great. And at least we know his name now."

"That would be good! I didn't want to choose a name until I knew what would happen. I keep calling him Dog."

Hank said, "They named him Johnson."

The dog lifted his head, cocking it to one side and fixing Hank with a puzzled gaze.

Tory said, "Johnson? How odd."

"You wouldn't believe what some people name their pets."

"It's not that." Tory put her wineglass down, and eased her foot out from under the dog's head so she could get up and go to the counter where she had put a small plastic bag. She drew out three CDs. "I found these at the library's used-book sale," she said, holding them up. They were all operas, Mozart and Verdi and Puccini. She slid the Puccini out of the pile. "It's *Fanciulla del West*," she said.

Hank leaned back on the small sofa, crossing one leg over the other. "Now that *is* odd," he said. "Dick Johnson, if I remember correctly."

"Exactly. The hero. Minnie's lover." Tory laid the case aside, and came back to sit down in the armchair once again. She bent over the dog and lifted his chin on her hand. "Is your name really Johnson? Do you like it?"

The dog's tail beat against the floor. When she released him, he put his head over her foot again. It was possessive, in a way, but it was also comforting.

"Nice," Hank said, smiling down at the dog. His eyes were very dark, gleaming with firelight. "One of the things I love about dogs—some dogs, anyway—is their empathy."

Tory patted the dog again. "Johnson," she mused. "It's so— prosaic, I guess."

"Apparently Puccini didn't think so." Hank chuckled, then held up his empty glass. "Mind if I have another?"

"Please do. Help yourself." As he rose and moved back toward the kitchen, she said, "You know, Puccini didn't choose the name. It was from the Belasco play. I remember reading that Puccini didn't like any of the names—he thought they were ugly. Unmusical. Especially Minnie."

"You're an opera buff." Hank sank back onto the couch. "Me too." His height made the small couch look ridiculous. Having company, in fact, made Tory uncomfortably aware of how shabby the cottage was. She thought of her own beautifully appointed living room, her shining kitchen with its glass-fronted cabinets full of china and crystal, and felt a twinge of nostalgia.

Distracted by it, she said, "I love opera. A little too much, my son would say—" She very nearly clapped her hand over her mouth when she realized what she'd said. She fumbled for her wineglass to cover her confusion, and it went flying, spilling what was left in it over the braided rug. "Oh, damn!" she exclaimed, jumping up. She hurried to grab a wet towel from the kitchen. When she got back, Hank took the towel and crouched above the rug, first soaking up the wine, then scrubbing at places where small stains showed. In moments, there was nothing but dampness to show where wine had spilled.

"You need a fresh glass," he said, smiling up at her.

Her cheeks burned, but she nodded. "So clumsy," she said. "I'm embarrassed."

"Don't be." He picked up the dropped glass, got to his feet, and went to wipe it clean and refill it. From the kitchen, he said, "You were telling me about your son?"

Tory clenched her hands together in her lap, chagrined at her slip. She had managed, all these weeks, to tell no one anything about her private life. Even Iris had ceased asking her. And now, this strange, tall man had come into her house and she had blurted out the very secret she needed to keep.

He came back, and handed over the wineglass. She said, striving for a casual tone, "He's grown now," as if that meant there was nothing to say.

"You don't look old enough to have a grown son."

She couldn't meet his eyes. She let her gaze drift to the paperweight, still resting where Iris had left it on the coffee table. It didn't help. Looking at it only reminded her of her dreams. A silence stretched, broken only by the dog—Johnson—yawning, turning on his side to lie flat on the rug. She wanted to say something, to fill the void, but she couldn't think of anything safe.

"Well," Hank said at last. "It's getting late. I'd better go."

Tory knew she had been rude. She hadn't asked him anything about himself, about his life or his family. She said awkwardly, "It was so nice of you to come and tell me."

"Thanks for the wine." He rose, unfolding his long frame with some difficulty from the little sofa.

"Do I—do I just keep him, then? Johnson?" She rose, too, and the dog lifted his head to watch them both.

"That's up to you," he said. The look on his face had changed, and she was afraid she had offended him. "Otherwise he'll have to go to the shelter. They'll try to adopt him out, but—"

"No," she said hastily. "Oh, no, I'd love to keep him. He seems to like it here."

"Yes, I would say he likes it here." They both looked back at Johnson, who had put his head down on his paws. Hank pulled on his coat as he walked to the door. "Let me know if you need anything for him," he said as he put his hand on the doorknob.

"I will. I—" Tory wanted to say something else. She felt tongue-tied, fearful of offending this nice man, but more fearful of saying something to give herself away. "I really appreciate it," she finished, knowing it wasn't enough, wishing she could manage more.

He nodded. "Right. Good night, then."

"Good night, Hank."

Tory stood by the window, watching the SUV back out of the short driveway. She waited until it was gone before she pulled the curtains, as if that would erase the inadequacy of her conversation. The little house seemed emptier than ever when she was alone again. She picked up the wineglasses and carried them to the sink. Her own was still half full, but she poured it out. She scooped up dog food from the bag the reluctant Shirley had given her, and filled the dog dish. Johnson jumped up at the rattle of kibble in the dish, and padded into the kitchen.

Tory watched him munching for a moment, but she was thinking about Hank. In all the years since her marriage had ended, there had been no men in her life. Kate had tried, once or twice, to introduce her to someone, but Tory had been busy with her practice, with raising Jack, with keeping up her house. As Kate had said, with a shake of the head, she was naturally solitary. But this—this utter emptiness—it was all but unbearable. Everyone she loved thought she was dead, and in a way, she *felt* as if she had died. As if the Tory Lake she had always been was gone, buried, truly vanished.

Who would Paulette Chambers be? Was there ever to be any happiness for her? Or, failing happiness, peace?

Johnson went to sit by the front door, and Tory guessed he needed to go out. She pulled on her bedraggled jacket, and the two of them went out again, side by side. They crossed the road to go down to the dark beach, where Tory stood shivering inside her jacket, waiting as the dog sniffed the sand and lifted his leg on pieces of driftwood. More lights shone now from the houses up and down the beach, people arriving for their Christmas holidays. As she and Johnson went back through the gate, the light from the cottage's windows seemed muted, cooler than the lights in other people's houses. Tory paused for a moment, looking at it. She knew it was her imagination, but that didn't alter the impression.

"How did it get to be this way, Johnson?" she asked aloud. He wagged his tail and panted. "Right," she told him. "It just happened. It's not fair, though." His ears turned toward her. "This is why lonely people have dogs," she said. "So they're not talking just to themselves." He grinned at her, and she tugged at his ears. "I'm glad they couldn't find your people," she whispered as she opened the front door. "I know it's selfish, but I don't care. It's the best thing that's happened to me in quite a while."

She hung up her coat, then added a small log to the fireplace. She stood in front of it, thinking, watching the flames begin to flicker around the new piece of wood. Johnson flopped onto the rug again. Silence filled the cottage, broken only by the crackle of the fire and Johnson's occasional sigh.

Tory went into her bedroom to find the CD player Iris had given her. She carried it out, and set it beneath the lamp, where the cord could reach the outlet. She took the Mozart CD—*Don Giovanni*, with Octavia Voss singing Donna Anna—and put it into the machine. The familiar overture began. She leaned against the fireplace, listening for several moments, thinking how much like an opera her life had become. When Donna Anna began to rail at Don Giovanni in the first act, Tory suddenly straightened, and went back to her bedroom.

She opened the bottom drawer of the bureau, and took out the file that had lain untouched for two months. She carried it back to the fireplace, her heart thudding with the urgency of her wish to wipe it out, to make it go away. She moved the screen, and knelt in front of the fire, the folder in both hands. Her heart raced even faster as she held it out to the flames, an offering to whatever power there might be that could remove the story of Ellice Gordon from her conscience forever.

The corners of the folder had just begun to char when she snatched the file back, and pressed the sparks from the cardboard. She sat back on her heels, her mouth dry, the pounding of her heart beginning to ease. The dog was sitting up now, watching her, as she laid the folder to one side, and replaced the fire screen.

She stood up, retrieving the folder from the floor. She sat on the sofa, and opened the file on the little table, moving the paperweight to one side to make room. Ellice Gordon's statistics— birth date, occupation, marital status, health insurance—were on an evaluation sheet stapled to the inside front of the folder, and her own notes, pages of lined paper, were clipped opposite, neatly dated, the most recent on top. She smoothed them with her hand, but she didn't read them. There was no need.

The CD stopped after the first act of the opera. In the silence, Tory closed her eyes, one hand on her own notes, the other pressed to her heart. Ellice had trapped her, cornered her with the deft cruelty, the merciless determination of a sociopath. She should have known, should have seen. Should have reported her before she could act on her fantasy. Before she killed a man who was, as far as she knew, innocent of any wrongdoing. Before she could threaten Jack.

Jack. Oh, God.

Tory's eyes flew open, and she leaped up to dash across the living room to the kitchen. Johnson leaped up, too, sensing some sort of crisis. Tory groped through her bag for her cell phone. She held it in her hand, staring at it, and then she dialed.

She didn't stop to think about what time it was in the east. She didn't even know what time it was here, in her lonely cottage on the Oregon coast. She only knew that she had to hear his voice. She couldn't bear not knowing. She couldn't bear it for another moment.

Jack jumped when he heard his phone ring. He couldn't think where he was, why he was asleep sitting up instead of in his bed—and then he remembered. The house was cold and dark around him, and when he pushed the afghan off his legs, the hatchet slid off the couch and clattered on the floor.

Jack, half asleep, staggered toward the kitchen, where he had left his cell phone in the tray where they always kept keys and pencils and pens, the flotsam of daily life. Beneath his sneakers, the sound of broken glass and the sharp fragments of shattered china brought him fully awake.

The phone had rung four times already. On the fifth it would go to voice mail. It wouldn't matter, really, except . . . something made him hurry, made him lunge across the darkened kitchen to seize it and push the button. He was still leaning across the granite counter, his belly pressing against its sharp edge.

"Hello?"

The hiss of an open line greeted him.

He said again, his voice scratchy with sleep, "Hello? Who's

there?" There was no answer except a gentle click, the sound of the connection being broken.

He tried again just the same. "Hello?" And then, softly, hopefully, "Mom?" But the line was dead.

He crunched across the floor to turn on the light. He had to squint against the sudden glare as he looked at the phone for the number that had called him. 503. Where was that prefix? He didn't think he'd ever seen it before.

He could just redial, but that didn't seem like a good idea. It could be whoever had trashed the house. Or it could just be a wrong number, the simplest explanation. Everyone got wrong numbers from time to time. It was rude for the person—especially at one in the morning—not to apologize, but if the caller was embarrassed at the mistake, or just thoughtless, it could be—

Jack dropped the phone into his pocket and hurried upstairs to his computer, turning on every light along the way. He did a reverse phone search: 503 was in Oregon. The number, though, wouldn't come up, and an advisory at the bottom of the page told him it was probably a prepaid cell phone. For a fee, he could find out where it had been sold. It would be a start.

He pulled the phone out and looked again, then wrote the number down on a sticky note. He pressed the note onto the edge of the computer keyboard, then got up, slowly, to make his way back downstairs.

It was one-thirty. He couldn't call the Binghams before seven at the earliest, or maybe eight. He was wide-awake now. In fact, he felt jittery and dry-mouthed, as if he'd just drunk a double espresso. The pizza he'd eaten churned in his stomach. He went out to the garage refrigerator for a soda, and on the way back he picked up the push broom and dustpan. Might as well get to work on the mess. There would be no more sleep tonight.

Tory held the phone in her trembling hand after hanging up on her son. He had sounded sleepy. With a stab of compunction, she saw that it was after ten, meaning it was after one at home. Was he home? Was he at school? She had no way of knowing.

But he was okay. He had answered his phone, and he was okay. She dropped to her knees, buried her face in Johnson's soft fur, and wept. She sobbed aloud, with all the drama of a diva's theatrical weeping. She cried for a long time, and Johnson lay still, supporting her, waiting for her. When at last she stopped, the dog lifted his head to lick at her tears.

19

❦

Sì, tutto in un istante io vedo il fallo mio. . . .

Yes, all in one moment I see my wrongdoing. . . .

—Pinkerton, *Madama Butterfly*, Act Three

Tory opened her eyes, not sure for a moment where she was. She was shivering with cold, the chill of midnight, with the wintry ocean air seeping through the shutters and glass of the picture window. She had fallen asleep on the little sofa, and when she sat up, pain shot through her neck and shoulders, forcing her to full wakefulness.

Johnson lay at her feet. He lifted his head and regarded her solemnly, his eyes shining faintly in the darkness. Tory remembered crying herself to sleep against his silky fur, then, for some reason, curling up on the sofa. The file still lay on the coffee table, and the paperweight rested precariously at the edge. The gold butterfly was invisible in the darkness.

Tory knew she should go to bed. She had promised to be at the flower shop in the morning. Perversely, she wanted to stay where she was, thinking of hearing Jack's voice, contemplating the almost-destruction of Ellice's file. She padded into the bedroom and got the zippered sweatshirt and the extra blanket from the foot of her bed. She put a fresh log on the fire, and stirred the embers until it began to burn. She opened the shutters, despite the cold, so she could see the dark ocean beyond the window, and then she went back to the sofa. She collected the pages of the file and slid them back inside. She tucked the blanket around her feet, and curled up on the sofa again. Johnson sighed, and put his head on his paws. Tory gazed at the water for several moments before she felt a weight against her thighs.

She looked down. She had, evidently, taken the paperweight into her lap, and was cradling it between her hands. It seemed to vibrate against her skin, to echo with memories. It was easy, in the middle of the night, in the darkness and silence, to explore them.

Her fingers caressed the cool glass, and in her mind she saw the things of the past—an ocean voyage, a wedding in a tiny church, a village with dirt lanes and donkey carts.

Tory wondered if Nonna Angela had felt these things, and if that was why she kept the paperweight with its gold butterfly out of her granddaughter's reach. She wished she could ask her now.

Tory let her head fall back against the top of the sofa, and closed her eyes. She pictured Nonna Angela's wrinkled face, her bright black eyes, her aureole of gray hair. She remembered the softness of her veined hands, and faintly—because it had been such a long time—the welcoming cushion of her lap as she rocked little Tory and told her stories of a village by a lake.

Tory's mother had resented her Italian mother-in-law, complained of her ignorance and her "Catholic superstitions," as she called them. She had bitterly opposed Nonna Angela coming to live with them, but at least in this one thing, Tory's father had put his foot down. Tory couldn't remember the words now, because she had been little more than a toddler, but she knew there had been a harsh argument, her father losing his temper, her mother eventually withdrawing to her bedroom for hours, or it could have been days. Tory couldn't be sure, but it seemed, to her child's perception, that Nonna Angela came and her mother disappeared, all at the same time. Nonna Angela moved in, bringing her cracked cardboard valise full of surprises to delight a child. For the all-too-brief years that followed, Nonna Angela was Tory's one constant parent, her defense, her solace, and her confidante.

Except for the paperweight, Nonna Angela allowed Tory to

explore anything she possessed. A sweater, already old when Nonna Angela was a girl, became a cloak for a captured princess. A funny long skirt and a faded black hat turned Tory into a witch for Halloween. There were bits of cheap jewelry, a dried-up nosegay of white flowers pressed flat between the pages of an Italian Bible, and there was a wooden St. Francis, the paint worn from its brown robe, which Nonna Angela said Tory's father played with as a boy.

There was a photograph in a wooden frame, showing a bright-eyed young woman standing next to a tall, fair-haired young man in uniform. Behind them was a stone church, and in the distance, glistening with sunlight, a broad lake edged with reedy marshes. Tory had to practice saying the name of the lake, but she did it again and again until Nonna Angela said she had it right. Massaciuccoli. Nonna Angela had learned to swim in Lake Massaciuccoli, and her family fished there before the war.

Nonna Angela didn't tell Tory about the war. Tory dreamed of it. She was five, and had been sleeping in her grandmother's room one stormy night. She woke up screaming from a dream of bombs and fierce men with guns. Tory knew nothing of such things, but her Nonna Angela did. She knew them all too well. She remembered every detail as if it had happened the day before instead of forty years ago, and thunderstorms always brought it back to her.

Nonna Angela comforted the little girl, soothed her weeping, held her close until she calmed. She murmured endearments, but she didn't try to tell her granddaughter that her dream was just a nightmare. She couldn't say there were no monsters, tall cruel creatures with fierce eyes who invaded people's homes and brought terror and destruction with them. When Tory wept that she had seen people burning, Nonna Angela could only hug her, and murmur into her tumbled hair, *"Lo so, bimba, lo so."* I know, little one, I know. I remember.

The little girl had dreamed her grandmother's dream, plucked it all out of her mind as neatly as if she had seen it herself. It was the first sign of Tory's fey.

20

※

So ben: le angoscie tue non le vuoi dir;
so ben, ma ti senti morir!

I know well: you don't want to speak of your sufferings;
I know well, but you feel like you're dying!

—Musetta, *La Bohème*, Act Two

In two days, Zoe and Tory established a routine at the flower shop. Zoe, upon learning that Tory was an early riser, clapped her hands. "Fantastic!" she exclaimed. "You can open up then, and I can stay in bed until I feel human!"

"Well—sure," Tory said hesitantly. "If you'll just tell me what I need to do."

"Easy squeezy," Zoe said. "I'll give you the keys, you open the door, smile at the other crazy people who like to get up early, and take as much of their money as you can get." She gave her scarlet grin, and Tory couldn't help but smile in return.

"Mom's stuck in Portland till next week," Zoe explained. "But I told her we had the situation under control."

"She doesn't even know me," Tory said.

Zoe shrugged, and reached for a box of dry-cut flowers. "Your cred is good, thanks to Iris," she said. "And hey—what's that in your yellow bug out there?"

Tory followed her gaze. She had parked the Beetle on the street, just in front of the shop. Johnson sat in his favored place, the front passenger seat, his long nose stuck out the window, his wide black nostrils quivering. "Oh," Tory said. "That's the—I mean, that's my dog. Johnson."

"Johnson?" Zoe said. "Cool! Does he like people?"

"He seems to. I haven't had him very long. I didn't feel right leaving him home all day."

"Why don't you bring him in?"

"Well, I—I thought, a place of business . . ."

"Nah! Cannon Beach is a dog town," Zoe said. "Mom has a papillon that goes everywhere with her. I'd have a dog myself if it weren't for going off to U of O soon."

And so, with startling ease, the pattern was set. Tory came in early, opening the shop in the near-darkness of a coastal winter morning, Johnson panting at her heels. She swept up the litter of leaves and stems and bits of ribbon Zoe had created the evening before, and she opened the register and turned on the fairy lights adorning the window and the holiday displays. She dusted shelves and restocked supplies. Just before ten she took the dog for a walk on the side streets of the town. At ten she turned the door sign from "Closed" to "Open," and a trickle of customers began to come in after having breakfast at one of the downtown cafés.

For two days, Tory kept her cell phone in her pocket, close at hand. She both hoped and feared Jack would try calling the number back, and when he didn't, she was disappointed and relieved in equal measure. She had put the file away again in its bottom drawer, but looking at it had reminded her of Ellice's reptilian gaze, and of her chilling lack of affect as she recited everything she knew about Jack.

When the shop was still quiet, as she busied herself readying things for the shoppers who would come, Tory admitted to herself she was relieved when her phone died, her prepaid minutes gone. Ellice was a police officer. She had access to all sorts of information Tory couldn't imagine, and it was possible, Tory thought, that she could monitor Jack's calls. Did you need a warrant for that? Was a disappearance enough cause? She didn't know. When she thought of the chance she had taken in calling, her stomach quivered with uneasiness. She had been reminded, looking through the file, of how intelligent Ellice was. So often the case with the sociopathic personality—but of course, in her naïveté, she hadn't believed her client was a sociopath. She had convinced herself she was just a woman with a difficult life whose response to its challenges was anger.

Anger. Ellice was like the big, dark woman in her dream, the embodiment of pure, untrammeled fury. Neither of them seemed to need a reason. They only needed an outlet.

Now, on her fourth day as an employee, Tory settled Johnson on a rug behind the counter and began tidying the gift wrap and ribbon racks. There was a steady stream of cars rolling up and down the main street of the town now, as Christmas approached. People strolled to and fro in the cold sunshine, reading the posters for the theater across the street, buying coffee and pastries, stopping to point at things in shop windows. They wore mufflers and knit caps and thick jackets. Tory found, to her surprise, that she looked forward to ten o'clock, when she had to unlock the door and open the shop, when people would come in and she would have to smile at them, offer assistance, wrap their purchases, make small talk. This thought made her pause with a roll of embossed red foil in her hand.

Where had Ice Woman gone?

Even as she thought that, the old feeling of premonition pierced her, the dull, sudden pain running from her breastbone to her spine. Johnson, as if he felt her unease, rose to his feet, and came around the desk to stand beside her. Tory put the roll of foil in its place, and turned slowly toward the door to see what was coming.

The chilly December sun glinted on his silver hair, and he had to bend a little to see her beneath the holly wreath decorating the glass door. He waved, a little awkwardly. She waved back, and hurried to unlock the door for him. "Hank," she said. "Good morning."

He grinned at her. "Good morning. How's our patient?" Johnson, tail waving a welcome, padded forward to nose at Hank's hand.

"He's fine, I think," Tory said.

"And you?"

"I'm—I'm fine, thanks." She felt awkward herself, like an adolescent not sure of how to behave. It happened sometimes—not often—that her premonitions were not so much warnings as acknowledgments, an occasional recognition of something important about to happen. She stood back for this tall, nice man to come into the shop, and she wondered when she would know why her fey vibrated so in her chest.

As she locked the door again, Hank stood looking around the colorful shop. Like everyone else, he wore a heavy coat. Its thickness made his legs look even longer and leaner than before. "I tried to call you, but I got a message saying the number isn't working anymore."

"Oh, I guess—yes, it died. It was just one of those prepaid things. I'm going to have to get a new phone."

"Well, be sure and let me know the number when you do." Hank pulled a small, expensive-looking camera from his pocket and held it up. "Shirley's doing a calendar," he said. "Photos of our patients, you know—one of those promotional things. It'll be on the Web site, too."

"Oh." Johnson sat down in front of Hank, as if he thoroughly approved of the idea.

Hank patted his head. "I thought it would be best if I came," he said. "You and Shirley didn't seem to be quite—" He shrugged, and chuckled.

"She doesn't approve of me," Tory said. "Maybe it's the red hair?"

"She wants me to be organized, and she thinks people should have to make appointments in advance," Hank said. "She doesn't seem to understand that we need to be grateful for every bit of business we have."

Johnson panted and smiled, and Tory said, "Looks like Johnson is happy to have his picture taken."

"Why don't I take a picture of the two of you together?"

Tory stiffened. This was it, then. This was the warning her fey was trying to give her. She took a shallow breath, expecting the sensation in her chest to subside. It didn't.

"Hank," she began, then stopped. She looked away from him, around at the red and green and silver decorations, the fairy lights twinkling in swags of greenery and miniature Christmas trees. It all seemed to have gone cold, somehow. It mocked her. How could she have thought, even for a moment, that she could forget it all? That she could make friends with people, live normally? She felt his gaze on her, questioning, possibly offended. But she couldn't look into his face. There was an edge in her voice when she spoke again. "Okay if you just take the dog's picture?"

There was a frozen pause. Tory, to cover her embarrassment and anxiety, bent to smooth Johnson's hair and adjust his collar. Hank hadn't said anything, and when she finally summoned the courage to look up into his face, his dark eyes told her nothing. He said, with that gentleness that was so striking in a big man, "Right. Just the dog."

Tory straightened, and as Hank took the camera from its case and adjusted the lens, she took several steps back, well away from Johnson. The flicker of Hank's eyes told her he saw this, and a corner of his mouth twitched, but she couldn't tell if it was from amusement or, more likely, irritation.

Johnson sat patiently, the perfect model, smiling up at the camera while Hank snapped four or five pictures. When he was done, he put the camera back into its case with deliberate, precise movements. Johnson, evidently sensing that his job was done, padded back to his blanket behind the counter and lay down with a gusty sigh.

Hank dropped the camera back into his pocket. He nodded to Tory. "Thanks," he said. "We appreciate it. We don't have all that many patients yet."

He turned toward the door, and Tory hurried to unlock it for him. She glanced at the clock behind the counter, and saw that she would need to open the shop in five minutes in any case. She pulled the door open, and Hank started through it.

The sensation in Tory's breastbone intensified. She said, impulsively, "Hank. Wait."

He stopped in the doorway, one hand on the doorjamb, the other in his pocket. He looked remote now, his face composed, his eyes gleaming slightly with the sunlight splashing through the door. "Yes?"

Tory felt as if she couldn't breathe past the pressure in her chest. "We don't really know each other," she said. "But you've been more than nice to me—and I haven't behaved very well."

Hank's eyelids dropped a bit, as if in acknowledgment, and the set of his mouth softened. "You don't have to explain anything to me, Paulette," he said.

"I do." Tory folded her arms, pressing them close to her ribs, and tried to take a deeper breath. "I have to at least say that— that it has nothing to do with you."

That quirk at the corner of his mouth showed again, just briefly. "I'm pretty sure," he said calmly, "that I'm the only one here."

Tory sighed, releasing her arms, turning her face up, closing her eyes against the glare of the cold sunlight. "I have baggage you wouldn't believe," she said. The pressure in her chest released so suddenly she almost gasped. She couldn't think what else she had meant to say.

When he didn't answer, she turned her head away from the light and opened her eyes. He was watching her with a steady dark gaze. "I have a little baggage of my own," he said. "Don't you wonder why a guy my age is just starting out as a vet?"

"I—I didn't really know you were just starting out," she said. From behind the counter she heard Johnson sigh and roll onto his side. She was distinctly aware of being close to Hank, close enough to catch the scent of the soap he used, and the faintest tinge of something medicinal. His coat had fallen open. Beneath it he wore a blue denim shirt and a tie printed with dogs of a dozen breeds. It was crooked, and she had to put her hand behind her back to stop herself from straightening it.

"I'd bet," he said, turning his head now to look out into the street, "that every person who makes it past adolescence has a story of some kind. I do. Evidently you do."

It was the sort of thing Tory the therapist might have said. She stepped back a little, away from the beguiling male scent of him. "I just didn't want you to think I was—that I'm just—" She clicked her tongue. "Rude," she finished, in exasperation. "Even though I've been rude to you at least twice now."

He smiled at her. "Okay, then," he said. "I have to get to the office now, Paulette. I do have some actual appointments this morning."

"That's good."

"It's great, actually."

A trio of women, laughing, adorned with Christmas pins and earrings, walked up to the door of the shop. "Are you open?" one of them asked.

"Oh, yes." Tory stepped aside, out of the doorway. "Please come in."

When they had trooped past Hank, he said, "Hey, Johnson, thanks for the picture." The dog's tail sounded a farewell, beating against the floor. "That's a really nice dog," Hank said. "I'm glad you two found each other."

A moment later he was gone, long legs striding up the sidewalk. "Hey," Zoe said from behind Tory. She had just come in from the back of the shop, and was unbuttoning a vintage plaid wool coat. Her red lipstick clashed violently with the orange pattern of the fabric, and she had stuck a red-and-white candy cane into her hair. "Who's the heartbreaker?"

Tory glanced after Hank, but he had already disappeared around the corner. Zoe elbowed her. "Hey, Paulette?"

Tory closed the door against the cold air. "That," she said, "is Johnson's doctor."

"Whoa," Zoe said cheerfully. She pushed the candy cane

deeper into her waxy black spikes. "Johnson, you are one lucky dog."

The winter sunshine gave way in the afternoon to a layer of dark clouds that rolled up over the horizon and hid the early sunset. When Tory and Johnson left the shop at five, dusk already enveloped the town. The lights of shops and cafés and taverns garlanded the main street of Cannon Beach, glittering through the gloom. Tory opened the car door for Johnson, and he jumped up into his usual post. She paused for a moment, looking up and down the street, decorated now for the holiday. It was lovely, and it made her heart ache. She should be baking and decorating now, anticipating Jack's return for the holidays, enjoying the lull in her work as her clients did the same. There would be a rush of them after Christmas, of course, as there always was. The holidays brought out the worst in everyone.

And the best. It was important to remember that.

She went around to the driver's side of the Beetle and climbed in, but she didn't start the engine right away. She sat, one hand absently twined in Johnson's fur, and thought about what had happened this morning. Her fey had been prompting her to do something. She wished she understood what it was.

She started the motor, switched on the headlights, and eased the car out into the street in a U-turn. She didn't drive toward the cottage, but turned left, toward the veterinary clinic.

There were cars in the parking lot: Hank's white SUV, a tired-looking brown Honda, a couple of others. Tory turned into the lot, and said to Johnson, "I won't be long." He whined, but he stayed where he was as she turned off the motor and opened her door.

Shirley glanced up as she came in. Tory forestalled her question by saying, "Hi, Shirley. I don't have an appointment, but I wanted to speak to Hank for just a moment."

"He's with a patient," Shirley said with a certain truculence.

"Yes, I see you're busy tonight." Tory nodded to her, and sat down on the long banquette next to a stack of *Dog Fancy* maga-

zines. "I'll just wait till he's free." She smiled, picked up a maga-
zine, and pretended to read. She didn't need her fey to see that
Shirley didn't care for her one bit. She wondered what that was
about. It couldn't just be about appointments.

There was no one else in the waiting room. The doors to both
exam rooms were closed, and behind one of them Tory heard a
dog yipping, and someone soothing it. Before long the other door
opened, and a woman with a cat in a carrier came out, saying
something over her shoulder to Hank. He came just behind her,
dressed as before in jeans and a medical coat. He was answering
the woman, taking a pen out of his breast pocket. When he
caught sight of Tory, his composure broke, just a little. He lost his
train of thought, gave his head a shake, then led the woman to
the counter, where he wrote something on a pad and handed it
to her.

Shirley was taking the woman's payment, running her credit
card, filling out a form. Hank crossed the waiting room to Tory.

"Hey, Paulette," he said. "Johnson okay?"

"Yes. Listen, I can wait. I know you're busy."

He smiled. "I've been busy all day. Just like a real vet."

Tory smiled back at him. "I'm so glad." Tory stood up, laying
the issue of *Dog Fancy* neatly on top of the stack. "I just came to
ask you to dinner, Hank. Tonight, if you can. Another night if
that's better."

His eyebrows rose, and for a moment she thought he was
going to refuse. She wouldn't be surprised if he did. Mostly
Hank had met Ice Woman, not the real Tory. Or even Paulette,
whoever that was.

He smiled again, a different smile this time. He looked younger
when he did it, and the weary lines of his face smoothed.

The woman with the cat carrier was at the door. She said,
"Thanks again, Dr. Menotti."

He spoke to her, then turned back to Tory. "Tonight, then,"
he said. "What can I bring?"

"Nothing. And I won't spill the wine."

He chuckled. "I'd better bring some just in case."

"Just come in about an hour, if you're free."

"Perfect." He regarded her, his dark eyes seeming, as they had before, to see right through Paulette to the heart of her that was Tory. "Maybe we can unpack a bit of that baggage."

Tory's fey didn't stir.

It had been so long since Tory cooked for anyone but herself that she felt a bit anxious about it. She wasn't sure about the broiler on the ancient stove at the cottage, but she thought, if it didn't work, she could always pan fry a steak. She stopped at the market, with Johnson beginning to get restive in the car, and bought steaks and onions and asparagus. She found fresh rolls in the baking section, and remembered at the last minute to buy butter. She splurged on a good bottle of Barolo. If she was going to make amends, she thought, she might as well do it right.

She laid the table with her Costco silverware and plates, and brought out the vintage wineglasses and napkins. The broiler, it turned out, worked just fine. Hank showed up with a marrow bone for Johnson and another bottle of wine, and they drank a glass while she sautéed onions. Hank, it turned out, was handy in the kitchen, and by the time they settled at the scarred Formica table, she had forgotten her anxiety. They ate in silence for a few moments, and Tory thought how food always tasted better in company. Even the sullen company of her son had made her dinners better.

The storm began while they ate, torrents of rain beating on the roof. Tory went to build up the fire a bit. Hank opened the Barolo, and they drank some of it with the steaks. When the food was gone—every bit of it—they took their glasses into the living room and sat by the fire. "I could close the curtain," Tory said.

"No, don't. I like watching the storm."

"I do, too."

For a time there was only the sound of the rain and of Johnson energetically gnawing at his bone. Hank set down his glass, stretched his long legs out in front of the tiny sofa, and put his hands behind his head. He said, "I've just realized you don't have a computer."

"I've never used one."

"Ah. A Luddite."

She smiled. "If you like. I prefer to think of myself as a classicist—I like fountain pens and nice stationery, too. The engraved kind, with thick paper and matching envelopes." He smiled his understanding of this, gazing out into the rainstorm. Tory, taking in his clear-cut profile, suddenly understood why Shirley resented her. "You're not married," Tory said.

"No. Never."

"Shirley's hoping—" She stopped. It seemed a terrible invasion of poor Shirley's privacy, especially when she wasn't here to speak for herself.

Hank laughed. "I know," he said. "But I can't think what to do about it." He looked across at her, where she was curled up in the old easy chair. "You're not married, either."

"No. I was once, though."

"Divorced?"

"Yes." She felt on safe ground here. "Well, he's dead now. I divorced him when he went to prison, and then he crashed his car right after he got out. He was killed instantly."

His eyes glowed with sympathy. "That's awful, Paulette. I'm very sorry."

"It was awful at the time," she said. "But I was young. I got over it." She tilted her glass, watching the dark wine swirl this way and that. "I really did," she added. "I got completely over it. My son, though—"

"Tough on him."

"He never knew his father, and for a long time he blamed me for that."

"Not now, though?"

Tory hesitated. It was here, she thought, at this point, that danger lurked. She didn't trust herself to be able to judge what was safe and what wasn't. She'd made too many mistakes.

"It's okay," Hank said. "You don't have to talk about it."

"It's hard to talk about."

"I can see that." He put his feet up on the table and folded his arms. "So I'll tell you a bit about me, if you're interested."

"Please," she said softly.

"The reason I've never married," he said, watching for her reaction, "is because I was a priest. And before you ask, yes, a Catholic priest. For ten years, not counting seminary."

Tory blinked, and said, "Wow."

"Not what you were expecting."

"Not even close."

"I don't suppose you're Catholic," he said.

"As it happens, I am. My grandmother was an Italian Catholic, and she took me to Mass with her every week until she died."

"Do you still practice?"

Tory looked away. "I did," she said softly. "Until I came here."

He waited a moment, and when she didn't go on, he uncurled himself from the too-small sofa and walked to the window. He stood looking out into the storm, the rain coming in fat drops that shimmered with reflected firelight as they slid down the glass. "Faith is a strange thing," he said, half to himself.

Fé, she thought. A thrill of recognition made her shiver.

"I didn't lose my faith," he went on. "But I did lose my calling."

Tory wished he would turn to face her as he talked, so she could look into his eyes as she had her clients', let her intuition help her to understand. She stood up, and went to stand opposite him beside the window. "That must have been very hard for you," she said.

Still looking out into the rain, he nodded. His face was still, his mouth set in a straight line. "It felt like a tragedy. As if—as if I had lost myself."

"And medicine?"

He lifted one shoulder, and the corner of his mouth twitched. "My new calling."

"It makes you happy."

His gaze came back to hers then, and held it. "Happy enough," he said.

She looked up into his face, and although it only shone with firelight, not the revealing sunlight of her home office, her intuition told her the rest of his story. He hadn't spoken of the resentment and rejection and loneliness that had been part of all of it, but she could feel it. She had the strangest impulse to put her arms around him, to comfort him.

It was a strong impulse, and she might have done it, but he turned again to gaze out into the rain-soaked night, and she resisted. She said instead, safely, "Thank you for telling me, Hank. I think you're going to love your new calling."

"I think so, too," he said. He turned, putting his back to the window, and smiled down at Johnson. "Off to a good start, right, Johnson?"

The dog beat the braided rug with his plume of tail.

21

Piangerà tanto tanto!

She will weep so much!

—Suzuki, *Madama Butterfly*, Act Three

Chet knocked on the front door, and Jack, a broom and dust-pan in his hands, went to open it. "Hey, Chet. Thanks for coming."

"Of course, Jack. I'm glad you called, but I didn't—" Chet took one step into the hall, and stopped, staring at the mess of the living room. "Oh, Christ."

"Yeah. And I've cleaned up the worst of it."

"Hell, Jack. When you called, I really didn't understand what—I mean, this is more than just a break-in. This was—this was *deliberate*."

Jack managed a sour laugh. "Yeah. Someone meant to do as much damage as possible."

"This happened yesterday?"

"Yeah. I was downtown doing a few errands, and when I came back—this." He gestured at the mess of glass and pottery and smashed wood in the living room. "It's even worse in the kitchen. Someone pulled down Mom's pot rack, broke up all her china and glass—it's a real mess." *It's going to break her heart.* But he couldn't say that.

He had thought it through as carefully as he could. He had made lists of possibilities. He had tracked down the location where the cell phone had been sold. He had tried to call the phone back, when he judged it to be a decent hour, but got a message saying the number was no good anymore.

Still, he was going there. He didn't care that Christmas was coming. He had to find Tory, and this destruction—this attack—was the push he needed. He just had to do something about the house first. And think of something to tell Kate and Chet.

He led the way into the kitchen, and listened to Chet's horrified exclamations. Jack had made a start on cleaning up the glass and china, but there was no way to fix the real damage, the hole in the ceiling where the rack had hung, the banged-up appliances, the broken plaster and drywall.

"Son, we're going to have to rebuild the whole kitchen," Chet said heavily. He stood in the middle of the ruin, his hands on his hips, his pudgy cheeks flushed with anger. "Have you called the cops?"

"I called them last night. That deputy showed up—Gordon, her name is."

"I don't think I know her."

"She was at the memorial. One of Mom's clients, I guess. She gave me an incident number for the insurance company."

"Good. We'll need that."

The inclusive pronoun touched Jack, and he felt a wave of misgiving. He wished he could tell Chet what he was planning, but he didn't dare. He was sure Chet and Kate would try to stop him, and he didn't want to be stopped. No one else was going to do anything, that was obvious. Certainly not the police, not if every time something happened they sent that woman to the house.

No. It was going to be up to him, and he'd put it off long enough.

"Look, Chet," he said. He hated to lie, but he couldn't see any other way. "The thing is—I'm supposed to go to a friend's house for—for the holidays. I was hoping you could help me at least fix the door to Mom's office. That way I can close up, make the house secure while I'm away. When the insurance money comes, I'll get started on repairs."

Chet gave him a worried glance. "A friend's house, Jack?"

Jack tried to make his eyes round and innocent. "Yeah. Friend of mine in Oregon. He heard about . . . well, he heard the news. He's a buddy from college."

Chet nodded, seeming to accept this. He turned in a slow circle, examining the mess, then stepped to the connecting door and opened it to look into Tory's office. "Jesus," he said softly. "This guy meant business."

"Yeah." *Or she did.* At the thought, Jack felt that tingle in his head, that weird sensation that was beginning to feel normal.

Chet pursed his lips, and scanned the room. "You'll need new drywall, paint, and so forth, but that can wait, you're right. What we need to do right away is get a new sliding glass door. I'll get the tape measure out of my car."

"I have one here, Chet." Jack reached into the drawer under the wall phone, and pulled out a big tape measure. As his hands closed on it, he had a sudden, sharp memory of Tory, a carpenter's pencil in her teeth and the tape measure in her hands, her eyes intent as she measured for shelves in the garage. It made his eyes sting, and Chet saw.

He stepped toward him, and Jack was afraid for a moment he might embrace him, but he only put one hand on his shoulder. "Hey, son," he said heavily. "This is a hell of a thing, after what you've been through. I'm really sorry."

Jack handed him the tape measure, and when he could trust his voice, he said, "I'm okay. I'll be okay."

"It's a good thing you're going to spend the holiday with a friend," Chet said. "Hanging around this empty house is no good. And then this—" He shook his head as he took the tape measure from Jack's hand and started into Tory's office. Jack snagged a pad of paper and a pen as he followed. "Just let us know where you're going to be. I know Kate will worry otherwise."

"I'll give you my cell phone number. You can call me anytime."

"Well . . ." Chet hesitated, and Jack thought he might have to invent a friend, a phone number, some other way for them to reach him. The problem of the door distracted Chet before he could ask another question. The frame was screwed to the siding of the house, and he began fussing with how it would come out. They measured, and Jack wrote down the figures.

Before they left the house, Chet said, "I know a company in town that does security systems. You should put one in."

"Okay." At least Chet and Kate would feel better if he did that. "If you think so."

"When are you going?"

"Well, they—uh—invited me for the whole week of Christmas. I thought I'd head out there a couple days before. Not until I can close the house up, though."

"We'll get that taken care of by tomorrow. You could go anytime, really. Kate will want to drive you to the airport, though."

"No need for that, Chet. I'll catch a ride with a friend."

Chet frowned at this, and Jack supposed Kate would have something to say, too, but that would be okay. He might have taken a chance and told them the truth, but that persistent feeling in his head, the tingling that had so surprised him on the train and which troubled him more and more every day, persuaded him that the fewer people who knew his plans the better.

Which meant no one.

Chet was as good as his word. By the end of the following day, a new sliding glass door sparkled at the entrance to Tory's office, and the security company had come out to install a straightforward alarm system, the kind that alerted a monitoring company if it was triggered. While they worked on wiring and sensors and installing a keypad, Chet helped Jack cart the ruined pot rack and splintered cupboard doors out to a spot behind the house, where it could all rest until the snow was gone and a truck could come up the hill to cart it away. Jack had already cleared up the glass and pottery and china shards and filled two large garbage cans with them.

He wrote down his cell phone number for Chet, and handed it to him at the end of the long day. "Thanks for your help," he said. "I'll come and help out around your place sometime."

Chet clapped his shoulder. "No need for that, son," he said. "Now that I'm retired, I need stuff to do anyway." He glanced back at the kitchen, which looked wounded, with its gouged ceiling and missing cabinet doors. "When you get back," he said, "after Christmas, we'll put everything right again. A few months from now, you won't know anything happened here."

Jack shook Chet's hand and said good-bye. He made a circuit of the house, checking that every door and every window was locked. It was as neat as he could make it, considering the damage. Chet was wrong about one thing, though. He would always know something had happened here, and so would Tory.

There was no peace in the house now, no feeling of welcome or comfort. It was a fanciful notion, he supposed, but the house seemed to have lost its heart. It reminded him of a wrecked car he had seen once, a beautiful Jaguar that had been smashed up in an accident. The cat on the hood was the only thing that appeared to be intact, while all the grace and power of the car was ruined. The house felt that way to him now. Ruined.

He went into his bedroom and shut down his computer. He couldn't find the sticky note with the cell phone number on it, but it didn't matter. The number was firmly set in his memory.

His duffel bag, already packed with a couple of shirts, an extra pair of jeans, some shorts, and his shaving kit, waited in the Escalade. When he was sure everything was locked, he went out to the garage, set the alarm on the keypad, and shut that door, too.

He stood for a moment, listening, before he got into the car, pushed the button for the garage door opener, and started the engine. He backed out, but he watched the garage door close all the way before he turned the Escalade and started down the long, snow-covered driveway. When he reached the bottom of the hill, he looked carefully to see that there was no patrol car parked among the trees or on the shoulder before he turned out into the road. He didn't turn toward town. He turned farther uphill, toward the park, and he kept an eye on the rearview mirror until he was safely away from the neighborhood.

He wasn't going to fly, though he felt bad about deceiving Chet and Kate. He didn't want to go to the airport, put his name on a flight manifest, use an easily traced credit card. In any case, he was pretty sure he was going to need wheels when he got near the Costco store on the coast of Oregon that had sold the cell phone. He was going to drive all the way across country. It was a long trip, and he could hear Tory's voice, in memory, reminding him to be careful.

He would. He would drive with great care, because he had to get there. There was plenty of room for him to sleep in the Escalade when he got tired. He had cashed a check so he could pay for gas without using his credit card. It would have been nice to have company, but he had Tory's CDs in the console and a good radio.

He plugged his cell phone into the car charger, but he turned it off. He didn't want to take a chance on anyone calling him when he was supposed to be in the air, flying to spend Christmas with a friend and a family.

At another time, in different circumstances, he would have liked to spend Christmas that way. He remembered, though it had been five years since he'd seen any of them, what the Garveys' Christmas was like, all noise and mounds of wrapping paper and the kinds of cookies and candy Tory wouldn't have in her house. He had, brat that he had been, flatly refused to eat the fruitcake Tory made each year. Instead, he went to the Garveys' to play with all the toys and gadgets they got at Christmas, and made himself sick on luridly frosted Santa Claus cookies bought at Walmart or some such place.

He wished, right now, he had a slice of that fruitcake. Once, when Tory wasn't around, he had tasted it. It was buttery, full of nuts and dried fruit, steeped for weeks in advance in brandy. Thinking of it now made his mouth water.

"Okay, Mom," he said aloud in the dark car. "You win. Next Christmas, fruitcake."

It made him feel a bit better to envision another Christmas, a return to their own traditions, Midnight Mass, Christmas breakfast, modest but thoughtful gifts. He took one of the CDs out of the console without looking at it, and popped it into the player as he crested the hill that led into the state park. The strains of one of Tory's favorite operas, *Madama Butterfly*, began.

Jack had come into the living room once, and found his mother staring out the front window as she listened to Un bel dì, an aria so beautiful and heartrending that even a kid who liked heavy metal had to be touched by it. She hadn't heard him come in, the sound of the front door covered by the soprano's soaring voice and the swell of the orchestra.

He had seen her reflection in the window, hand pressed to her mouth, tears streaming down her cheeks. He wished now, driving away from their home in the darkness, that he could go back to that time, break through his own resistance, put his arms around her. How alone she must have felt! Did she ever weep with her friend Kate? He doubted it. Her control, as far back as he could remember, had been absolute.

When the overture to *Butterfly* ended and the first faintly Japanese melodies began, he felt strange, listening as he drove alone through the night. He felt as if there was no one in the world but himself. There were no headlights behind him, no cars passing him. There was only the road unfolding before him, a concrete ribbon running up and down hills, around bends, over bridges, and beneath underpasses.

And the great thing was, now that he was headed west, the tingling in his skull had eased at last. He knew—he *knew*—this was the right thing to do.

22

Demonio! Taci!

Demon! Be quiet!

—Edgar, _Edgar_, Act One

Autumn wore on toward winter in Torre with days of pouring rain alternating with days of cool sunshine. All Souls was coming, and after that, Christmas preparations would begin in earnest. The Puccinis had been in Milan for weeks, and when they returned, the maestro declared there would be no guests, no hunting, no distractions. "I _must_ work on Mademoiselle Minnie," he said. "Everyone is after me to see the score, and I have _nothing!_"

Doria and Zita cast each other a glance as they cleared the table. Elvira, grunting a little as she pushed herself up, said, "Giacomo, you always say that. Everything will be fine."

"This time it's true," he grumbled. "They'll say I'm a hack. It's what they all think." He rose, too, feeling in his shirt pocket for his Toscano cigar.

"Well, Giacomo, tonight it is quiet and peaceful. You can work."

"We'll see," he said. "We'll see. We should have stayed here, and not gone to Milano at all."

"Come now," Elvira said, tossing her napkin onto the table. "We can't stay in Torre all the time. We would never see anyone!"

"I like that," he said. "Too damn many people in Milano, anyway, and they all want something from me." He stuck the cigar in his teeth, and looked around the room. "Damn it, Elvira, where is my matchbox?"

Doria was just taking the linen napkins to launder. She glanced at her mistress. "The matchbox is on the *signore*'s desk," she said. "In the studio."

Elvira waved her hand. "Get it, then, Doria. Don't make him wait."

"No, signora." Doria hurried into the studio and collected the matchbox from where it sat beside the butterfly paperweight. She carried the box back into the dining room, meeting Puccini halfway. She took a match from the box, struck it, and held it for him as he puffed on his cigar. He blew a cloud of smoke over her head; then, with one of his sudden changes of mood, grinned and winked at her before he walked past her into the studio. Doria, flushing a little under the narrow regard of her mistress, put the matchbox on the table and picked up the napkins. She turned toward the kitchen, but she found Elvira in her way.

Elvira's arms were folded beneath the shelf of her bosom, and her cheeks were reddened by the port she had just drunk. Her black eyes glittered in the way Doria had come to know meant trouble for everyone.

She had taken every care not to anger her mistress since her return, and she couldn't think what she might have done just now to set her off. She paused, clutching the soiled napkins. "Signora?"

"Don't think I don't notice," Elvira hissed.

"*Cosa?* Notice what?" Doria took a half step back.

"The way you look at him," Elvira snapped. She kept her voice low, and Doria knew she didn't want Puccini to hear. "You flirt with him, batting your eyes like that, doing little favors. I want you to stop it!"

Doria swallowed, remembering her resolve to keep her temper. She tried to speak mildly. "Signora, I didn't—" She faltered when Elvira raised one big hand, the fingers spread. Doria took another half step back, away from the threat of a slap.

How was she supposed to behave in the face of such treatment? She could have drawn Puccini's attention, but already the sound of the piano reached them, the work resuming, and that was what mattered. It didn't matter what Elvira thought or did, as long as the maestro could go forward with his opera, and she could stay here, in Villa Puccini, smoothing his path.

She let her gaze drop to the floor. "I'm just going to help Zita with the dishes."

"Very well." Elvira lowered her hand, and stood aside. As Doria passed her she said, in a harsh whisper, "But you watch yourself, my girl. I know your type."

Doria, though it galled her, looked back at Elvira and said, as demurely as she could, *"Sì, signora,"* and went on into the kitchen.

A storm had begun to build during dinner, with flickers of lightning off to the east. Just as Zita and Doria finished their kitchen chores, rain began to patter against the windows, and the rising wind shook the shutters. Zita said, "This will be a bad one." Far in the distance they heard a soft roll of thunder, like a bass drum just beginning to tune.

"I hope it doesn't disturb the maestro," Doria said. Puccini had been hard at work for the hour since dinner, and she knew he would go on long past midnight. She smiled at Zita. "Mademoiselle Minnie must be behaving herself tonight!"

"Hah!" Zita exclaimed. "I should think she'd do as she's told."

Doria laughed at that, and stood with her hands on her hips, surveying the clean kitchen with satisfaction. "You're off to bed?" she asked Zita.

"Sì, and you should be, too."

"Soon. There's just the table linens to iron, so they'll be ready for the morning."

"Do them tomorrow, Doria *mia!* Go to your bed! And besides—" Zita paused, glancing upward, where they could hear the creak of Elvira's heavy footsteps. "Besides, didn't she tell you not to iron at night?"

A crash of dissonance on the piano made them both startle, and they heard a curse from the studio. Doria said, with a shrug, "She did, Zita. But if there are no table linens, she won't like that, either. I'll just do enough for the breakfast table."

"Well—" The music started again, a fragmented and halting progression of chords beneath a melody in octaves. Zita scowled. "Well, see you're very quiet. And hurry!"

"I will. It shouldn't take long."

With the irons heating on the stove, Doria gingerly set up the board, careful not to bump anything or make any noise. She had turned off the lights in the kitchen, and she meant to work with just the light from the pantry. She thought, as she spread the tablecloth over the board, that this would be a pleasant chore under normal circumstances. She liked seeing the hot iron smooth the wrinkles in the linen, and she liked the scent of soap that rose from the cloth under the heat. It was routine, but it was made delightful by the music wafting from the studio. The intermittent, nearly inaudible beat of the thunder was, she thought, a little like gunfire, of which there was evidently so much in *La Fanciulla del West*. Perhaps it would be an inspiration!

She forgot, as she listened to the rich sounds of the piano, to be quiet. She had begun to recognize the melodies of this opera, and it seemed the maestro was growing confident. Doria paused, the iron held above the tablecloth, listening as he played all the way through a scene, the different voices coming through, picked out in different registers, the flowing harmonies so like his usual work and yet—somehow, in a way she wasn't educated enough to understand—different, more subtle, more continuous. The iron went cold in her hand as she stood there, rapt, and she reached to put it back on the stove, to pick up the other one.

She was distracted, and it was dark in the kitchen. As she reached across the ironing board with the iron in her hand, still following the melody unfolding at the piano, she lost her grip on the heavy iron. She tried to grasp it as it fell to the floor, but she was too late, and it burned her fingers as it slid through them. The iron clattered on the floor, and Doria thrust her burned fingers into her mouth with a gasp of pain.

From the studio, the maestro called, "What was that?"

Doria, her heart in her mouth and her fingers stinging, hastened toward the studio to explain to him. She cast a wary glance up the staircase, then dashed through the dining room. Puccini was standing now, his hair disarrayed from running his hands through it, a cigarette dangling from his lips. "I'm sorry—" Doria began, just as he said, "Are you all right?" He reached out to take her reddened hand with an exclamation.

"How dare you!" Elvira shrieked from the doorway to the studio.

Doria and Puccini both jumped, and the cigarette fell from the maestro's lips to the carpeted floor. He swore, and bent to snatch it up, and Doria whirled to face Elvira, holding her burned fingers with the other hand.

"Right here under my nose?" Elvira shrilled.

"Elvira—" Puccini began, but she cut him off with a gesture worthy of any diva standing center stage at La Scala.

Her voice was as sharp and cutting as the edge of a saw. "I know what's going on here!"

Doria said, "Oh, no, signora, it's not—" but she never finished her protest. Elvira took one long step to reach her, and backhanded her across her face. Doria fell, her elbow scraping the carpet, her head banging against the wall behind her.

Puccini shouted, "No!" and seized Elvira's wrist before she could strike Doria again.

Doria pushed herself up on her hands, her burned fingers blazing with fresh pain. Elvira was screeching something, and Puccini's voice thundered fury. He dragged his wife out of the studio and up the stairs, shouting at her all the way. The house itself seemed to shudder with the force of their argument.

Zita, in her dressing gown, appeared in the doorway. She bent to help Doria up, and together they scrambled out of the studio, through the dining room, and into the kitchen.

Doria whispered, "I burned my hand! I burned it on the iron, and the *signore*—he tried to look at it, that's all, and he—then she came down and she—"

"*Lo so, lo so,*" Zita muttered. "Never mind. Never mind now." With an arm encircling Doria's waist, she led her to the sink. She uncovered the butter dish and smeared a generous dollop of yellow butter over the burns. "There, there. This will feel better soon."

From upstairs they could hear Puccini berating his wife, Elvira answering with nerve-grating cries. Zita drew Doria into her own bedroom to wrap the burned fingers in a clean handkerchief. They waited there together, huddled on Zita's bed, until the voices above them reached a crescendo and then, abruptly, ceased. They heard the slam of a door, footsteps on the stairs, and Elvira weeping noisily.

When the house was quiet, Doria crept back to her own room. She wriggled out of her clothes as best she could with one hand, and got into bed. She lay there, her fingers throbbing. She wished the music would resume, but the only sounds were those of the wind and rain and the occasional clap of thunder, echoed by the quick beat of her own heart.

The next morning, an enormous bank of storm clouds hid the rising sun. Lightning glinted behind it, making the wall of cloud glow like an enormous curtain lit by footlights. Thunder still rattled and rumbled across the sky. *Not gunfire now,* Doria thought irrelevantly, as she dressed and drew a brush through her hair with her sore hand. It was more like cannon, great thumps and bumps that made the windows creak.

Ignoring the theatrics in the heavens, Doria and Zita began their morning chores, creeping about the kitchen and the dining room like mice fearful of waking the cat. Zita set the bread to rise, and Doria laid the table for breakfast, careful to do everything just the way Elvira liked it. She carried the dogs' food out to them, and dashed back to the house just as the rain began. Raindrops, fat and cold, spattered the zinc screens. One flash of lightning seemed to be right over Villa Puccini, and the following roll of thunder shook the windows. A moment later, the electricity went out, leaving the house in shadow.

Doria hurried to lay a fire in the studio, and to light the oil lamps kept for such contingencies. She was just on her way to the kitchen to refill the saltcellar when she heard the uneven, limping tread of Puccini on the staircase. She stopped where she was, watching him descend.

He was dressed in his hunting coat and tall boots. He tramped to the gun rack without speaking, and seized one of his long shotguns. He tucked it under his arm, and pulled his wide-brimmed hat from its peg. He nodded to Doria. "No breakfast for me this morning. Tell Zita, will you? I'm going out to the island."

"Not in this weather, signore!" she exclaimed without thinking.

He scowled. "It's the weather in this house that's unbearable. Better a good clean rainstorm." He tramped out through the front door, leaving Doria staring after him.

Zita came to stand beside her, and together they watched Puccini walk through the rain to the boat dock. They heard the roar of the engine in his motorboat just as a fresh onslaught of lightning and thunder exploded over Lake Massaciuccoli. The house shook with it, and the dogs, left behind in their kennel, began to howl. The floor above creaked with Elvira's footsteps moving this way and that. Doria moved to the kitchen cupboard for the box of table salt, but her burned hand hurt so she could hardly twist the top off the saltcellar.

She heard Elvira's heavy step on the staircase. She put the saltcellar aside, and stood with her hands twisted in her apron. Zita was on the point of coming through the doorway into the kitchen, but she fell back to allow her mistress to precede her.

Elvira looked as if she had aged ten years in a single night. The flesh beneath her eyes was baggy and dark. She wore a shirtwaist and a long plaid skirt with a thick woolen shawl around her shoulders. She bulked in the kitchen doorway like a massive ship in a tiny harbor, turning this way and that as she fixed her two servants with a baleful gaze. "I know what you all say about me," she said hoarsely. "You say I'm crazy. That I throw fits."

"No, no, signora," Zita began, but Elvira cut her off with a gesture.

"The *signore* is out?" she said in a colorless tone.

"*Sì, signora,*" Doria whispered. "He went to the island. He took his gun."

"Good. Doria, get your things. I want you gone before he comes back."

Doria stiffened. "What? Why?"

"I've had enough of your tricks."

"That's not fair!" Doria cried. "I didn't—"

"Giacomo doesn't see it, but I do! I want you out of my house!"

Doria couldn't think of the right words, the diplomatic ones, the calming ones. She could only blurt, "Signora, if you will just listen to reason!"

"Reason?" Elvira hissed. "How dare you?"

"I didn't mean—I only want to—"

"You think I will keep a servant who speaks to me this way?"

"I only mean—if you would only think—"

Elvira said hoarsely, "You! You, the village slut who can't stay away from my husband."

Fear and anger mingled in Doria's heart. She protested, "It's not true! I've told you over and over, it's not true!"

"I have my pride! I know who I am and what I deserve!" Elvira pressed her hand, with its long, thick fingers, to her breast. She didn't appear to notice that her corset was twisted askew. The shelf of her bosom was tipped sideways, making her look even more like a ship listing to one side. "I will not have a little viper like you slithering around my feet, Doria Manfredi!"

"You have to let me explain—"

"Oh, yes, yes. You love to talk, don't you, Doria? You love to talk to my husband! You do your ironing late at night, so you can be near Giacomo, though I've ordered you not to do that! I hear you, late at night, talking, talking on and on. You give him no peace."

"*I* give him no peace?" Doria spread her hands, desperate to find her way through the maze of argument. "It is not *I* who—"

Elvira snapped, "Don't you dare!"

Zita tried again to intervene. "Signora," she began, but Elvira said, "Quiet! I'm not talking to you!" A peal of thunder rattled the second-floor shutters, and the rain intensified, hammering the roof, spattering the windows. "Go now, Doria. Fetch your things." When Doria didn't move at first, Elvira took a threatening step toward her. "Do I have to throw you out myself?"

Doria, shocked and defeated, backed away from Elvira toward her bedroom. She fumbled with the doorknob once, twice, before she could turn it and go in. Once inside she stood staring at her few possessions, her brushes, her prayer book, her extra dress, her only coat. She couldn't think how to collect them, what to do with them. She couldn't believe, even now, that Elvira meant it, that after all the times she had lost her temper and railed about this or that imagined offense, her mistress had really turned her out of the house. Doria kept thinking Elvira would call her back, change her mind.

Puccini could not have known what his wife meant to do. Surely, he could not have known. If he had, would he have fled, taken his gun and gone out in his boat? She couldn't believe it. She wouldn't.

Zita came into Doria's room when Elvira's heavy footsteps had clumped out into the studio. Elvira sometimes stood beside the mosaic fireplace, one hand caressing the inlaid mantelpiece as she gazed out over the lake, watching for her husband to return. Doria had always felt sorry, seeing her like that, her big feet splayed on the pretty carpet, her thick shoulders tense with impatience and longing. How terrible it must be to love someone so much that it drove away reason and dignity! How sad to be a woman to be avoided, a woman famed for her bad temper and jealous rages!

But now, sitting on her narrow bed and staring up at Old Zita's wrinkled, sorrowing face, Doria had no room in her heart for pity. Elvira Puccini had thrown her out, after her years of service, dismissed her on a baseless suspicion. "Zita, where will I go? What will I do?"

Zita crouched beside her, taking her hands and squeezing them in her old, dry ones. "You will go home to your mamma, of course," she said soothingly. "Until the *signora* comes to her senses."

"Mamma won't have me," Doria said sadly. "She said so."

"Of course she will. That was only talk."

"She will say I should have kept quiet. It's what she always says."

"I will go with you, and explain. The *signora* is crazy; everyone knows that!"

Doria thought perhaps her heart would break into pieces. She was Butterfly, helpless little Cio-Cio-San. A girl with no power. She hadn't asked much of her life, she thought, only this work, service to the maestro, the music! But Villa Puccini was her Sorrow, to be taken away from her even though she had given her life to it.

She said, "I don't know if Mamma will listen to you, Zita. She's a hard woman."

"*Lo so*," Zita said grimly. "Emilia's had a hard life."

"Do you think the *signore* will be angry with his wife for doing this? Will he make her take me back?"

Zita scowled. "Hah. Who knows what rich people will do, Doria?"

Sick at heart, Doria reached under the bed and pulled out the satchel she had carried here on her very first day at Villa Puccini, nearly six years before. She folded in her dress, her nightdress, her few bits of lingerie. She hesitated over her spare apron, then took that, too. She put her hairbrushes on top of it all, and closed it.

She followed Zita out to the kitchen and then to the back door. They put on their coats, and Zita picked up the big umbrella. She also, with a quick glance over her shoulder, took up her shopping basket, and filled it with two jars of tomatoes, a bottle of olive oil, a tin of tea sent from Babington's in Rome, and a loaf of bread. "The *signora* would not want you to go back to your mamma empty handed," she said. Doria tried to smile at this, but her lips trembled.

Together, the two of them went out the back door and into the rain-sodden garden. Zita put up the umbrella, and, laden with the basket and Doria's satchel, they trudged up the muddy lane toward the Manfredi home. The villagers of Torre came to their doorsteps and windows to watch them, and Doria hung her head. Tongues would wag today. Rumors would fly. Her mother would be furious, and Father Michelucci would be disappointed. Even Zita couldn't know how her heart ached.

Only Cio-Cio-San, poor little Butterfly, could have understood her feelings.

23

La mia mamma, che farà s'io non torno? Quanto piangerà!

My mother, what will she do if I don't return?
How she will weep!

—Jake Wallace, *La Fanciulla del West*, Act One

Jack took care making his way out of Vermont, across New
York, and south to Pennsylvania. He kept a close eye on his
rearview mirror. He bought a map at a service station to supple-
ment the GPS, since he wasn't certain what destination to pro-
gram it for. He used the cash he'd brought, and for two nights he
slept in the car, rolled in his sleeping bag, finding deserted state
parks and campgrounds to park in, and watching to be certain no
one observed him. By the time he skirted the south end of Lake
Michigan and headed north into Wisconsin, he was sure no one
was following him. *She* wasn't following him.

He kept his cell phone in the car charger. Once or twice a
friend called, but he didn't speak long. He promised himself he
would call Chet and Kate in a day or so to reassure them. He
pressed on toward the west, using the map to choose the fastest
route. He had to change the radio channel often as stations faded
in and out. Once he came upon a classical station that lasted long
enough for him to hear Octavia Voss sing "The Song to the
Moon" from *Rusalka*. Tory loved that aria. He yearned to see her,
headphones fixed over her head, tears on her cheeks as she gave

herself up to the music, and he swore to himself he would see that again.

There was plenty of snow, but the roads in Wisconsin and Minnesota were well plowed, and he only had to slow his pace a few times. Christmas lights shone along main streets of towns and from remote farmhouses. They blinked garishly in convenience store windows. He ate fast food mostly, but once or twice, when he couldn't face another greasy hamburger, he stopped in a grocery store and bought oranges and bananas. He cleaned up in rest stops and gas station bathrooms, and promised himself a motel room when he reached Montana.

The long, long hours of driving forced him to be alone with his thoughts. His mind spun with images and regrets and tumbled memories of things he wished he'd done differently, until at last he blew out a breath and said aloud, "No way, man. You'll end up as crazy as Gramma. Take it from the beginning."

It was a good way to pass the hours, it turned out. Tory the therapist, he reflected wryly, would have approved. He disciplined himself to look at his twenty years in order, to try to figure out what had gone wrong between himself and his mother, what he had done and, in fairness, what she had done—or not done—to let this rift grow between them. He had a good memory. He thought back to when it had all started, when he was thirteen or fourteen, and worked his way forward through the years.

He remembered jumping on the trampoline in the Garveys' backyard, he and Colton bouncing together, falling, laughing even when they bounced right off onto the grass. He had banged his head on the steel support where the canvas was suspended. His forehead swelled, and his eye turned black and blue in a quarter of an hour. Mrs. Garvey had glanced at him, saying offhandedly, "There's ice in the freezer if you want it," then turning back to whatever she was doing. He had been amazed at that. His mother would have insisted he hold an ice pack on the bruise, would have lectured both him and Colton about the dangers of getting wild on the trampoline and, if it had been Colton with the black eye, called his mother to tell her. When Tory came to pick him up that day, Mrs. Garvey was nowhere to be found. Colton had looked a little shamefaced about that, facing Tory's worried frown with a shrug and reddening cheeks. Tory had refused to let Jack go back to the Garveys' again until she learned the trampoline was gone.

He remembered a baseball game one spring evening. Colton's dad had practiced all the sports with him, football, soccer, basketball, and baseball, and Colton was a great hitter. Jack remembered the shame of his own strikeouts, the agony of a dropped ball in center field. They'd won the game anyway, when Colton smacked one completely out of the park, and he had stood by watching Colton and Mr. Garvey high-fiving each other. When Tory came up, she said something or other, he'd made a good effort, at least he'd tried, something like that. He remembered how his throat had burned with humiliation at the other guys hearing these lame excuses for his failure. He had snapped at her that she didn't know what she was talking about, and he remembered with painful clarity how the smile had frozen on her face, how her slender shoulders had stiffened, and how high and tight her voice was when she turned to greet one of the other parents.

There were good times, too. They had made a trip to New York when he was fourteen, and wandered the streets together staring at the buildings they recognized from films and television, going to a Broadway show of his choosing, attending only one classical concert. He had enjoyed that, actually, and had liked the way the patrons of that theater glanced at his pretty mother, how smart she had sounded chatting with their seatmates about the music.

His eyes began to burn as the sun set ahead of him, beyond the flat fields and low silhouettes of the little Minnesota towns he drove through. He had better stop. He'd be no good to his mother if he fell asleep and crashed the damn car.

And he remembered, as he started looking for a safe place to park, how cautious she had been about his driving, how he had chafed under her constant reminders, how he had badgered her to let him take the car to school—an old Volvo station wagon, embarrassing, but at least having four wheels—and how rarely she had allowed it.

By the time he was driving, of course, the Garvey family he so admired had broken up. Mrs. Garvey's negligence, Mr. Garvey's infidelity, had all led to disaster for Colton and his little brothers. Jack had seen it for what it was, even as a teenager. He understood he had been wrong about them, that their family was no more ideal than his own single-parent household. Why had he never told his mother that? She had never spoken of it except for offering to take him to say good-bye to his friend on the day the Garveys left town.

Jack found a city park with a gravel lot in a tiny town on the western edge of Minnesota, but the moment he turned off the engine, he knew it would be too cold to sleep in the car. Snow blanketed the grassy area around him, and bent the boughs of pine trees with its weight. Frigid air crept in through the doors of the car the moment the heater went off. He'd have to splurge on a room. He wouldn't be any good to Tory if he turned into a Popsicle, either.

He pulled out his wallet and counted what he had left. He was pretty sure he could do it. He would be out of money by the time he reached Oregon, but that didn't matter. The important thing was to get there, undetected, and search for Tory.

There was a motel in the little town, a dilapidated-looking place with cabins arrayed around a snowy parking lot. There was no one in the office when he stopped, but a sign said to ring for service, so he did. A sleepy woman with old-fashioned plastic curlers in her hair came out to the desk, had him sign the register, and gave him a key. She looked curiously at the cash he gave her, but she didn't say anything other than to direct him to a room. He took the key, said a polite good night, and went out to take his duffel bag from the Escalade.

The room was the most depressing place he'd ever been. The sheets were threadbare, there was no television, and the shower emitted only a weak stream of water. Still, it was good to be off the road. Jack stood under the shower for ten minutes, scrubbing his hair with hand soap and rubbing himself down, glad to be clean after three days of roughing it. He put all the blankets the room provided on the bed, and he inspected the sheets before he climbed in between them. He laid his head on the pillow, and listened to his stomach gurgle. He had only had a banana since lunch. He closed his eyes, longing for eggs and sausage and pancakes. That made him think of the kitchen at home, always stocked, something ready in the fridge for quick meals. Another good memory, and one a guy only appreciated too late.

In fact, he thought, yawning, turning on his side, Tory's house had been the most efficient he'd ever seen. As different from the Garveys' house as it could be, of course, and that had been part of his problem. . . . As he grew warm under the blankets, his thoughts drifted sleepily. Images from his days of driving jumbled with thoughts of school, of his friends, of the classes he hadn't finished. His stomach gurgled emptily, and he thought of the savory smell of Tory's lasagna winding up the stairs and into his bedroom while he sat at the computer—

His eyes opened abruptly. Sleep slid away from him, and he lay staring up at the flyspecked ceiling of his lonely motel room.

The computer. The note with that cell phone number on it.

Why was he thinking about that now? What had happened to it?

Or, he wondered with a chill that matched the icy Minnesota air, who had taken it?

24

❦

Non più, fermate!

No more, stop!

—Fidelia, *Edgar,* Act Three

Emilia Manfredi opened her door to a bedraggled trio. Father Michelucci now held the umbrella, but it wasn't wide enough to protect Doria and Zita and himself. All three were wet at the edges, elbows and necks and faces. Doria's satchel dripped with rain, and her boots were muddy. She hung back behind the others now, beyond the shelter of the umbrella, and the rain dripped from the limp brim of her hat to run down her forehead, adding to her misery and shame.

Her mother stood back to let them enter. The priest said, "*Buon giorno,* Emilia." She didn't answer.

Zita, in the little silence, said tentatively, "*Buon giorno.*"

Emilia spat, "*Penso di no!* I don't think so."

Doria shuffled in after the others, her head bent. As Father Michelucci and Zita took off their coats and hung them on the pegs by the door, Doria busied herself unbuttoning her boots and kicking them off. Her stockings were wet, too, but she kept them on to hide her long toes. She stood to one side as the priest sat down and her mother and Zita sat opposite them.

Zita glanced up at her. "Doria," she said in her rusty voice. "There's tea in my basket. Why don't you make a pot for us?"

Doria hurried to fill the kettle, glad of something to do. She felt as if her mother's angry gaze would burn right through her.

Emilia sighed and folded her hands on the table. "What has she done?"

It was Zita who answered. "*Niente,*" she rasped. "Doria has done nothing. Elvira Puccini is a madwoman."

Emilia turned her gaze to the priest. "Father?" she said, in a voice as hard as stones, a voice that made Doria's heart shrink even as she put the kettle on to boil.

She looked up and saw Father Michelucci steeple his fingers beneath his chin. Worry lines pulled at his forehead. "Emilia," he said. "Giacomo is very happy with your daughter's work. But his wife—"

"Doria works for the *signora!*" Emilia snapped. "It is her job to make her happy!"

At this unfairness, Doria's neck stiffened. She whirled to face her mother. "I work for them both!" she cried. "I do everything in that house!" She cast an apologetic glance at Zita. "Almost everything. Zita does the cooking."

"*È vero,*" Zita said, nodding so that her gray hair, frizzier than ever in the wet, fell out of its pins. She pushed it back with her bony hands. "It's true. Doria does everything in that house but the cooking. Can you imagine, Emilia—"

"It's a good job," Emilia said stubbornly. "She could find a way to—"

Father Michelucci put up a hand, and Emilia stopped. He said gravely, "I don't think so, Emilia. I don't think there's a way." With a glance up at Doria, he added, "I don't think it's safe for Doria to be there any longer."

Emilia gave a snort of disbelief. "Not safe? What nonsense!"

The priest's cheeks reddened. Doria said, "Mamma, don't speak to Father Michelucci that way!" The kettle whistled, and she turned away to pour the boiling water over the tea leaves. When she turned back, she saw that her mother had folded her arms as tightly as she now folded her lips, restraining herself.

"When the *signore* comes back," Zita said, "he will speak to his wife. Signor Puccini is fond of Doria."

"Fond," Emilia muttered.

"*Sì,*" Zita said. Her hair fell down again, and this time she left it where it was. "*Sì,* he is fond of Doria, but the *signora* imagines every girl in the world is after her husband."

"She is very unhappy," the priest said.

"Hah! Unhappy?" Zita said. "*Pazza.* Crazy."

Doria poured the tea, and carried the cups to the table. She put one in front of her mother. "It's very good, Mamma," she said softly. "It comes from Roma, a shop near the Spanish Steps."

"Did you steal it?" Emilia said sourly.

Zita said, "A gift, Emilia."

"From whom?"

Zita's smile was both waspish and triumphant. "From Signor Puccini! It was sent to him by an admirer of *Madama Butterfly.*"

There were a few moments of peace as they sipped the tea. Doria poured a cup for herself, but she stood beside the stove to drink it. After a time, her mother looked up at her. "You must go back, Doria. Apologize."

"Apologize for what? I didn't do anything!"

Father Michelucci pursed his lips, and his frown lines deepened. "Emilia, listen to me. I think it's best Doria is not in Villa Puccini anymore."

"Why?" Emilia turned her angry gaze on the priest.

"Mamma—" Doria began, but her mother ignored her.

"Why is it best?" Emilia demanded. "Why is it better for her to come back here, where I still have children to feed and clothe, a house to keep? Her brother tries, but Rodolfo can't support us all!"

"I don't want to speak ill of Elvira," the priest said, choosing his words slowly. "She is one of my parishioners, after all, and I know she has—I know she suffers."

Zita snorted, but he bent his gentle glance on her, and she didn't speak.

"Some of her sufferings are imaginary," the priest said. "Many are not."

"If Doria has given offense—" Emilia began.

Doria stamped her foot. "I haven't, Mamma! You're doing just what the *signora* does. She accuses me, and she won't listen when I tell her it's not true. You can ask Signor Puccini!"

Father Michelucci gave a slow nod. "I will go to Villa Puccini myself," he said. "I will speak to both of them."

Doria said, "It's not that I don't want to go back, Mamma. I do. But I can't—"

"Let us see," the priest said, and his worried gaze came up to Doria. "Please. Let us just wait and see." A fresh rumble of thunder underscored his words, and Doria shivered.

After Zita and Father Michelucci departed, Doria presented the gifts from Zita's basket to her mother. She didn't say anything, nor did Emilia. Doria went to carry her satchel back to the room she had always shared with two of her youngest brothers. She was searching out corners to stow her clothes and her hairbrushes when her mother appeared in the bedroom doorway.

"Doria," she began.

Doria straightened, and faced her. "Yes, Mamma," she said warily.

"You are my daughter. My girl. You can stay as long as you like."

"*Grazie*, Mamma."

"But I want to know the truth."

Doria's jaw ached suddenly, and she found she was gritting her teeth. She put down the clothes in her hands, and crossed the room to face her mother, her little fists braced on her hips. "*Ascolta*," she said, in a tone as hard as any Emilia Manfredi had ever produced. "Listen to me, Mamma. The maestro is like an uncle to me. Or a big brother. He has been kind, and he talks to me as if I matter. As if what I think, or what I feel, *matters*."

"That's not—"

Doria interrupted. "I told you before, Mamma. I am not the

signore's lover. I have not been in his bed, nor he in mine. I am as much a virgin as when I left your house to go to work at Villa Puccini, when I was only fifteen. If you care anything at all for me, you will believe that!"

Her mother gazed at her for a long moment, and Doria stared back at her. The two of them, Doria thought, were like a pair of hound bitches at that moment, taking each other's measure, deciding their territory. In the end, Emilia gave a sharp nod, turned about, and went back to the kitchen. Doria closed the door behind her before she collapsed on to one of her brother's cots and put her head in her hands. She sat there for a long time, trying to think of a way to make things right. Wishing the maestro would come back to Torre.

When the feeling came, she wasn't sure of it at first. It was a vague itchy feeling that began in her long toes, as if tiny ants were biting at her feet. It spread up her ankles and into her calves, becoming a tingle that seemed to bloom in her chest. Once, she had touched a frayed cord of one of the electric lamps in the villa, and this same sensation had run through her hand and up her arm, but it had gone no farther. It was like that in a way, a distinctly physical energy, a slender line of fire that made her shiver with surprise. Mostly it reminded her of how she had felt listening to Caruso sing in the maestro's studio, when the whole of Villa Puccini vibrated with his celestial voice, his high B flat making the glassware shiver and the walls resound—and causing Doria's breastbone to vibrate in sympathy. Now she pressed her hand to her chest, wondering.

It lasted for perhaps a minute while she sat there, her breathing quickening, her body trembling before this strangeness. When the feeling subsided she rose slowly to move to the little octagonal mirror that hung over the dilapidated chest of drawers. She peered into its murky depths, and she wondered, Was this her *fé*, come at last?

"Not much good," she muttered to her reflection, "if I don't know what it means."

25

In quell'azzurro guizzo languente sfuma un ardente scena d'amor.

In that blue flicker, an ardent love scene vanishes.

—Rodolfo, *La Bohème*, Act One

Tory woke with an odd sensation in her toes that seemed to spread up into her shins, as if her legs had fallen asleep. She was surprised to see that she had slept right through the night for the first time since arriving in Cannon Beach. Johnson lay in what had become his usual position, curled against her, a node of warmth and comfort. She lay still for a moment, wondering at the unusual feeling, but before she could analyze it, it was gone. She turned on her side, and ran her hands over Johnson's sleek head, pondering the latest installment of her dream.

Installment was the right word, she thought. There was something sequential about the dreams, as if one led to the next, even though the events were shadowy, the characters made of gossamer, elusive creatures of imagination. If this was her subconscious at work, its message was both subtle and obscure.

She sighed, and pushed back the covers. Johnson raised his head, ears forward. She patted him. "You're always ready for the day, aren't you?"

For answer, he gave her his doggy smile, and leaped off the bed to race to the front door. "Wait just a minute, my friend," she called. "I can't go straight outside like you can!"

When she was ready, her coat pulled on over a pair of jeans, the two of them emerged from the cottage into a cold gray morning. Johnson bounded off toward the beach the moment she opened the gate. Tory followed more slowly, yawning and pushing her fingers through her hair. The rain of the night before had stopped, but everything was wet, the dirt of the lane, the sand, the long grasses that fringed the beach. A thin fog shrouded everything, so it all looked mystical, a fantasyland of indistinct shapes and shifting mists.

She and Johnson were halfway to the big rock when she heard the bells chiming their Sunday invitation from the Presbyterian church. The sound seemed amplified by the fog, or perhaps it was that there were no other morning sounds as yet. Tory lifted her head to listen, and thought of Hank. Tall, gentle, charming Hank. Who had been a priest.

They reached Haystack Rock, and Tory strolled around it while Johnson sniffed at the tide pools, his flag of a tail waving gently. The bells faded away, and she supposed the service had begun. Did Hank go to Mass, she wondered? There was no Catholic church in this town, but she had seen a sign for one a short distance away. It would be nice, she mused, as she and the dog headed back up the beach, to go to Mass. To hear the ritual prayers, to kneel with the congregation, to listen to the music. She thought of the communion wafer being offered in Hank's long fingers, and something strange and oddly familiar shivered in her belly.

It had been a long, long time since she had felt anything like that. It seemed incongruous that now, when everything in her life was a desert, she should meet someone like Hank, who made her feel—well, made her feel *something*.

She glanced up, and realized that the sun was well up above the fog. She hurried Johnson back up the beach and in through the gate. She was due at the flower shop soon. It would be busy today, only two days from Christmas Eve.

As she was making her coffee, she thought about Christmas. Nonna Angela had always taken her to Midnight Mass, and she had continued the tradition, attending at Our Lady of the Forests, where Father Wilburton led a contemplative service that always appealed to her. Jack had stopped going with her a long time ago, but she had kept on, feeling centered by the ritual, comforted by the words of promise. She often imagined that Nonna Angela was with her at those times, a gentle and loving presence.

Perhaps she—

The thought, whatever it might have been, died unborn. With her hands still on the coffeepot, she remembered, in a rush, the rest of the dream.

November and December in Torre were unusually cold that year. The sun shone without warmth, and the shallows at the edge of Lake Massaciuccoli crackled with ice crystals. Puccini had removed himself to Rome, and everyone in Torre knew why.

Old Zita came to Emilia Manfredi's house one chilly evening when her work was done. She had brought *biscotti* she had baked that day, and she sat with Emilia and Doria drinking coffee as she listed her complaints about her mistress. When she reached the end, she exclaimed, "She's as mad as one of those loons that nest on the island!"

"Yes, everyone says so," Emilia said. Doria listened in resigned silence. It seemed pointless to talk about it, yet talk they did. "They say half the village heard them arguing," Emilia went on. "Did you know that?"

Zita sucked her breath in, a disgusted hiss. "I could have guessed. I thought her ugly voice would break the crystal in the dining room."

Emilia leaned forward eagerly. "We're too far away to hear. What did they say?"

"The usual things," Zita replied. Emilia poured more coffee into Zita's cup, and Zita stirred a lump of sugar into it. "Mostly about him neglecting her." She took a sip of coffee, then said with a shake of her frizzy hair, "What that woman needs is a good fucking. I could tell her she's not going to get it from him that way, but she would never listen!"

Doria looked away, her cheeks burning.

"And so," Zita said triumphantly, setting her cup down with a bang, "he can't work this way, he says, so off he runs to Roma. He claims this new opera is the reason!"

"La Fanciulla del West," Doria murmured, but Zita didn't hear her, and her mamma was intent on the details of the Puccinis' argument.

"He left me alone with a madwoman! No one will come to work there now. Not even her children will come to see her. Even Tonio found someplace else to celebrate Christmas."

Doria crumbled a biscuit in her fingers. Emilia said, "Do you know, Zita, she told Giorgio the butcher that Doria is pregnant. Then she told that little tart Nuncia, at the café, that Doria seduced her husband, took him into her bedroom late at night when she was supposed to be ironing. She called my Doria a whore and a slut, right there in the café where anyone could hear, and now Doria won't go out of the house because people whisper behind her back!"

Zita put her wrinkled hand over Doria's smooth one. "Doria *mia,* you mustn't mind what people say." She patted her hand, over and over. "Or what they think," she finished.

Doria's eyes stung, but there would be no more tears. She had wept them all.

When the first gossip and taunts reached her, she had cried over every hurt, every insult. It was much worse than she had ever expected, a constant barrage of rumors and whispers and slights. She couldn't go to the café or to the market. She even stopped going to church. Foolishly, Doria had thought Elvira's attacks would stop once she left Villa Puccini. If anything, they had worsened. The viciousness of them shocked her. She had no way to fight them. She had no way to prove herself, and now she felt emptied by the struggle, like a sponge wrung out and left to dry on a shelf.

"Father Michelucci spoke to Signora Puccini," Emilia said. "He might as well have saved his breath. She has never forgiven him for that shameful wedding."

"But that wasn't the priest's fault! That was Puccini!"

"As you said," Emilia whispered, and she touched her palm to her forehead, her eyes rolling. *"Pazza."*

"Hah," Zita said sourly. "The great Puccini! He ran away like a little boy afraid of a spanking. Ran away without a thought for poor little Doria!"

At this, Doria roused herself. "Oh, no, Zita. *Non è vero!* He wrote to me."

Zita blinked, startled. Emilia said sharply, "What good is a letter, Doria? Did he send money? Did he promise your job back?"

Doria sighed. "No, Mamma. You know he didn't."

She felt Zita's gaze on her sharpen. "What did he say, Doria? In his letter?"

Doria lifted one shoulder in a half-hearted shrug. "He said he was sorry about me leaving Villa Puccini. He said—"

"He said," Emilia pronounced with bitter clarity, "that his damned opera would never be written if he stayed here, and that he knew Doria would understand!" She pounded her fist on the table, and the coffee cups rattled in their saucers. "Why should Doria understand? That's not her job! All my girl wants is to do her work and to be left alone by his witch of a wife!"

"Lo so, lo so," Zita said, shaking her frizzy head. "Doria is a good girl. He should have done more for her."

"But I do understand," Doria said, in a voice so slight both older women leaned closer to try to hear.

"What?" Emilia demanded. "You understand what?"

"I understand the maestro needs to work on *Fanciulla*. In New York, they're asking for it, and he's having such trouble over it. When the *signora* distracts him—"

"Distracts him!" Emilia exclaimed. "What about what she's doing to you? To us? Do you know, Zita," she said, raising her eyebrows dramatically, "that my son threatened to kill Puccini for seducing his sister?"

"Very proper," Zita said, "that an older brother should defend his sister's honor."

"The only thing that stopped him," Emilia proclaimed loudly, "was Doria convincing him. Telling her brother there is no reason for him to go to prison over something that didn't happen!"

Zita crossed herself. *"Grazie al cielo,"* she said fervently.

Doria slumped in her chair. That had been a terrible day, with her uncles in a rage and her brother storming around the house and threatening to buy a gun—where he would have found one, she didn't know, unless he went to Villa Puccini and took one of the *signore*'s shotguns. She had sworn on their father's grave that she was not the *signore*'s mistress, and finally Rodolfo had calmed down.

"Better Rodolfo should shoot Elvira than the *signore*," Emilia said.

Zita said darkly, "Puccini should never have married her."

"There were the children," Emilia reminded her. Zita nodded, and took a biscuit from the plate. It was a circular argument, back to the same old thing.

Doria pushed away from the table. "I'm going to lie down," she said.

Her mother said, "Doria, you never come out of your room anymore! You can't spend your life in there."

Zita tried to catch Doria's hand, but Doria gently freed herself. "Thank you for coming, Zita," she said. "You won't forget to feed the dogs?"

"No, no, of course I won't. Don't worry. It will all pass, Doria *mia*, you'll see."

"Sì. It will pass. I'm sure you're right." Doria tried to smile at Zita, at her mamma, and walked on heavy feet to her room. She shut the door, and lay down on the bed to stare at the ceiling.

She had lied to Zita. The truth was that she was quite sure Zita was wrong. Her *fé*, vibrating in her toes, made her certain. She had felt it when the letter came, and she felt it when she heard the murmurs behind her as she walked down the lane into the village.

She could no longer live in Torre. Elvira, with her money and her power and her position, would drive her from her home with lies and gossip. Despite hours on her knees at the shrine of the Virgin, she was going to lose this battle.

Like Butterfly, kneeling on the hill above the harbor, she waited in vain for her hero to rescue her. She was alone.

As she unlocked the shop and she and Johnson went in, Tory reflected that though she had never put her faith in interpreting dreams, she had always trusted the subconscious for guidance in healing trauma and restoring balance. She had to think there was meaning in this succession of dreams. It could be a stress response, but it felt like much more. It felt as if, on some level she couldn't access during her waking life, she was working something out. Were the characters in the dreams archetypal, representing her own conflicting feelings?

Or perhaps being alone so much was making her imagination work overtime.

She stroked Johnson's head. He had already flopped onto his rug with the ease of one who knows his role. "Do you dream?" she asked him as he smiled up at her. "Do you dream of whoever you started out with? Do you have nightmares about getting lost?" He beat his tail against the floor, then rested his chin on his paws. She patted him again, then straightened, found her apron and tied it on, and began getting the shop ready for the day.

Business was brisk, as she had expected. Tory and Zoe hardly had a chance to talk before a steady stream of customers began to flow through the shop. Zoe stayed behind the counter, busy with poinsettia arrangements and holiday centerpieces. Tory helped customers choose gifts, wrapped them, and hurried to restock shelves when they started to look bare.

"Mom will be here tomorrow," Zoe said, in a brief lull when they were the only ones in the store. Johnson, from his blanket beside the counter, lifted his head as if this news interested him. "About time, too! I don't know what we would have done without you, Paulette." She bent to tug gently at Johnson's ears. "Or you, either, Johnson me lad."

Tory cleared the counter of ends of clipped ribbon and slivers of bright wrapping paper, sweeping them into the wastepaper basket. "It worked out for all of us," she said.

"Whew! That's the last one for today." Zoe set a fresh arrangement, a gay display of white roses and red carnations and thick candy canes, into the refrigerated cabinet to wait for pickup. "It's a good thing. My fingertips are practically raw."

"That's beautiful, Zoe," Tory said. "You're wonderful at this."

"Thanks." Zoe stepped into the back, and returned a few moments later with two steaming cups of tea. "I think we need this. There'll be another rush toward closing."

"Thank you," Tory said fervently. "I do need it."

Zoe hopped up on the counter and sat swinging her yellow cowboy boots. She eyed Tory over the rim of her cup. "So-oooo," she said, with a scarlet-lipped grin. She had pinned a sprig of holly amid the black spikes of her hair, and she wore red-and-green-striped tights. "Are you going to tell me about Dr. Darling, or will I have to hear it from that bitch Shirley?"

Startled, Tory laughed, and Zoe pointed a red fingernail at her. "There, now!" she said. "I knew you'd be gorgeous if I could get you to smile."

"Zoe! I've been smiling at customers all day!"

"Not the same," Zoe said breezily. "Not the same at all. So tell me. How was your date?"

Tory leaned against the counter, her teacup cradled in her hands. "We didn't have a date."

"You had dinner, I know that."

"You weren't kidding about small town gossip, I guess."

"Nope. I grew up with it, and trust me, it's better than CNN."

"Zoe, you're an original."

"That's the idea." Zoe pushed her spikes up with her fingers. "So you're not going to tell me?"

"There's nothing really to tell. We did have dinner."

"And wine?"

Tory laughed again, and sipped her tea. "I always have wine," she said.

"That's my girl!" The bell over the door tinkled, and Zoe slid off the counter, her florist's apron fluttering. "Back to the salt mines. Why do we say that, I wonder?" Without waiting for an answer, she turned to greet the new customers coming in from the fog. The mist had persisted all day, wreathing the Christmas lights up and down the street in shifting silver haloes.

Tory drank the rest of her tea, then took Johnson's leash from the coat hook and clipped it on. She led him through the back room, where jumbled cartons and boxes crowded together with a vacuum cleaner, a big plastic garbage can for flower clippings, and other flotsam and jetsam. In the alley behind the shop she let Johnson sniff for a few minutes while she tipped her face up and let mist collect on her eyelashes.

Three days till Christmas. The fog around her seemed to swirl with memories, the rush of her clients having a difficult time over the holidays, the cheerful press of shopping and baking, the de-light—and the torment—of choosing gifts for Jack. Midnight Mass, a tree, cards arriving in the mail, swapping fruitcakes with Kate. Christmas carols, *Messiah* on the radio, kitschy decorations and colored lights, crystalline snowfall that made everything look clean and new.

Ellice Gordon had taken that from her. Had stolen it all, with the singular selfishness of the sociopath. Tory would spend Christmas without her son, and that would be no Christmas at all. The colored lights mocked her, and she understood the despera-tion some of her clients had felt as the holidays drew near.

Johnson pressed close against her knee, sensing her misery. She knelt beside him, encircling his neck with her arm. Her cheeks were wet, and she wiped them on her sleeve. "It's just the fog," she whispered to Johnson. He nuzzled her neck and gave a little anxious whine. She hugged him tighter. "Don't worry, Johnson. Everything's okay."

But it wasn't.

26

❦

Mentisci! Sì! Finisci!

You lie! Yes! Finish!

—Minnie, *La Fanciulla del West*, Act Two

It was late when Tory pulled the Beetle into the driveway of the cottage. She hadn't eaten much, but she didn't feel hungry. She decided to take Johnson out on the beach, hoping he wouldn't need to go again before morning. She bundled herself in her down coat. It was ragged at the edges now, a bit embarrassing, but all she had. She wore her knit cap and a scarf she had picked up on a sale table. She tied a red bandana around Johnson's neck. "I know it doesn't really help keep you warm," she told him. "But it makes me feel a bit better." He licked her cheek, and trotted to the door in anticipation.

The dog led the way out through the little gate and down to the damp sand. It was too dark and foggy to see the water, though Tory heard the crash of the waves off to her right. She trudged after Johnson as he circled to the south, his favorite route. Lights twinkled from the houses to her left, faint stars of white and red and green, blurred by the mist. Here and there she could make out the shapes of Christmas trees in picture windows, limned by even fainter lights. Johnson circled back every few moments to make sure she was following.

The pain she had felt that afternoon had only slightly subsided. Ice Woman, she thought, was well and truly melted. Talking with Hank, accepting the affection of the dog, chatting with the ebullient Zoe and making herself smile and be courteous to customers, had all conspired to dissolve the casing of ice that had protected her for so long. It was, in truth, a demonstration of the advice she gave unhappy clients. Live. Move. Talk. Act like you're alive, and you'll begin to feel that way.

She hadn't known, when she told them that, how much it could hurt.

When Johnson had enough of racing through the gray darkness, they made their way back to the cottage. Tory gave the dog his dinner. She debated opening a can of soup for herself, but nothing sounded good. Not even the half-empty bottle of wine appealed to her. It was as if, the flatter and leaner her belly got, the less she wanted to put in it. She put a CD into Iris's player, and set a fire in the fireplace, then curled up in the easy chair with Johnson at her feet to listen to the Bach Christmas Oratorio, her latest find from the library sale shelves.

She bent forward to pick up the paperweight, nestling it in her lap as she settled back. She traced the gold outline of the butterfly with her fingertip, and tried to picture her grandmother, tried to remember the sound of her voice, speaking with her heavy Italian accent as she told the story of the paperweight being handed down in the family. She had warned the young Tory to take care with it when it came to her. The glass was fragile, she said. And it was important. A symbol of family. Of history.

Tory deliberately closed her eyes. It was time to finish whatever story was being told to her in her dreams. To listen to what her subconscious was trying to say. She was ready, she thought. She had to be.

When Zita came down the lane, the day before Christmas, Doria was in the bedroom, smoothing freshly washed sheets on the cots her brothers slept in, plumping their pillows. She heard Zita's knock, and the clatter of the kettle as Emilia set it to boil. She stood behind the half-open bedroom door, a pillow in her hands, to listen to Zita's news.

"He's back," Zita said. Doria, behind the door, leaned forward to hear better. He was back? Puccini had returned?

Zita went on. "She drove him half mad with her letters and calling him on that telephone. I had to stand there in the kitchen and listen to her begging him, promising him all sorts of things. You never heard a woman so pitiful!"

"I thought he was angry at her."

"Oh, he is, he is. They barely speak, even now. But on the telephone—she shouts into it, you know, though that screech of hers could probably reach all the way to Roma without any wires to carry it. She cried, and swore she would let him work on his opera. She told him the children won't come unless he's here, and she went on and on about how she would be all alone for Christmas."

"And what about Doria? Will he do something about Doria?"

Doria heard the clink of coffee cups, the sliding of the saucers. She leaned her forehead against the splintery edge of the door, listening, hardly breathing.

"*Non lo so*, Emilia. If they speak of her, it's not in my hearing."

"Perhaps, in time?"

"I hope so. I certainly hope so!" And then, in a rough whisper, "How is she, Emilia? How is our little Doria?"

"I'm worried about her, Zita. She doesn't eat, and she hardly speaks. She scurries around, cleaning things that aren't dirty, scrubbing things that don't need it. She fixes things. There's not a broken hinge or cracked board in the whole house. That's nice, but it's not natural, a young girl behaving this way."

Doria straightened and pulled back from the doorway, easing the door shut as silently as she could. She went to the window on the far side of the bedroom, and peeked out through the curtain. There were two women passing by in the dirt lane, scarves pulled forward over their foreheads against the intermittent spatter of rain, shopping bags over their arms. As they walked by, they cast furtive, curious glances at the house.

They made Doria furious. These people were her neighbors. They had known her from infancy. Now they watched her with narrow eyes, bent their heads to murmur together as she passed them, whispered behind her back in the shops and the café. She couldn't bear the thought that they believed Elvira Puccini's slanders.

Half the village was on her side, her mother assured her. That half believed the Puccini woman was out of her mind with jealousy. They told stories of the scenes she had created in Milan and Lucca, and said she didn't dare show her face in those places.

But the other half of Torre's citizens had seized on the excitement. They believed Doria had been seduced by Puccini—or had, as Elvira claimed, seduced him. They repeated the names Elvira had called her—slut, slattern, and worse. It was bitterly unfair.

What Doria wanted, she thought, was so modest. She wished only to return to her pretty bedroom behind the kitchen at Villa Puccini, to clean and wash and iron, to help Zita in the kitchen, to serve at table, and to listen to the music at night.

Elvira Puccini could never understand such simple desires. Elvira had five houses to live in! She wore beautiful clothes and she rode in fast automobiles. She could go anywhere she liked, without asking anyone. She could stay in hotels, eat in restaurants. She had been to Paris, and to New York, to Rome, even to London! She had no idea what it meant to be a poor girl who had never traveled beyond the boundaries of her village.

Doria lay down on one of the beds, and stared up at the pattern of cracks in the low ceiling. She could smell panforte, and thought that Zita must have made an extra one for the Manfredi family. She knew how it would look, how it would taste, rich with nuts and fruit and butter. Today, she should have been slicing panforte in the kitchen at Villa Puccini! She should have been setting it on the cut-glass dessert plates, pouring out tiny glasses of *limoncello* to go with it. She should have been serving the *signori* and their family, seeing them off to Mass, laying the table for Christmas breakfast.

She wanted to be doing that, not making beds for ungrateful little brothers. She wanted it so much it seemed her very desire should make it possible. Surely that was fair? Surely it was not too much to ask that she should have this simple wish satisfied?

She sat up suddenly in bed, propelled by a rush of righteous energy.

Perhaps the maestro would insist. After all, he had only just returned. There would be time. He was busy, no doubt, with his opera, with soothing Elvira's fears, with the children and grandchildren come for the holiday. Surely he meant to make the *signora* send for her.

Perhaps, she thought, if he were to see her, he would remember how fond he was of her, how they had talked through his long nights of pain. Perhaps, if he remembered all of that, he would make Elvira bring her back to Villa Puccini. She wouldn't have to apologize! Doria would forgive her without that, if she would only allow her to return!

The idea made Doria leap from the bed to stand in the middle of her bedroom, her body suddenly thrumming. She felt edgy and stimulated, as if she had drunk too much coffee, but it felt good to have a plan. It felt good to have hope!

She pressed her hands together for a moment, thinking, then crossed to the row of wooden pegs to pull down her best dress and shake out the wrinkles. She took her good shoes from the corner where she had set them, and checked the soles to be certain they were clean. She found her gloves, and her black stockings, and laid everything out. The wool of her good black coat was worn thin, but that couldn't be helped. She had mended the rents in the skirt, and she had brushed it only two days before. She had steamed and shaped her black felt hat, too.

Now all she needed was a bath!

She hurried out into the kitchen. Her mother and Zita broke off their conversation, staring at her in wonder as she dashed about, building up the fire in the stove, tugging the tin tub in from the porch. Emilia said, "Doria? What are you doing?"

Doria, pumping water into the kettle, spoke over her shoulder. "If he's back, Mamma, he should see me, be reminded of how the villa needs me!"

Zita said cautiously, "Doria *mia*, it's true that we need you, but I'm not sure the *signora*—"

Doria whirled to face her, her hands on her hips. She tossed her head. "It doesn't matter about the *signora!*" she cried. After the dark bedroom, the December day seemed almost too bright to bear, cold sunlight glinting off every surface so her eyes stung with it. "The maestro is back!" Doria said triumphantly. "He will see to everything!"

And though Zita shook her frizzy head in doubt, and Emilia scowled and fretted, Doria would not be persuaded. She pressed on with her preparations, filling the tub, fetching the soap and shampoo and a towel. All that was needed was for Puccini to be reminded! The moment he laid eyes on her, he would remember his promise, and she would be back where she belonged.

Christmas morning dawned clear and cold in Torre. Doria rose early to brush her hair out of its plaits, and twist it up into a shining neat bun. The family gathered noisily, Emilia scolding everyone to wash, to dress properly, to polish their shoes. She sent them back into the bedroom time and again, and they ran in and out, banging drawers, dropping shirts and socks, smothering laughter and curses. Doria dressed with the greatest care, and when the church bells began to ring to call the people to Mass, she put her hat on and thrust the pin through. Her mother eyed her, and nodded. "You look good, Doria."

"*Grazie,*" Doria answered.

As she shrugged into her coat, Emilia pulled the collar up around her chin. "That will hide the shiny places," she said, and Doria said again, "*Grazie.*"

Her mother led the way, and Doria and her brothers trailed after her into the lane.

As they walked to San Giuseppe, Doria held her head high, avoiding the curious gazes of her neighbors. She refused to worry about what they were thinking. She thought instead about the Christmas of last year, of 1907, the forest of candles flickering in the church, Father Michelucci looking happy and proud of his crowded little church, and its most famous congregant on his knees at the communion rail. Doria had ducked in just in time for the first hymn, after making everything ready at the villa. After Mass, she had kissed her mother, then hurried back to Villa Puccini ahead of the family. The nativity scene had been laid out in the studio, and in the dining room Doria helped Zita arrange her sumptuous breakfast, the panforte waiting in all its glory under a lacy sprinkle of the finest ground sugar. Doria meant to do all of that again. Surely Puccini's return was a sign for her! She would offer a special prayer to the Virgin to make it so.

The Christmas Mass was always a joyous one. Doria loved hearing Father Michelucci chant the paternoster, his flock behind him with bent heads. Incense and candle smoke filled the church, and the crush of bodies—nearly every citizen of Torre—made it warm as toast. The Manfredis sat near the back of the church, but Doria could see, in the very first pew, the crown of one of Elvira Puccini's elaborate hats, a purple velvet affair with a sweeping white feather. Next to her was her daughter, Fosca, in a stylish hat with a great scarlet bow. Her little daughters, Franca and three-year-old Biki, Puccini's great favorite, sat beside her, also dressed in Christmas finery, with crocheted scarves draped over their hair. Beyond them was Puccini, his hair and mustache freshly trimmed. Tonio was there, too, and Fosca's husband. Everyone had decided to come after all.

In the pew behind the Puccinis Old Zita sat, her back very straight, wearing her ancient brown hat that always looked as if it had been squashed flat by the wheels of a donkey cart.

Doria, filing up to the communion rail among the crowd of her neighbors, kept her eyes down, but she tingled with awareness of the Puccinis' presence. She knelt to receive the host from Father Michelucci's hand. When she stood up again, she put up her chin, and paced back down the aisle as if her old black hat were as grand as Elvira's purple creation.

When Mass was over, she filed out of the nave with her family. She dipped her fingers into the font and made the sign of the cross as she stepped out into the chilly sunshine. The painted walls of Villa Puccini rose directly in her line of sight, and Doria tried to think, as she went down the steps, that it was a good omen. Her brothers hurried ahead up the lane, eager for their Christmas breakfast. Emilia followed more slowly, and Doria, still hoping, walked more slowly still.

"Doria!" Her heart leaped. The Virgin had heard her prayers! It was Puccini's smoke-roughened voice, calling to her from the crowd. She stopped, letting people push past her.

Her mother turned, and came back to her to take her arm.

"Doria, wait a moment!" he called again.

"Mamma, wait," Doria said, freeing herself from her mother's grasp. Puccini was pushing through the crowd toward her, and Elvira was nowhere to be seen. "It's Signor Puccini."

Emilia turned with her daughter, and they watched the crowd part respectfully for Puccini to make his way through. When he reached them, Doria dropped a curtsy, and Emilia imitated her, though her face was a thundercloud. *"Buon natale,"* Doria said. She savored the moment, everyone around her watching the famous maestro come to greet her. She linked her gloved hands together, and said primly, "How are you, Signor Puccini?"

He grinned at her, acknowledging the formality. "Well enough, thank you, my little nurse." He nodded to her mother. *"Buon natale,* Signora Manfredi." She gave him a chilly nod, but he seemed not to notice, focusing his attention on Doria. He took one of her hands, and held it. "Doria, you're so thin! Tell me you're not ill!"

"No, no," she said. She tossed her head in the old way, confident now that all would be set right, that her plan was proceeding. "I'm never ill, maestro, you know that."

"No, you're always the strong one!" He bent his most affectionate look on her, squeezing her hand in his strong fingers. "Signora Manfredi, you have a fine girl in your Doria. I don't know what I would have done without her after my accident."

Doria heard her mother draw breath, and she feared she was about to say something sharp. Doria elbowed her, and Emilia, though she cast her daughter a sidelong glance, merely curtsied again and said, *"Grazie, signore."*

Doria said, "Maestro, how is Mademoiselle Minnie coming along?"

Puccini, still holding her hand, patted it. "It's kind of you to ask, Doria. Mademoiselle Minnie is a tyrant, as you know! She is beginning to behave, though she's taking a long time about it. I think she will—"

Father Michelucci emerged from the church at just that moment. Elvira was at his side, with Fosca and her little daughters. Doria pulled her hand free. "Signore," she interrupted him. "I believe your wife is—"

But it was already too late. Elvira had seen them through the crowd, the people having cleared a space around Puccini and the Manfredis.

Elvira Puccini never shrank from an audience. She had struck Corinna with her umbrella right in the public street. She threw tantrums in restaurants or hotel lobbies or anywhere she happened to find herself when something outraged her. The curious eyes of the residents of Torre del Lago meant nothing to her. Now, she bore down on her husband and Doria, plowing through the throng like an ocean liner through a crowd of fishing boats. She was already shrieking by the time she came close enough to seize Doria's arm with her big hand.

"You little whore!" Father Michelucci gave a wordless exclamation at the offensive word, but she paid him no attention. "You dare show yourself here, in church, Doria Manfredi? You bring shame on your mother!"

"Elvira! *Silenzio!*" Puccini bellowed. She didn't even look at him.

Doria gasped, and tried to pull her arm free, but Elvira's temper was out of control. Her fingers were like a vise, squeezing, bruising, and her face was dark and distorted. Her great purple hat tilted, askew on the mass of her hair, and threatened to fall over one eye.

Emilia cursed at Elvira and grabbed at her hand. Puccini shouted at her to let Doria go. Still Elvira's grip didn't loosen, and as Emilia

staring eyes, accusing, gloating. She wasn't sure if the dream had ended because she woke up or because the person at the center of it had collapsed, but she had been glad when it was over.

When she went to the bureau for her sweater and jeans, she gazed at the bottom drawer where Ellice Gordon's file rested, and anger sparked in her chest.

When Tory and Johnson came back from their beach walk, Tory was startled to see Iris's white Acura parked behind her Beetle. She and the dog came in through the gate, and Tory could see Iris inside, drinking coffee at the kitchen table. The door was unlocked, and she pushed it open to reach for the towel she kept beside it. Iris got to her feet when she saw her, and crossed to the door as Tory bent to rub sand from Johnson's coat.

"I hope you don't mind," Iris said. "It was so cold out. I let myself in."

Tory did mind, rather a lot. As curious as Iris was, she was perfectly capable, she suspected, of nosing around. Tory couldn't say that, of course, nor did she want to. She said only, "You made coffee."

"Brought it. A thermos." Iris stepped back so Tory and Johnson could come in. "Would you like some?"

"Yes, that would be great. I need to hurry a bit, to get down to the shop."

"I know. I just wanted to drop by and invite you to dinner tonight. A very small gathering. Betty's back, and she and Zoe are coming."

Tory took a cup from the cupboard and helped herself from Iris's thermos, covering her hesitation. And her irritation. Finding Iris in her house had felt strange, and she needed to sort out why that was. There was only one object in the house she needed to keep hidden, and surely Iris wouldn't have gone through her bureau.

As if sensing that something was amiss, Iris picked up her car keys with a brisk rattle. "I'll leave you to it," she said. "But dinner after the shop closes, if you can."

Tory held the coffee cup in both hands. "Iris—"

Iris put up her hand. "Don't worry, Paulette. Love to see you, but it's up to you. Open invitation." She pulled on her oversized parka as she walked to the door. She put her hand on the knob, and gave Tory a half smile. "Hank Menotti is coming, too," she said. It didn't feel, to Tory, like an afterthought.

"You know Hank?" she blurted. She felt, again, as if something private had been laid bare, as if Hank was her special secret. It was all so silly, so childish, that she found herself saying with a rush of self-reproach, "Iris, of course I'd love to come. Tell me what I can bring."

It wasn't until Iris had pulled away in her car that Tory realized her landlady probably thought it was Hank's presence that made her accept the dinner invitation. The thought rose in her mind, too swiftly for her to suppress it, that it was probably true.

She stood beside the window, gazing at cold-looking seagulls tossing on the surface of the ocean, and wondered if she would ever be able to behave normally again.

Iris was just a friendly person who liked to get people together. She liked to cook, and to see people enjoying her good food and her pretty house. She wouldn't snoop, Tory told herself. She was just outgoing, curious. There was no need to be paranoid, and no need to be rude.

Still, when she went through the bedroom to take her bath, Tory opened the bottom bureau drawer to make certain the file was still there, undisturbed.

On her lunch break, Tory went down the street to one of the boutiques that catered to tourists. She was tired, she told Zoe, of sweaters and jeans. Zoe had pointed her to the shop she liked best, and said with a grin, "Nothing like new clothes to perk a girl up! And there's Dr. Adorable to think about, right?"

"It's not that, Zoe," Tory protested.

"Nah, of course not." Zoe winked. She was wearing vivid green eye shadow and layers of mascara that turned the wink into a feat of feminine engineering. "Just leave Johnson with me while you go find something to make you look pretty. We'll be fine, won't we, big guy?"

The prices in the boutique were daunting, but on a sale rack, Tory found a long-sleeved, long-skirted dress in an emerald-green fabric that looked more or less like silk. She held it up in front of her, admiring the shimmer of the gored skirt. It seemed the right length, so she took it into a cramped dressing room to try on.

She wriggled out of her jeans and pulled off the thin red sweater she had been wearing to work. She paused, staring at herself in the long mirror. She had never been so thin. Not even during the awful days when Jack's father was on trial, when she had thrown up every morning before going off to the courtroom. Now she could see her hip bones, and when she lifted her arms, the outlines of her ribs. Her collarbones were sharp and prominent, something she hadn't noticed before. The red hair made her skin look startlingly pale, and the scar on her arm was a jagged bluish line.

"You look like a real refugee," she whispered to herself.

"You doing okay in there, miss?" The saleswoman had come to stand outside the dressing room. "You want another size?"

"Oh, I—I don't know yet. Just a minute."

"Okay. Just let me know!" The woman's heels clicked away on the floor. Tory took the green dress from its hanger, and slid it over her head.

It was a bit loose around the neck and waist, but the length was perfect, the hem swirling just above her ankles. It had a wide belt with a gold-tone buckle. Tory cinched that in, blousing the bodice fabric above it. She tried to get the effect by standing as far away from the mirror as she could. Hoping for a better look in a bigger mirror, she slipped out from behind the curtain.

The saleswoman pounced. "Wow, that was meant for you!"

Tory gave her a doubtful look. "I don't know. It's a bit big—"

"That color, with your hair! Really great," the woman said. She pointed to a three-way mirror in one corner. "There, go have a look. I love it, though, and it's a great price."

Tory padded to the mirror in her bare feet. As she turned before it, she realized she had no shoes to wear with a dress. The saleswoman had already noticed the same thing, evidently, and she returned to Tory carrying a pair of black pumps, holding them up to tempt her. The bell beside the door tinkled, and she set the shoes down, saying, "Take your time," and went off to greet another customer.

Tory didn't need much time. The dress really did suit her. The material was soft against her skin, and the touch of shine would look nice in candlelight. She put her hands to her short hair, tousling it a bit, then stepped into the pumps.

"You look beautiful in that." It was the new customer, with the saleswoman beside her.

The saleswoman nodded. "It's perfect."

Tory couldn't argue. At least for this dinner—and to see Hank Menotti again—it was indeed perfect. She bought the dress, and the shoes, too, carrying them back to the flower shop in a big red shopping bag with a painting of holly on it. Zoe seized the bag, took everything out, and exclaimed over it. As she folded the dress back into its tissue paper, she said, "Hey, Paulette. You can use my makeup kit if you want."

Tory chuckled, already feeling she was in danger of acting girlish. "I don't think I will, but thanks, Zoe," she said. "How about if I just wear some lip gloss?"

"Suit yourself," Zoe said. "Dr. Darling probably likes that natural look, anyway." And then, tilting her head to one side, she added, "You do rock the look, Paulette. You really do."

This rendered Tory speechless, her cheeks flaming. Zoe guffawed, and turned back to a complicated arrangement of greenery and candles and miniature red roses.

Tory put the red bag down behind the counter. Johnson sniffed at it and wagged his tail as if he approved. Tory patted him. For the moment, with a new dress and shoes to wear, and a dinner to look forward to, surely there could be no harm in a single evening without worry.

* * *

Iris's party was in full swing when Tory arrived. She was a little late, having locked up the shop and gone home to change and to feed the dog. When she rang the bell, a woman with crimson lips, a daunting mane of silver hair, and enormous gold earrings opened it.

"Paulette! You must be Paulette!" she cried. "Look, Zoe, Paulette is here."

Zoe, resplendent in a strapless red dress, came into the foyer. "Paulette! Great. Mom, Paulette. Paulette, Betty."

Tentatively, Tory put out her hand. "It's nice to meet you."

Betty shook her hand with a fierce, plump grip, and drew her into the house. Music played, pop recordings of Christmas songs. Candles burned everywhere, and garlands of greenery hung from every lintel and banister. Tory, slipping out of her black coat, hung it on the coatrack, and turned to face a bewildering riot of color and people. The "little dinner party" appeared to have gotten out of hand, with five people she didn't know already drinking wine by a heavily decorated Christmas tree, and the refugees she had met at Thanksgiving leaning on the holly-festooned mantelpiece, talking together. Iris came to the kitchen door in a Mrs. Claus apron, waved once, and disappeared.

Betty was talking, but through the noise of the music and voices, Tory could hardly hear her. She felt tongue-tied in the face of so much festivity. Betty was saying something, waving a beringed hand, then smoothing a Christmas sweater over her generous figure. Tory couldn't make out the thrust of the conversation, so she merely nodded. Zoe saw this, and leaned forward to say in her ear, "It doesn't matter, Paulette. Mom loves to talk. You wouldn't get a word in anyway."

Tory found Iris in front of her, a glass of red wine in her hand. She gave it to Tory, handed her a cocktail napkin, and said, "Glad you could make it! Sorry it turned out to be so many people," and was gone again, leaving Tory looking around for a corner to fade into. One of the refugees nodded to her from his place by the fireplace, then returned to his conversation. Tory moved to one side of the doorway to the living room, and stood with the wineglass in one hand, the napkin in the other, feeling awkward and exposed. The raucous music scraped her nerves, and when she sipped the wine, it tasted thin and sour in her mouth. She looked down at her green dress, and tried to recapture the feeling she had had when she bought it. Now, in the moment, it eluded her.

"You look beautiful."

Tory started. She hadn't noticed him in the room, but looking up into Hank's familiar face was such a relief that unexpected tears stung her eyelids. He had leaned down to speak to her, and the clean soapy scent of his skin tingled in her nose, an oddly intimate sensation. "I would have picked you up," he said. "But Iris wasn't sure you were going to come."

Tory dropped her gaze, fearful her eyes had reddened. "Iris knows everyone, it seems."

"She brought her cat in to see me. I guess that puts me in her circle."

Tory looked up again when the sting of her eyes had subsided, and she gave him a smile that almost felt steady. "You're one of the refugees."

He nodded. "So I'm told."

"Me too. At least, I was on Thanksgiving."

He lifted his glass to her with his quiet smile. "It's good to see you, Paulette. And I meant it—you look lovely."

"I haven't worn a dress in a long time."

"You're one of those women who looks good in anything. I've always wondered how you do that."

Her cheeks warmed, and she was saved from having to reply to the compliment by the appearance of Zoe in a swirl of red fabric and the clink of a dozen silver bracelets on her arm. "You must be Dr. Menotti! I've been waiting to meet you!"

Tory, relieved Zoe hadn't called Hank "Dr. Precious" or some other creative name, introduced them. Hank shifted his glass to shake Zoe's hand. Betty appeared to be introduced, and to flutter her eyelashes at Hank. Soon after, Iris announced dinner and everyone streamed into her dining room.

The long table was set with Portmeirion china and a half dozen pillar candles in red and green. Tory faltered briefly when she saw that place cards were at every plate, but it turned out Iris had seated her next to Hank. As he held her chair, she sank into it with gratitude for Iris's thoughtfulness. Nosy and bossy her landlady might be, but she was also sensitive and kind.

Suddenly, with Hank beside her and a festive table spread before her, Tory was ravenous. The baked salmon, rice pilaf, roasted beet salad, and fresh rolls were delicious. She filled her plate, and before she knew it, had emptied it all. She sat back, one hand on her stomach, marveling at how much she had eaten. "Oh, goodness," she said. "I stuffed myself."

"Good to see you eat," Hank said.

Startled, she laughed. "No one's said that to me in years!" she exclaimed. "If ever."

"That's something a lonely person would say." He touched her hand where it lay on the table. "Everyone needs someone to care whether they eat or not."

She smiled up at him, liking the way the candlelight gleamed on his cheekbones. His eyelashes were dark and thick, a striking effect on so masculine a face. She said impulsively, "Does anyone worry about whether you eat, Hank?"

He leaned closer to her, his elbow touching hers. "Not lately."

"Does that mean you're lonely, too?"

He shifted to face her. "Not right now," he said. The corner of his mouth twitched in that way she was coming to recognize. "This is very nice, I think."

"It is." She glanced around the table, and Zoe caught her eye with a saucy wink that made her laugh again. "Iris throws a mean party. I think she likes getting people together. It's like—her mission, or something."

"We would call it her charism, in church language."

"Would you? What a lovely word that is."

They were quiet for a moment, comfortable together. Hank finished the wine in his glass, and set it down. "You should let me cook you dinner one night," he said. "I make the best spaghetti *amatriciana* you've ever had."

"That sounds wonderful. You do seem like someone who could cook."

He gave a one-shouldered shrug. "Well, my kitchen is a bit small here, but I manage. I live over the clinic, for now."

"Do you?" She was about to say something about knowing what that was like, living in the same place you work, but she caught herself.

The conversation around them was a steady stream of noise, encasing the two of them in a bubble of privacy. Hank pushed his plate away, and turned in his chair to face her, one elbow on the table, the other hand on the back of her chair. The posture was both masculine and protective, and it made Tory's breath catch in her throat. Bemused, she watched the candlelight flicker in his eyes, and she felt something soften in her middle, something that allowed her to relax her spine, to lean ever so slightly closer to his warmth.

"Tell me how things are going with your clinic," she said.

"Good," he answered, nodding. "I've been busy." Then, wickedly, "Shirley says hi."

"She does not!"

He laughed, and she felt his wine-scented breath on her cheek. "No, she doesn't. I try not to talk to her about my social life."

"I do think that's best," Tory said, with mock sternness. "She'll be handling your social appointments, too!"

He grinned, and propped his chin on his hand, keeping his eyes on her. It occurred to her that everyone was treating them as a couple. That they were behaving like a couple. A little thread of guilt over that wormed its way through her. She couldn't be doing that, could she? Not with—not when Jack thought she was—

At just that moment, Hank said, "Paulette. I told you my story, but you haven't told me yours. How did you become one of Iris's refugees?"

Tory's heart skipped a beat. She had a sudden, vivid vision of Ellice Gordon's black gun, the flat look in her eyes as she recited what she knew about Jack. *Oh, no . . .* Tory's hand, lying on the table next to the fork she had laid down, began to tremble, and her voice shook when she said, "Hank, I just—I don't know—"

He leaned back, not abruptly, not dramatically, but just enough to break the circle where she had felt, for a moment, safe. Connected. He was quiet for a moment. When he spoke, his voice was even. Too even. It chilled her, despite the warmth of the room. He said, "Never mind. I shouldn't have asked."

She dropped her hands to her lap and twisted her fingers together. "I can't talk about it," she said in a little rush. "I want to, but I can't."

He withdrew his arm from the back of her chair, and reached for his water glass. "I shouldn't have pushed you."

"I—no, Hank, you don't understand." She glanced sideways at him, at his unsmiling face, the shuttered expression that had come into his eyes.

"No, Paulette," he said quietly. "I don't. But there's no reason I should."

"If I were able to tell you," she said, whispering now, speaking too fast, too urgently, "I would. If I were going to tell anyone, it would be you." His eyebrows rose, but she shook her head. "Hank, it's just not—" She had been going to say "safe," but she caught herself. Even that was giving away too much. She finished weakly, "It's just not possible."

"Forget I asked," he said.

Her throat tightened so she couldn't answer. Someone spoke to Hank on his other side then, and he turned away from her. She saw Iris get up to clear the table, and she pushed her own chair back to go and help, her feet dragging, the swish of her pretty green dress around her ankles no longer giving her pleasure. The bright colors of the decorations, the glimmering candles, the gay music all had lost their luster. She collected plates, smiled automatically, accepted an apron from Iris as she went to the sink to rinse dishes and set pots to soak. She helped serve tiny dishes of peppermint ice cream with Christmas tree cookies, but when she sat down before hers, she couldn't eat it. She felt Hank's eyes on her from time to time, but he didn't say anything more.

Tory was startled, as the front door opened for the first of the departing guests to go to their cars, to see snow on the lawn and in the street. It fell in shimmery flakes that reflected the red and green lights from Iris's front window. The shrubs and lawns glittered under the streetlights.

"I didn't know it could snow here," Tory said to Iris.

"Sometimes," Iris said. "Won't last, though. Never does here on the coast."

Tory retrieved her jacket from the coatrack, and dug her car keys out of the pocket. She thanked Iris, and was surprised to find herself in the older woman's embrace, Iris's lined cheek pressed briefly to hers. She felt oddly violated, as she had when she found Iris in her house, but she knew that wasn't fair. She managed to smile, and not to pull away too soon.

When she reached the front step, she found Hank waiting for her. She said artlessly, "I'm glad you're still here."

He arched an eyebrow. "Are you?"

She put her hand on his arm. "Of course I am. I was hoping to wish you a merry Christmas before you—we—"

"I'm going to follow you home," he said. "The snow will make the streets dangerous."

"There's no need, really. I'm used to snow driving."

"Are you?" He smiled, but it wasn't the easy smile he had bestowed on her at the dinner table. He said in an offhand way, "Well, just the same, Paulette. The snow here is really slippery, because of being so close to the ocean." When she still hesitated, he said, "Look. You don't have to talk to me. Just let me follow you, for my own peace of mind."

Tory nodded, mute and embarrassed. He walked her to the Beetle, held the door for her, and then went to his own car and got in. She started her engine, backed out of the driveway, and waited for him to pull out behind her before she turned her car for home.

His headlights followed her steadily back to the cottage. She turned in, shut off her motor, and climbed out. Hank pulled in after her, but only, it seemed, to back up, to turn back to the road. She hurried up to the driver's side of his SUV, her pumps sliding dangerously on the icy driveway. He stopped, his engine idling, and slid down his window.

"Hank," she said. She bit her lip, searching for something to say. "Hank, I—come down to the beach with me. With us, I mean. Me and Johnson. I know it's late, and a little cold, but . . ."

The corner of his mouth twitched. "It's freezing," he said.

"I know. Johnson has to go out, though, so I . . ."

With deliberate movements, he switched off his engine. He reached into his backseat for a thick parka before he opened the door and put his long legs out. "Get the dog," he said, smiling at her. "But you'd better change those shoes."

Johnson, released after the long evening, leaped over the doorstep and out into the yard, where he paced the inside of the fence, glancing back impatiently as if to see what was keeping Tory. Hank stayed with him while she slipped out of her dress and into warmer clothes. When she emerged, the three of them walked out through the gate and down to the beach. There was no snow here, but the wind from the ocean was as cold as Tory had ever felt it. She walked close to Hank, not taking his arm, but glad of the warmth, and the shelter from the wind his height gave her.

They strolled for a time, not speaking, listening to the waves wash against Haystack Rock. Johnson ran in exhilarated bounds, making big circles around them. When they reached the rock, they stood in the lee of it, out of the wind, and watched the dog sniff the tide's edge.

Hank said, "Christmas Eve tomorrow. Hard to believe it's here already."

"It always seems to come too fast."

He said, "A very different Christmas this year, I think. For both of us."

She glanced up, and met his intent gaze. That half-forgotten feeling trembled in her belly again, and she put her hand on his arm. He covered it with his own, pressing it against his sleeve, his eyes on her face. "Hank," she said. "You're really—I mean—" She broke off, shaking her head. "This is like high school," she said. "I was never any good at it then, either."

"It's not like high school for me," he said, laughing. "I went to a seminary school."

"Oh, my god. I never thought of that!"

He turned her hand, and held it in both of his. "So we're a little awkward. Let's try anyway."

She gave him a rueful smile. "I just wanted to say how glad I am that I met you. How very nice you are."

He chuckled, dropping her hand, putting his long arm around her shoulders. He pulled her close enough to press his cheek against her windblown hair. She leaned against him, closing her eyes. His chest was warm, and his hand on her shoulder was strong and sure. She wished she could hold this moment, preserve it like the gold butterfly frozen forever in sea-green glass. She wished she didn't have to open her eyes and remember who she really was, why she was here, what dread hung over her.

It was Johnson who broke the mood. He trotted up to them, bumping their legs to get their attention. Tory opened her eyes. The dog smiled up at her, winding around the two of them, smearing them both with cold wet sand. Hank released Tory, and she, laughing now, said, "Johnson, stop it!"

"I think he's trying to tell us to get out of the weather," Hank said.

"It's a good idea." Tory patted the dog, and her hand came away covered in sand. "Come on, Johnson. Let's get you inside and toweled off."

"I'll help you," Hank said. As they headed up the beach toward the lights of the cottage, he took her hand. His skin was smooth, his fingers strong and warm. She found, when they reached the gate, that she regretted having to let it go.

She brought a towel to the front step. Hank scrubbed Johnson from head to tail, then shook the towel out over the thin layer of snow that covered the yard. "That should do it," he said.

Tory, feeling shy again, stood awkwardly in the doorway. "Can I get you anything?"

He was brushing sand off his coat. He looked up and smiled. "It's late," he said. "I have clinic hours in the morning, even though it's Christmas Eve."

"And I'll be at the shop."

"What are you going to do for Christmas, Paulette?"

She shrugged. "I don't think I'm going to do anything."

"That's not good." He wasn't smiling now, but looking at her intently. "Why not come to Mass with me?"

She was suddenly, sickeningly, overwhelmed by a flash of memory from her last dream, people on the steps of a church, shouting, threatening each other. A rush of panic made her heart thud in her ears. She said, with more force than she intended, "No! Oh, no, I—I don't think—I don't really—" She wanted to say something that might make sense, something that would soften her refusal, but she couldn't think what it would be.

He said softly, "It's okay, Paulette."

"I'm so sorry," she said, weakly, but meaning it.

"Don't be sorry. I just wish you wouldn't be alone for Christmas."

"I'll be okay," she said. He hesitated, looking at her. She thought for a moment he might kiss her cheek, but he touched it instead, the slightest brush of his fingers as he said good night.

As he turned toward his car, she called after him, "Merry Christmas, Hank."

He glanced back. "And to you."

He lifted one hand to her as he drove away, and she gazed after him, wishing . . . wishing what? Wishing he wouldn't leave.

Wishing it could all be different. Wishing she had met this lovely man at a better time, a time when she was free.

This was another way Ellice Gordon had hurt her, an unexpected wound. The anger that had flickered in her breast earlier that day grew into a flame.

28

✦

Sorda ai consigli, sorda ai dubbi,
vilipesa, nell'ostinato attesa raccolse il cor.

Deaf to all entreaties, deaf to doubting, humiliated,
blindly trusting to your promise, her heart will break. . . .

—Sharpless, *Madama Butterfly*, Act Three

For weeks after Christmas Doria never left her mother's house. Not even to celebrate *capo d'anno*, the new year of 1909, could she bring herself to face the people of Torre. Father Michelucci took to calling every day, and for that she was grateful. Otherwise she saw no one.

The priest knew all the news of the Puccinis. The *signore*, in a towering temper at Elvira's behavior on Christmas morning, had left Torre when their children did, leaving Elvira alone in Villa Puccini. Elvira was, Father Michelucci said, worse than ever. Her dresses were dirty, because no one but Zita would work for her now, and Zita flatly refused to do her laundry. Elvira's eyes were wild, and at night, her neighbors saw her stalking through the empty house, talking to herself. People had taken, Father Michelucci said, to ducking into doorways or alleys when they saw her coming. She prowled the lanes of the village, seizing people's arms, recounting her stories to anyone and everyone who would listen.

Doria said, "Stories about me?"

"About everyone, including her husband and her children. She imagines that everyone is against her, that everyone is plotting to harm her."

Emilia poured more coffee for the priest, and then for herself. She set a biscuit on his saucer, but Doria saw she took none for herself, and she felt a rush of shame. There was little money for flour or sugar without Doria's modest salary. She had tried to make this up to her mother, darning socks and mending towels and linens until her fingers were sore, but such efforts brought in no money.

Emilia scowled. "Those children of hers can't stand to be with her, and I don't blame them. But one of these days she's going to do something really crazy, and then they'll be sorry!"

"I've written to Giacomo," Father Michelucci said. "I have his address at the Hotel Quirinale. He's so angry at Elvira he won't even discuss her."

"I hope he's working on his opera," Doria said. She thought of him at his piano, candlelight flickering on his face, music emerging from his pencil one painful, tentative note at a time, the notes piling up, collecting, finally coalescing to make magic. She missed that magic, missed lying in bed at night and hearing his melodies and harmonies take shape in the studio. Surely she missed Puccini more than his wife did.

"His wife needs him here!" Emilia pronounced.

"She would only shout at him," Doria said. "Then he can't get anything done."

Emilia tutted. "Family is more important than any opera."

But Doria shook her head. "The *signore* can't help it if his wife is crazy. He tried to stop her, Mamma, you saw him."

"Hah," Emilia said, sounding for all the world like Zita. "You mark my words, that woman will harm herself one of these days."

Father Michelucci gave an unhappy sigh. "Or she will harm someone else," he said.

It was the very next day, the twenty-fifth of January, that the message came from Villa Puccini. Emilia, still on the doorstep, called, "Doria! You have a letter! The Puccinis' gardener brought it!"

Doria was washing clothes on the icy porch. It was a nasty chore in the winter, because no matter how hot the water was when she poured it into the tin tub, it cooled quickly. It made her long for summer, when she could wash the family's clothes in the warm waters of the lake. She dried her reddened hands on her apron, and hurried into the kitchen, where Emilia had laid the envelope on the table and was standing to one side, her hands clasped hopefully beneath her chin.

Doria could see instantly that the letter was not from Puccini. It was from Elvira.

With trembling fingers, she picked it up and held it, gazing at the *signora*'s handwriting, with its extravagant loops and scrolled capitals.

"Doria!" her mother cried. "Open it, for pity's sake! What does it say?"

Doria, biting her lip, slid her finger under the flap of the envelope and drew out a small sheet of beige notepaper, elaborately embossed with the Puccini initials. She read the note quickly, then read it again, hardly believing what she saw.

"What is it? What is it?" her mother begged.

Doria lifted her eyes to her mother's, her heart lifting with wonder. "Mamma," she said hoarsely. "The *signora* wants to see me!"

"Why? Does she want you back?"

Doria read the note a third time. "He must have written to her. Perhaps he even called her on their telephone! She doesn't say that exactly, but she says she wants to talk to me."

"I hope she means to give you your last two months' wages," Emilia growled.

"*Non lo so*, Mamma, but she wants me to run an errand for her on the way, and I'm to come now. Today!"

"Then you'd best change your clothes, Doria. I won't have you running through the village in that wet apron."

* * *

Doria washed her face and hands in the basin, comforting herself as she shivered under the cold water with the thought that perhaps, soon, she could take a nice hot bath in the tub at Villa Puccini. She had pressed her best shirtwaist, and darned the moth holes in her woolen skirt. She had sewn the sleeve back onto her coat. Her shoes were spotless, and she had washed her black stockings just the day before. She brushed her hair up into its bun, perched her hat on top, and thrust the hat pin through. She smiled all the while, chiding herself for giving up hope. She should have known Puccini would not abandon her. She should have known he would take his wife in hand, sooner or later.

Her mother eyed her carefully, nodded without speaking, and opened the door for her. Doria, feeling as if the world had changed overnight, caught up a string bag and rushed out of the house. The *signora*'s letter requested her to pick up some disinfectant at the chemist's. Surely that meant she had a job for her to do at the villa! No doubt it was some task she couldn't manage on her own, and she had realized at last how much she needed Doria to help her.

A cold drizzle began the moment she was out the door, but she didn't care about that. She felt buoyant, as if the summer sun had broken through winter's clouds just for her, come to burn away the cloud of despair that had enveloped her since Christmas. A surge of brittle energy drove her steps until she was almost running up the lane. Though she felt curious eyes following her, that didn't matter, either. Soon enough she would regain their respect.

In her hurry she nearly tripped over the sill of the chemist's shop. She caught herself, and stood for a moment inside the door, out of breath, looking around for what she needed. When she spied the proper shelf, she crouched to reach for the brown bottle, neatly labeled, tucked away beneath boxes of starch and bluing and peroxide. She carried it to the counter, and set it down with a decisive gesture.

"Put this on the Puccinis' account," she said, with self-conscious pride. "The *signora* needs it." It felt grand to say that again.

The chemist was a round, balding man who wore thick glasses and always had ink and chemical stains on his hands and the cotton coat he wore over his vest. He frowned over the disinfectant, and pushed his glasses higher up his nose. "This is corrosive sublimate," he said. "Chloride of mercury."

"She asked for it particularly," Doria said. "For mold, I expect. Could you hurry, please? She's waiting for me."

He lowered his glasses again to peer doubtfully at her. "It's all right, signore," she said. "I have her note. Would you like to see it?"

He hesitated, but he shook his head. "No, no. I know you. Doria Manfredi, isn't it?"

"*Sì, signore!*" Doria bounced impatiently on her toes. "Could you wrap it? And hurry, please. I don't want to keep Signora Puccini waiting."

"Hmph," he said, and she supposed he, too, had heard the stories of Elvira's behavior. "*Va bene.*" He took the bottle of tablets, wound a strip of brown paper around it, and tied the whole with a bit of string. He held it out to Doria across the counter. As she took it, he said, "This is dangerous, you know. Be careful with it."

"*Sì, signore!*" Doria smiled, dropped a curtsy, and scurried out of the shop and down the lane toward the lake and her beloved maestro's golden tower.

Old Zita met her at the back door. Doria threw her arms around her, making Zita say, "Hah! About time you cheered up, Doria *mia*."

"The *signora* sent for me, Zita! When the note came, I thought perhaps it was from Signor Puccini, sent from Roma, but—" Doria hurried in through the pantry, unbuttoning her coat as she went, unpinning her hat. "But I think a note from the *signora* is just as good, don't you? She even asked me to run to the chemist's for her." She kept the package under her arm as she hung her hat and coat on the rack. "Should I put on an apron, do you think? Or should I wait until she offers me my job back?"

"Is that what the note said?" Zita asked. "That she wants you back?"

"Well—not exactly, at least not yet. She says—" Doria stepped into the kitchen, and stopped, staring around her. "*Mamma mia,* what have you been doing?" Things were stacked everywhere, lamps and books and ashtrays and empty picture frames.

"She's cleaning," Zita said sourly. "She says when the *signore* returns, everything must sparkle. All these things"—she waved one wrinkled hand—"all of these have to go down to the church to be given away. A fresh start in Villa Puccini, she says. A new broom sweeps clean! She's ordered all sorts of new things from Milano." She dropped her voice. "She says she's getting rid of everything that ever troubled her."

"I don't know if the *signore* will like that. Some of these things are his."

"*Lo so, lo so,* but it's not my problem. She'll have to explain to him." Zita tapped her temple and rolled her eyes. "*Pazza,*" she whispered. "Worse than ever."

"Where is she now?"

For answer, Zita pointed her finger up at the ceiling. Doria nodded. "I'll take her some tea," she said. "Oh, and her package." She took it from under her arm and set it on the counter next to a jumble of things she had dusted many times. She wouldn't mind a few of them going away, really. So many little gifts from people all over, given to Puccini in appreciation! They did take up a lot of space and gather an impressive amount of dust.

She filled the kettle and began to gather the tea things, fill the creamer, set a tray with a pretty cup and saucer from the breakfront in the dining room. At the last moment she decided the apron was a good idea. Zita lent her one of hers, and though it was a little short, it was clean and pressed.

She put the package on the tray next to the teacup, and carried everything up the narrow stairs. She stopped outside the bedroom door, and called in her most polite voice, "Signora Puccini? It's Doria. I came as you asked me to, and I have the package from the chemist's."

The door flew open with a bang, making Doria start, and the tray tilt in her hands. She stared at Elvira Puccini, hardly recognizing her as the same strong woman who had assaulted her on the church steps on Christmas Day.

The roots of Elvira's hair showed shockingly gray. Her cheeks were sallow, and her eyes glittered so that Doria wondered if she had taken opium. Her shirtwaist was stained across the bosom, and the hem of her skirt had come loose to drag unevenly on the floor. She had an enormous black shawl around her shoulders. She looked, indeed, like a madwoman.

But the words she spoke were just the ones Doria wanted to hear.

"Doria, good," she said. Her voice was not the crow's caw, but a hoarse whisper that was almost inaudible. "You're back. Come in." She turned, and waved her hand at a cluttered dressing table. "Put it there, and sit down."

Doria's knees felt weak as water, and though she meant to demur—she knew very well the housemaid did not sit down to have tea with the mistress—she thought if she did not set the tray down quickly, she would drop it. With her elbow, she moved the clutter of perfume and lotion bottles aside enough to make room. She could see the *signora* truly had need of her. The bedroom was a mess, bed unmade, curtains wrinkled and dusty, everything in need of a good scrub. The room smelled sour, as if something had been spilled and not cleaned up. The new broom, it seemed, had not yet reached Elvira's bedroom.

With the tray safely settled, she turned, linking her trembling hands in front of her. *"Buon giorno, signora,"* she said carefully. "I was very glad to get your note." She had decided, as she scurried toward the villa, that she would not expect an apology. Surely Elvira was humiliated enough, especially if the *signore* had ordered her to take Doria back.

Elvira sank onto the chaise longue. Her corset shifted when she did, and Doria was sure it was fastened wrong. "Sit, sit," Elvira said, pointing at the stool before the dressing table. Her hand shook, and there was a tremor in her head Doria had never seen before.

Doria said gently, "Oh, no, signora, but thank you. I've brought you some tea—and your package from the chemist's."

"I want you to have tea with me," Elvira said. "And I will tell you what Giacomo has written from Roma."

Doria bit her lip in an agony of confusion. A housemaid did not sit down with her mistress. But Elvira looked so ill! And Puccini would want Doria, his own nurse, to look after his wife, wouldn't he?

Again, Elvira pointed a wavering finger at the dressing table stool with its lacy flounce and padded seat. Her lips parted, and Doria saw with a shudder that they were wet, that her teeth were not clean. "Signora," she faltered. "There—there is only one teacup. I didn't think—"

Elvira forced her lips into a parody of a smile. "Go get another," she said. Her gaze skittered away from Doria, around the untidy room, but it seemed to Doria she saw nothing. She had a letter in her hand, a much-creased envelope with a sheet of paper half out. Doria wanted to take it from her, to see if it had the crest of the Hotel Quirinale at the top. Perhaps it was this very letter that had forced Elvira to send for her!

She backed toward the door. Elvira half rose from the chaise, but Doria waved a hand to stop her. "Please, just sit, signora. I'll be right back." She dashed down to the kitchen for another cup and saucer. She and Zita didn't speak, though Zita raised questioning eyebrows. Doria shrugged, rolled her eyes, and hastened up the stairs once again.

She knocked on the half-open door, and went in. Elvira was on the chaise, her arms folded tightly around her, as if she were cold. She was staring at the dressing table, her lips working as if she were talking to herself. Or praying.

Doria said, "Signora?"

Elvira started. "Oh! Doria!" She stared at her for a moment, her eyes wild. "Tea, good. Yes, tea. I—" She pointed a ragged fingernail at the dressing table. "You see, I've already poured you a cup. Give me that one, and I'll—" She struggled to rise, unfolding her arms and pushing herself up from the chaise. "I'll pour for myself," she said, crossing the room on unsteady feet. She took the fresh teacup, and placed the other one, half full, into Doria's hands.

Doria wanted to protest, to tell the *signora* to let her do the serving, but a tingle had begun in her toes, a prickling that spread up her ankles and calves. Her *fé*.

She held the half-full teacup, bemused by the sensation in her legs. Elvira poured tea for herself and carried it back to the chaise. Elvira lifted the teacup to her lips, then produced another ghastly smile. Her eyes had gone flat, like those of one of the water snakes that squirmed among the marsh grasses at the edge of the lake. They made Doria shiver. "Drink your tea," Elvira insisted, her voice rasping as if she were the heavy smoker and not her husband. "Do sit down, Doria, and drink your tea."

Still Doria hesitated, caught between the creeping sensation of her *fé* and Elvira's strange behavior. Elvira snapped, "Oh, do as you're told, girl!" For that moment, she sounded like herself, but she caught a noisy breath, as if she hadn't meant to speak that way, and she held up the envelope. "From Giacomo. Drink your tea, now, and I'll read it to you."

At last Doria sat down, crossing her tingling ankles beneath the lacy stool. There was no time to think about what her *fé* was trying to tell her. Elvira pulled the letter from the envelope, but her eyes never left Doria until, obediently, Doria drank the tea.

She didn't drink much. It tasted awful, though she had made it herself, and she wondered if it was too old, or if there had been mold on the leaves. She hadn't noticed any, and surely Zita would not have moldy tea in her kitchen. Elvira sipped her own tea, and seemed not to notice anything amiss.

But then, Elvira Puccini had gone mad. Zita was right. The only thing to do now, Doria thought, was to humor her. And to get the *signore* home to see that she had proper care.

"Drink, drink!" Elvira said, and drained her own cup as if to demonstrate.

"I would like to hear the letter," Doria demurred. She pretended to take another sip, but even where the liquid touched her lips there was a nasty sensation. She put the cup back on the tray, and folded her hands in her lap.

"Oh, the letter, the letter," Elvira said irritably. "It's just the usual, but I'll read it to you."

To Doria's great disappointment the letter was, indeed, just the usual. The maestro wrote about struggling with *Fanciulla,* about the terribly wet, cold weather in Rome, about some people he and the *signora* both knew, whom Doria had never heard of. She listened closely through to the end. The letter wasn't long. There was no mention, as she had so hoped, of herself.

So why had Elvira asked her to come? Surely not just to bring something from the chemist's! Doria looked around for the bottle of disinfectant, but she didn't see it. Elvira must have put it somewhere while she was in the kitchen.

While the *signora* was folding the letter back into its envelope, Doria rose. She gathered the teacups—her own still a quarter full—and lifted the tray to take it back downstairs. She waited a moment, hopeful Elvira would speak to her about her job. Elvira, however, seemed to have forgotten her. She gazed down at the envelope in her lap, smoothing it over and over with her fingers, her lips working again as if she were reciting what she had just read. Doria went to the door, and opened it with her elbow while she balanced the tray with both hands.

She paused in the open doorway. "Signora?" Elvira didn't look up. "Signora!"

Finally, Elvira lifted her head, and fixed Doria with a vacant expression. "What is it?"

"You asked me to come here today, signora," Doria said. As an afterthought, hoping it would help, she curtsied. "I thought perhaps you were going to give me my job back."

Elvira's eyes sharpened, focused, glared. "Your job back!" she said in a grating voice.

"*Sì, signora,*" Doria said. A sudden pain of nerves shot through her stomach, but she held her ground. "I want to come back, and I can see you need me." She nodded at the turmoil of the bedroom.

"I don't need you," Elvira said, her voice rising, the black crow squawking. "A little whore like you? You're never coming back here! Never! Do you hear me?"

Doria's stomach clenched, and she thought she might be sick, right there in Elvira's bedroom, right on her beautiful Turkish carpet. She clutched the tray against her, the cups and teapot clattering together, the tea she had not finished slopping over the surface. "Why did you ask me, then?" she demanded. "Did you send for me only to insult me one more time?"

"*Esatto!*" Elvira cried, leaping up with sudden energy. She threw up her arms, and her shawl flapped around her like great black wings. Crow's wings. "One more time! One *last* time!" she shrieked. "Go home now, go back to your ignorant mother and your filthy hut! You will never bother me again!"

Doria didn't move for one long, frozen moment. Then, with a deliberate gesture, she turned the tea tray over in her hands. The teapot, the painted cups and saucers, the creamer and the bowl of sugar fell to the floor with a gratifying crash. Porcelain, pottery, and glass shattered. Sugar flew everywhere, and the teapot burst into pieces as if it had been struck with a hammer.

"You," Doria Manfredi said to Elvira Puccini in a loud, clear voice, "are truly the *strega* they say you are. I pity the *signore* that he has to suffer you. Thanks be to God *I* will never lay eyes on you again!"

Leaving the mess where it was, white cream blurring the red and green and purple design of the carpet, she spun about, and ran down the stairs to strip off Zita's apron, seize her coat and hat, and dash out into the rain.

Her fury and resentment turned to pain with shocking swiftness. She stumbled as she navigated the muddy lane toward her home. She passed several people, but she didn't speak to them, didn't look at them. She knew they were staring at her, but she didn't care. She only wanted to reach the sanctuary of her own house. It seemed to take hours to get there, though it could only have been minutes. By the time she finally staggered over the sill into her mother's kitchen, her stomach felt like it was on fire.

Emilia met her at the door. "What happened? What did she say?" But Doria could only shake her head. She half fell into the house, still in her coat and hat, clutching her middle with her arms. "What is it?" her mother said, her voice shrill with anxiety. "What's wrong with you?"

"I don't know," Doria groaned. "My stomach hurts so much, Mamma! It's awful!"

"But, Doria, you were fine when you left—what happened? Did you eat something?"

Doria shook her head, and collapsed onto a kitchen chair. A cramp seized her, and she gasped. Another followed, the pains so close in succession she could hardly draw a breath between them. Emilia said, "Tell me what happened!" but Doria couldn't speak.

There was agony in her belly now, coming on so fast and so fiercely that it was beyond anything she had ever felt in her life. She pulled up her knees, groaning, twisting to find a position that didn't hurt.

"The doctor! I'll fetch the doctor!" her mother cried. In moments she was gone, hurrying down the lane with only a ragged umbrella to protect her from the rain.

Doria hardly knew she had gone. She gasped and shuddered under the onslaught of pain, a pain that writhed in her belly like a live thing, a live beast with teeth and claws. She fought it for a time, there on the chair, and then found herself on the floor, curled into a ball, without remembering how she had gotten there. She thought she cried out, but she wasn't sure. In the midst of one particularly brutal spasm, the light faded around her, and for a time she knew nothing.

She woke again to a steady torment, and to the sounds of voices coming through the front door. Her mother. The doctor. She wanted to call to them, to beg for help, but all that came from her mouth was an agonizing grunt as her belly contracted, the live pain gripping her with devilish strength. She could barely see Dr. Giacchi as he bent over her, or feel the pressure of his hands and her mother's pulling her up, cradling her between them, maneuvering her into the bedroom. She knew what the doctor was spooning into her mouth, though, and she swallowed it greedily. The laudanum burned down her throat, but the sensation was nothing compared to the agony of her stomach, the bite of a flea contrasted with the bite of a tiger. Dr. Giacchi's medicine reached down into her belly to soothe the beast there, to ease the cramping at least a little. She gave a sob of relief and slipped into unconsciousness.

Doria woke in darkness, roused by her own groans. The pain had returned with more strength than it had before, intensified by the respite she had gained. Her mother appeared at her side, to bathe her forehead with vinegar water and chafe her wrists, to weep over her daughter's agony. Dr. Giacchi had left a dose of laudanum, and Emilia administered it, but this time it seemed to do little to help.

Emilia said, over and over, "Doria, what happened? In the name of God, what happened?" but Doria, writhing in misery, couldn't tell her. She could barely remember, in truth. The all-consuming pain drove everything from her mind.

It went on and on, until the sun rose behind the thick rain clouds. Emilia kept the curtain drawn, but rain-tinged light illumined the bed on which Doria suffered, twisting and turning in search of surcease. Vaguely, she was aware of her brothers staring at her through the doorway, though Emilia wouldn't let them come in. The doctor returned, and gave her a larger dose of laudanum, which helped a little. Zita came, and sat beside her bed for a long time, stroking her forehead, rubbing her back between spasms of pain.

Doria's mind was foggy with laudanum, her thoughts blurred by pain. She knew Zita was there. She knew something had happened, something with the *signora*, but she couldn't remember it. In the evening Dr. Giacchi came once again, with more laudanum, in a greater concentration. For a little while then she was better, the pain receding enough that she could listen to him telling Zita and Emilia that the chemist said Doria had bought poison at the *farmacia*. She heard the word as if from a great distance.

Suicidio.

No! It wasn't true! That much she knew, that much she could remember. She struggled toward consciousness to deny it, to explain, to tell them she would never—

Her mother misunderstood the strangled sounds she made. "Oh, Doria *mia!*" she shrieked. "Why would you do such a thing? She wasn't worth it, that *strega*, that creature! I'll kill her with my own two hands if—if you—" She broke off into wild weeping, and Doria, helpless in the grip of her torment, could only listen, and mourn for her.

Another day passed, and another. The agony of her body became a constant, as regular as the rhythm of the unceasing rain on the roof, of the lapping of the lake against the shore, of the visitors who came to hold Emilia's hand and speak to her in low voices of the offenses of Signora Puccini and what the Manfredis could do to win justice for Doria.

By the fourth morning, Doria lay limp, exhausted by the pains that now wracked her whole body. She was too tired to fight them. She let them buffet and torment her, but she didn't resist. She took the laudanum when it was offered. She drank the other draughts the doctor prepared, but if they made any difference, she couldn't tell. It had begun to seem like a dream, a nightmare, dark and foreboding, an endless round of whispering, weeping, praying, and pain.

Zita came again, and knelt beside Doria's bed, stroking her hand. "I brought you something, Doria *mia,*" she said sadly. "The *signora* is off to Milano. She says it's a shopping trip, but I think she's afraid to stay here. Everyone says this is her fault, that she drove you to it." She stroked Doria's hand, and her voice broke a little. "*Bella,* can't you speak to me?" When there was no answer, she went on. "She left me all those things to box up for the church, but I kept something for you. I know you always liked it. I thought it might cheer you a little."

Doria felt something cool and smooth tucked under her fingers. It did feel familiar. Her fingers curved around it, and she managed to lift her eyelids enough to see Zita's face bending close to hers. Zita was weeping tiny tears that glistened in the dim light as they coursed along the seams of her wrinkled face.

Doria breathed, "Don't cry, Zita."

Zita said brokenly, "I *will* cry for you, Doria *mia*. Of course I will cry for you!"

"I didn't do it," Doria said thinly.

Zita misunderstood. "We all know you didn't do it!" she said in a rough whisper. "That crazy woman wouldn't believe you, wouldn't even believe *him*—"

Doria didn't have the strength to argue. It wasn't what she had meant, but what did it matter now? They would think what they would think.

She let her eyes close again, but she felt the butterfly paperweight cupped in her palm, and she was comforted.

Father Michelucci came to administer the last rites. She could no longer open her eyes by then, but she heard his sweet, familiar voice, felt the touch of his hand as he made the sign of the cross on her forehead with the blessed oil. Her lips barely moved in the amen.

They would bury her outside the churchyard, she supposed, where those who had committed mortal sins were laid to rest, but that didn't matter, either. The Virgin knew she was not a suicide. The Virgin also knew that Doria, like Her sacred self, was a maid untouched.

And the Virgin knew that Elvira had killed her. Cruelly, heartlessly killed her. Put the poison in her teacup, persuaded her to drink it, then fled the village so she wouldn't be here when her victim died.

There was nothing to be done about it now, nothing but to leave it to God and pray for release. She cradled the paperweight against her, a reminder of her beloved maestro, and she awaited the moment.

29

❧

Tienti la tua paura; io con sicura fede l'aspetto.

Persist in your fear; I, with sure faith, await him!

—Butterfly, *Madama Butterfly*, Act Two

Jack turned south at a town called Astoria, where the Columbia River drained into the Pacific Ocean. It was early morning, and traffic was light. Holiday traffic, he supposed. Christmas lights bloomed here and there, flowers of red and blue and green, blurred by fog.

He felt as if he had been driving forever, the hours stretched to infinity by solitude and the monotony of his circling thoughts. Now, relieved to have reached the coast, he drove along a twisting, ice-slicked highway between forested hills. To his right, where there was a break in the trees, gray breakers surged toward the land. Huge rocks thrust up here and there from the spume-filled water. From the highway he saw picturesque hamlets nestled along bays and inlets. Scraps of snow persisted in shadowed spots, but mostly there was fog, sometimes so thick he had to turn on his headlights, sometimes in scraps and tatters, drifting ghostlike among the evergreens.

He had played through every CD in Tory's collection, the Mozart symphonies, the Bach Brandenburg concertos, the Verdi Requiem. As he caught sight of the signs warning him of the towns he had marked on his map, he turned off the music. It was Octavia Voss singing Puccini arias, and he liked it, but he needed to focus. He had a good idea of where he was going, but he would need luck. And his newfound intuition. He was pretty sure he could be more sensitive to his instincts in the silence.

He stopped for gas in a town called Seaside. The cell phone could have originated there, but as he watched the attendant pump his gas, he felt certain—a certainty that was as much physical as emotional, marked by that tingling sensation in his skull—that this wasn't the right place. He wasn't there yet.

It was when he handed over his money—his cash was almost gone—that a prickle sprang up on his neck. He turned, and saw a car, its engine running, waiting at the edge of the gas station parking lot. He rolled up his window, just stopping himself from twisting in his seat for a second look. He bent forward to start the engine, allowing himself a single glimpse in the rearview mirror as the motor turned over. The goose bumps spread over his shoulders and down his arms.

He had seen that car before. Where had it been? Not on the freeway, he was certain. Astoria, perhaps. He hadn't taken any particular notice the first time. It was just a car, almost aggressively neutral-looking, a beige sedan with no distinguishing features. Jack didn't have a lot of experience, but he thought it looked like a rental.

He pulled the Escalade out onto the highway again, keeping an eye on the sedan. At first it didn't move, and he hoped perhaps he'd been wrong. Five minutes later, with a sinking feeling in his stomach, he spotted it, several car lengths behind him and in a different lane, but definitely there.

"Fucking sticky note," he muttered.

All he had to aid him in his search was the telephone number of the cell phone that had called him, and the information he had been able to glean about its location. But she—she was a cop. She had taken the sticky note, and consequently had all sorts of resources he couldn't even imagine. He had been naïve to think he could outwit her. Childish.

"Dammit!" he said, pounding the steering wheel with his fist. A glance in the mirror showed him she was still there, the neutral beige of the rental car standing out among the black Priuses and red SUVs. "Damn you, what do you *want?*"

His temper in full spate, Jack stomped on the accelerator. The Escalade downshifted, all its power rising to his challenge as if the car, too, had lost its temper. He passed several cars and a truck as if they were standing still. He flew past a sign for a town called Cannon Beach, and one named Arch Cape. When he reached a place called Manzanita, he slowed, a little worried about the highway patrol. He looked into his rearview mirror once again, but he didn't see the beige sedan. A viewpoint was ahead, with an enormous silver-and-blue RV parked in it. Its driver and passengers were out of the car, leaning over a low stone wall to admire the fog-shrouded vista.

Jack stepped on the brake, cleared the traffic to his right, then spun the Escalade into the tiny gravel-strewn parking lot. He parked the car in the shade of the RV. Spectacular cliffs fell away to the ocean on his right, the water hidden now by the mist. On his left, the RV hid him from the highway.

Cautiously, he climbed out of the car. His sneakers crunching on the gravel, he walked toward the restraining wall where the tourists, muffled in thick jackets and wool scarves, were pointing down at the cliffs, chattering together as they peered into the mist. Jack hung back, taking shelter behind their vehicle. When he saw the beige sedan fly past the viewpoint, he barely restrained himself from an exclamation of triumph.

He spun, gravel sliding beneath his toes, and hurried back to the Escalade. He was in the car, and had just started the motor again when he realized that the tourists had climbed back into their RV. They were beginning the laborious process of backing and turning to return to the highway. The RV blocked his own view of the road. There was steady traffic now, and the RV would be slow to accelerate. The big vehicle waited for a break in the stream of cars, and Jack, fuming, had to wait behind it.

Probably no more than three minutes passed while the RV's driver watched for his moment, but they felt like three hours to Jack. When he finally was able to accomplish his own merge into the traffic, his heart was pounding so that perspiration broke out on his chest and forehead. He drove south at a moderate speed, watching for an exit where he could reverse direction and drive back to the north.

He found an exit about five miles on, and left the highway. He turned left at the end of the exit, and followed the signs on the surface road toward the entrance to the northbound lanes.

He was already on the highway again when he realized she had found him. His head buzzed with that feeling he had come to recognize. He glanced in his rearview mirror, and saw that the beige car was right on his bumper, so close he could see her through the windshield. Her brush of sandy hair and the silhouette of her wide shoulders were clearly visible in the gray light slanting through the side windows.

He was tempted to see if the Escalade could outrun the sedan, but he gritted his teeth and restrained the urge. He was so close to his goal now. He could feel it. It would be better to face her than to have her follow him. He would have it out, get it over with before he found his mother. He was afraid of her, of course, but that fear made him angry. He was calm enough to recognize that, but angry enough not to care.

"Just do it!" he muttered, and spun the wheel at the first turnout he saw.

He could have chosen a better spot. He saw that right away. The exit led into a two-lane road that ran alongside the highway before twisting up into the forested hills. He didn't want to move that far away from a road he already knew, so he swung the Escalade onto a wide triangle of gravel that looked as if it might be meant for parking construction trucks. The beige sedan was right behind him, shuddering onto the gravel as it turned and stopped. He was trapped, his access to the road blocked behind him, a grassy water-filled ditch ahead of him.

Jack took one tight, deep breath, and opened his car door. The warning bell dinged, telling him the key was still in the ignition. He pulled the key out just far enough to silence the bell, but left it where it was. He jumped down onto the gravel, leaving the door open behind him. He stalked toward the sedan, though his nerves shrilled with dread. He didn't want to wait for her to approach him. He wanted—somehow—to take control of the situation. She was probably armed—she was a sheriff's deputy, after all, and could no doubt carry a gun on an airplane if she wanted to—but there was nothing he could do about that. She could as easily have shot through his car window, if that was her intent, as she could out here in the open.

She opened her own door slowly, and stepped out with a deliberate motion. Jack stopped several feet away, and put his hands on his hips. Seeing her made his anger grow until it swallowed his fear. He felt well and truly pissed off, and that was a hell of a lot better than being terrified.

She was wearing a black denim jacket that hung to just below her waist. He couldn't see her gun, but he felt sure it was there. She leaned on her open car door and surveyed him.

"How'd you find me?" he asked.

"That's a stupid question, Jack," she said. "You don't strike me as a stupid kid."

"The cell phone number," he said.

"Obviously. If you could trace it, it was nothing for me to do the same. The only question is, where is it now? Where is *she* now?"

"I don't know," Jack said. He dropped his fists from his hips, and thrust his hands into the pockets of his jeans. "Even if I knew—" He shrugged.

"What do you think you're going to do?" she asked. "Visit every pissant little town in the area code?"

Jack shrugged again. "What are *you* going to do?"

"I," she said with icy calm, "am going to let you lead me to her."

"I'd drive the goddamn car into the ocean first."

At that, she laughed. He eyed her with distaste. She wasn't ugly, exactly, but her face was unpleasant, as if the eyebrows and the nose and the mouth didn't work together somehow. He hadn't noticed that before. Or hadn't paid attention.

Jack said, "What is it you want, deputy?"

"Same as you. I want to find Tory."

"But why?"

She was still leaning on the open door, but she straightened, and let her gaze drift out into the misty distance. "Not that it's any of your business," she said casually, "but Tory betrayed me. Let me down."

Jack said, "I'm not much of a son, but I know one thing about my mother. She never lets anyone down. Ever."

"Bullshit." Ellice stepped away from the sedan, and closed the door with a decisive click. "You don't know anything about it."

"Tell me, then."

She laughed again, a mirthless bark. "What, are you the therapist now?"

Jack didn't bother trying to answer that. He could feel, in the buzzing of his head and in the hollowness of his belly, the danger of this woman. She didn't want to kill him. At least she didn't want to kill him yet. Not till she got what she wanted.

He had to lose her somehow. He stood where he was, trying to think what to do. He said, after a moment, "Well, deputy. I'm no therapist, obviously. But you want my diagnosis anyway? I think you're batshit crazy."

She stiffened, and her right hand moved toward the pocket of her jacket. "Better watch what you say, Jack."

He stood still as stone, though his muscles trembled with the desire to flee. "You trashed our house. Searched through our mail. Followed me out here—what did you do, fly? Get on an airplane to go after a woman who was probably only trying to help you?"

"She didn't help me."

"Maybe," Jack said, proud of the evenness of his voice, "you're beyond help."

Ellice Gordon's face flushed scarlet, and she smacked the roof of her rental car with the flat of her freckled hand. "Where's Tory?" she shouted.

"Don't know!" Jack shouted back.

She said, "Goddammit," and started toward him, freckled fists clenching, muscles bulging in her long jaw.

Jack whirled, and with one leap, he was in the Escalade again. He saw her reach in her pocket as he jammed the key back in the ignition, turned it, slammed his door, and stamped on the accelerator. He couldn't back up, because the sedan blocked his access to the road. He went forward, jolting over the edge of the gravel patch, down into the drainage ditch with a bruising bump, skidding on the wet grass as he drove up the far side to reach the surface road. As he turned back the way he had come, he blessed Tory for having all-wheel drive and great tires. His wheels slid on the slick asphalt, then abruptly found traction. The car lurched forward, throwing him back against the headrest as its engine roared as if in triumph, as if it knew how important this was.

There was a stoplight and a Y intersection where the road met the highway entrance. Jack ignored both. He crossed the verge in the most illegal fashion possible, bridging the distance between the two-lane road and the highway with bone-jarring speed, taking his chances on cops and traffic.

It worked. He drove much too fast for the foggy conditions, but he was out of sight of the beige sedan in seconds. He kept on, breaking the speed limit by a good twenty miles an hour, his heart thudding in his ears, his mouth dry, every sense fired by adrenaline.

After a few moments he began to slow the car, glancing in his rearview mirror over and over to make sure she hadn't caught him. His breathing eased and his heart ceased its pounding. Now he could feel it. The buzz in his skull, the alarm of his fey. It grew until he thought he couldn't stand it. It was so intense it was almost audible.

He was close. He had to be close. He pulled into the right lane.

He clicked his cell phone to check the time, but it was dark and lifeless, the battery dead. As he fumbled in the console for the charger, he drove past the exit for Cannon Beach. Instantly, the buzzing intensified until he thought his head might explode.

He knew. He slowed, looking for a place to get off the highway, reverse direction one more time. It took a few minutes of driving through a fog-blurred landscape until he found one. He took it, circled back, and drove south again as fast as he dared.

30

Finiamola! Bisogna che giustizia sia fatta!

Let's end it! It's necessary that justice be done!

—Rance, *La Fanciulla del West*, Act Three

She was dead. The girl in the dream was dead, and Tory knew it the moment she opened her eyes the morning of Christmas Eve. She cried out, and sat straight up, her hands pressed to her face. Johnson startled and leaped from the bed, then turned to stare at her. She stared back at him, watching his hackles rise in alarm. She had never seen that in him.

"Oh, my god," she whispered. "She killed her."

Johnson whined. His tail stretched straight out behind him, not up and waving as it usually was. She lowered her hands, and took a slow breath. She had frightened him. When she swung her legs out and put her bare feet on the floor, his hackles lowered. His tail rose, but it didn't wag. He sat down, his black eyes fixed on her with what she could only feel was wariness.

Tory reached for her zippered sweatshirt and pulled it on as she padded out into the living room. Johnson followed her, but when she opened the front door for him to go out, he sat down again, his gaze never leaving her face.

"Okay," she said in a low tone. "I get it. I'm sorry I scared you." She closed the door, and went into the kitchen to start coffee, but found herself with the filter in one hand, the scoop in the other, staring blindly out into the mist that enveloped the beach, the rock, even obscured her own front gate. Shreds of snow still clung here and there, and lacy patterns of ice gleamed on the window glass. The dream was distinct in her mind, an impression of unbearable pain, of helpless sorrow, of the sickening shock of becoming a victim.

She saw again, as if it had not been a dream but something real, the eyes of a murderess glittering with fury, and she knew, with a sudden and overwhelming certainty, what these dreams were telling her.

The girl in her dreams had relinquished her power. She had let a madwoman control her life, and it had cost her everything. Tory was doing the same thing, and she saw now, with a clarity that cut to her soul, how great a mistake she was making. Her fey was telling her there was no time to lose.

She knew, belatedly, what she had to do. But she didn't think she could do it alone.

Before the coffee had even begun to perk, she had her new cell phone in her hand. She stood staring blindly into the fog as she waited for someone to answer, waited and waited until she heard the recorded message. "You have reached the Cannon Beach Veterinary Clinic," Shirley's voice said. "Our office hours are—"

Christmas Eve. Was no one there?

Her heart pounding so she could feel it in her toes, she looked at the clock. It was only seven. Too early.

She pushed her hands through her hair, trying to think. Did she have another number? Could she—

Oh, yes. He lived over the clinic, he had said that. With an exclamation, she rushed to the bedroom to throw on a sweater and jeans, to brush her teeth, to drag a comb through her hair. She opened the drawer in the bottom of the bureau and lifted out the file. She pulled on the dilapidated black down jacket, grabbed her keys and Johnson's leash, and hurried out toward the Beetle, the file tucked under her arm. "Breakfast later," she told the dog. "Sorry about that. We have to hurry."

Johnson seemed relieved by the sudden action. He trotted at

her heels, stopping only for his morning pee before they went out through the gate. He leaped into the car, taking up his usual position, facing forward as she started the motor.

She drove as quickly as she dared over the icy streets toward the veterinary clinic. She saw that Iris had been right. Most of the snow was gone, dissolved into the dry grass and cedar chips of the flower gardens, but the streets shone with rime, and twice her tires slipped, sending the little car sliding sideways. Johnson panted, fogging the windshield. The engine was too cold for the defrost to work. Tory had to wipe the glass clear with the edge of her hand.

Fortunately, it was too early for much traffic. She pulled into the gravel parking lot in front of the veterinary clinic, and with a rush of relief, saw that lights shone from the windows above it. The SUV was parked to one side, but there were no other cars.

The rush to get here had distracted Tory. Now, her legs trembled as she stumbled around the car to clip on Johnson's leash. He jumped out, but he kept a little distance from her as they walked around the clinic in search of a door to the apartment above. "It's okay," she told him. "It's going to be okay." She hoped it was true. Her throat was dry, and her heart had not eased its thudding. The dog followed at her side, but she was sure her rough awakening and her sudden panic had infected him. His customary smile was absent. His mouth was closed, and he kept his eyes straight ahead.

The door to the apartment—at least she hoped that's what it was—was on a small landing at the top of a short stair. A tiny spruce tree in a clay pot rested in one corner, and someone—Hank, she supposed—had draped it in curling red ribbon. She gave it the briefest glance as she led the dog up to the door and lifted her hand to knock.

The door opened before her knuckles could strike it. He stood there, tall and steady, eyebrows raised. He put out his hand, and she gripped it hard, as if it were a lifeline in an angry sea. "I need help," she blurted. "Hank, I really need help."

He pulled her gently in through the door. His hand felt so strong and warm and steady that it made her throat ache. "The coffee's on," he said in his deep voice. "Tell me what's wrong."

She found herself, moments later, seated in a pleasant little dining nook with a built-in table and padded benches under a window. The apartment, like the clinic below, still smelled of fresh paint and new carpet. Hank set a bowl of water down for Johnson, then brought two cups and a coffeepot to the table. He sat opposite Tory. "Cream?"

"No," she said. She cradled the hot coffee cup in her hands to hide their shaking.

"Does the dog need food?"

"Yes."

"Okay, we'll take care of that in a few minutes. Tell me what's up."

"Hank—I've lied to you. I've lied to everyone."

The corner of his mouth curled. "Paulette, you haven't told us anything, so I doubt there could be much you've lied about."

"Oh, there is!" she said bitterly, clinging to the coffee cup. "My name, to start with."

"Really." He tilted his head, regarding her. "You lied about your name?"

"I did. My name isn't Paulette Chambers at all. I took it out of the phone book—well, the Chambers part. Paulette comes from *La Rondine*. I don't even know why—I just thought of it." She stopped, uncertain how to go on.

He said quietly, "Okay. You're not Paulette. What name shall I call you?"

"I'm Tory. Victoria, but everyone has always called me Tory. Tory Lake."

"Tory. That's nice. It suits you." He sipped coffee, sitting with his elbows on the table, his long legs stretched beneath it. Johnson lay a little distance away, his head on his paws, watching them.

She hesitated, casting about for a way to tell her long story. All she could do, she decided, was begin at the beginning. If she could find the beginning. She pulled the file out of her bag, and laid it on the table between them. Hank glanced at it, but he made no move to open it.

She drew the cup close to her so she could stare into the shining dark surface of the coffee as she started to talk. "I'm—that is, I was—a therapist. A counselor. In a small town in Vermont." She spoke quickly, feeling the pressure of the dream, the warning it carried, the overwhelming sense of danger that had impelled her here.

"One of my clients did something very bad, and I made a mistake. I knew she was having fantasies, but I never thought she would act on them. She seemed angry, but not violent, just dealing with feelings of abandonment and betrayal. These fantasies—I just couldn't believe she would actually act them out. I didn't call the police as I should have. A man died, and it's my fault. My client has never been investigated, and that's my fault, too."

Hank listened quietly, watching her face. When she glanced up she saw the angle of the cold sunshine glinting on his silver hair, and she was, somehow, encouraged. "My client—this woman, a sheriff's deputy—she threatened my son. She knew everything about him, where he goes to school, which dorm he was in, what he did and where he went when he came home. She said, if I reported her—she said he would be next. She admitted she shot this man, just because she wanted to, and she said, if I told anyone, she would shoot my son. I knew she meant it."

He nodded, but he didn't speak. She looked away again, down at the dog, then back into the coffee cup. She spoke even faster, feeling the pressure of time passing, some terrible event looming over her—and Jack. "She cut me," she said matter-of-factly. "I still have the scar on my arm. She meant to kill me, that was obvious. I tried to get away from her, and she forced my car over a riverbank. I managed to jump out, and then I hid in the water until she was gone. I took some money from my house, nothing else. I walked away through the woods, and no one knows anything about what happened to me. I'm certain everyone thinks I'm dead."

She paused, and took a sip of coffee to put some moisture in her mouth. At this movement, Johnson lifted his head, and it felt as if he was urging her to go on. "I came here to Cannon Beach," she said, "just because it seemed a likely place to stop driving. I created a life, a story, everything a lie. All this time I haven't done anything about Ellice Gordon. She could have hurt someone else. She could even hurt my son." She glanced up again, into Hank's uncritical gaze. "Jack," she said. "His name's Jack. He's only twenty."

"Jack."

"I called him once," she said, her voice a little unsteady for the first time. "About two weeks ago, I think. I hung up right away, but I heard his voice. He was okay then. I don't know where he was, though, at school or at home. I didn't dare—you see, Ellice said if I told anyone, if I reported what I knew, she would shoot him next, the way she shot that poor man." She passed a hand over her eyes. "Hank, I've made it even worse. All this time, I don't know if Ellice might have done it again—I don't know what happened. I should have—I don't know what I should have done. I couldn't think."

"And you were all alone," he said quietly.

"I should be used to that," she said with a shrug. "But I—I just ran. I probably should have gone straight to the police, but the trouble is—she *is* the police. If I called the sheriff's office, they'd take her part. Were they going to believe me, take action in time? She could have gotten to Jack so fast—I didn't know what to do."

"What's changed, Pau—I mean, Tory? What brought you here, now?"

"I've been having these dreams." She looked down at her cup again, wondering why she had ever thought he would believe her. He would probably think she was out of her mind. "The thing is, Hank, I have—I'm—" She drew a sharp breath through her teeth, and looked up again. "I have something my grand-mother called my little fey. My intuition. I used it all the time as a therapist. No one knows that, really—I didn't talk about it much—but it was helpful. I'm afraid I counted on it. But with El-lice—it failed me."

The eyebrow again, but no comment.

"These dreams started soon after I came here. I brought something of my grandmother's with me, and it's in the dreams, too, but the dreams—I couldn't think why I was having them, until now. Now I know. My dreams are warning me that I have to deal with Ellice. I can't put it off any longer, and I can't take any more chances. You don't have to believe me about the dreams," she added hastily. "I would understand that. But I have to do something. I have to report her, and before I do that, I have to get my friends in Vermont to make sure Jack is safe."

"We'll call them."

Tory spread her hands. "Yes. But if I call, if they hear my voice—the shock will be—I guess I thought you might do it for me. So she and her husband will understand. You always seem to know the right thing—that is, you could try to explain why I haven't let them know—it's been awful not being able to—" She dropped her hands. She had run out of words, and she could only sit across from him, shaking her head.

"You know her number?"

She nodded, mute and miserable.

He unfolded himself from the bench and crossed the kitchen to where a telephone hung on the wall beside a small, new-looking refrigerator. He lifted it from the base and carried it back to the table. "Tell me her name, and her husband's name," he said as he held out the phone to her.

"The Binghams. Chet and Kate." It felt strange saying their names aloud, as much a confession as everything else had been. She took the phone in a hand that shook so she could hardly press the buttons, but when she handed it back, she felt as if she had taken a huge step in the right direction, on the right path.

She heard the phone ring, and Kate's voice—so far away, so

small through the telephone—answering. Hank said, in a quiet, steady voice, "Mrs. Bingham? Good morning."

Tory put her hands to her cheeks, and pictured Kate with the phone in her hand. She glanced at the stove clock in Hank's kitchen, and realized it was ten-thirty in Vermont. Kate was probably busy with her baking, wrapping presents, getting her house ready for Christmas.

He went on. "My name is Hank Menotti. I'm calling from Cannon Beach, Oregon, and I have some news for you. It's very good news, but it's going to be a shock. Is your husband there?" A pause. "Good," Hank said easily. "It would be good if he's right there with you. But remember, this is the best possible news to hear." His voice vibrated, ever so slightly, but in a way that Tory thought must give confidence to the person listening. "I'm calling about your friend Tory. Yes. Yes, Tory Lake."

Hank spoke at length with Kate, and then repeated it all to Chet. Tory pulled up her knees and rested her forehead on them. Tears streamed down her cheeks to dampen her jeans. Johnson rose from his place in the kitchen and padded over to her. He crowded under the table so he could rest his chin on her foot, and now his tail beat gently, slowly, against the floor. Tory listened, her throat aching with the sobs she was holding in, as Hank patiently answered the Binghams' questions.

At the end, when it seemed there was nothing else he could tell them, he handed the phone to Tory, got up, and walked away down the hallway. Tory heard a door close just as she said, her voice tight with emotion, "Hello? Kate?"

Her friend cried joyously, "Oh, my god! Tory, my god! I can't believe it. Is it really you? What a Christmas present!"

"Kate, I have so much to tell you, and I'm so sorry about—about all of this, the way you must have felt, this phone call—I'm just so sorry. Something very bad happened, and I'll try to explain all of it, but right now we have to hurry. Can you find Jack? Can you get him to stay with you until—well, until I settle something? I don't think it will take more than a few days."

"Tory, of course we would, but Jack's not here. He's gone out to visit a friend, somewhere west. Oh, Oregon, Chet says—but wait, that's where you are! He's spending Christmas with the friend's family, he said."

"What friend?"

"He didn't tell us that. He left us his cell phone number. He's been gone—what is it, Chet? Right, about five days. Oh, my god, I can't believe I'm talking to you!"

"He didn't say where?" Tory asked. "When is he coming back?"

"Honey, he said he was going to fly, but Chet went over to check on the house, and it looks like he took the Escalade."

"He drove? Out west?" A sudden pain pierced Tory's chest. She dropped her feet to the floor and pressed her hand over the spot where her fey had stabbed her. Her voice caught in her throat so she could hardly speak. She choked, "Are you sure, Kate?"

"As sure as we can be, Tory—oh, this is all so strange." Kate's voice turned thready, and she said unevenly, "Oh. Oh. I feel a little woozy!"

"Kate, I'm so sorry. I wanted to call you—please believe me, I really couldn't."

"Tory?" It was Chet's voice. "Kate has to sit down a moment. This is so—it's unbelievable!"

"I know. Hi, Chet. I'm terribly sorry."

"That's okay, honey. It's okay. When we've had a chance to process all this, I'm sure we'll understand."

"I hope so. Is Kate okay?"

"Yes. She's just—dammit, Tory, this is really wonderful! Just as your friend said, the best possible news!"

"Chet, we'll talk about everything, but—I have to find Jack. You're sure he took the car?"

"It's not in the garage. At the moment, that's all I know."

"I'll call his cell. I'll have to hang up now, Chet, but—I'll call you as soon as I possibly can. Please don't tell anyone. Not anyone! It's very important. And again—I'm sorry to have put you through all this."

"Sweetheart." She heard the tightness in his voice. She pictured him, fatherly, kind, standing in Kate's bright kitchen. Fresh tears started in her eyes. "Just come home safe, okay?"

"As soon as I can."

Tory closed her eyes when the call ended, trying to assess what her fey was telling her. Jack. A friend in Oregon. Christmas with another family.

She didn't believe a word of it.

The sounds of Johnson munching kibble filled Hank's little apartment as Hank and Tory dialed Jack's cell phone number again and again. The only answer was his cheery recorded "Hey! Leave a message!" Tory couldn't think what she could possibly say to a son who had thought for two and a half months that his mother was dead, so she didn't say anything.

Hank said, "Maybe his battery's dead."

Tory's chest still ached with the effects of her fey. She said, "It's awful not knowing where he is." The irony of that was not wasted on her, and she saw in the twist of Hank's mouth that he understood it, too.

He touched her hand. "Let's take the next step. He's going to be okay."

With trepidation, but driven by the conviction she had woken up with, Tory nodded. Hank said, "Where shall we start?"

31

E come sarà giunto, che dirà?

And when he has arrived, what will he say?

—Butterfly, *Madama Butterfly*, Act Two

Tory paced the floor in the cottage, with Johnson watching her uneasily. She had called Zoe to tell her she had an emergency to deal with. Hank had promised to come as soon as he completed the couple of appointments he had scheduled for the morning. The clinic was closing at noon for the holiday. The fog had thickened, fresh clouds of it rolling in from the sea, isolating the cottage in folds of mist. Tory tried Jack's phone again and again, with no result, until at last she forced herself to stop. She tried not to think of what might be happening in Vermont, the sheriff's office buzzing over Hank's phone call, Kate and Chet upset, Ellice aware and alert that something had happened.

She tried, especially, not to imagine terrible things happening to Jack, but in this she failed utterly. She pictured a car accident, or a robbery, or a kidnapping. She imagined him lost somewhere, and tried to tell herself he could really be with the family of one of his friends. The thing she feared most—Ellice Gordon and her gun—she closed away from her mind, but the idea of it lurked there just the same, like a child's imagined monster awaiting its opportunity to pounce.

On one of her circuits of the cottage, she picked up Nonna Angela's paperweight, holding it in her palm, taking comfort in the familiar smoothness. She stopped by the window to gaze out into the fog, but she could see nothing. Her heart sped until she thought she could hear every beat. To drown it out, she clicked on the CD player. The opening bars of the overture to *Madama Butterfly* sounded, masking the thudding of her pulse.

The file folder—Ellice Gordon's file folder—lay on the cracked Formica table. They had made photocopies in Hank's clinic, on the machine behind Shirley's counter. They had already mailed a set to the sheriff's office. She had the receipt in her pocket.

She tried Jack's phone again. She couldn't help it. She must have dialed it a dozen times already, but she dialed it again, punching the numbers instead of using the redial, as if the extra effort might make a difference.

"Hey! Leave a message!"

Oh, Jack, sweetheart. Where are you?

The time on her cell phone said eleven-thirty. Hank wouldn't be here for at least another hour. Now, after all these ponderous weeks, she could hardly bear the slowness of passing time.

She turned the music up louder, and stood leaning against the wall beside the window, butterfly paperweight in her hand. Johnson, ears twitching nervously, rose and came to her. He pressed his nose against her thigh, and she crouched down to put her free arm around his neck. She murmured into his fur, "I'm sorry. I'm so sorry," but she knew very well it wasn't the dog she was apologizing to.

As Jack coasted to a stop at the end of the exit to Cannon Beach, a billow of fog rolled over the road, obscuring the street signs and the buildings. His shoulders ached with tension. He wouldn't be able to see the beige sedan if it found him again. He could barely see the road ahead of him, only headlights and taillights warning him where other cars were. Through the murk, holiday lights gleamed red and green, and lighted Christmas trees sparkled here and there in a front window or a fog-shrouded garden. He drove slowly over a small bridge and down into the town, looking for somewhere he could park, perhaps someplace safe to ask for—ask for what? What could he say? *I'm looking for my mother. . . .* It was impossible.

But his intuition was still with him. His fey, just like his mother's. He drove tentatively on through the fog, following what seemed to be the main street of the town, past a market, a flower shop, a few boutiques, all open for last-minute Christmas shopping. He kept on, into a residential area where streets and lanes led into foggy neighborhoods, and hoped he would know.

When he felt the impulse, he pulled the Escalade out of the main road and into a side street. Warily, feeling hyper-alert, he turned off the engine, and turned off the headlights as well.

Before he could decide whether this was a good place to get out, the beige sedan rolled past him. Its lights were off, too, and through the mist he could just make out the profile of Ellice Gordon. He knew that strong jaw, the beak of her nose. She was turning her head back and forth, searching.

How had she found him? It made no sense. Surely with the fog . . .

He glanced down at his cell phone, glowing now in the charger. Cell phones had GPS, didn't they? It had never occurred to him to disable it, nor would he have known how to do it if he had thought of it.

It was too late to undo that now. Jack pressed himself back against the headrest until the sedan swept by and was swallowed up in the fog. He waited another minute, two, to be certain she didn't come back. Then, cautiously, he opened the car door and climbed out. He left the cell phone where it was, eager now to get away from it.

He turned down the nearest street, heading toward the ocean at a jog. He buttoned up his coat as he went, and turned his collar up against the damp. His neck prickled, making him glance over his shoulder. He stopped abruptly, his heart lurching. The beige sedan had come back, had turned into his side street. It was rolling to a stop opposite the Escalade.

She had found him after all. Adrenaline jolted through Jack's veins.

He whirled to his left, and dashed up the nearest alley. He dodged garbage cans and stacks of lawn furniture. He jumped a low wire fence, cutting across someone's dried-out grass, and made for the beach. He couldn't see the ocean through the shifting fog, but he could hear the crash of the waves and the deep call of the surf up ahead.

He ran, his sneakers digging into the wet sand. Mist collected on his eyelashes, droplets rolling back into his hairline. To his right, above a low ridge of dunes, lights glowed softly through the fog. To his left, an edge of foam marked the surf line. Up ahead, dim at first through the fog, then looming large and dark, was a giant rock, its feet washed by the surf, its craggy shoulders shrouded by mist. Jack raced toward it, driven by the sure conviction that Ellice would be coming after him.

There was something uncanny in her ability to follow him, something that defied logic, that had nothing to do with technology. It was as if she was connected to him in some obscure and indefinable way. Ever since the first time he saw her, on the steps of Our Lady of the Forests, and every time he had encountered her since, what had happened between them had felt inevitable. Inescapable. It was weird, and he hoped he would be able to think it through one day. The only thing he knew for sure was that he had been right. Ellice was up to her neck in all of this— whatever it was.

He ran toward the big black rock, and circled around to the north side of it where he stopped, hands on knees, to catch his breath. The air was thick and chilly in his lungs, and the sound of the ocean filled his ears.

He straightened, and peered around the dim beach. He couldn't see more than twenty yards in any direction. His sneakers were heavy with wet sand, and the wind from the ocean chilled his wet cheeks and sent rivulets of moisture running down his neck. He backed up as far as he could without stepping in the foam-edged surf, so the rock's bulk sheltered him from the worst of the wind.

He thrust his hands in his jacket pockets and bent his head, listening for the sounds of footsteps.

What he heard instead made him pull his hands free and lean forward, cupping his left ear with one palm.

Music. He heard music drifting down the beach.

Specifically, he heard an opera.

Jack's lips parted as he strained his ears to hear. Puccini, he was sure of it. The second act of *Butterfly*.

Tory's favorite.

He abandoned the cover of the great rock and dashed across the beach, up toward the dunes and the dirt lane that ran behind them. His skull throbbed, tugging him, guiding him. She was here! There was no time to doubt his fey. None of it made any sense, anyway, but it didn't matter now. He only had to follow the music, Tory's signature music, and his long journey would be at an end.

She was here. She *had* to be here, or all of it was for nothing.

Tory set the paperweight on the coffee table before she opened the door to let Johnson out into the yard. Gray drifts swirled over the gate and haloed the Christmas lights in her neighbors' windows. The dog sniffed for a moment, nosing the brown grass and the thin shreds of snow at the bases of the fence posts. The soaring melodies of *Butterfly* rolled out through the open door. She supposed the neighbors wouldn't like it much—it was hardly Christmas music—but just now she didn't care. Her nerves were stretched to the breaking point. It was as if all the fear she had suppressed for so many weeks had suddenly broken through, making her heart pound and her throat ache with tension.

She had done it. She had done what she needed to do, with Hank's help. The sheriff would have Ellice's file the day after Christmas, and that would be a great relief. She had set things right.

But if Jack weren't safe, if he were harmed in any way, she couldn't imagine she would ever feel joy again.

Johnson barked, a deep, harsh sound that made Tory jump.

She had never heard him do that before. It sounded like an alarm. A warning.

She squinted, trying to see through the fog. A shape was approaching, a tall, broad-shouldered figure. Tory stiffened. "Johnson! Come here!" she whispered, beneath the swell of the music.

The dog didn't move. He faced the beach, his expressive tail straight out behind him, his head high and his ears pricked forward.

The shape came closer, so Tory could make out a shock of blond hair, a dark jacket. Whoever it was paused, peering through the fog, finding the lane, taking tentative steps up it.

Tory gasped, and dashed across the yard to the gate, leaving the door of the cottage standing open behind her. Her heart thudded in her throat, stealing her voice. "Jack!" she choked. She threw the gate open, swallowed, and called again. "Jack, here! I can hardly— oh, Jack, my god! What are you doing—Sweetheart, I'm here! Right here!"

He lifted his head, a smile beginning on his face, and he started to trot toward her.

She could hardly breathe, watching him come. He was bigger, surely, and he looked older than she remembered. His fair hair shone through the fog, and even at a distance she recognized the brilliant blue of his eyes, wide now in his pale face, glimmering with surprised tears.

He cried, "Mom!" His voice cracked and broke like a boy's as he dashed across the lane toward her. "Mom, it's really you! God, I—"

"Jack! What are you doing here? How did you—Are you okay?"

Their words tumbled over each other as she reached the gate and opened it. He looked so familiar it hurt, the fronds of hair falling over his forehead, his smile broadening as he saw her, the smooth strength of his stride. The suddenness of it all, the overwhelming relief of seeing him well and whole, weakened her knees, and made tears of relief start in her eyes, too. He had almost reached her, his arms lifting to meet her own outstretched ones.

He said, with a sound halfway between a laugh and a sob, "Jeez, Mom, what did you do to your hair?"

"I—"

She never finished her answer. She didn't have the chance to fold him in her arms as she had longed to do. Even as she was about to touch him, about to hold the reality of her son close to her, another figure emerged from the mist.

It was a nightmare come true. Ellice Gordon, tall, dangerous, vicious, appeared behind Jack. It was what Tory had dreaded for weeks. The reality was terrifying.

But this time she would not flee. She would not cower, nor would she hide.

The weakness left her knees. Her spine stiffened and she set her shoulders. She dropped her arms, stood aside, and said, "Jack. Go inside." She pointed behind her, through the gate to the open door of the cottage.

Johnson began to growl, a low, chilling sound. His nape bristled, and he contrived somehow to look larger than he usually did, taller, broader, fiercer. His lip curled, but not with his usual smile. It lifted to show his long white canines, and he went on growling, a rumble deep in his chest.

Jack twisted his head to look behind him, and when he saw the enemy he, too, turned to face her. He took only a single step backward, enough to carry him through the gate. The two of them, Tory and Jack, stood shoulder to shoulder as they watched Ellice Gordon stalk toward them, stiff-legged. She wore jeans and a black denim jacket with big zippered pockets. As she came near them, she dipped her hand into one of the pockets and drew out her gun. She held it so it dangled, black and ugly, beside her thigh. Tory's skin crawled, and she heard Jack's hiss of indrawn breath.

"Sweetheart," Tory whispered. "Go in the cottage."

"No way."

"You need to call the police."

"She *is* the police, Mom."

"Not anymore, she isn't." She pulled him back one more step so she could slam the gate between them and Ellice. It wasn't much protection, she knew, but it was something.

Ellice crossed the lane and stood with her legs braced, smiling across the closed gate, her pale eyes the same color as the shifting mist. "Smart kid you have there, Tory," she said.

Tory had listened to that uninflected tone for hours, sitting in her office. It irritated her now, fanned the flame of her anger. She felt her own lip curl, and she wished she had teeth like Johnson's to show.

She answered in a hard voice she barely recognized, "I know that." Her anger burned in her throat. She gathered herself, muscles tightening, preparing. She was angry at Ellice for disrupting her life, for threatening Jack. She was angry at herself for waiting too long to take a stand. As her fury grew, she felt like Johnson, taller than before, fiercer than anyone thought she could be. She was afraid of the gun, but that wasn't important. Jack was what was important. She said, through gritted teeth, "What do you want, Ellice?"

The gun twitched at Ellice's side, as if it had a life of its own. Johnson's growling grew louder, and his body, close to Tory's leg, vibrated like a coiled spring. Tory moved slightly, trying to put herself between Ellice and Jack. The dog moved with her.

Ellice's thin lips curved in a feral smile. "What did you do with my file, Tory?"

Tory felt Jack shift slightly behind her. He said in an undertone, "She broke in. Ransacked your office." The gun twitched again in Ellice's hand.

"We've just sent photocopies of it to the sheriff," Tory said. "This morning. We sent all of it." Jack drew a breath, and she realized she had said "we." Her voice sounded sharp and cold, like the blade of a knife. Like the blade Ellice had scarred her with. "He'll have it in twenty-four hours."

Ellice's freckled knuckles whitened as her grip tightened on the gun.

"It's over," Tory said. "You have to face it, Ellice."

"No."

"Yes. You can't run from it now."

Ellice's eyelids flickered. "You tricked me."

"I did not. It was the other way around."

Ellice's face suffused, her freckles disappearing in a rush of blood to her cheeks. She raised the gun, and it wavered right and left, its black muzzle like a searching eye, choosing first Tory, then Jack, then, as if aware there was a real threat, Johnson. "You're just like all the others," she said, her voice rising, shaking. "I trusted you, and you betrayed me."

Jack said tightly, "Put the gun down."

Tory said, "It's okay, Jack. Ellice doesn't want to shoot me. Or you."

Ellice barked a laugh. "You haven't learned anything yet, have you, Tory?" She steadied the gun, pointing it at Tory's breast. "You think you know so much, know-it-all therapist! All your theories and questions and suggestions! You don't have any fucking idea what I might do!"

Johnson surged forward against the closed gate, his growl becoming a snarl. Ellice startled, and turned the gun in his direction. Behind Tory, Jack's breathing quickened, whistling in his throat.

Tory said in a steely voice, "Ellice, if you fire that gun, you won't feel better for long. You should have learned that." She wanted to put a hand on Johnson's collar, to pull him back, but she wasn't sure if that would make things worse.

"You're not my therapist anymore, Tory."

"I'm not your enemy, either."

"All I have are enemies," Ellice said. The gun looked enormous, the muzzle like a cannon, black as death, holding them all frozen in place.

"There's still a chance for you," Tory said. She glared at Ellice, measuring the distance between them, judging the angle of the gun and how she could block it.

As her heart began to race, time slowed. She could see every movement of Ellice's eyes, the beat of her eyelids, the thread of her pulse in her freckled throat. She felt herself rise on her toes, ready to move. It was like being poised at the edge of a precipice, ready to leap into the abyss. Physical danger, at this moment, meant nothing. It didn't seem real. She was no longer afraid even of the gun.

She said, in that knife-sharp voice, "Put the gun away, Ellice. I'll help you—"

"No!" Ellice swung the gun up, away from the dog, past Tory, aiming now at Jack. "No one can help me."

Tory said, "Jack. Back up, and get in the house."

He said, "No, Mom," but she snapped back, "Do it, son. Please." She stepped directly in front of him. The coolness of the air at her back told her he was finally doing it, moving, backing away.

The muzzle of the gun swung to follow him, and Tory seized her moment. She lunged forward, thrusting from her toes, her hands out, open and ready. She hit the gate with both palms, throwing all her weight behind the movement. The gate slammed open, the gate she had repaired so it swung smoothly and swiftly on well-oiled hinges. It struck Ellice a hard blow in the middle of her thighs. There was a sound to the impact, brief and sickening, as hard wood struck flesh and bone. Ellice stumbled backward, grunting, losing her balance, nearly falling.

The gun went off.

Tory's ears rang with the sound of it. It made a dull, aching clap, like that of someone striking an untuned kettledrum. Glass broke somewhere behind her, and at the same moment Johnson, freed by the open gate, charged forward with a roar like that of an angry lion. It was a sound so strange and wild Tory wasn't sure it came from the dog.

Ellice struggled to regain her feet. She tried to point the gun at Johnson, to stop his rush, but he was on her before she could gather herself, leaping at her with his teeth bared, his hackles stiff. His teeth sank into her arm, the very arm with the gun, as if he understood what she was trying to do.

Ellice emitted a hoarse scream. Tory shouted Johnson's name, and leaped after him. She spared a fraction of a second to look back, to see that Jack was safe on the step of the cottage, and then she seized Ellice's wrist with all her strength.

She could never have done it without Johnson. He had bitten Ellice deeply. Blood soaked the black fabric of her sleeve and ran down over her hand. Still he held her clamped in his jaws, snarling through his closed teeth, scrabbling at her with the claws of his front feet.

Tory found Ellice's wrist with her two hands, and twisted. Ellice's blood was slick under her fingers, but she persisted, gripping, squeezing, using all the strength of hands accustomed to wielding hammers and wrenches, hatchets and saws.

Ellice's fingers opened. The gun came free, clattering to the gravel of the driveway. Tory released Ellice's wrist to grab for it, bending, scrabbling along the rocks with her fingers until they encountered the cold metal. She straightened, holding the weapon in her two hands. It was heavy, as she had expected it to be, and she gripped it with all her strength. She took a single step back, bracing her feet wide apart, and pointed the weapon at Ellice.

The trigger was beneath her right forefinger. For one furious, suspended moment, Tory thought of pulling it. She could have done it. She anticipated the feeling of doing it, the stiffness of the trigger, the sound of the report, the thud of the bullet striking Ellice's body. If Johnson had not been there, his teeth still fastened to Ellice's arm, she might have done it. It was possible to do it. There was time, plenty of time, but she would always be grateful, later, that she hadn't.

Ellice was still screaming when she went down, toppling backward onto the gravel. The impact jarred the dog's teeth from her arm, but he wasn't done with her. He attacked. She covered her head with her arms, wailing now as he bit at her wrists, her head, searching for exposed skin as if he were a wolf, or a tiger, a creature accustomed to violence. She was a strong woman, a big woman. When she caught him a blow with her knee, he fell to one side just long enough for her to scramble to her feet. He lunged at her ankles, snarling, gobbets of bloody foam flying as he tried to find purchase on her boots.

The scene, and the sounds, were visceral. Primitive. Nothing in Tory's life had prepared her for this conflict. Her breath hissed through her gritted teeth as she followed the battle, keeping the gun trained on Ellice. If Ellice dared to take a step toward Jack, if she so much as glanced at him, Tory promised herself she would fire. She would do it, consequences be damned. She would pull the trigger, and be done with this madwoman.

But Ellice, with a sobbing cry, lurched to one side, regained her balance, and fled toward the beach.

In three long, unsteady strides, she vanished into the fog. Johnson was right behind her, snapping and snarling, his tail straight as a sword behind him.

Their noises faded with astonishing swiftness, leaving Tory with the gun gripped tightly in both hands, pointing at nothing. The music had stopped sometime during the fight, and now her ears vibrated at the sudden, shocking silence. Still she held the gun, trained on the billowing mist that had swallowed her enemy.

She didn't know when it was that Jack reached her side. He put a warning hand on her shoulder before he stretched his other arm around her for the gun. He took it carefully, gently from her. There was blood on it, and when she looked down at her hands, they were dark, too, and sticky. She waited to feel something about that, about having Ellice Gordon's blood on her hands. No feeling came.

She watched Jack do something with the gun, manipulating it with a deftness that surprised her. It became two harmless pieces, the clip of bullets in one hand, the empty gun in the other. Tory had no idea how he had learned to do that. She glanced down at the beach, where Ellice and Johnson had disappeared, and she began to shiver.

Jack wrapped his strong arms around her—when had they gotten so long?—and they stood together, listening in tense silence for some sound from the fog.

"I need to go after the dog," Tory whispered.

"No," Jack said.

"I do. I need to get him back."

"It's not safe."

"But he's—he's my dog. He saved us."

Jack shook his head, blinking in amazement. She understood, distantly, that Johnson must be a great surprise to him. He said, "Mom, do you have a phone? I forgot mine in the car. We have to call the police."

"Oh. Oh." She swallowed, and tried to steady her breathing. "Yes, I do have a phone—I bought a new cell phone. It's on the counter—" Tory turned to look up at her boy. A man now. She would have to understand that, somehow. "Oh, my god, Jack. I have so much to tell you, and I'm so sorry—"

"I'm sorry, too, Mom. I have a lot to say to you. But later." He kept an arm around her shoulders, and guided her up to the door. He was like a dear stranger, much-beloved but much changed, and she felt the strength of his arm with a sense of wonder that was oddly disorienting. He said, "Call the cops now."

She dialed the police, and stood, trembling with unspent adrenaline as she made her report. When she was done, and when she had answered their questions, they asked her to stay on the line. She stood, the phone in her hand, waiting to see what would happen next. Dried blood crackled on her fingers and dropped in crumbs to the floor.

Jack looked around the cottage curiously. "You've been living here?"

"Yes. Johnson and I."

He frowned. "Who's Johnson?"

A laugh bubbled up in her throat. She put the phone against her chest, and pressed the back of her free hand against her lips, fearful that if she started to laugh, she wouldn't be able to stop. That Jack would think she had lost her mind.

Several moments passed before she trusted herself enough to say, "Johnson—Johnson's the dog. My dog."

32

꧁

Ora permetta che accenda il lume, tutto è passato.

Please allow me to light my candle: everything is all right now.

—Mimì, *La Bohème*, Act One

The police arrived just ahead of Hank, lights flashing lurid red and blue through the mist. Hank's SUV swept around the corner, headlights stabbing through the fog. He parked crookedly behind the patrol car and leaped out, leaving the door open behind him. He didn't quite run, but he moved more swiftly than Tory had ever seen him move, long strides that carried him past the police car. He reached Tory, standing on the step of the cottage, before the policemen could open their doors. His face was tight with anxiety, and his hands came up to grip Tory's shoulders, her arms, as if to assure himself she was in one piece. She had the impression he was barely restraining himself from pulling her close to him, cradling her against his chest.

He said in a low voice, "You're all right?"

Tory nodded, a motion she was sure looked shaky and uncertain. She didn't feel uncertain, though. She felt triumphant. Transcendent. Hank took her hand, and she wound her fingers through his with a fierce grip. "My hand's dirty," she said. "It's got blood on it."

He said in a low, intense tone, "Just so it's not yours."

"Absolutely not."

Behind her, she felt Jack's surprised movement. Hank's eyes

came up to look past her, to take in the surprise of Jack standing just inside the door. He said, "This must be Jack."

Jack said, "Yeah. That's me." He put out his hand, and Hank reached around Tory to shake it. Jack regarded Hank with frank curiosity. "Who're you?"

"Hank Menotti. Your mother's friend. It's great you're here. It's—it's wonderful."

There was no time to explain anything. The patrol officers came in through the gate to stand in the little yard, looking up at the trio in the doorway, taking cautious glances around at the quiet neighborhood. The squawk of their radios was muted, but it felt intrusive to Tory, and she was glad when they turned them down, touching their shoulders as they moved closer. They were both middle-aged and paunchy, and she had the irrelevant thought that they looked more like grocery clerks than police. They looked far less threatening than Ellice Gordon. Less threatening than she herself had felt, such a short time ago.

"Which one of you folks called?" an officer said.

Tory stepped down to meet him. "That was me," she said. All at once, embarrassingly, her teeth began to chatter. She folded her arms tightly against herself.

"You had an intruder?"

"Yes." Tory turned to Hank. "Johnson's gone, too. I don't know where he is!"

"Johnson?" the officer said warily. "Who's that?"

"That's P—I mean, Tory's dog," Hank said. With a sidewise glance at Jack, as if to apologize for taking control, he went down the step, and put his arm around her shaking shoulders. "Officers, you should come in out of the cold."

"Sir," the older officer said, "if you had an intruder, we'd better get someone out looking for him."

"Her," Tory and Jack said together.

"Her?"

"She's a sheriff's deputy," Jack said. "Not in uniform. Tall, light hair, black denim jacket and blue jeans."

"Is she armed?"

Jack said, with obvious relish, "Not now."

"I have to find Johnson—" Tory said. She freed herself from Hank's arm, and edged toward the gate.

"We won't be able to find him in this fog," Hank said.

"Hank, he went after her. After Ellice. He bit her, and then he was chasing her. . . ."

He held her back, the pressure of his hand gentle but firm. "We'll look as soon as we can, but first we'd better explain the situation."

The police officers glanced at each other. One moved up the step and into the cottage. The other one spoke into his radio as he walked back toward the patrol car.

Jack held the door as the officer and Hank walked past him, but still Tory hung back, peering toward the beach, trying to see something, anything, through the fog. "I could just go a little way, call him—"

"It might not be safe out there," Jack said.

Hank said, "Jack's right. No one should be wandering around out there until we're sure."

Tory followed the men into the cottage, but she left the door open a crack, hoping. It felt awful to leave Johnson out there in the mist, to not be able to hear him or see him. She felt as if part of her had been forgotten. Had been abandoned.

Hank and Jack were right about the danger. She knew that. There were people waiting in her kitchen, waiting for her to make sense of a senseless situation. She had to find a way to tell them what had happened and why. She would have to postpone her worry over the dog.

At least Ellice couldn't shoot him.

The officer was standing beside the table, staring at Ellice's service revolver where it lay in two parts on the cracked Formica. Next to it lay the file, clearly labeled with Ellice Gordon's name. The officer bagged the two parts of the gun and labeled them, and pulled out a notebook. As he settled into one of the chairs, the wail of a siren sounded, growing louder as it approached.

Hank pulled out a chair for Tory, and she sank into it, still shivering. He waved Jack into a chair beside her, then stood to one side, leaning against the counter, his arms folded across his chest. He seemed to preside over everything, not only because he was taller, but because he seemed more contained than anyone in the room, even the officer. He caught Tory's eye, and gave her a measured nod of encouragement.

She looked around at them all, the police officer with his pencil poised, Jack with that strange look of relief and amazement, Hank's calm face. She began to speak for the second time that day, disgorging the weeks of secrets and tension in a steady voice, pausing now and then in search of the right word, the most economic expression.

It took a long time, beginning with Ellice's first appointments in her home office. She was interrupted once, when the other officer came in to confer with his colleague, then went out again to talk to the new ones who had arrived. The revolving lights on the patrol cars cast red and blue shadows through the picture window, and Tory watched them as she talked.

She described everything that happened, outlining everything she knew up until Ellice Gordon disappeared into the fog with a furious dog in pursuit. She held nothing back, not her escape, the unregistered VW, the invented name and history, the false Social Security number, the broken-off cell phone call to her son. She recounted, to the best of her ability, the lies she had told, the truths she had omitted.

She glanced up once to see Jack nodding as if it all made sense to him. She pressed on with her tale, giddy with pride at his presence, with relief at his acceptance.

The officer asked questions, wrote down her answers, reducing the immensity of her experiences to a few scribbled words. He called it a statement, and told her she would need to come in to the police station to repeat it in detail to a clerk and then sign it. The familiar, hideous weapon that had spent so many hours locked in her file drawer, that had caused such pain and fear, lay on her table, disarmed, impotent. The officer said Ellice's beige sedan was already being impounded, dragged away through the fog.

When the policeman asked if Ellice had another weapon, no one knew the answer. Tory's heart clenched at the thought that if Ellice had another gun, she could still hurt Johnson. She had to quell a powerful urge to get up from the table, run outside, call the dog's name.

She knew they wouldn't let her go. She clenched her fists beneath the table, and went on talking. She spoke for an hour, until there was nothing left to tell, no questions left that she could answer. Not until she was certain Hank had kept a copy of all the pages in Ellice's file, securely locked up in his clinic, did Tory hand the original over to the policeman, and accept a receipt in exchange. They were on the point of leaving, taking the file and Ellice's gun with them, when she remembered the sound of breaking glass she had heard from the yard. She stopped, halfway to the door, and gazed around her.

"The window," she said. "Didn't a window break?"

"Why did you think so?" the officer said. "We've been all over the house. Everything seems okay."

"But I heard glass break, I'm sure I did. When Ellice fired her gun."

Jack pointed toward the coffee table in front of the little sofa. "It wasn't a window, Mom," he said. "It was the paperweight. The one with the butterfly."

She turned to look.

The bullet must have caught it right in the middle. It lay in glowing green shards, the threads of gold exposed to the light so they gleamed softly against the shattered glass, the butterfly outline smashed beyond recognition. The piece of Murano glass, the family heirloom so lovingly carried from Tuscany by a hopeful bride, was ruined.

Tory gazed at it, wondering why she didn't feel anything, not sorrow, not regret, not even amazement that Ellice had managed to destroy the only valuable object in the house. It was, she thought, only an object, with a history and with emotional ties she might mourn one day. For now, all she could think was how close that bullet must have come to Jack. He had been standing near the open door, and if Johnson hadn't leaped on Ellice . . . She felt a fresh rush of anger, but there was nowhere to direct it.

Jack said, "That sucks, Mom."

"It's not important."

"It was kind of a strange thing to bring with you. You didn't take anything else."

"Yes, it was odd. I don't know how it happened. I just found it in my pocket, once I was already—away."

She crossed to the coffee table, and crouched to pick up one of the biggest of the fragments from the old carpet. She straightened, holding the bit of glass in her palm. It felt dead now, as if the life that had radiated from it, life absorbed from the people who had touched it, carried it, admired it, had drained away.

It didn't matter. All that mattered was right here with her. Jack was here, and safe. Hank was standing in the entryway, a steady, warm presence. There had been a great shift in the shape and structure of her life, and as she looked up at the two of them, so different, but so dear, anything and everything seemed possible. She dropped the bit of glass onto the table.

The full-throated bark from the beach coincided with the faint click of the glass on the wood. Tory whirled to face the open door just in time to see Johnson, pink tongue and long ears flying, bound across the lane, leap over the fence—he had been with her all these weeks, and she hadn't known he could do that—and race up through the yard and in the front door. He tumbled against her legs.

She fell to her knees, and threw her arms around the dog, hugging him to her. Johnson licked her cheek, and nuzzled close to her, covering her in sand and mud. "He's wet," she said. "Salt water—Hank, he's been in the water!"

Hank disappeared into the back, and returned with a towel in his hands. He started to rub the dog down, and it was clear Johnson was wet to the skin. Tory said, "He never went into the water before!"

Jack came to stand over them. "He looks like he's okay, though, right?"

Hank said, "I'll check him over, but yes. He looks like he's okay."

Tory clung to the dog's neck and thought that it wasn't just Johnson who was okay. Everyone—everything—was okay. All the weeks of anxiety and fear, of worry and guilt, had evaporated in the span of a few hours. It felt enormous, a transformation too big to take in, as if a theater curtain had dropped, and risen again on a completely different scene. She was no longer afraid, no longer lonely, and she would be able to set everything right after all.

It was strange, Jack thought, to realize that, despite all the drama and disruption, it was still Christmas Eve. It appeared that this tall, silver-haired man had invited Tory to Midnight Mass, and she wanted to go with him. When they asked Jack, it seemed right for him to go, too.

It was the first time he'd been in church since Tory's memorial, and he couldn't have imagined anything less similar. Hank knelt in the pew next to Tory as if it was the most natural thing in the world. Jack, feeling awkward and out of place, sat beside them. He gazed at his mother, her shocking red hair brilliant in the flickering candlelight, and listened to the familiar hymns and carols waft around them.

Despite himself, he felt soothed by the scents of incense and candle wax, the familiarity of white choir robes and scarlet vestments, the recitations of the old, old texts. Hank and his mother went to Communion, and though he didn't, he found himself with his head bowed, soaking in the peaceful atmosphere of the crowded church, beginning to believe the crisis had actually passed.

* * *

It had been a weird day from start to finish. He had listened to Tory talking on the phone to some people she had been working for, explaining. When she hung up, she told him word of the attack had already spread through Cannon Beach. Hank had piled Johnson into his car to take him to the clinic for a bath, and Jack sat across from Tory at the disreputable-looking kitchen table, drinking tea and trying to make sense of all that had happened.

Jack could hardly take in that his mother had been living here, in this shabby little place, for so long. "Those people, Mom." He pointed to the framed photographs that rested on the narrow mantel. "Who are they?"

She gave him an apologetic smile. The red hair, hanging in a ragged fringe over her forehead, made her look like a girl, slightly rakish, a bit punk. If she hadn't been his mother, he thought ruefully, he might have actually liked it. She said, "I don't know who they are, sweetheart. I bought them in an antiques store."

"And this house—it's nothing like you."

"That was the idea, actually."

"I only found you because of the music." At her raised eyebrows, he pointed to the little CD player resting prominently on the counter. "You were playing music. *Butterfly*."

"Oh, my god. You're right." She rested her chin on her hands, gazing at him. "Jack, I can't believe you're here—that you came all this way alone."

"You mean, the way you did?"

She laughed, but then she shook a finger at him. "You have to go back to school! I never thought you'd drop out."

"Well, don't worry. I haven't dropped out. I'm on leave."

"I thought Kate and Chet would keep an eye on you."

"They did. Or they tried." He pulled his teacup closer. "You won't believe this, but I had a hunch, Mom. Almost right after they told me you were—" His voice caught in his throat, and he had to clear it. "They told me you were dead. That they thought you had drowned. But something—I just knew you weren't."

"Oh, dear. Not the fey!"

He grinned over the edge of his teacup. "I hope not! I still don't believe in it. Or, I guess I don't want to believe in it. But it brought me here."

She smiled, but she glanced past him at the mound of broken green glass on the coffee table in the cramped living room. "Well. I guess we just have to be grateful."

They called the Binghams, and each of them spoke, reassuring Kate and Chet they were safe, that details would be forthcoming, and wishing them a merry Christmas. When that was done, Jack spoke the question that was uppermost in his mind. "Mom—this dog—and Hank? I don't know what to make of any of it. You've never done anything like this before."

"It all just sort of—happened," she said lamely. "Things have been messy."

"Hank seems like a good guy. And the dog rocks!" He added, "I gather you're keeping him."

She chuckled. "The dog? Or Hank?"

He grinned at her, liking the flush of pink on her thin cheeks. "I'm good with both of them, Mom."

"Well, the dog is staying, at least. Hank is just a friend."

Jack let that pass without comment.

While Jack went back to take a bath, Tory turned to the kitchen. There wasn't much there beyond a carton of cream and a package of frozen fish. She was just despairing over the lack of food in the house when Hank returned with a silky-clean Johnson and a bag of sandwiches and fruit from his own kitchen.

Tory went back to the bedroom to let Jack know food had arrived, and found him sound asleep on her bed. Gently, she closed the door, and stood for a moment with her palm against it, treasuring the sensation of having him under her own roof, however temporarily.

When she turned, she saw Hank watching her with an expression that was hard to read. She went back to meet him, looking up into his dark eyes with a smile. "He's so grown-up," she whispered. "I hardly know him."

"He's terrific," Hank said. He put an arm around her shoulders, and led her back to the kitchen. "A wonderful young man who came looking for his lost mother."

"I feel like we're starting over," she said. "I can't say that where he can hear me, though. He hates it when I talk like a therapist."

"You'll just have to talk like a mother, then."

"Yes." Tory accepted a sandwich, and laid it on one of the napkins Hank had brought. "He likes you, Hank."

"I have to be a surprise to him."

"No more than the dog!" she said, laughing. "I'm supposed to hate dogs."

"I think you've surprised your son in many ways."

"Yes. I guess I have. I hope that's a good thing."

There had been no sign of Ellice. The police called twice to report on their searches of the beach and the surrounding neighborhood. There was a trail to follow, Ellice's boot prints, marks of Johnson's paws in pursuit, but they ended at the waterline. The fog dispersed to reveal a pale blue sky above the gray ocean, and the tide came in early in the afternoon to wash away any remaining evidence.

Now, as Tory and Hank and Jack filed out of Midnight Mass with the throng of other people, she found herself pausing at the top of the steps of St. Peter's. She thought, or she imagined, that she saw a tall figure among the crowd, someone with a brush of sandy hair. She stood on her tiptoes to see better, but whoever she thought she had glimpsed either wasn't there, or had disappeared into the darkness. She settled back onto her heels, frowning.

"What is it?" Hank asked.

"Nothing," she told him. "Really—nothing."

She told herself, as the three of them walked down the steps together, that she could not spend the rest of her life watching for Ellice Gordon. A gentle sensation in her chest, not the flashing pain of her premonitions, but a feeling of warmth and comfort, assured her she wouldn't need to.

Iris's open house was a jolly occasion, the Christmas tree blazing with lights, a huge bowl of cranberry punch on the table, and platters of cheese and crackers and Christmas cookies in every shape and color. Tory wore her green dress again, with the black pumps. Jack and Hank both complimented her before she pulled on her battered black down jacket. Iris met them at her door with a raised eyebrow and a terse, cheerful, "Glad you're in one piece, Paulette!" That brought a surprised glance from Jack, and Hank and Tory both laughed.

Zoe was there a moment later, aglitter with gold bracelets and the longest earrings Tory had ever seen. She embraced Tory, effusing over the drama of the story, then pulled back to look Jack up and down. "Sweet," she said, flashing her scarlet smile. "A fresh face in town." Tory made introductions, and Jack was gone a moment later, towed off by a gleeful Zoe.

Tory said, "Iris, I have a lot to tell you, but I don't think this is a great time."

Iris shook her head. "We'll talk tomorrow. Or the next day. It doesn't matter." She pressed her cheek to Tory's, and nodded to Hank. "Everybody has a story. Didn't I say that sometime or other?" A moment later she was off to the kitchen.

Hank said, "Punch or wine?"

"Oh, wine, I think," Tory said. He nodded, and slipped off through the crowd to the sideboard where bottles and glasses were lined up and waiting. Tory waved to several people she recognized, but when Hank came back, they found a quiet corner to stand together and watch the shifting crowd of people. Tory took a sip of wine, and let her head fall back against the wall.

Hank looked down at her. "Tired?"

Tory smiled up at him. "A bit. You must be, too."

"A lot happened yesterday."

"I don't know what I would have done without you, Hank."

"I'm glad I was there. But Jack did just fine."

"Yes." Tory straightened, looking around for her son. She found him laughing with Zoe behind the Christmas tree. The two of them looked young and silly and happy. A surge of joy swept her, an intense feeling that made her heart flutter. She pressed her free hand to her throat in wonder at the sheer perfection of it.

Hank said quietly, "It's okay to be happy, Tory. You've earned it."

She turned her head, and found his shoulder very close to her cheek, temptingly close. She let her cheek touch the fabric of his shirt, just for an instant. "Thank you," she said quietly.

They drank wine, and nibbled at Iris's excellent food. They sang carols when someone went to the piano and started playing. They chatted and laughed with two of Iris's refugees, who also seemed to be in a holiday mood.

Jack and Zoe found them, and Jack asked if he could take the Escalade. "There's another party Zoe wants to go to," he said. "Hank, do you think you could give Mom a ride home?"

"Of course."

As they watched the two young people go out the front door, Tory suddenly laughed.

"What?" Hank asked.

"I was going to tell Jack to be careful. Jack, who just drove all the way across the country by himself!"

Hank nodded, smiling. "A very grown-up thing to do."

"Well, he is twenty. He's a man, I know, but it's hard to think of him that way."

"What mother ever sees her children as adults? Twenty, thirty . . . I don't think it matters."

"It matters to the children, I suppose. I wouldn't know, though. No one worried much over me, not after my grandmother died. Maybe that's why I fussed over Jack so much."

"Maybe. Or maybe you just love him."

She sighed. "Let's go, Hank, shall we? It's a nice party, but I have a lot of thinking to do in the next few days."

They found their hostess and said good night. Iris said, "Call me, Paulette."

Tory assured her she would. As Hank went to retrieve her coat, she said, "Iris, I don't want you to be shocked when I tell you my story."

"Not easy to shock me," Iris said comfortably. "But you can try."

On an impulse, Tory hugged her, receiving a strong embrace in return before she and Hank went out into the starlit darkness.

At the cottage, Tory let Johnson out into the yard. "I never knew," she said lightly to Hank, "that he could jump the fence. He could have done it a hundred times before yesterday."

Hank leaned against the doorjamb, the light from the living room outlining his lanky form. "He didn't want to, Tory. He's your dog now. I've seen it before with rescue dogs—when they find the right person, they get attached quickly."

"I feel a bit guilty about it—but I'm really glad you didn't find his people."

The corner of his mouth twitched. "I stopped trying," he said. "I withdrew the search request."

She sighed, watching the dog make his circuit of the little yard. She gazed beyond him, out into the darkness of the beach, where the glimmer of the ocean was just visible in the starlight. When she felt Hank's touch on her arm, she turned, and saw he was holding out a package. It was rectangular and rather heavy, wrapped in white tissue and tied with silver ribbon.

"It's a present for you," he said. "And you're *not* to say you didn't get me one, because that doesn't matter. I only give presents when the right one jumps out at me, and this one did."

She took the gift, smiling because she had been going to say exactly that. "I didn't shop. I didn't expect to celebrate Christmas at all."

"I know."

Johnson trotted back toward them, and they went inside and closed the door against the chilly night air. Tory took off the down jacket, saying, "I never want to see this thing again!" Hank chuckled, and she settled onto the easy chair to unwrap his gift.

It was a biography of Giacomo Puccini. The cover showed the composer in middle age, handsome, mustached, his dark eyes gazing out of the portrait, a burning cigarette between his lips.

"Hank, it's perfect!"

He was sprawled on the too-small sofa, his long legs stuck under the little coffee table. The bits of the Murano glass paperweight still lay there, scooped into a pile. "I knew you'd like it," he said.

"I've never read his biography, isn't that strange? I think I know all his music. Thanks so much—I'm going to enjoy this very much."

Hank yawned. "You're most welcome, and merry Christmas."

"You should go and get some rest."

"I don't know," he said. "I think I'll wait until Jack comes back."

"Oh, Hank," she said with a laugh. "That could be awfully late! Those two looked like they were ready to have fun."

He turned to face her, his dark eyes narrowing. "Tory," he said. "No one knows where that woman is. I don't think you should be alone."

Tory traced the photograph of Puccini with her finger. "I think I know where she is," she said. She paused for a moment. "I think she's dead, Hank. I think she went into the water."

"Why do you think that?"

"I have a feeling."

He shook his head doubtfully. "A feeling," he said.

"It's what I do," she said, and grinned at him. "It really is! You'll have to get used to it."

He pushed himself to his feet, bent, and kissed her cheek. His lips were warm and smooth against her skin, and she found herself wishing he would do it again. "Let's have dinner tomorrow," he said. "You and Jack take the day. Talk things through."

"That would be a good idea. We have to make some plans."

Tory stood up to walk him to the door. She took his arm, and he looked down at her with his gentle smile. She felt the strength of his arm under her hand, the warmth of his body so close to her, and she wanted to say something, explain to him how she felt. There were no words, and so, in silence, she lifted her face to his.

This time he kissed her lips, firmly, confidently, and she pressed close to him. She felt as if a barrier between them had been shattered, crumbled to dust, and there was nothing more to hold her back.

He whispered against her hair, "Don't make plans without me. Please."

She put her arms around his neck, and kissed him again before she pulled back to look into his eyes. "Don't worry, Hank," she murmured. "I couldn't make plans without you. Not anymore."

33

*Per sognie e per chimere e per castelli
in aria, l'anima ho milionaria.*

For dreams and visions and castles in the air,
I have the soul of a millionaire.

—Roldolfo, *La Bohème*, Act One

Tory dreamed one more time of the girl who had died. The dream didn't wake her as the others had done, but rather seemed to go on and on through the night, an endless vision of a small stone church and a coffin draped in evergreen branches resting before the altar. She seemed to be watching from some vantage point near the ceiling of the church, seeing the dark coats, the black hats with their drooping brims and bits of veil that trembled throughout the funeral Mass. Women sobbed, with handkerchiefs pressed to their faces. Men hung their heads, holding their hats in their hands. It was a gloomy scene, and very still, with none of the drama that had so colored her earlier dreams.

Tory, the watcher, felt nothing as she watched the mourners file past the coffin, touching it with their hands as they passed. She was neither sad nor happy, neither bitter nor glad. She was just—nothing. Neutral. An observer.

She didn't wake until the chilly December sunshine slanted through her bedroom window, and Johnson stirred and yawned. The only remnant of the dream was the scent of incense that seemed to linger around her, though she knew that couldn't be.

Tory slipped out from under the covers and pulled on the zippered sweatshirt. She shushed Johnson, hoping Jack, in his sleeping bag on the floor in the living room, wouldn't wake. Still in her stocking feet, she let the dog out into the yard, and sat on the cold front step to watch him make his usual circuit.

It was odd, she thought, as she watched her breath cloud in the cold air. All the dreams had been strange, but this one was different. It felt—conclusive. Like an ending. Perhaps the end of her crisis had something to do with that.

Or perhaps it didn't.

She had stayed up too late, reading the book Hank had given her. Propped up on pillows in bed, she had meant to skim through the book first, and go back later to the beginning to savor the details of Puccini's life, the triumphs and failures, the gossipy anecdotes and documented scandals. When she happened upon the story of Doria Manfredi, however, she slowed her pace. She read every detail, all the way through, then read it a second time, her scalp prickling uneasily at the resonance.

A young girl, a housemaid in Villa Puccini, had reportedly been driven to suicide. According to the account, she had bought poison at the chemist's, and taken it. The girl's family sued Elvira Puccini for hounding the girl to her death, and Elvira had been convicted, though Puccini later paid the family a substantial amount of money in order to keep his wife out of prison. The book claimed there had been a suicide note, though no one knew what had become of it. Puccini had threatened to divorce Elvira for what she had done, and the couple only reconciled after months of pleading and persuasion by the family.

Johnson came padding back to the step where Tory sat. She rubbed his ears, and pulled him close for warmth. "I don't know what it all means, Johnson," she murmured. "Or if it means anything at all." He scraped her cheek with his long pink tongue, and she chuckled, wiping it with her sleeve. "You're probably right," she told him, pressing her chin to the top of his smooth head. "It was just a dream. They were all just dreams."

As she let the dog back into the house, she caught sight of the small cardboard box that now held the shards of the Murano glass paperweight. She tried to tell herself there was no point in carting the shattered pieces back to Vermont, but she couldn't bring herself to leave them. She padded into the kitchen, touching the box with her fingertips as she passed it, and wondered if this was, after all, truly the end.

Tory and Jack chose the first of the year as a good day to depart. Her rent was paid up through the end of December, and though Iris assured her she would happily grant her a few days as thanks for all the repairs she had done, Tory thought it made a good start on a new year and a new direction for them to set off on the first of January.

"Breakfast at my house before you leave," Iris decreed, and that seemed like a good idea, too. They gathered around her table for eggs Benedict and plates of smoked salmon and toasted baguette slices. Zoe and her mother were there, and Hank, of course. The cat had been tucked away upstairs so Johnson could come in and lie on a rug near the front door. "No rushing," Iris said. "You might as well not head out until the roads are dry."

Jack and Tory were content with that. They expected to take a week to get back to Vermont. The Escalade was outfitted with half a dozen audio books, food for Johnson, the few things Tory wanted to keep.

The yellow Beetle was now in Zoe's proud possession, though the paperwork still had to be straightened out. The rest of the items Tory had bought for the cottage she left there. "If you have renters, they can use them," she had said.

"Including the family photos?" Iris had asked slyly. "Paulette Chambers's history?"

Tory had chuckled, and given a helpless shrug. "No, I'm keeping those," she said. "Those poor people have already been sold to strangers once, and I don't think it should happen again."

"What a story," Iris said. "You could be an actor. Or a fiction writer."

It had all come out, bit by bit, so everyone now knew everything. They still had trouble remembering to call Tory by her real name, but the drama of the tale evidently overrode any feelings of resentment at her deception, and there was abundant sympathy for what had happened to her.

Of Ellice Gordon there had been no sign. *In absentia,* she was charged with murder, but Tory could have told the sheriff's department not to bother. She knew Ellice was gone.

So did Jack.

"She's dead, Mom," he had said one evening, when he had come in from seeing a movie with Zoe.

"Who?" Tory asked.

"Ellice Gordon."

"So you feel it, too."

He nodded, and the smile that had been on his face when he first came into the cottage faded. "It's uncomfortable," he said. "Knowing things you shouldn't know."

"Sometimes," Tory said. She had been sitting in the old easy chair, a small fire crackling beside her, the Puccini biography open on her lap. She closed the book, and folded her hands on top of it. "Sometimes it's uncomfortable," she agreed. "Often it's helpful."

"You can't count on it, though."

"No. Nonna Angela told me that, a long time ago. She told me not to depend on it. Just to use it when it comes along, and be grateful."

Jack threw himself onto the little sofa, and propped his feet up on the coffee table. He said, staring at the scuffed toes of his sneakers, "How do you live with it? I mean, never knowing when you're going to get that feeling?"

"I guess," Tory said, "you just live with it like you live with anything else that's part of your nature. Like being short, or tall, or shy, or . . . whatever."

He cast her a sidelong glance from beneath his eyelids. "Is that therapist talk, Mom?"

"Being a therapist is part of *my* nature, Jack."

"I know," he said, and she saw he was smiling, his eyes closing as if he felt perfectly relaxed. "Are you going to be a therapist again?"

"Yes, I think so. I hope so. I have a few kinks to work out, since I didn't report Ellice's crime. I'll speak to Chet's lawyer when we get back, but the circumstances work in my favor, I think."

"You're good. It would be a waste for you to give up your practice."

The compliment made her cheeks warm, and she was glad he kept his eyes closed, his head tilted back against the worn fabric of the sofa. She could watch him unhindered, admiring the young man he had so swiftly become. She said, "I'm going to need a new license, of course."

He said, "Easy squeezy."

"Now you're quoting Zoe!" She laughed.

"Yeah. She's pretty quotable."

"I know. She's one of a kind."

"She sure is." There was a pause, and then he said, still with his eyes closed, "I'm sorry about the house, Mom. I never expected that."

"Of course you didn't. How could you?"

"I'll help fix it up."

"No, you'll go back to school."

"Well—yeah. I guess so. The house is a mess, though." He opened his eyes and turned his head toward her. "It's just—ruined, Mom. All your pretty things, your kitchen . . . You'd never feel the same there."

"It's too bad, that's for sure. But it will make it a bit easier to let it go." She had meant it. It was hard to think of selling her house, parting from Chet and Kate, but she knew it was the right thing to do. They could come and visit her in Oregon. And she needed no reminders of Ellice Gordon.

When it was time for them to leave, everyone pulled on coats to follow Jack and Tory out into the chilly morning. The rain of the night before had given way to the familiar low cloud cover. The wet leaves glowed gently in the gray light, and in the distance the tip of Haystack Rock thrust up against the grayness like a big black thumb. They all trooped out to Iris's driveway, where the Escalade waited. Tory handed Iris the key to the cottage, and said a warm thanks. Zoe, in a bright yellow vintage coat and purple plaid scarf, hugged Tory and said, "I'll be seeing you soon. Jack's asked me out to visit over spring break. Hope that's okay by you!"

Tory was still speechless from this announcement when Hank came to help Johnson jump up into the back of the car. He settled him with his blanket and a stuffed toy he'd brought from the clinic, then came around to the front to hand Tory up into the driver's seat. Jack stood by Iris's garage, teasing Zoe, making her laugh. Tory fastened her seatbelt, then unfastened it so she could settle her purse—the same old fake leather drugstore purse—near her hand, and put a CD in the player.

When everything was settled, she turned back to Hank. "Thanks," she said, as he adjusted the seatbelt over her shoulder.

"You're welcome." His deep voice was as calm as always, but the pressure of his hand on hers had an urgency about it. "Drive carefully."

"I will, Hank. We will, I mean."

"Call me every night."

She smiled at him, and leaned to kiss his cheek. "Okay," she said. "Every night."

"If you're not back in three months," he said, "I'm coming to get you."

She chuckled. "Ah, a deadline. Okay! I've been warned."

The passenger door opened, and Jack hopped nimbly up. "Show on the road, Mom!" he exclaimed.

"Right." It was time. She put the key in the ignition.

"Keep an eye on her, son," Hank said, and Jack gave him a thumbs-up.

"Hank—" Tory began, but sudden tears closed her throat, and she had to blink her eyes against them.

He leaned in to kiss her cheek. "No worrying," he said. "We'll talk every day."

She swallowed, and managed to say, "Right. No worrying."

He stepped back, and closed the driver's door, touching the glass briefly with his fingertips. She had to look in the rearview mirror to back out, to turn the car, to face toward town and the highway. At the last minute she looked back to see, through a mist of tears, all of them standing on Iris's steps, waving good-bye. She thought she would never forget the picture they made: Zoe's scarlet grin, Iris's gray hair whipping around her face, and Hank's lean figure towering over them all.

Jack inclined his seat as far as it would go and leaned back, his hands behind his head. "You didn't find this place by accident, did you, Mom?"

"No. I don't think so."

"It's great. I love it. I may just join you here—once I finish school, that is."

She sniffled, and smiled across at her son. "That would be lovely, sweetheart. Really lovely. You know you'd always be welcome—if you think you might like it."

"Yeah," he said. "I think we have some time to make up."

She smiled at that, blinking away her unshed tears. She wheeled the Escalade through town, past the flower shop and market and beachfront hotels, over the bridge and out toward the highway. Behind her, the dog sighed, and flopped to one side to sleep away the journey.

THE GLASS BUTTERFLY

Louise Marley

ABOUT THIS GUIDE

The suggested questions that follow
are included to enhance your group's
reading of this book.

Discussion Questions

1. Tory Lake's practice as a therapist was enhanced by her psychic gift, which she called her "fey." In what way did her fey help her protect herself from Ellice Gordon? In what way did it fail her?

2. Giacomo Puccini often referred to his wife, Elvira, as his "policeman." Does that resonate with the character of Ellice Gordon, since she's a sheriff's deputy? Can you see other parallels between the memories Tory has of Torre del Lago in 1908 and her current crisis?

3. Tory, with nothing but a bit of cash in the lining of her coat, has to create an entire new life, symbolized by the photographs of strangers she buys and displays as if they were her own family. Have you ever wondered what it would be like to start your life over as someone else? Do you think you could do it?

4. The presence of the butterfly paperweight is a connecting thread running through the plot of the book. The paperweight belonged to Puccini and then, briefly, to Doria, before it was passed down through the Manfredi family to Tory. In what ways does the butterfly symbolize the relationships between the principal characters?

5. Classical music, especially opera, is Tory's passion, the one area in her life that allows her to release her emotions. Doria Manfredi also loves opera. Iris Anderson loves jazz, and Jack Lake likes rock music. Do you think musical preferences help to define characters? In your discussion group, who likes which kind of music?

6. Doria Manfredi lived at a time when servants were all but slaves to their employers. In the remote village of Torre

del Lago, Villa Puccini offered the best possible job for a girl of low birth. What other life choices could Doria have made? Can you understand why she would tolerate Elvira Puccini's abuse in order to hold on to her job?

7. In what ways does the dog, Johnson, help Tory to heal?

8. Tory's son, Jack, is shocked to find that he, too, has the fey he has previously dismissed, and is not completely happy about it. Do you think Nonna Angela was right when she told Tory that the fey was both blessing and curse? Have you ever had a psychic or intuitive experience you couldn't explain?

9. *Madama Butterfly* is one of the most famous and most beloved of all operas. Can you see why Doria Manfredi identifies with Cio-Cio-San, the little Butterfly?

10. Are you convinced, at the end of the book, that Ellice Gordon is gone for good, or do you think this is an instance in which Tory's fey—and Jack's also—might fail them?